What the Sh

M J Lee has worked as a university researcher in history, a social worker with Vietnamese refugees, and as the creative director of an advertising agency. He has spent 25 years of his life working outside the north of England, in London, Hong Kong, Taipei, Singapore, Bangkok and Shanghai.

Also by M J Lee

DI Ridpath Crime Thriller

Where the Truth Lies
Where the Dead Fall
Where the Silence Calls
Where the Innocent Die
When the Past Kills
When the Evil Waits
When the Guilty Cry
When the Night Ends
What the Shadows Hide

MJ LEE
WHAT THE SHADOWS HIDE

CANELO CRIME

First published in the United Kingdom in 2023 by

Canelo
Unit 9, 5th Floor
Cargo Works, 1-2 Hatfields
London SE1 9PG
United Kingdom

Print ISBN 978 1 80032 932 4
Ebook ISBN 978 1 80032 931 7

Cover design by Tom Sanderson

Cover images © Arcangel, Alamy, Shutterstock

Look for more great books at www.canelo.co

Printed and bound in Great Britain by Clays Ltd, Elcograf S.p.A.

MIX
Paper from
responsible sources
FSC® C018072
FSC
www.fsc.org

For Mike and Janet. Enjoy

Sunday, August 24, 2008

Chapter One

He knew he was near death.

He'd seen his grandmother standing in the corner of the room hiding in the shadows, beckoning him to join her, waving as she always did with her right hand, saying, 'Come along, hurry up, why are you always so late?'

And then she had gone.

Vanished.

He shook his head, trying to clear it. Was he seeing things or was this all real?

The heat was unbearable. A dry, coarse heat that made his throat rasp like sandpaper as he tried to swallow whatever saliva remained in his parched mouth.

He tried to raise his head from the mattress laid over the wooden floor, but gave up when the effort became too much. Next to him, his sister lay, her hands clasped in front of her as if in prayer.

What had they done to deserve this?

He inched his head towards her lips, listening for the sounds of life, but there were none. She hadn't moved for a long time.

Was she still alive?

He doubted it. He heard no breathing. No whimpers. No cries of pain. Nothing.

He wasn't sure how long they had been in this room. A small window high up in the apex where the wall met the roof was the only source of light during the day. The candle had been used very quickly, too quickly.

At first, they had been certain someone would come for them, shouting at the tops of their voices for hours on end, finishing the bottle of water far too quickly.

But there had been no response, no cavalry arriving, no knight in shining armour to rescue them. The person who had locked them away was no longer there, no longer cared.

The days had passed, or were they mere hours?

Sleeping and waking.

Sleeping and waking.

Sleeping and waking.

Losing all track of time and themselves. Hunger and thirst gnawing at their bodies, drowning their souls.

She had been full of energy at the beginning, urging him to force open the door with his bare hands.

He had tried tugging at the handle, beating on it with his fists, clawing at the solid wood, losing his fingernails, the door still intact at the end of hours of struggle.

She had lapsed into silence then. A zombie-like state, staring into the distance, her eyes unfocused, cradling the empty bottle of water like one would a baby.

Through their chapped lips, they had talked about their memories of childhood lived in two different places.

For him it was a day tobogganing with the neighbours when he was eleven on some slopes out near Alderley Edge. The neighbour was German and she knew exactly what to do, teaching her son and him all the ways of making the sledge go faster.

He never saw the boy again, his family moved away soon after to live in Hale and never came back.

For her it was a first kiss. A fevered, wet exchange of spit behind the bleachers at her school, the boy boasting to his friends later he'd 'had' her.

It had been embarrassing when his sister had decided she needed the toilet. He had turned his back when she used the bucket in the corner that had been provided. Nothing came of course, there was nothing left to come.

Later, after his sister had lain down, he had tried to scratch a message into the plaster with the cap of the water bottle.

But his mind could not focus, his strength was diminished, he couldn't form any words, couldn't even work out what to write.

After hours of effort, all he had to show were a few meaningless scratches, half-formed words, unformed ideas.

Before she fell asleep, his sister had stared longingly at the empty bottle of liquid placed next to the feathers she had brought with her.

A bluebottle had disturbed him when he was sleeping, buzzing around his head. Had it been incarcerated with them? The three locked away in their own version of hell?

He had spent hours trying to catch it, but without luck. Each time he thought he had it, it would dart away, just out of reach.

He could hear it now, as he lay there, his sister dying or dead next to him. Buzzing up in the rafters, trying to find a way out.

There was no exit. He had tried to shout but the words wouldn't form in his throat, the bluebottle would never hear them.

He wasn't going to last much longer, he knew that.

Hadn't his grandmother already come for him?

He opened his eyes and saw the small window at the point where the roof and the walls joined. He could see a distorted moon through the thick, cobweb-sheathed glass.

Or was it the sun?

His eyes wouldn't focus and he knew the end was close.

The end. At the beginning of his life.

Through his cracked, parched lips, he whispered the words his grandmother had whispered to him.

'Father, father, why have you forsaken us?'

Thursday, June 17. Modern Day.

Chapter Two

Mrs Challinor waited for the court to quieten before turning to face the jury and speaking in a quiet but firm voice.

'Ladies and gentlemen of the jury, I am now going to sum up this inquest for you in my role as the coroner. I must remind you that any inquest is a three-stage process; the findings of fact, the answer to "how" and the verdict in the form of your conclusion. A narrative statement can also be appended to your verdict if you so desire. Let me take you through the three stages in detail.'

She coughed twice and reached for the glass of water in front of her. The air was still in the court, the fans placed in front of the jury and the legal counsel simply moving the hot air around rather than chilling it.

The coroner carried on speaking, still wearing her black woollen jacket and tailored shirt despite the heat.

Detective Inspector Thomas Ridpath looked around the Coroner's Court. The family sat next to the empty witness stand, the wife dressed in black, a handkerchief still pressed to her red eyes. In front of her, the solicitor impassively listened to the coroner. On the table next to the family, almost touching, the barristers representing both the council and the East Manchester Hospital Trust leant forward like whippets waiting for the command to run.

All were suffering in the insufferable heat.

Ridpath was there in his capacity as coroner's officer, on call in case Mrs Challinor needed him. It was just one of the many duties he had to perform.

She continued speaking without looking at the notes on the laptop in front of her.

'You have heard all the evidence in this case, including that of the witnesses in court, documentary evidence, photographs of the location and items of property such as the rope and chair, apparently used by the deceased to end his life. Your findings must be based solely on the evidence you have heard or seen in court. You must ignore anything else, including media coverage of the case. It is irrelevant.'

She stopped for a moment, checking each member of the jury.

'The next point I cannot emphasise enough. This is not a trial; it is an inquest into a death, an inquiry to find out how Mr Owen Davies died. It is not concerned with attributing blame, it is simply to establish the facts of the man's death. To put it briefly, the "how" of how he died.'

A snuffle from Owen Davies' wife. The coroner glanced across at her, a look of pity crossed her face and then she seemed to steel herself to continue.

'In order for you to determine the facts, you must make an assessment of the evidence. Some has been agreed, some has not. But you must decide. What evidence do you accept and what evidence do you reject?'

Ridpath watched as Jenny Oldfield, the office manager, moved to the side of the jury box, placing a stack of papers next to the jury foreman. These were the copies of the summing-up.

'The evidence has been directed towards answering four questions: Who was the deceased? And when, where and how did he come by his death? Once you have made your findings in relation to the four questions and reached a conclusion you must record these and sign one copy of the Record of Inquest. You have copies of this form in front of you and must complete all the sections.'

She paused again, letting her words settle in the minds of the jurors.

'I shall deal with the first question as there is no dispute over the facts and you will enter them on your record. The date and place of death was April 4, 2022 at 7 Helmand Road, Levenshulme. The name and surname of the deceased was Mr Owen Davies and he was male. His date and place of birth was April 4, 1957 in Sale, Manchester. He was at the time of his death unemployed but had been recently a marketing director for a scientific instrument company.'

She paused for a moment.

'Don't worry if this is too much information for you, it is all repeated in my written summation. If you need any guidance or help, please don't hesitate to contact myself or any of my staff at any time.'

She looked down, checking her notes on the laptop for the first time. 'The medical evidence stated the cause of death was a hypoxic brain injury, the result of hanging. There has been no dispute about the finding in the case. You should therefore enter that medical cause of death in section two. In the next section, this is where you should record when, where and how the deceased came by his death.'

A little cough as Mrs Challinor cleared her throat. 'I shall now review the evidence in the inquest.'

For a second, Ridpath remembered the details of the case. Owen Davies had hung himself in his garage on his birthday, two days after being released from psychiatric care. This was despite the professed concern of his wife to case workers and the local health authority that he intended to harm himself. It had been difficult for Mrs Davies to hear the details of his death repeated again and again in court. Ridpath had watched her gradually descend into her own private hell. It was she who had discovered the body, trying in vain to cut it down.

Mrs Challinor had tried to make the process as easy as she could but it was obvious there had been numerous failings by the local authority, the health trust and the doctors. It was a case where nobody had come out of it smelling of roses; all had been tainted by the stench of an unnecessary death.

He focused back into Mrs Challinor's voice.

'In this case, there are three possible conclusions. The first possible conclusion is suicide. You may reach this conclusion if, on the evidence, you are sure Mr Davies took his own life and intended to do so. The second possible conclusion is an open verdict. You may reach this conclusion if you are satisfied on the basis of the evidence that it is probable Mr Davies deliberately suspended himself by a rope, but he did not intend the outcome to be fatal. In other words, he died as an unintended consequence of his actions. The third conclusion is in the form of a short narrative verdict and is appropriate where either you cannot decide Mr Owen's state of mind or you find his mental condition caused him to be incapable of forming an intention.'

Ridpath heard her cough once again. Was she coming down with an illness or was it just the heat? The coroner again reached for a glass of water to help clear her throat before continuing.

'I have added a short questionnaire to help you decide if a narrative conclusion is necessary. For example, was an absence of community mental health records or a delay starting medication a contributing factor? And were there failures to respond to an obvious risk of self-harm such as indications of depression and mood swings? What about the lack of response to Mrs Davies' emails? Should there have been better follow-up for a recently released patient? You may decide these questions are relevant in Mr Davies' death, or you may decide they have no bearing. That is your task as a jury.'

Ridpath knew this inquest would not finish that day. There was far too much for the jury to decide. It was one of those sad cases where a man's death could have been prevented if only somebody had acted rather than simply passing the buck. He had slipped in between the cracks in a system stretched to breaking point.

He glanced at the clock. Four thirty p.m. Mrs Challinor was close to completing her summary now. He had heard the last words so often standing in this court.

'Before you retire to consider your findings, I must repeat the warning I gave you before. You decide this case solely on the evidence which you have seen and heard in this court. Do not do your own research or look anything up on the internet. This is most important. You must reach, if you can, a unanimous conclusion, one with which you all agree. There may come a time when I can accept a majority decision and if so I shall call you back into court.'

She glanced at her watch. 'It is now too late for you to record your verdict today. We will return tomorrow at nine a.m., and you can deliberate and return a verdict when you have reached a conclusion. I thank you in advance for your work as a jury.'

Mrs Challinor stood up and announced, 'Mr Ridpath, could I see you in my office now?'

Ridpath wondered what she wanted and why it was so urgent she'd announced it in open court. Had he made a mistake in his investigation of the case?

Chapter Three

Mrs Challinor's office was as tidy as ever; the files neatly stacked to once side, an empty inbox and a pristine blotter. As Ridpath entered, she was typing away on her laptop, her black jacket now hanging neatly on a hanger in the corner.

'I'll be with you in a second.'

He stood there waiting as she finished her notes with a flourish and turned to look at him. 'That was a difficult inquest, but I think we got there in the end, don't you?'

'It wasn't easy, particularly for Mrs Owens.'

'No, poor woman, having to live through it all again. But as long as the jury come to the right conclusion, I hope it will have been worth it. The local health authority was incompetent at best. It looks like I may be writing a Regulation 28 notice to them, the third in recent months.'

A Regulation 28 was a report following an inquest if it appeared there was a risk of other deaths occurring in similar circumstances. Also known as a Preventing Future Deaths report, it required any organisation to reply within fifty-six days to say what action they planned to take to reduce the risks identified by the coroner.

'Have they replied to any of the others?'

'Not yet. I'll send a follow-up note with a copy to the chief coroner.' She shook her head. 'I'm beginning to lose patience with them.'

'It looks like all aspects of the National Health Service are under pressure, mainly due to shortage of staff.'

She frowned. 'When a man dies there are no excuses, Ridpath, only immediate remedies to prevent it happening again. My worry is this particular health authority is incapable of putting into place the simplest measures to alleviate its problems.'

Her anger was palpable. But her face softened. 'That's not why I asked you to see me. Claire Trent has requested you be briefed on a job.'

Ridpath was both a serving member of the Major Investigation Team at Greater Manchester Police and the coroner's officer for East Manchester. As such, he often had to juggle both roles, managing his time and his responsibilities to both his bosses.

'I checked your workload and I've agreed. The case she wants you to work on has a particular interest for me.'

'No problem, Coroner.'

'Apparently she too is short-staffed at the moment.'

'It seems like a common theme. When am I supposed to be briefed?'

'I'm not your secretary, Ridpath, you will need to sort it out yourself,' she said abruptly, before quickly smiling and saying, 'Sorry, that came out as curt. I have something troubling me at the moment.'

'Can I help?'

'Definitely, but not yet. I don't want to send you on a wild goose chase until I have sorted out the facts. I'll know more after this evening.'

'What's happening then? Are you sure I can't help?'

She stared at her notepad for a long time before answering. 'I've spotted something which is troubling me, but I may just be imagining it, drawing a conclusion that isn't there. I need to gather more evidence first...' her voice trailed off, before she focused back on him. 'I've let it slip for the last week, but with this inquest finishing, I can concentrate on it again. You start the work Claire Trent has assigned you first and then I will be able to tell you more.'

'It all sounds mysterious. Are you sure you don't want to tell me now?'

'Not yet – let me do a little more digging. Now off you go, Ridpath, don't you have work to do?'

'Always, Mrs Challinor, always.'

Chapter Four

Sophia Rahman, Ridpath's assistant, was waiting for him went he returned to his office.

'Shall we go over the numbers for tomorrow's work-in-progress meeting?'

'Just a sec.' He picked up his mobile and called Claire Trent's office. She answered the call after two rings.

'Mrs Challinor has told me you have something for me, boss.'

'We're swamped and I need you to supervise a case.'

'Shall I come over now?'

There was the rustling of a page down the other end of the line. 'Not now, I have drinks with the Manchester Chamber of Commerce at seven, followed by a presentation on new property developments in the city and their impact on policing structures.'

'Sounds fascinating.'

'Don't be sarcastic, Ridpath, it doesn't suit you.'

'Nine a.m. tomorrow morning, then?'

'It's in my diary. Don't be late. I have a budget planning meeting for 2024 at ten and after that forward planning for 2025 to 2030.'

'Sounds like United, they're planning to sign a forward too.'

'As I already said, humour doesn't suit you, Ridpath. Be there tomorrow.'

'What's it about...?'

The phone went dead in his hand.

Detective Superintendent Claire Trent, otherwise known as his boss, didn't sound a happy bunny. And, given the extent of the bureaucracy at GMP, he wasn't surprised. There seemed to be interminable meetings about everything from the shape of the lockers to the ordering of staples. 'Rather her than me,' he said out loud.

'What was that?' asked Sophia.

'Nothing, just talking to myself.'

'Apparently, it's the first sign of madness.'

'Nah, the first sign of madness is when you start looking forward to budget meetings.'

'That reminds me, Mrs Challinor has pencilled one in for you on Thursday.'

'You're joking?'

She shook her head, and then nodded. 'The look on your face...!'

'Don't joke, Sophia, you nearly gave me a heart attack.' A shudder ran down his back. A bureaucrat no doubt, walking over his grave with a form in hand.

The interminable bureaucracy of both the police and the coroner's office was a constant bugbear for Ridpath. He recognised the need for it, just hated doing it. Luckily Sophia seemed to revel in the detail of the innumerable forms which had to be completed whenever a death occurred. If she ever left, he didn't know what he would do. Suffer a slow lingering death by bureaucracy, probably.

'Earth to Planet Ridpath. Do you want to go over these WIP forms now?'

She handed the typed spreadsheets to him. There had been fifty-two deaths in their area of Greater Manchester last week.

'I've indicated the deaths we may need to look into. Mrs Challinor has already arranged inquests for most of them.'

Ridpath sat down. Sometimes, there were elements of bureaucracy he couldn't avoid. This was one of them. Together, they went through the details of each death, highlighting those where more investigation on Ridpath's part was needed, and where Sophia had to follow up with the relatives of the deceased.

Finally, they finished the spreadsheet.

'I'll stay tonight and amend this before tomorrow's meeting. With a bit of luck I should be able to get away before seven this evening.'

Ridpath raised his eyebrows.

'Before you ask, I *do* have a date and it *is* with a human being.'

'Isn't this a second date?'

'Fourth actually.'

'Sounds serious.'

She smiled and looked up and to the left. 'Could be, we'll see.'

'Does the mother know?'

'Not yet. She thinks I'm at a macrame class.'

'Oh what a tangled web we weave…'

'Not funny, Ridpath. I'll tell her eventually, just not now. Asian mothers are like mushrooms, they tend to function better in the dark. Going out with an Irish man is not on the list of things she needs to know.'

Jenny Oldfield bustled into the room, her strong, acrid perfume and orange lipstick preceding her by at least ten feet. 'Is the WIP ready yet?'

'We're just doing it now. It'll be ready later this evening.'

'Good, I'll schedule the meeting for Monday afternoon when the coroner is free.'

She was about to leave when Ridpath spoke. 'How is Mrs Challinor?'

Jenny frowned. 'You should know, you've just had a meeting with her.'

'That's why I'm asking. She seemed… well… distracted.'

'We're busy, plus it's budget time, and Mrs Challinor hates dealing with the council's finance people.'

'Don't we all.'

'But *you* don't have to do it, Ridpath.'

'Lucky me.' He paused for a moment, before asking, 'So you think she's fine? She mentioned she was looking into something recently. Did she tell you about it?'

'No, and even if she had, you know I wouldn't mention it until she did. Why don't you ask her, Ridpath?'

'I just did.'

'And her answer?'

'She would tell me when she was ready.'

'There you go then. Have a good evening both of you.'

Jenny left the room, closing the door behind her with a loud thud.

'What was all that about?'

'I don't know, Sophia, but something is going on with the coroner, and I'm going to find out what it is.'

Chapter Five

Eve was already at home when Ridpath arrived back. She was eating a jam sandwich and drinking milk, still wearing her school uniform. A little of the strawberry jam had stuck to the side of her face.

'How was today?'

'Same old, same old.'

'What happened?'

'I went to school, I sat in lessons, I came home. End of story.'

It was one of those uncommunicative days, when the teenager in her was at its worse. He tried again with a different tack.

'Something must have been good about today. Tell me one good thing that happened.'

Eve thought long and hard. 'Fiona Sims fell over and cut her knee playing netball. She cried her heart out.'

'Is that good?'

'If you knew what a bully she was, you'd realise karma was only getting its own back.'

'I'm not sure karma is supposed to work like that.'

'Whatever. What's for tea? I fancy the sausages we bought at the weekend.'

'The vegan ones?'

'Of course. Meat is murder, Dad.'

She was going through her vegetarian phase. It usually lasted about a week before the desire to murder a bacon sandwich reached its peak and she succumbed, only to feel immensely guilty when she took her first bite.

'I'll grill them for you, but I'm going to have the pork and apple myself. I'll add a salad just to make it slightly healthy.'

'You know pigs are actually considered the fifth-most intelligent animal in the world, even more intelligent than dogs? According to studies in the United States they are capable of playing video games with more focus and success than chimps.'

'Hang on, some scientist gave a pig a video game to play and it won?'

'According to the studies.'

'What was it? Hogs of War? Swine Fever? Or was it a *board* game? Boom tish!'

'Sometimes you can be so embarrassing, Dad.'

'Just sometimes. At least I'm making progress.' Ridpath strode over to the fridge taking out the separately packed sausages. 'Where did you learn about pigs anyway?'

'Biology. We're studying the relative intelligence of species now. Mankind is way down the list.'

'Now that doesn't surprise me.'

She pointed upstairs. 'I'm going up to do homework with Maisie.' They often did homework together online even though Maisie's home was less than half a mile away. The wonders of Facebook Messenger and the internet.

'OK, but the sausages and salad will be ready in twenty minutes.'

He heard her stomping upstairs like a sumo wrestler, the house reverberating beneath her feet. Was there anything heavier than an eighty-six pound teenager?

He put the sausages under the grill. While they cooked he could just check to see if the WIP had arrived from Sophia.

Thirty minutes later, a girl's voice came from upstairs. 'Dad, is something burning?'

'Shit, shit, shit.' He ran back into the kitchen, noticing wisps of smoke drifting upwards from the grill.

'No,' he shouted, 'just the sausages cooking.'

'Smells like they're burning, Dad.'

He pulled the grill pan towards him and saw six charred and blackened fingers of sausage staring back up at him. He walked to the door and shouted upstairs, 'I don't fancy sausages anymore. How about I order pizza from Rudy's?'

Eve appeared at the top of the stairs and shouted down accusingly, 'You burnt them, didn't you?'

Ridpath looked down at the grill pan still in his hand, the lumps of charcoaled sausage reprimanding him. He thought about trying one before deciding the bin was probably the best place for them.

'I was distracted.'

'By the TV?'

'No, a heart attack in Burnage.'

She seemed to think about this for a moment, her thirteen-year-old eyes looking up and left processing the information, before finally answering, 'Pizza sounds great.' She shook her head and pointed back towards her bedroom. 'I'm going to finish my homework.'

'I'll call you when it arrives.'

The only answer was a loud tutting followed by the slamming of a bedroom door.

Thirteen-year-old girls have that unerring ability to make you feel terminally incompetent. Despite being an inspector in the Greater Manchester Police. Despite also being a coroner's officer attached to East Manchester's Coroner's Court. Despite having a record of solving important crimes and running major investigations. To her, he was still just Dad, with all the fallibility the word invariably conjured up.

It hadn't been easy for her over the last five years. First his bout with cancer, myeloma to be exact. He'd gone through all the pain of chemotherapy with a death sentence hanging over his head. He had finally been placed in remission and went back to work, but then his rock, his love, his wife and Eve's mother, Polly, had been killed and their world destroyed.

It had been a difficult time for both of them, and he often wondered if his daughter had handled the death of her mother better than he had handled the death of his wife.

Had she been forced to grow up too quickly?

He didn't know.

She had returned to him from her grandparents' house five months ago, but not without sitting him down first and giving him the inevitable talk, sounding more like a thirty-year-old than a teenager.

'Look, Dad, you can't treat me like this—'

He tried to speak but she stopped him by raising her hand.

'—let me finish. You can't send me away, bring me back and then send me away again, whenever it suits you or life becomes difficult.'

He wanted to tell her both their lives had been threatened during an investigation into a death in custody at a police station. He had sent her to her grandparents' for her own safety, but he knew from the look on her face it was his turn to listen, not speak.

'I either live with you or I live with my grandparents. Personally, I would prefer to stay here. This is my home and, since Mum died, we only have each other to rely on. There's nobody else. So we're in this together, Dad, or we're not, come hell or high water. You need to make up your mind. I'm not a thing to be placed somewhere else when work gets a little too difficult or you suddenly feel I'm a burden to you.'

'You're never a burden to me, Eve… but…'

At that moment, Polly's face flashed through his mind. He missed her every day, the absence like a pain in the centre of his chest that would never go away.

'No buts, Dad, this isn't a time for buts. We're in this together or we're not, it's simple.'

'My work…' he said feebly.

'You've got a job like thousands of other single dads up and down the country. They manage, some better than others. We need to make it work, Dad.' She sighed. 'Look, I realise your job sometimes involves working late or long hours, but I can handle it. I've grown up.' A slight pause. 'I've had to grow up. We can make it work, Dad.'

For the first time, he heard a pleading in her voice. The thirty-year-old had become thirteen again. She just wanted to come home.

He made a decision.

'OK. No more going back to the grandparents, Eve, you stay here, come hell or high water.'

'Forever?'

'Well, maybe not forever… just until you start drawing your pension.'

So she had moved back in five months ago. Sometimes, he would be able to pick her up from school. At others, he had given her a key and allowed her to come home on her own using the tram. It was his way of saying she was old enough to be trusted. But if he was going to be home particularly late, she would get a lift with Maisie's mum, Angela, and stay there doing her homework till he picked her up. It took a bit of planning, but somehow it worked, and they both felt comfortable with the arrangement.

The pizza arrived forty minutes later. A veggie campana for her, a rocket and parmesan salad to share and a cinghiale for him. But where they found wild boar in the middle of the Manchester suburbs always puzzled him.

She was by his side even before he had carried the boxes through to the kitchen.

'I'm starving, I could eat a horse… Don't say it, Dad.'

'Don't say what?'

'Don't say what you were thinking.'

He unwrapped the packaging, bringing out the pizzas and the salad. This was almost a healthy dinner for him.

'So you're a mind reader now?'

'You were thinking horses aren't vegetarian.'

She had him in one. That was exactly what he was thinking. She would make a great copper.

'Am I right or am I right?'

'It's time to eat,' he said decisively. 'You want some Coke with it?'

She shook her head. 'Just water. I'm off carbonated drinks, too much sugar.'

He grabbed a beer from the fridge for himself and sat down beside her. 'Maths sorted?'

She tucked into her salad while he tore off a slice of pizza, folded it in half and took a large bite, far too large.

'Yeah.'

This was usual. He asked her about school every day, but received grunts if he was lucky and one-word answers when she was feeling particularly talkative. He decided to change tack.

'Olivia Rodrigo's coming to Manchester.'

She suddenly came alive. 'When? Can I go, please? Does Maisie know?'

He tried to calm her down. 'It's a Sunday, July 3, at the Apollo. You want me to get tickets?'

'Yeah, duh, she's brilliant. "drivers license" is a classic. And she loves purple just like me.'

'OK, I'll try and book the tickets for us.'

A frown crossed her face. 'You're not coming too?'

'I thought I might join you and Maisie. See what all the fuss is about?'

'Fuss? This is music, Dad, not fuss. Bowie is fuss.'

'Careful, you're treading on a minefield mentioning Saint David, particularly when you want me to buy the tickets.'

'But my friends might be there.'

'And dads are embarrassing?'

'Just a bit.'

'OK. I'll take you and wait outside till it's finished. Monday is a school day, so you need to be back early.'

'A deal. Let me go and tell Maisie.'

Taking her pizza with her, she clomped back upstairs, slamming the bedroom door once again.

Ridpath smiled. He loved making her happy. He knew this was probably overcompensation for the death of her mother, but he didn't care. If a dad couldn't make his daughter happy, what was the point of being a dad?

He took another slice of Rudy's pizza and bit down into it. The sudden flood of taste in his mouth reminded him he hadn't eaten all day. This morning, his trousers had felt so loose he'd tightened his belt one more notch. He needed to look after his diet better, as his daughter so often nagged him.

He took another bite and pulled up the doctor's report on the heart attack in Burnage. It wasn't pleasant reading.

Chapter Six

The coroner had chosen the cafe in Altrincham carefully. This person mustn't be spooked, not yet anyway. The place was busy enough she could lose herself among the other patrons but not so packed she couldn't have a quiet conversation.

Mrs Challinor had even invented a reason for the meeting; she was just looking for feedback into the coronial process from independent operators. How could they make reporting easier? Was there anything they could streamline? What timelines could reasonably be expected?

Hopefully, the person she'd invited for coffee wouldn't realise what her real purpose was until deep into the meeting. She was taking a risk, but it would be worth it if she confirmed her suspicions.

She had arrived fifteen minutes early to give herself time to find the right seat and settle her nerves. At least the formal aspects of the Davies inquest were now finished and all that remained was the jury's verdict. With a bit of luck it would come tomorrow and then she would be free to pursue this properly.

Sitting down at a table facing the door, she wiped her damp hands on a tissue and rearranged the notes in front of her, checking them one more time.

She had first noted the anomaly by chance. A conversation with the coroner for Cheshire over dinner at a conference six months ago was followed a day later by a request from Lancashire for information about the same person.

Normally, she wouldn't have noticed anything was wrong, but the coincidence of those two events happening so close together had started her searching. And then, also by chance, she had been working on a postponed inquest when the person's name came up again.

Three times in as many days. Was it just a coincidence?

At first she thought it was her imagination, or simply her determination to not make the same mistake again.

That mistake had been Harold Shipman. Although she hadn't been directly involved, she still blamed herself, and the whole coronial system, for missing so many deaths of elderly women for so long.

How many had the doctor in Hyde murdered? Nobody knew for sure. At least two hundred seemed to be the closest guess anybody could make. The inquiry into the deaths by Dame Janet Smith had made a number of recommendations, few of which were actually implemented on the grounds of cost.

Nothing had really changed in twenty years. For Mrs Challinor, it meant they had to be vigilant so a case like Shipman's never happened again.

It was why she was sitting in this cafe waiting for her guest to arrive. All her research had led her back to the same person, again and again. At least four murders, perhaps more, in the last fifteen years.

Was this person involved or was something else happening?

She tapped the table nervously. For a moment she was regretting not inviting Ridpath too. Should she have told him about her suspicions?

Probably, but he had a lot on his plate at the moment. She had to make sure first. After tonight's meeting, she would let him know, bring him in.

She wiped her hands again. Not like her to be so nervous.

The door to the cafe opened and her guest stood in the doorway.

Mrs Challinor stood up and put out her hand. It was the first time she had shaken hands with a murderer.

Friday, June 18

Chapter Seven

Detective Superintendent Claire Trent was waiting for him in her office. 'You're late,' was her greeting.

'Sorry, traffic. The A56 was chocka.'

'No excuse, be early next time.'

Ridpath spotted another man sitting opposite his boss, somebody he'd never met before.

'How is Mrs Challinor?'

'Busy as ever. The one thing people don't stop doing is dying, even in a recession.'

'I heard she was doing some investigating of her own…'

Ridpath watched as Claire Trent sat forward, obviously fishing for information.

'Is she?' Ridpath replied vaguely. 'News to me.'

His boss frowned, obviously unhappy with the answer. 'Anyway, I didn't invite you here to talk about the coroner.' She pointed to the silent man. 'This is Steve Carruthers from Police Scotland. He's just joined us in Manchester. And by 'us' I mean both Greater Manchester Police and MIT. This is your new DCI.'

The new Detective Chief Inspector stood up and held out his hand. 'I heard a lot about you, Ridpath, some of it even complimentary.'

The accent was broad Scots; the harsh tones of Glasgow, not the soft burr of Edinburgh. The man was short, not more than five foot six and slim, with the scent of a smoker about him. His handshake was firm without being vice-like.

'You must have been talking to my mother, sir.'

'Call me Steve, I hate all that "sir" boloney. And I haven't got round to your mother yet, she's next on my list.'

'That'll be difficult. She passed away a few years ago.'

'I won't bother her then, not for a few days anyway.'

At least he had a sense of humour, unlike his predecessor, Paul Turnbull. Ridpath wondered what else his boss had told Carruthers.

'Take a seat,' she ordered. 'Steve wants to brief you on a job.'

The DCI handed him a beige folder with a long list of numbers on the cover. A case file.

Carruthers was staring at him. 'I've heard you're a bit of a maverick who cuts corners but gets the job done.'

Ridpath said nothing, opening the folder and looking at the first page.

'I have nothing against mavericks myself. Every force needs one or two. Those investigators who can look at a case and see a new way to tackle it rather than a time-server who follows the police manual like it was an IKEA instruction book. This job should be right up your alley.'

The report was titled 'Executive Summary'. Ridpath laughed to himself. So he was an executive now, news to him. Ridpath read the first paragraph.

> **While clearing an old warehouse prior to its demolition, workers broke into a sealed room and discovered two dead bodies, a male and a female, arm in arm.**

'I remember reading about this in the *Evening News* six months ago. Didn't the site foreman want to cover it up but one of the workers rang 999?'

'That's the one. Didn't want his construction schedule to be messed with. Sometimes I despair of these idiots...'

Ridpath read on.

Post-mortems on the bodies revealed both the deceased were in their late teens and had probably been entombed in the room roughly fifteen years ago. But the exact date has still not yet been confirmed.

'Entombed?'

'They were walled up in a closed room and left to die, Ridpath. A little water, no food, just each other,' said Trent.

'That's why the press have called it the Romeo and Juliet murders,' added DCI Carruthers.

Ridpath read on.

No wallet, ID or phone was found with the bodies. Speculation as to the identity of the two victims has been rife. Students? Runaways from a care home? Young lovers? But extensive investigations have not revealed their identities nor the reason for their incarceration.

Were they entombed voluntarily or were they walled up against their will? Scratches and marks on the door and the walls indicate the incarceration was involuntary; they had tried to escape. Traces of the man's nails were embedded in the wood of the door.

Ridpath turned the page. There was just one more paragraph.

Manchester Central's Criminal Investigation Department (CID) under Chief Inspector David Meredith was put in charge of the case. But despite a large team, inquiries with previous owners of the building, extensive publicity and calls for help from the public, even a spot on the BBC's *North West Tonight* programme, no headway has been made. The victims are still

unknown and, so far, no suspects have been identified.

'Meredith? I don't know him.'

'Another new hire. This time from South Yorkshire. He came across with the chief constable.'

Ridpath nodded and read the file one more time. At the end, in a pocket, he found two photofit pictures of a young man and woman.

'Those were our best attempts at a likeness of the victims,' explained Carruthers, 'We're treating this as murder.'

'Could it be some sort of weird suicide pact?'

Trent coughed. 'Here's the pathologist's report – you'll realise why we ruled out suicide. We're calling the two victims Female A and Male B.'

'Catchier than Romeo and Juliet.' Ridpath quickly scanned the document, noticing the signature at the end was signed John Schofield. At least he had worked with the pathologist before.

When he had finished, Trent continued speaking. 'As you can see the room was locked from the outside and then a brick wall was built to cover the doorway with the wall plastered over to conceal it. If the building hadn't been due to be demolished, Female A and Male B could have lain there undiscovered for another fifteen years. Both victims were drugged, probably to prevent their escape.' She glanced across at DCI Carruthers and he took the hint.

'We'd like you to take over the case, Ridpath, see what you can make of it.'

'We are extremely busy in the coroner's office at the moment...' Ridpath played for time, desperately trying to assess whether this case was a poisoned chalice. It was six months old and such cases were notoriously difficult to solve.

'Mrs Challinor was reluctant to release you, saying you were busy, but once I mentioned this case, she agreed. Apparently she is also the coroner for this case, and will be postponing the inquest while we complete our inquiries.' Trent spoke forcefully, closing the folder in front of her and sitting back in her chair.

'Won't I be stepping on Meredith's size tens?'

It was Steve Carruthers who answered this time. 'Probably. But this is an instruction from the chief constable. It's a high profile case and he wants it solved. There's another visit soon coming from Her Majesty's Inspectorate of Constabulary...'

GMP had been put in special measures last year by the Inspectorate for a long list of of failures including not recording crimes properly and slow response times.

Ridpath rubbed his nose, finishing Carruthers' sentence for him. '...and the chief constable would like a win to show he's making a positive difference, particularly as the Met is now in special measures too.'

Trent glanced at her DCI. 'See, Steve, I told you Ridpath was aware of the politics of police work. It's only the naivety with which he uses the knowledge which lets him down.'

It was as if he was no longer in the room.

'We're giving you eight days, Ridpath. Get moving and get a result. Consider it a little test of your capabilities.'

'Any support?'

'Who do you want?'

'Chrissy Wright and DS Parkinson.'

'The usual mob?' said Trent.

'I prefer to think of them as an investigative team.'

'You've got them. But keep us updated on your every move. I don't want either myself or DCI Carruthers to find stuff out before you tell us. Communication is key, Ridpath, and remember the chief constable will be sitting on my shoulder watching everything.'

'Got it.' Ridpath held up the folder. 'Is this it?'

'Well, Meredith, has a lot more...'

'...but you haven't told him I'm investigating his case yet.'

'No, we thought we'd leave the pleasure to you.' Carruthers turned to DSU Trent. 'You were right, he does understand the politics of police work.'

Ridpath stood up to leave.

'One last thing,' Trent said, fixing him with a stare. 'Find out what Mrs Challinor is up to. I don't like coroners stomping around our territory. It could lead to problems.'

'I don't know what Mrs Challinor is doing, boss, she hasn't told me.'

'And even if she did, you wouldn't tell me?'

Ridpath didn't answer, holding up the folder instead. 'Shall I get on with this job, boss?'

She nodded. 'You have just over a week – don't screw it up.'

Ridpath walked out of the room, closing the door behind him. As he did, he saw Trent and the new DCI talking in low voices. He couldn't catch what they were saying, but whatever it was, it probably wasn't good news for him.

Chapter Eight

'Right, Chrissy and Emily, we have a job.'

The other detectives in MIT looked up from behind their computers, before quickly returning back to their screens at the mention of new work.

Chrissy Wright ran out from behind her desk wearing a Manchester City scarf around her neck despite it being the middle of summer and the football season at least one month away. 'About bloody time. If I have to go through crime stats for Stalybridge one more time, I'm going to become a United fan.'

DS Emily Parkinson also joined him as he searched for an empty meeting room, finally finding one.

'What is it? I have a stabbing in Moss Side but it's just a question of dotting the i's and crossing the t's. The gang's WhatsApp messages show communal action before the attack.' She sniffed once, dabbing at her nose with a paper handkerchief. 'Bloody hay fever. Pumped full of antihistamines and I'm still a wreck.'

'Haven't the gangs realised we can read their phones?'

'Well, none of them is going to win Brain of Britain.'

He showed her the folder. 'We've been asked to look into the Romeo and Juliet case.'

'The couple found in the bricked-up room? They were discovered six months ago.'

'I know, but Manchester CID have hit a brick wall.'

Chrissy covered her mouth with her hand. 'Brick wall, Ridpath, really?'

He realised what he had said and quickly rephrased. 'They've hit some obstacles in the investigation.'

'I remember reading the newspapers when the bodies were discovered. They'd lain in that warehouse untouched for nearly fifteen years. What do they expect?'

'They expect progress, Emily. And by "they," I mean the sixth floor.' He pointed upwards.

'Oh, it's one of *those* jobs,' she said knowingly.

'Do you want the good news or the bad news?'

Emily and Chrissy looked at each other, saying at the same time, 'The good news.'

'We've been given a free hand and all the resources we need to get to the bottom of this. The chief constable wants a result before the next Inspectorate of Constabulary report.'

'There must be a catch,' said Chrissy.

'The inspectors are coming soon. We have eight days to make progress.'

She whistled. 'That's a pretty big catch.'

'So let me get this straight,' said Emily, tapping the desk in front of her, 'Manchester CID have had this for six months and made no progress, and we get just over a week to clear it up?'

'That's it.'

'Sounds perfectly reasonable to me. Classic GMP. So what are the next steps?'

'Chrissy, I'd like you to dig up everything Meredith and the team have discovered so far. The case number is written on the folder. Email Emily and me the files when you have them. A little light reading for this evening. Can you also check on HOLMES and see if there are any similar cases in the last fifteen years or so? No – make it twenty years, just in case.'

HOLMES was the Home Office Large Major Enquiry System, which logged and compared all major crimes in the UK. It was starting to show its age, but in the absence of anything else, it was one of the best tools they had.

'Won't Meredith and his team have already done it?'

'Probably, but I would rather trust Chrissy's ability to manipulate the data than some plod from Central.'

'What do you want me to do?' asked Emily.

'I want you to come with me to the crime scene. Let's see what we have.'

'Won't it be destroyed by now?' said Chrissy. 'I thought they were going to build one of those new skyscrapers that have been shooting up like mushrooms after the rain in Manchester. Last time I was in the city centre there were more building sites and cranes than there were people. Looked like they were creating more monstrosities.'

'Listen, our job is to investigate a crime, not to comment on the architectural progress of Manchester in the last decade.'

'Progress?' Chrissy snorted.

'Aren't half the buildings owned by City's owners? Some Abu Dhabi development corporation?' said Emily.

Chrissy didn't answer, making notes in her book instead.

Was there something going on between the two of them? Ridpath decided to ease the tension. 'It won't hurt to take a look anyway.'

'When are we going?'

Ridpath stood up. 'There's no time like the present.'

Chapter Nine

Of course, Emily had to have a cigarette before they went to the crime scene. They both stood outside Police HQ in the area assigned to the pariahs who were still smokers.

Ridpath stood downwind, inhaling the secondary smoke from her cigarette. He had promised Eve a year ago he would give up smoking. And, except for a slight lapse last November, had kept his promise. Anyway, secondary smoke didn't count, did it?

Off to the left, on his own, he could see DCI Carruthers checking his phone and smoking. Their eyes met for a second and his new boss nodded, but stayed where he was.

'What do you think of our new man?' he asked Emily.

'Seems all right. Gave us all a speech yesterday which was refreshingly free of the usual copper-speak or corporate bollocks. But I guess the bar is pretty low after Turnbull.'

'Have you heard what happened to him?'

Turnbull was their ex-boss, with whom Ridpath had a few problems. Or, more correctly, Turnbull had problems with him.

'I heard he's a superintendent with the Lancashire force.'

'They must be desperate.'

'Shit always rises to the top. After the cuts of the last decade, all the forces are short of experienced staff so they're poaching from each other, and the Met hasn't even started yet. Wait till the new commissioner realises what a mess it's in and starts looking for new people.'

'Would you go and work in London?'

'I might.' She held up her cigarette. 'Try out the smoke in the Smoke for a while. I'm not getting any younger and GMP don't look like they'll promote me soon.'

'You're a good copper, Emily, they'll see it soon enough.'

'But we seem to be lead by the blind, and I'm running out of patience.'

'Hang on in there. See how Carruthers turns out.'

She frowned. 'I don't know, Ridpath, sometimes with all the shite, I just think it's never going change.'

'You think it would be different elsewhere?'

'No, but *I* would be different elsewhere. GMP has pigeon-holed me as another permanent detective sergeant. Jesus, Rhona Cartwright was promoted last week and she was in the same class as me at Edgeley Park. It's like I'm treading water, going nowhere fast. In fact, I'm gradually sinking.' She stomped out the cigarette beneath her sensible shoes.

'Do you want me to have a word with Claire Trent?'

Emily shook her head and laughed. 'That could make it worse. And what about you? Aren't you still a probationary inspector? What is it now, three years?'

Just before being diagnosed with cancer, Ridpath had been promoted to inspector. Normally the probationary period would last a year. In his case, it had been allowed to go on much longer.

'You know all you have to do is attach yourself to a successful collar.'

'Or be seen to be attached to success?'

Ridpath smiled ruefully. 'There is that. It's amazing how many unsolved cases suddenly have nobody in charge of them.'

'Is that what we have with this one?'

'Perhaps, but it's up to us to change it.'

'A crime which happened nearly fifteen years ago? You do know the chances of us cracking it in just over a week are about the same as United winning the league this year.' She held up her hand, using the fingers to form a zero.

'You *are* in a bad away, aren't you, Emily? You should know United's chances are far less than zero.'

DCI Carruthers walked past them, going back into Police HQ, checking his watch.

'I would have thought you'd be in Central Manchester by now, Ridpath.'

'Just going there.'

'Aye, well good luck. Old cases are never easy to crack.' He turned to Emily. 'And you are?'

'DS Parkinson, sir.'

'Call me Steve or guvnor, DS Parkinson.'

'Thank you, sir, and you can call me Emily,' she said cheekily.

Carruthers coughed quietly. 'Right, Emily, you're part of Ridpath's team?'

'On this case, sir.'

'Good luck. We're counting on you.'

He walked away up the steps, vanishing into the dark heart of Police HQ.

'You didn't have to rub his nose in it.'

'Says the man who, ever since I've known him, has bent every rule from every boss in MIT.'

'I haven't.'

'You have, Ridpath. Every. Single. Time.'

'Yeah? Well, the case and the victims matter, not the fragile egos of some ambitious wannabes who'd sell their grandmothers for a promotion. Sometimes people forget that the real job is to stick crooks inside, not to climb up the ladder in GMP.'

'God, you sound like me.'

He tilted his head. 'Let's get going before you infect me even further with your bolshiness.'

'Welcome to the Liam Gallagher school of policing, Ridpath.'

He walked towards his car, singing 'Wonderwall'.

Emily ran after him, joining in on the chorus, both of them imitating the man's nasal Manchester voice perfectly.

Chapter Ten

I hadn't slept all night.

Had she discovered me? Or was this just a fishing expedition?

I know she had been looking into our operation, I'd seen the first indications over two months ago. It wasn't difficult to discover she had been asking questions, too many questions.

As soon as I found out, I researched her.

It's remarkable how lax public officials are with their information. Almost as if they don't know how to keep anything secret. Her home address was easy to find over the internet, posted in the newsletter of some professional organisation – Women in Law. You would think if they were legal professionals they would know better than to reveal such important personal information.

I scoped out her home, followed her patterns of behaviour, the details of her life plain to see. There's often something more enjoyable in the planning and research than in the execution itself.

But how had she found me?

I'd covered my tracks. None of the other deaths had ever been traced back to me.

Why her? Why was she the one asking questions?

Was it the deaths in Manchester? Had I made a mistake all those years ago, and it was now catching up with me?

When the bodies had been discovered six months ago, I read the papers, watching for news, waiting for any announcements. I knew they were getting desperate when they broadcast an appeal on the local BBC news programme. I even sent in a tip, anonymously of course. Our local undertaker received a visit from the police and was taken in for questioning.

Nasty man, he deserved every second of the grilling they gave him.

And then out of the blue, I received an invite over the phone.

'Let's meet up for a coffee at the end of the week. I'd love to pick your brains about a revision to the forms for death certificates issued by independent clinics. I'd like to make the whole process far easier and more streamlined.'

I knew it was rubbish from the moment she opened her lying mouth.

But I went anyway. Better the devil you know than the one you don't.

After the initial introductions the whole atmosphere changed. She asked me a direct question.

'Your clinic has been involved in giving evidence in quite a few different inquests in recent years. Why is that?'

How had she pulled the information together? The inquests were in different parts of the country. What had she noticed? What had I missed?

I shifted uncomfortably in my seat before answering. 'Just one of those things, I suppose. Our patients do come from all over the country. In the last ten years alone, we must have treated over fifteen thousand people. It is inevitable we are called to attend inquests in Coroner's Courts.'

I could see she wasn't convinced by my answer. She sipped her coffee, looking at me over the top of her spectacles, her grey hair like Medusa's in the lights of the cafe.

'But it is strange, wouldn't you agree? The verdict in three of these inquests was unlawful killing by a person or persons unknown. One other, the one I am involved with, dubbed the Romeo and Juliet deaths by the papers, is still under investigation by Manchester police.'

So it was the warehouse deaths. How had she discovered my involvement?

'Don't you find it a little strange that your clinic was involved in all three inquests?'

'I have no control over the conclusions reached by coroners or their juries during an inquest,' I answered, avoiding the question.

She had smiled at me then and licked her lips like a boa constrictor staring at a fat chicken who had wandered into her domain.

'Of course you don't, but it is rather strange, isn't it?'

We finished soon after, going our separate ways with all the false niceties only true enemies can exhibit.

Has she worked it all out? How had she discovered me? What mistakes had I made?

I'd covered my tracks so well, making sure that I left behind no trace of my involvement in the deaths.

I spent the rest of the night lying awake, thinking it through, reliving every last second of the meeting in the cafe.

I think she has somehow linked me to the deaths in the warehouse. But she can't have any evidence, can she? It would all be circumstantial. So long ago now, I can hardly remember. They were my first, and I took no pleasure in killing them.

If she had any proof, there would have been a herd of coppers with her last night. But she was alone. Is this just a pet project? Is she flying solo?

I think she is. But I can't take the risk any longer. Last night's meeting was warning enough. Time to bring her down to earth.

Too much is at stake. All my work over the years would be wasted. I can't allow that.

Not now, not ever.

Time to sort her out.

Time to take care of business.

Chapter Eleven

The old warehouse in which the bodies had been found was now covered in hoardings announcing an 'exciting new mixed retail, commercial and lifestyle habitat, perfect for twenty-first century living'.

'What's that?'

'What's what?' Ridpath answered as he parked on the double yellow lines in front of the building.

'"Twenty-first century living"?'

He thought for a moment. 'It probably means thirty storeys of thin-walled rabbit hutches with an achingly trendy cafe/restaurant/art gallery at the bottom and a mortgage transferable to your grandchildren.'

Emily stepped out of the car. 'I checked out a flat in New Islington last week. Over four hundred grand for two bedrooms with a view of some bins.' She looked up at the small print on the poster. '"One-bedroom units available at the special price of £388,888." Jesus, that's three times the cost of my flat. And why such a strange price?'

'Aimed at Chinese buyers. The number eight sounds the same as good luck in Chinese.' Despite being born and bred in Manchester, Polly, Ridpath's deceased wife, had been a devout believer in Chinese traditions. She had spent many hours educating him on the details of Chinese geomancy, feng shui and fortune-telling. No amount of him saying what a load of old poppycock it was could ever shake her belief in the old ways.

Ridpath locked the car door and checked the area. Most of the street had already been demolished and tarmacked over to create a series of windswept car parks. A few buildings remained, decrepit and run down, quarantined as unacceptable in the new Manchester. The new stuff was as soulless as the architects who had designed them. He was all for regeneration of the city but did it have to be so ugly and so depressing?

'Now that's the Manchester I remember.' He pointed to a large mural painted on one of the few buildings left standing.

'Who is it?'

'Who is it? *Who is it?* It's only Ian Curtis, isn't it? My one claim to fame: he was born in the same hospital as me. Stretford Memorial on Seymour Grove. Mind you, I didn't arrive kicking and screaming until twenty-five years after him.'

'He looks vaguely familiar. Wasn't he a singer or something?'

'Singer? He was a chronicler of the end of punk and the beginning of Manchester music as we know it. Joy Division and New Order started the new movement, making the city cool.'

'Manchester's cool? In winter, maybe.' She looked around her. 'So he's to blame for all this. It's no wonder they put his face on the side of a building.'

'Oi, you can't park here. We've got a delivery.' A large red-faced man had rushed out through a hole in the hoarding.

Both Ridpath and Emily pulled out their warrant cards. 'Detective Inspector Thomas Ridpath. And you are?'

'Phil Turner, site manager.' The man stuck out a large, dirt encrusted hand.

Ridpath ignored it. 'We're here to look at the crime scene on the third floor.'

'Again? I thought you lot had finished here months ago.'

'It's still an ongoing investigation.'

The man bowed slightly and waved towards the open door in the hoarding. 'Be my guest. But you'd better get a move on.'

'Why?'

'It's coming down tomorrow.'

'What?'

'This.' He pointed backwards at the building, then spoke slowly, as if educating a child. 'The whole lot coming down. Boom.'

'You can't do that, it's a crime scene.'

'Not any more it isn't.' He reached into his oversized neon green jacket, pulling out a stuffed planner. He flicked through the pages before selecting a sheet of paper. 'Here's the official release.'

Ridpath read through the paper. It was a letter dated June 14 from Chief Inspector Meredith stating the address on Port Street was no longer designated a crime scene by the police and was released back into the ownership of Intrepid Manchester Properties Ltd, incorporated in the British Virgin Islands.

'When are you starting demolition?'

'Like I said, tomorrow. Two days from now this is going to be a car park.'

Ridpath looked around. 'Just what the area needs, huh?'

'Exactly,' answered the man without irony.

'What's the rush?'

He shrugged his shoulders. 'Orders from the boss: Pull it down.'

'Is it still safe to enter?' asked Emily.

'As houses. The Victorians knew how to build this stuff.'

Ridpath looked up at the old warehouse, seeing the elegant Victorian brickwork and green-tiled frontage. In the centre, above the door, a chiselled plaque proudly announced it was built in 1887. He couldn't help but wonder how many people had walked through these doors when Manchester was the centre of the world's cotton manufacturing and exporting, a hive of industry.

He moved towards the hole in the hoarding, then stopped. 'Were you here when the bodies were found?'

'Yeah, not one of our best days.'

'What happened?'

'The lads were clearing the building. They found a bricked-up room on the third floor. We called the police and they've been hovering over the place like flies round shit ever since. Romeo and Juliet the papers called them. Just two dead bodies getting in the way is how I see it.'

Ridpath pointed towards the building. 'Anybody inside?'

'Two men clearing away the rubbish.'

'Were they the ones who found the bodies?'

'One of them was, Barry. We had to let the other one go.'

'The one who reported it to the police?'

Turner nodded. 'He was a student anyway.'

'We'll need to speak to Barry.'

'Be my guest, he's just getting rid of your stuff.'

'Our stuff?'

'The tape and plastic sheets. Didn't think you needed them any more.'

'What? You've cleared the crime scene?'

Phil Turner waved the paper. 'Not a crime scene any more.'

Chapter Twelve

Ridpath and Emily found the man they were looking for on the ground floor, stuffing what looked like crime scene tape into a large pink skip.

'Are you Barry?' asked Emily.

The man stopped what he was doing and turned to face them. He was tall with biceps the size of rugby balls bulging beneath a tight T-shirt.

'Who wants to know?'

They flashed their warrant cards. 'It's about the Romeo and Juliet case.'

'Jesus, I've talked to your lot about twenty times. Wish I'd never been anywhere near those bodies. I'm going to swing for Dan when I see him.'

'Dan was with you when you found them?'

The man nodded. 'He was the bloody idiot who reported it to 999. He should've done what Mr Turner said and just ignored them. Once the wrecking balls had been in, nobody would have been any the wiser.'

'But it's an offence not to report a death.'

'Do you think I care?'

'Why don't you tell us exactly what happened,' Emily interrupted, glancing over at Ridpath.

The man turned to face her, striking a pose. 'Like I said, I told your lot twenty times already. Why don't you ask them?'

'Tell us one more time, Barry,' Emily answered, 'for luck. Or we could go down to the local nick and do the interview there. Might take a few hours though, we'd have to book you in, check your past, previous offences, go through your history. It always amazes me what we find when we decide to look into somebody's past.' Emily took out her notebook. 'So what's it to be, Barry? Here or down the nick?'

Barry shrugged his shoulders and scuffed the ground with his feet. 'Telling you lot one more time won't hurt.'

'What's your full name?'

'Barry Hutchings.'

'And Dan?'

'O'Donnell, I think. He was a student, just working part-time over the holidays. Don't bother getting to know them.'

'So what happened?'

The man seemed to consider this and then spoke slowly. 'Mr Turner asked me and Dan to work on the top floor. The bastard always gave Dan the hard stuff to do. Meant we had to carry everything down three flights of stairs—'

'Woah, back up,' Ridpath held his hands up. 'What were you doing?'

Barry sighed and then explained as if he was talking to an idiot. 'Before the wreckers come in to take these old places apart, our job is to clear them. The boss makes money from the scrap. Get all the wood and metal we can find and sort it into separate skips. The rubbish left over always goes in another pile. Turner was in a hurry because the lads with the big balls were coming in the next day.' Barry looked around at the still standing brick walls. 'That worked out for him, didn't it?'

'So you went inside this building?'

'Yeah, the ground floor was a mess; broken windows, rubbish everywhere, exposed timbers where the old plasterwork had come away. Must have been used as a flophouse by the dossers at some point. There was an old fire made of bricks with a couple of broken sofas and some empty cider bottles. You have to be careful clearing these old places, you never know what you'll find.'

'So what happened?' coaxed Emily.

'We went up to the top floor. The place was much cleaner up there than down here. I pulled down a tarpaulin to let some light in—'

'You want to show us?' asked Ridpath.

They walked up some graffiti-strewn stairs. On the first landing, large neon letters shouted 'Graham Street Reds'.

'One of the local gangs marking out their territory,' explained Barry.

'Wasn't the place sealed as a crime scene?'

He shrugged his broad shoulders again. 'Can't stop the local kids getting in.'

Ridpath sighed. 'Let's go up.'

On the third floor, they walked to the end of the room. The windows had been boarded up but light shone in through two grimy skylights. One of them had been broken and pigeons had flown in, nesting in the rafters, their feathers dotted around the floor like snowflakes.

The room itself was open plan, probably a place for storing bales of worked pieces ready for export, not more than forty feet long and twenty wide. The sides of the room still showed the raw brick of their construction but the end gable walls had been covered in green plaster. Ridpath remembered the name of the colour. *Eau de Nil*. The waters of the Nile next to the canals of Manchester.

'When we walked up here, the place was dark, so I pulled down another tarp which covered those.' He pointed to the skylights.

'And what was here?'

'The middle bit was clear, just bare floorboards, but each end had stuff piled against it.'

'You'd think the previous owners would have already cleared it.'

'I dunno,' Barry shrugged his immense shoulders again, 'but somebody had already taken away the good stuff. I started going through the pile at this end and Dan started down over there.'

Ridpath looked to the far end. A hole had been knocked through the doorway to reveal a small room hidden inside. There was no evidence the police, or the bodies, had ever been there. All the paraphernalia that should have been guarding a crime scene had been removed.

'So the doorway was bricked up?'

'Yeah, your lot took most of the bricks away.'

'How did you find the doorway?'

'I didn't, Dan did.'

Emily rolled her eyes. 'How did Dan find the doorway?'

'He dug his way through a load of boxes full of old newspapers and rubbish in front of the wall. Looked like stuff from a house clearance; mops and brushes, an ironing board, an old table, and a chest of drawers. A load of crap basically. We were going to throw it all out. Then he saw an old green army blanket with those arrows in the corner covering a set of planks leaning against the far wall.'

'So what did you do?'

'I helped him pull it down, covering myself in dust, pigeon crap and old feathers, thought it might be worth a few bob. It was then we saw it.'

'What?'

'The wall had been plastered over but roughly, not a proper job, and the plaster was a different colour.'

'What?' asked Ridpath.

It was Barry's turn to roll his eyes. 'A different colour. We could see the shape of a doorway. I remember Dan saying there could be something valuable behind it.'

'The doorway wasn't hidden?'

'Once we'd cleared away the rubbish and the old army blanket covering it, you could see it as plain as I can see you two in front of me.'

Emily glanced at Ridpath. They were both thinking the same thing. Why hadn't it been discovered sooner?

Ridpath walked over and examined the opening. The few remaining bricks abutted the architrave surrounding the door.

They were a different colour and size from those in the rest of the room; a bright red versus a dark brown. Bits of old, off-white plaster still stuck to them.

Emily carried on questioning the big man. 'So what did you do?'

'I went downstairs to get a sledgehammer.'

'You didn't tell Turner what you had found?'

'Not yet. He was always taking the good stuff for himself.'

'So you used the sledgehammer...'

'It only took two blows and we were through, it wasn't well built, bit amateurish.'

'And what did you see?'

'Nothing, it was too dark. So Dan used his torch on his phone and we saw a door. We tried to turn the knob but it was locked.'

'What did you do next?'

Barry flexed his muscles. 'Used the sledgehammer on the lock. It didn't last long,' he said proudly.

Ridpath checked the architrave. 'Where's the door now?'

'I think your lot took it away.'

'What happened next?'

'Like I said, it was dark inside, so Dan crawled through with his mobile phone. It was like the man in the movies with the hat...'

'Who?'

'The man who discovers treasure with his dad, you know, Indian somebody or other.'

'He means Indiana Jones,' interrupted Ridpath.

'Right,' said Emily, smiling, 'so what happened next?'

'He crawled through the hole and the door and all I heard was "Jesus Christ".'

Ridpath stepped through the doorway. 'He'd found the bodies?'

'That's right, Sherlock. They were lying over there next to each other.' He pointed to the far corner without stepping into the room.

'You called Turner?'

The man nodded. 'He didn't want to call you lot, said it would put the schedule out.' He laughed. 'It's certainly done that. But Dan insisted and called 999.'

'Can you show us where exactly you found the bodies?'

The big man shook his head vigorously. 'I ain't going in there again. No way.'

Ignoring him, Ridpath squeezed through the hole, checking the edges of the bricks as he did, followed by Emily.

The room was small, only ten foot in length from the bricked-up door to the end wall and half the width of the floor. A small glass skylight high in the apex, where the wall met the roof, only let in a dull grey light despite the sun shining brightly outside. The room was stuffy and airless, the wooden floorboards swept clear, a small pile of dust and a brush in the corner.

'You've done a good job clearing it up. You can come round to my house and do the same, if you want.'

Barry didn't answer.

Emily looked. around. 'I wonder what it was used for?'

'Storing valuable materials? Or an office for the overseer?' answered Ridpath.

Emily moved to the corner. A vague chalk mark in the shape of two bodies appeared faintly on the floorboards in the corner. 'They were here?' she asked, looking back at Barry Hutchings. The big man was still standing outside the room, refusing to enter. He nodded his head.

The chalk-marked bodies seemed to be lying next to each other on their sides, face to face. Ridpath squatted down to get closer.

'We need to see the crime scene photographs. I hope they dusted the bricks they removed for fingerprints.'

'We still don't know who the two people were?' asked Emily.

'Not according to the briefing given to me by Claire Trent. They are still Female A and Male B.'

'Somebody must have missed them. In this day and age, two people can't just go missing.'

'You'd have thought so. But despite the appeals for information, nobody has come forward so far. At least nobody with a confirmed link to them.'

Ridpath took one last look around the room, imagining what it would have been like to have been locked up here with no food or water, slowly dying together.

Emily shivered. 'This place gives me the creeps. It's a tomb, not an office. The sooner they tear it down, the better.'

'But not yet, Emily, not till we've finished.'

'What does that mean?'

'I need to get a stay of execution on the place, at least for one more week. There may be something here everybody has missed.'

'You're going to have to move quickly, the wrecking crew is coming in tomorrow.'

'That's why we're off to see Chief Inspector Meredith immediately. If he signed the order, he can unsign it.'

Chapter Thirteen

'Who the hell are you to come in here and tell me what to do?'

'As I explained sir, DS Parkinson and I have been briefed to look at the Romeo and Juliet case to see if anything has been missed.'

'Briefed by whom?'

'Detective Superintendent Claire Trent of MIT, apparently under the express orders of the chief constable.'

Chief Inspector Meredith was sitting behind his desk, his shirt dazzling white. It was in startling contrast to his face, which was becoming increasingly red.

'You're going to check on my investigation!'

'Not really, sir, just a fresh pair of eyes to see if anything was missed.'

'Listen, sonny, I was a copper when you were hanging off your mother's tit, and your oppo here,' he jerked a thumb at Emily Parkinson, 'was just a stain on her father's underwear.'

'My name is Detective Inspector Thomas Ridpath, not "sonny". I must request you give me the courtesy my rank requires… *sir*.'

'We'll see about that.' Meredith snatched up his mobile phone and speed-dialled a number. It rang and rang before finally being answered. 'Hiya, mate, it's Dave. Look, I have some detective inspector here from MIT saying he's been ordered to look into my investigation. The two bodies found in the warehouse on my patch. The Romeo and Juliet case.'

Ridpath and Emily stood in front of the desk; they hadn't been asked to sit down.

Meredith was nodding at the end of the phone as something was being explained to him.

'Is it necessary, mate? You know me, I don't make mistakes. Everything is done by the book, that's why you brought me here.'

Another series of head nods and ah-has, followed by a long silence, and then, 'I understand.'

He put the phone down on his desk next to his hat with its rank prominently displayed.

'Apparently, you are not "looking at my case", as you so wrongfully described it, Inspector.'

'That's what I was briefed, sir.'

'Well, you were briefed incorrectly. Your role is to go through the documentation and the progress of the case prior to the arrival of Her Majesty's Inspectorate of Constabulary next week. You have been given eight days to deliver your report, is that correct?'

'It is, sir, but I—'

'You will receive the full cooperation and support of this division in your work, Inspector,' Meredith interrupted, 'reporting back to me with your conclusions.'

'With all due respect, sir, I report to DS Claire Trent and DCI Carruthers. If you want to see my report, I suggest you talk to them.'

'Oh, I will, Detective Inspector Ridpath, I most certainly will.'

'Good. In the meantime, can I request you rescind the letter you sent to the property developers allowing them to proceed with demolition. Given the arrival of Her Majesty's inspectors next week, it might look a little strange if they wanted to see the crime scene only to be told it was now a pile of bricks and dust.'

Emily glanced at Ridpath.

Meredith's head dropped to his chest and he appeared deep in thought. Finally, he spoke, almost whispering. 'It might be better to wait until they have returned to London. I'll send the letter today.'

'I suggest you call them first. The site manager's number is here.' Ridpath slid over Turner's card.

'I'll talk to the developer directly, I'm sure he'll understand. Ronnie Hardcastle is a fair man. Anything else?'

'I'll need all the documentation and files on the case.'

'I'll send them over to MIT this afternoon.' A long pause. 'You know my team and I spent six months working on this case, Inspector. We interviewed 376 people, looked into over four thousand leads from a television appeal and checked out 4,598 missing persons who vanished in the year 2008. You think you're going to solve it all in a week?'

'I don't know, sir, fresh eyes and all that. We can but try...'

Meredith stood up and held out his hand. Ridpath shook it, feeling the Masonic grip and touch on his palm.

'I'm sorry I flew off the handle, stress and everything.'

'Understandable, sir, nobody likes their investigation being reviewed.'

Meredith stared at him, trying to work out whether he was being sarcastic. 'A week, huh? Good luck – you're going to need it.'

Chapter Fourteen

'That was awkward.' Emily took another drag on her cigarette as they walked to the car.

'The old fiefdoms are still strong in GMP. This is my patch and stay off it or I'll string you up by your balls.' He inhaled the secondary smoke, enjoying the rich redolent tobacco smell of an Embassy extra mild. 'Sometimes, I wonder if we spend more time fighting each other than we do fighting crime. At least they'll preserve the crime scene in case we have to go back.'

'Where to next?'

'It's time to pay a visit to the pathologist, Dr Schofield. We need to know more about the bodies and how they died.'

'We could just read the post-mortem report.'

'Why bother when we can go straight to the source? I called him earlier, he can give us twenty minutes.'

'Aren't we going to eat, Ridpath?'

'Eat?' He spotted the teal blue sign of a Greggs on the other side of the road. 'How about a veggie sausage roll?'

Emily was about to say OK despite having already eaten six that week, when her phone buzzed. 'It's Chrissy, she's found the files on the GMP intranet for the case. She's going to compile them and send us the file name later.'

'Great, with them and Meredith's documents, we should have a complete case history. Has she checked HOLMES yet?'

Emily glanced at her phone. 'Her next job apparently.'

'Right then, let's get you the vegan special. I feel like a bacon sarnie.'

'You don't look like one.' She exhaled more smoke. 'That stuff will kill you, Ridpath.'

'Well, it certainly killed the pig. But there's something indescribably delicious about the taste of grilled bacon on a barm cake smothered in butter with just a splat of brown sauce.'

'You know I haven't eaten meat since I was sixteen?'

'You don't know what you're missing.'

'Clogged arteries, high blood pressure, excess salt, heart disease, pneumonia, diabetes, diverticular disease, and colon polyps.'

'Sounds delicious. I didn't know they had it on the Greggs menu.'

'Comes with a side order of chips.'

'Even better.'

After ordering the food, Emily devoured it in the car as Ridpath drove to the pathologist's office.

'Aren't you having yours?

'Later, I'm not hungry.'

'Cold bacon sarnie? You have to eat something, Ridpath.'

'You sound like Eve.'

'How is she?'

'Thirteen going on thirty-three.' He suddenly remembered he'd promised to pick her up from school today.

'Look, after this meeting, I may have to go to her school. I'll read the files later tonight.'

'No problem. What do you want me to do?'

'Follow up with Meredith on his documentation and go through the files yourself. Two pairs of eyes will help. Let's meet up tomorrow at nine at MIT,' he turned into the road leading to the mortuary. 'We're here.'

'Another visit to the morgue. Just what I need after eating a vegan sausage roll,' sighed Emily.

Chapter Fifteen

The following morning, I made my decision. I couldn't wait any longer, now was the time to act. Last night's meeting at the cafe had been the final straw.

I was at her home before six, scoping out the land, preparing my plan.

A quick recce and I saw a problem. She wasn't alone, a young woman was staying with her.

No matter, I'd seen her this morning walking the dog as usual. She would do the same later. People, no matter what their position, are creatures of habit. This one more so than most.

This was going to be new territory for me. Normally, I preferred to take my time, plan properly, make sure every base was covered and every angle taken care of. But with this woman, I had to act quickly. There was no time to waste.

Unfortunately, my methods would have to change for this death. A more pragmatic approach had to be taken.

Usually, I preferred to be far away when they died. It was a way of protecting myself and ensuring no investigators could ever associate me with the murders. Besides, I had no desire to see people die up close and personal. I much preferred creating life to destroying it.

I received no pleasure from doing what I had to do. It was work, not something I should, or indeed wanted to, enjoy.

But necessity is the mother of invention, as someone far smarter than me had once said.

It was necessary to kill her and the time was far too short to employ my usual methods. It would have to be quick: a firm strike with a hammer to the back of the head to render her unconscious, and then an injection with morphine to finish her off.

I would bring along a knife just in case she gave me trouble, but I didn't want to use it. No need to spoil her beautiful complexion. No woman deserved that.

I found the right place to make my move, a narrow lane less than a hundred metres from her home.

The weather was perfect, the nights long, the hedges along the lane overgrown, the verges untrimmed.

Perfect.

I nestled down. Now it was just a question of waiting. I was good at waiting.

In my job, you had to be patient; it came with the territory.

Chapter Sixteen

The entrance to the mortuary was as clean and lifeless as ever. But it was the smell which always disturbed Ridpath, making him gag involuntarily every time he entered the place.

He hated the feeling, hated being there, hated every brick and tile in the place. A feeling only slightly lessened when John Schofield, the pathologist, entered the reception area dressed in his usual uniform of bloodied scrubs.

'You'll have to excuse me,' he waved at his apron carelessly, 'a particularly stubborn liver, indelibly scarred with cirrhosis of course. A celebratory vodka and tonic was the end of him.'

'Remind me never to order the drink again, Ridpath,' whispered Emily.

'Now, how can I help you? You mentioned something about the Romeo and Juliet bodies?' Dr Schofield's high voice rose even higher at the question. The result of a childhood battle with Kallmann syndrome, a disease that stopped a person from starting or fully completing puberty.

'We've been asked to look at the case and wondered if you'd take us through your post-mortem findings.'

'No problem. I can give you twenty minutes – I have a suicide at three p.m. An overdose of bleach, not the easiest way to die.'

'Are there any easy ways to die?'

'In my sleep, enjoying a last dream of romping through the meadows listening to a Bach concerto would be my preferred way, but luckily for me, other people have different ideas.'

He led them a labyrinthine path through the post-mortem theatres and examination rooms, past covered gurneys where the vague outlines of what were once human beings lay beneath green plastic covers.

'As you can see, we're busy at the moment. Not enough fridge space. And with this heat…' He left the detectives to draw their own conclusion.

Finally they arrived at a small office hidden at the end of a corridor of labs. Ridpath had been here once before when he had interviewed Harold Lardner, the Beast of Manchester. The office had changed little since then.

The pathologist took off his apron, laying it casually across the back of a chair, and sat down at his desk, gesturing for Ridpath and Emily to sit opposite.

'You've read my report?' he said, typing in the password to his computer and selecting a file.

'I quickly scanned it,' answered Ridpath, 'but please take me through it as if you were presenting your findings for the first time.'

'I presume Chief Inspector Meredith is aware of your interest in the case, Ridpath?'

'He is.'

'I'm sure he is delighted at the thought of you checking his investigation.'

'Narked might be a better way of describing it.'

Schofield allowed the small twitch of a smile at the corners of his mouth. 'I can imagine. A meticulously turned out man, Chief Inspector Meredith. I would hazard his investigations are as meticulous as his clothes.'

'But after six months there has been little progress, hence…'

'…your involvement. Well, where shall I start?'

'The beginning always helps Dr Schofield,' said Emily sniffing loudly before taking out her notepad and pen.

Schofield stared at his computer as if to refresh his memory. 'I was called to the scene at eleven thirty-two a.m. on January 4. Two bodies, a male and a female, were found on the top floor of an old warehouse on Port Road. They had been deliberately walled up in a room next to the gable end.'

'What condition were the bodies in?'

'Desiccated, almost mummified.'

The pathologist turned his computer around so they could see the mortuary pictures. On each corpse the skin looked almost brown while the mouth was pulled back in a rictus grin.

'The atmosphere in the room was unique for Manchester in that it was almost free of humidity. I don't know what they stored there in the past but it must have been something sensitive to damp. In the years they had been lying there, these bodies must have suffered heat in summer and cold in winter, but throughout the time the environment remained dry. Hence the desiccated nature of the remains. If it had been damp, the bodies would have decomposed, leaving only skeletal remains, a gloop of adipocere fat and perhaps a smattering of hair. The room must have been effectively sealed because we found no evidence of rodent action on the bodies. They had been untouched since death.'

'And when was that, Doctor? When exactly did they die?' asked Emily.

'Difficult to determine an exact time or date of death. From the level of mummification, I would have estimated they died between twelve to twenty years ago.'

'But I saw a much more exact figure, nearly fifteen years according to the press.'

'I advised the police PR not to release the figure but they went ahead anyway.' Schofield clicked his computer. 'The corpses of both the victims were still wearing clothes when they were found. In the male trouser pocket was a tram ticket from Altrincham to Manchester dated August 18, 2008. Chief Inspector Meredith concluded the male victim had used the train on that day and the victims probably died around the same time.'

'But you don't agree.'

Schofield rubbed his nose. 'It is the most probable conclusion, but not the only one. Certainly, the presence of the ticket in a sealed room rules out the deaths happening before August 18, 2008. But, and it's a big but, the ticket may have lain in the man's pocket for a long time before he was killed.'

'It does seem the logical conclusion he travelled by tram on or near that time.'

'It is a probability, yes, but I prefer to deal in certainties. I like to keep an open mind on these things rather than commit to an exact date of death.'

Dr Schofield rubbed his nose. Was he suffering from hay fever too?

'There was one element that did narrow down the time of death though. We found some remains of Calliphora vomitoria, the common bluebottle, in the room next to the corpse. In this species of blow fly, the female deposits her eggs on a dead body. The pale whitish maggots soon hatch from the eggs and immediately begin feeding on the corpse where they were hatched. After a few days of feeding, they are fully grown. The normal duration spent in adult form averages ten to fourteen days; however, during cold weather, pupae and adults can hibernate until higher temperatures revive them.'

'So the room was full of flies when it was opened.'

'Apparently not, Inspector. You see, the larvae need soil or leaf matter to pupate. After two or three weeks, the adults emerge from the pupal stage to mate, beginning the cycle again. But as there was no ground soil in the room, they died out.'

'How does this help us?'

'Two areas: first, Calliphora vomitoria only lays its eggs from May to late September, so we know it was during this time the victims were placed in the room.'

'A pretty wide period, but it includes the date of the ticket, August 18.'

'What's the second area?'

'Interestingly, Calliphora vomitoria does not fly at night or lay eggs, so we know the victims died during the daytime. I've checked the weather for the day of the tram ticket; it was a bright, balmy Saturday with a temperature of twenty-one degrees centigrade and no rainfall. A rare day in Manchester.'

'What about the victims themselves, what did their bodies tell us? Any distinguishing marks?'

'Both the victims were extraordinary in their ordinariness. As you know, it is difficult to give an exact age for anybody – every body has a different rate of development. However, the male victim – I believe the police have named him Male B – his wrist bones were fused, which suggests he was over eighteen. The female victim's weren't, which suggests she was slightly younger, around seventeen perhaps.'

'Brother and sister, or lovers?' asked Emily.

'Unfortunately pathology gives no hint as to their relations, just their sex. Our forensic odontologist—'

'Your what?'

'A forensic dentist, for the layman. Through X-rays of the teeth, she confirmed the estimates of their ages. Of course, we shared the X-rays with the dental community but nobody came forward to identify the teeth.'

'And there were no other identifiers?'

'None at all. There was nothing outstanding about either of the victims; no bone breakages, no tattoos, no identifiable scars, nothing. All brain, liver and heart weights were within the usual parameters. As I said, extraordinarily ordinary. They were two healthy people, except they were dead.'

'That's why they have remained unidentified,' asked Emily.

'Probably. It's the differences which make us identifiable. A special operation scar, an unusual tattoo, an identifiable bone break. The closer they are to the mean, the more difficult it is to identify an individual.'

'But you were able to extract DNA?'

'Yes, eventually, from both victims. I believe Chief Inspector Meredith ran it through the National DNA Database but didn't get any hits. Nor did the CSIs find any other DNA at the scene.'

'None on the bricks or anywhere else?'

'Apparently not. The walls and door were covered in the victims' fingerprints but nobody else's. They had been sealed in the room for some time together.'

'A suicide pact?' said Emily out loud.

'Hardly likely given they were found in a bricked-up room, sealed from the outside.'

Emily blushed at the rebuke and scribbled in her notepad.

'And that's it?' asked Ridpath.

'Almost. There are two other things. Toxicology found traces of barbiturates in both their systems. Could have been amobarbital, pentobarbital, phenobarbital, secobarbital, and sodium thiopental as they are the most common examples. We couldn't break it down further. The barbiturate came from a bottle of water in their cell, traces were found.'

'So they were sedated. Were the drugs the cause of death?'

'This is the most distressing element. I think, but I can't be certain, they died of terminal dehydration. Not a pleasant death. The body is about sixty per cent water, and under normal conditions, an average person will lose about a quart of water each day by sweating and breathing. In the heat and under more difficult physical conditions, that amount increases.

'If it's not replaced over time and dehydration becomes severe, cells throughout the body will begin to shrink as water moves out of them into the bloodstream. The most affected part is the brain. As the brain cells shrink, changes in mental status will follow, including confusion, delirium and hallucinations. Without water, blood volume will decline and all the organs will start to fail. Kidney failure will ultimately lead to death as blood volume continues to fall and waste products that should be eliminated from the body remain. Those who die of thirst typically lapse into unconsciousness before death, which is slow and unpleasant.'

'Gruesome,' said Emily.

'How long would it take?' asked Ridpath, anxious to keep focused on the investigation.

'As a general rule of thumb, a person can survive without water for about three to five days. However, some factors, such as age and overall health, can affect the ability of an individual body to survive. In heat, especially in summer, the body uses water to produce sweat, which evaporates and lowers a person's body temperature. As I said, not a pleasant way to die. Some members of the Buddhist Sokushinbutsu sect in Japan historically practiced a form of self-mummification which in part is achieved by the forgoing of all liquid until death. Again, the desiccation of our victim's' bodies increases the likelihood that this was the cause of death.'

'Had they eaten before they died?'

'There was no food in either of their stomachs.'

Dr Schofield's eyes looked up and left as he remembered the post-mortem.

'It's probably the strangest case I've ever worked on. Good luck with the investigation.'

'You don't sound terribly encouraging.'

He shrugged his shoulders. 'These cold cases are hard, so little to work with. I wish I could help more.'

Ridpath frowned. 'Why would they go into the room in the first place? What took them to the top floor of an old Manchester warehouse?'

'I can't answer either of those questions, Ridpath. I think that's your job, is it not? One final thing before I forget...'

Both detectives sat forward, hoping for a vital piece of evidence from the pathologist.

'I'd get that hay fever of yours looked at, DS Parkinson. Plays havoc with the sinuses this time of year.'

Chapter Seventeen

'I don't think this is going to be easy, Ridpath,' sniffed Emily Parkinson. She was leaning on his car and for the first time Ridpath could remember, she didn't have a cigarette between her fingers. 'Two unknown victims, a man and a woman, both apparently healthy, died from dehydration after being shut up in a room. No ID on either victim and no forensic evidence to tell us who they are or were.'

'What about the tram ticket?'

'You're going to tell me there will be CCTV from nearly fifteen years ago? Nobody keeps images that long.'

'We still need to check.'

'And by "we" I presume you mean me?'

'Right first time. You're forgetting the DNA – Dr Schofield said they managed to find a viable sample from both the male and female victims.'

'But he also said the National DNA database hadn't found any matches. Last time I looked there were over five million people on their files. If one of our victims had ever been tested or arrested, they would have shown up.'

'Remember what the pathologist said: "They were extraordinarily ordinary." Perhaps neither of them were ever arrested or in trouble with the police. It does happen, you know...'

'But how often do murder victims have no DNA records? Plus no other DNA was found at the scene, certainly none of the killer's DNA.'

Ridpath scratched his head. 'By 2008, our killer would have been aware of DNA and its impact on crime cases. When did *CSI* start?'

'The American programme? I don't know, I'll check.'

'It doesn't matter. If no other DNA or trace elements were found at the scene, then we must presume our killer knew enough not to leave any trace behind.'

Emily frowned. 'Doesn't help us though, does it?'

'It just means we have to work harder.'

As he spoke, his mobile rang. 'Ridpath.'

'Hi there, it's Margaret Challinor. Sophia tells me you won't be in today.'

'Sorry, I'm just starting out on the job Claire Trent briefed...'

'The Romeo and Juliet case?'

'Correct, trying to get up to speed as quickly as I can. But it looks difficult.'

'I think I can be of help. Let's meet up sometime tomorrow and I can tell you what I've discovered.'

'Is this what you mentioned to me yesterday?'

'I think I've found something, but I'm not sure. Time to get you involved though.'

'Do you want to do it today?'

'No worries, tomorrow is fine. I'll call you, we can Zoom it if you don't want to come into the office.'

'Technology...'

'Don't be afraid of something new, Ridpath. It's there to make our lives easier. Call you tomorrow. Oh, and one more thing,' she added. 'The jury came back with a narrative conclusion to the Davies case. It looks like another Regulation 28 for the local health trust. It's time to come down hard on them.'

She rang off, leaving Ridpath staring at his phone. What had she discovered? And what had it to do with Romeo and Juliet?

'Challinor?' Emily Parkinson interrupted his thoughts.

'She may have something on our case.'

'Anything and everything helps. Meredith and his team have been working hard for the last six months,' she sniffed once again, loudly, 'and have got nowhere.'

'Then we'll work smarter. We need to know more about the case, we're just stabbing in the dark at the moment. We need to find something, anything, to give us a new lead.'

'Something Challinor has discovered or something Meredith and his team missed?'

'Both. The truth is out there somewhere. Two people don't just go missing without somebody knowing something.' Ridpath checked his watch. 'Come on, where do you want me to drop you? I need to go and pick up my daughter if I'm to avoid suffering the agonies of being sent to teenage Coventry.'

'A fate worse than death, if I remember from my own youth.'

'Don't I know it.'

'I'll go back to HQ. I need to see if Meredith has followed up on his promise to provide all the case files plus check in with Chrissy, see where she's at.'

'The third desk on the right as you go in.'

'Ha ha.' She opened the door on the passenger side. 'You'd better get a move on. Aggravating a teenager isn't worth the grief.'

'I'd rather take on a bunch of Salford heavies any day of the week.'

Chapter Eighteen

Eve was waiting for him when he arrived, sitting on the wall outside her school with her backpack at her feet. 'You're late, Dad,' she said, getting in the car.

'You're the second person to say that to me today. How was school?'

'Fine.'

'Is that all?'

'I went there, I studied. End of.'

It was going to be one of those conversations. 'Are you OK? You have a face like last week's washing.'

'What's with all the questions? I've had a shitty day and you keep mithering on at me.'

Ridpath stayed silent while the lights changed in front of him. 'Tell me about it. No judgement, I'll listen.'

She thought for a long time. 'It's just the idiots at school. One of them was saying all police were corrupt and racist. I said that wasn't true. And then she told me her cousin had been stopped and searched on the street while doing nothing, just because he was mixed race. How could I answer, Dad? All I could say was you were police and you weren't corrupt or racist. But then the pile-on started. Some of the other girls talked about stuff they'd heard or witnessed or had happened to other members of their families. Then somebody brought up the London policeman who murdered Sarah Everard and the two coppers taking photos of those dead women and sharing it with their mates. It was like I was arguing against the whole world. Then they didn't talk to me all afternoon, even Maisie was a bit iffy with me.'

Ridpath had wondered when this day would come, when his job would have an impact on her. 'Listen, Eve, there are always going to be stories about bad coppers and stories about good coppers. But the majority of the men and women I work with are trying to do their best in a difficult job.'

'I know, Dad, but how do I tell other people?'

'We are no different from the society we come from. It's just that when you become a policeman, people hold you to a different standard, a higher standard. And that's right. We need to be better than the people we police. Our job is to be better. Sometimes we don't reach those standards and we let the public down. It happens. But the standards don't change, we just need to try harder.'

'But don't you get sick of the abuse? Sick of your job?'

'Of course, everybody does, but can you imagine a world without the police? The strong would devour the weak. Our job is to protect people, to allow them to go about their ordinary lives without obstruction or being harassed by criminals. Every day my colleagues are out there on the streets of Manchester working, and ninety-nine times out of a hundred, they're doing it well. But it's the one time when we don't live up to our high standards that lets us down. People rightly remember and criticise us, and we need to do better, but could you imagine Manchester without the police? In the end, all your friends who criticised us, when they have a problem, the first thing they will do is ring 999. And we, despite their beliefs about us, will be there.'

She was quiet for a moment. 'Yeah, all of them would.'

Ridpath laughed, realising he was beginning to sound pompous. 'There endeth the first lesson from Dad.' He decided to change the mood. 'What do you want for dinner?'

'Something with meat and carbs. I had the vegetarian lunch at school today. Nut something or other with kale. Let me ask you one thing, Dad.'

'What's that?'

'Please don't ever give me kale. There is absolutely no need for something that tastes like fermented papier mâché.' She extended her pinky and thumb.

He understood this was some teenage gesture suggesting a promise. He did the same. 'No, kale, ever.'

'Solemn promise?'

'I swear on all the gods of food and Jamie Oliver. What do you want?'

'A burger? A thick beef burger with melted cheese oozing over the top.'

'Perfect. With fries and a fizzy drink. Let's go the whole hog.'

'Or in our case, the whole cow.'

Chapter Nineteen

It was never easy killing someone, but she had to die.

Ever since I heard she had been asking questions, it was only a matter of time before the situation had to be resolved.

Last night's meeting in the cafe had simply brought the timetable forward. I was certain she was flying solo, so she had to be eliminated before she communicated her concerns to other people.

The decision to kill her had been made — unfortunate though it was.

She arrived home from work at seven thirty p.m. and immediately took her dog for a walk. Thirty minutes from now, if she followed the patterns of previous evenings when it wasn't raining, she would round the top of the lane leading to her home.

The dog would be off foraging in the undergrowth as it usually did. No longer on the lead but enjoying the freedom to explore. She would call him back just before they reached the main road and he would return, tail wagging, bringing some treat he had found in the fields or the undergrowth.

The dog would pose no problem, a cocker spaniel never would. But, just in case, a can of pepper spray nestled in my inside pocket. One short blast in the dog's eyes and it would be yelping from here to next week.

The lane had been chosen for a number of reasons; the high hedges on either side were in full summer's growth and the lush verges were resplendent with wildflowers.

She would be placed on the carpet of St John's wort, white campion, common mallow and bird's-foot trefoil. Her death would be like a pre-Raphaelite painting; her curly hair spread among the wildflowers, her body limp and useless.

Death should be like art, don't you think? Having a beauty all of its own, unencumbered by artifice or deceit.

Right on time, she appeared at the top of the lane, hands at her side, deep in thought, the dog nowhere to be seen.

A shiver of anticipation ran through my body. This would be the first time I had killed anybody so close up, blood red in tooth and claw. Of course, I practised on animals first. The next door neighbours had even knocked on her door asking if anyone had seen their cat.

Not for a long time, had been my truthful answer.

And neither would they.

Checking the surroundings one more time; feeling the weight of the hammer in my hand, the round bag carrying the hypodermics and the feathers nestling in my pocket, the shears inside my jacket. A lock of hair would make a fine souvenir. I liked souvenirs, I had them from all my deaths. A little bit of each of them still with me.

Finally, the knife, recently sharpened, sat comfortably in its sheath, there in case it was needed, waiting for its stainless steel to be kissed by the late evening sun.

Strength was not important, planning was.

A blackbird was singing its song in a tree to the right. Over to the left, on the far side of a field, a farmer was cutting his grass for winter silage. But the noise of his tractor was loud and he wouldn't hear her screams. The sun was soft in the sky, the light casting a golden glow over this place of work. The long hot days of a lazy summer, when life could be given and taken away.

It's funny how you notice the smallest of details when a murder is being executed. It was as if my senses were tuned to perfection, hearing as sharp as a fox, eyes as keen as a hawk, all the cunning of an owl.

Everything was planned.

All was perfect.

The woman raised her voice, calling her dog to her, a concerned tone in its sharpness. 'Rufus, Rufus. Here, boy, come here.'

Was she worried about something?

She carried on walking towards me as the dog scurried out of the undergrowth, touched its nose to her booted legs and hurried off to discover some fresh, enticing smell.

She was getting closer. Now was the time.

I pulled my mask over my face and stepped out into the lane, putting hands in my pockets to hide the hammer, as if I was just out on an evening walk.

The anticipation of the moment growing inside me. Now was the time to bring it to consummation. There was no need, or time, to wait any longer.

She was less than ten feet away now. 'Good evening, Mrs Challinor,' I said.

Chapter Twenty

Ridpath settled down in front of his laptop. Eve was upstairs supposedly doing her homework but probably pottering around doing whatever it was teenage girls did when they relaxed. He'd heard her talking over the phone with Maisie, speaking in those impenetrable codewords and giggles which meant so much to them but left him clueless.

They'd picked up their order from the Laundrette on their way. A chorizo, bacon and pork burger for him and a signature cheeseburger for her. A year's supply of cholesterol in each bite.

Now he felt full and sated, ready to read the post-mortem report and notes on the case.

Emily had already texted him.

> Still nothing from Meredith. Shall I give him a call to remind him?

> No. Leave it until our meeting tomorrow. He's probably collating the material.

> Meeting tomorrow?

> 9 a.m. at HQ. Can you tell Chrissy?

He logged on to the GMP database and opened the file from Chrissy. A folder held the post-mortem report, interviews with key witnesses and a timeline on the case compiled by Meredith.

He read the post-mortem report first. It was exactly as Dr Schofield had told him. What was interesting were the crime scene photographs and a list of items found with the bodies.

Both victims were lying on thin mattresses facing each other, the man's hand resting on the woman's side. The bodies were desiccated, like the Egyptian mummies he had seen in a visit to the Manchester Museum as a kid. The skin dark, almost black, the hair thin and wispy, the hands shrivelled, claw-like. They were still wearing clothes; a T-shirt and trousers for him, jeans and a sweatshirt for her. Comfortable clothes perfect for a summer's day in Manchester.

An empty bottle lay next to them, with two feathers by its side. In the corner, a red bucket had been placed. Had the killer provided a toilet for them? Why wasn't it used?

He put three pictures side by side. It was almost as if the killer had wanted them to be at ease, to be comfortable. Why?

He checked other pictures from different angles. They were a parody of two humans, like something designed for one of George A. Romero's horror movies. The man with his arm protectively on the waist of the female.

Which one had died first?

From the attitude of their bodies, it was probably the female. How terrible to watch your own sister or lover die in front of you, yet be too weak to do anything about it.

Then it struck Ridpath. Why weren't there more signs of a struggle? Were they too sedated, or did they want to die together in that room?

One of the shots were scratches on the wall, probably made by the bottle top according to the scene of crime manager. Meredith had even brought in a coding expert to see if he could decipher them, but his professional opinion was that they made no sense.

A close-up of the door showed a piece of fingernail lodged in the wood. So they had tried to escape, but were perhaps too weak to succeed.

For a second, he tried to imagine what it had been like. Finding themselves entombed in the room and unable to get out. Surely they would have tried to break out. A close-up of the bottom of the door showed some scratches and indentions, suggesting someone had kicked the door more than once.

Ridpath wrote notes for himself in his book.

Why provide mattresses?

Was the killer trying to make his victims comfortable?

Why?

Were there any other traces of escape attempts?

Any messages anywhere?

Anything?

He imagined them settling down to sleep on the floor. What did they say to each other? What were their last moments like?

Wouldn't they have tried to tell somebody what was happening? A mark or a sign somewhere? A message on a wall?

He went back to look at the pathologist's report. Traces of plaster dust on the right hand. So the man had tried to leave them a message. But why had he failed? Was he so delusional by then that he thought he had left a message, when all he'd managed were indecipherable scratches?

He checked the list of items found in the room.

Two mattresses, both new, bought from IKEA.

A red bucket from B&Q.

One empty Evian bottle, traces of barbiturate found inside.

One bottle cap, the outside grooves containing traces of plaster dust.

A used candle in its holder, only a small nub of wax remaining.

A book of used matches.

Two dove feathers.

A tram ticket found on Male B dated August 18, 2008.

Clothes: Female A:

Abercrombie and Fitch shirt.

A pair of Levi's 501s.

Shoes made by Praed of Rome.

Underwear: Calvin Klein.

Male B:

Trousers from Next.

A Gap pocket T-shirt.

Nike Dunk Low shoes, new.

Underwear: Primark boxer shorts.

Laying down his pen, he gripped the top of his nose with his index fingers and squeezed. Did he have a headache starting? His eyes felt so tired.

He shook his head, trying to clear it. Time for a break, no alcohol though, just a cup of tea.

First he ran quietly upstairs to use the bathroom, but Eve was already there, sitting on the toilet, the door slightly open.

'Give me a bit of privacy, Dad,' she moaned before closing the door.

He shook his head. Living with a teenage girl could be difficult. Looking at crime scenes was far easier.

Chapter Twenty-one

As expected the use of her name stopped Mrs Challinor dead. She squinted her eyes, focusing on the face in front of her.

'Hello, how strange meeting you here,' she said.

Then the realisation struck her: it wasn't strange at all.

She turned and started to run, but the hammer was out of my pocket and swinging down onto her head before she could move.

It struck her lower than intended, just at the junction of the clavicle and the neck, missing the back of her head.

She screamed out in pain but didn't fall, moving to her right, away from the next blow. She dodged my swing, driving into my stomach, her head down, too close now to hit.

Landing heavily on the tarmac of the lane, the hammer tumbled out of my hand. Her grey hair writhed like snakes in my face as she tried to get on top of me.

She was far stronger than I expected, but she was fighting for her life. Before I knew it she was on her knees trying to scramble away.

I couldn't let her escape. She'd seen me, knew who I was, what I'd done.

Kicking out with the sole of the boot, my foot connected with the side of her stomach.

A squeal of pain sang from her lips. The hammer was here somewhere. On the ground by my side. Feeling it in my hand again, I swung towards her head, connecting with the temple.

She collapsed like a sack of potatoes onto the tarmac, lying still and heavy on the road.

This had to be finished this quickly, it was taking too long. Time to get it over with, I wouldn't get another chance.

The sound of the harvester had stopped. Had the farmer heard something?

She shook her head, tried to get up, to inch away. Would the women never lie still?

Two swift kicks settled her down again.

I got to my feet and stood over her. Killing someone up close wasn't easy. Grabbing her by the hair, I dragged her to the verge and its carpet of wildflowers.

I stood over her inert body and sank down, my knees straddling either side of her hips. I reached for the bag with the hypodermic, struggling to get it out of my pocket.

It finally came free and I was about to open it when her hand came up, the nails like talons digging into the skin on my neck, ripping off my mask. Her eyes widened as she saw my face.

Her claws swung round again, grabbing my hand. For what seemed like minutes, but couldn't have been more than a few seconds, we struggled over the bag, until finally it flew away somewhere into the hedge as she scraped three long scratches along the inside of my wrist above the glove.

I hit her across the temple with my fist. She wouldn't move again.

So it wasn't going to be an easy death after all. The needle would have been quieter, less painful, a long dream of death.

Now the hammer would have to be used. Shame, it was such a pretty head to crush. I did so want to avoid ugliness. I hated killing people, it was simply necessary.

It was her or me.

I stood up and reached down for the hammer lying on the road.

Just then the dog came out of nowhere, attaching itself to my leg, biting deep. I screamed, kicking out, trying to shake it off. The dog held on, its teeth piercing my trousers and sinking into flesh.

The pain shocked me into action. I brought my free leg round and kicked the dog in the chest.

It still held on, shaking its head as if killing a rat.

I kicked again, catching it flush in the chest. It flew away, landing on the side of the road, and then ran off in the direction of the woods, yelping loudly.

Ignoring the pain in my leg, I focused on the job.

Mrs Challinor was still lying there among the wildflowers, a thing of beauty.

I grabbed her hair and raised her head, exposing the throat. It seemed an apt way for her to die; the hammer crushing the mind which had asked so many questions.

I paused for a moment, enjoying the anticipation, feeling the weight of the iron as it bit into the head, into the skull, feeling the bone collapse, hearing the crunch, watching the pretty head vanish into a mush of blood and brains.

'I give life and I take it away.' I spoke the words out loud as I had done before. My grace, my benediction on those I delivered to death.

'Oi, you, what the hell are you doing?'

I looked over my shoulder. A burly man in blue overalls was running towards me. I glanced down at Mrs Challinor once more. Did I have time? Could I finish the job?

Blood was soaking her grey hair and dripping down her face. Her body was lifeless, still. Was she already dead?

I looked up again. The man was running down the lane, his heavy boots moving quickly, too quickly.

The man was too big to fight, I couldn't risk being caught. I glanced down at Mrs Challinor lying on the carpet of wildflowers, blood seeping from the wound in her head where I had kicked her.

'Oi, you,' the man shouted again. Just ten yards away now.

Flinging the hammer at him, I jumped up, kicking Mrs Challinor once more in the head before running back to my motorbike parked beside the tree, my escape route planned, as everything else was, well in advance.

The man followed for a few yards before turning back to check on Mrs Challinor.

Another time, another day.

She would have to wait for me a little longer.

And then I remembered the bag with the hypodermic in the hedge. Would the police find it? Definitely, if they searched.

I had to get it back.

Chapter Twenty-two

After the encounter with his daughter in the bathroom, Ridpath fled downstairs to make himself a cup of tea. No alcohol yet, not when he still had Chief Inspector Meredith's timeline to wade through.

His mind went back to the crime scene photos and the pathologist's report. Who had bricked them up in the small room and why?

Such a horrible way to die; minds confused with hallucinations and dreams, lapsing slowly into a coma as the organs gradually shut down, toxins building up until death became inevitable.

Who would do that to another human being?

And then it struck him. Why kill them that way? Why not just take a gun and shoot them? Or use a knife, or even give them an overdose of pills? Why lock them in a room?

He shook his head, trying to clear it of the image of the two dead bodies lying side by side, the woman's hands clasped in front of her.

Perhaps she had been praying, but he wondered if it had been for life or for death.

His thoughts were interrupted when he was joined by Eve.

'You need to make some noise coming up the stairs, Dad, you're too quiet.'

'You could try closing the door.'

'You could try whistling.'

'Which song should I use. Something by Olivia Rodrigo, "Drivers License" perhaps?'

'Not a bad start, certainly better than Elvis whatshisname, or Bowie.' She opened the fridge door. 'Do we have any snacks?'

The eternal hunger of a growing teenager.

'But you've only just had an enormous burger for your tea.'

'That was three hours ago, Dad,' she explained as if talking to an idiot. She took out some cheese and went to the bread bin to make herself a sandwich.

The whistling of the kettle was joined by the ringing of his phone. He glanced down at it, seeing a number he didn't recognize, and decided to ignore it, pouring the hot water onto the teabags, nestling in the pot.

The phone continued to ring, annoyingly, before stopping, then starting again.

'You better get that, it might be important,' said Eve between mouthfuls of Wensleydale cheese and bread.

Reluctantly, he picked it up. 'Ridpath...'

A distressed woman was on the other end of the phone, crying. 'It's Mum, she's been attacked.' The voice was almost incoherent.

'Please take a deep breath and tell me again.'

He could sense the woman trying desperately to control her emotions, taking deep breaths. 'It's my mother, somebody attacked her.'

'Your mother?'

'Margaret Challinor, the coroner.'

Chapter Twenty-three

Ridpath accelerated down the M60 on his way to the hospital. It had taken him a few minutes to get the full details from Mrs Challinor's daughter, Sarah.

Apparently, the coroner had been attacked near her home and taken to A&E. He had spoken to Eve immediately.

'I need to go out.'

'Who was it? Mrs Challinor?'

'No, her daughter. I don't know when I'll be back, so...'

'You want me to go to Maisie's? I can stay here in the house on my own, I'm not afraid.'

'You know I can't leave you alone, it wouldn't be right. You're too young.'

He picked up the phone and rang Maisie's mum, Angela. 'I'm sorry, but an urgent job has come up. Can Eve stay at your house tonight?'

'We'd love to have her, but we're off to the Lakes for the weekend early tomorrow morning.' A slight pause. 'Would it be OK if Eve came with us? She could stay with us tonight. Maisie would love to have some company. It's not easy being an only child.'

You're telling me, thought Ridpath. 'I'll ask her.' He put the phone to his chest. 'Maisie and her family are going to the Lakes for the weekend, would you like to join them?'

'Would it make it easier for you?'

Ridpath thought for a moment. He wanted Eve to stay, but he knew the truth. 'Yes,' he answered.

'That's great, tell Mrs Wells I'd love to go.'

'Hi there, she'd love to join you. Thank you so much, you don't know how much of a relief it is I can rely on you.'

It had happened once before; at the beginning of spring, Eve had stayed with them when Ridpath had to go to Derbyshire to work for another coroner. It was one of their solutions which allowed Eve to live with him permanently.

'We're camping, so she'll need her rucksack and sleeping bag. We'll pack the extra tent for the two of them. Maisie will be so chuffed.'

'Did I hear we were camping?' asked Eve.

'Fraid so.'

She smiled. 'Oh well, there's a first for everything.' She ran upstairs to pack her stuff and ten minutes later was down in the living room all ready to go, hiking boots and all.

'You look great.'

'I wish you were coming too.'

'So do I, but you can tell me about it all when I pick you up on Sunday.' He gave his daughter a hug. 'Look after yourself, kiddo.'

'Don't worry, Dad, just do what you have to do. I'll try to enjoy myself.' She rolled her eyes. 'Me camping, who'd a thunk it?'

He'd dropped her off, thanking Angela and her husband Rick profusely. Eve had gone into the house without looking back, already excited at an unexpected chance to spend a weekend with her best friend on earth.

Ridpath parked up at the hospital and ran into A&E. He recognised Mrs Challinor's daughter sitting all alone in the crowded waiting room.

He strode over to where she was sitting and she looked up, tears flooding her eyes. He immediately sat down and put his arm around her shoulders.

'Oh, Ridpath, it's terrible…' she snuffled.

'What happened?'

'Mum took the dog for a walk. About half an hour later I heard the sound of police sirens out on the lane near the house.

You know how quiet it is where we live. I went out to have a look and there was Rufus, waiting outside the house, but no Mum.' She stopped, trying to hold back her tears.

'It's all right, take a few deep breaths.'

Sarah Challinor closed her eyes, concentrating on her breathing. Around them, the A&E department was busy with a constant flow of patients being wheeled in on gurneys and wheelchairs, greeted by doctors or nurses who performed a quick triage of their injuries, deciding in seconds whether they needed immediate care.

'I ran up the lane and saw Mum lying on the ground being treated by the medics. She was just lying there, her hair muddied and torn, her face covered in blood... the police said she'd been attacked. They asked me her name. I told them it was Mum... how stupid is that?'

'Don't worry. Where are your children?'

'With their father. It's his week with them...'

'Has the doctor said anything to you?'

She shook her head. 'I wanted to be with her but they ushered me out, asking me to wait.'

'OK, let me find out what's going on.'

He walked over to the receptionist. 'I'd like to find out about a patient, a Mrs Margaret Challinor.'

'And you are?'

He took out his warrant card. 'Detective Inspector Ridpath. I believe she was assaulted.'

The woman checked her computer. 'Mrs Challinor is presently being X-rayed.'

'Can I speak to her doctor?'

'Dr Ahmed is extremely busy at the moment.' She glanced across at the lines of people waiting to be seen and the others lying in the corridors on gurneys.

'It's important I see him. Just for a few seconds,' he added.

'I'll see what I can do.'

'Thank you.'

Ridpath returned to Sarah. 'How is Mum?' she asked plaintively.

'She's being X-rayed at the moment – that's all I was able to find out. They're obviously checking for injuries sustained in the assault.'

'Why, Ridpath? Why was she attacked?'

For once in his life, Ridpath didn't have an answer.

Chapter Twenty-four

It took an hour and a half before a doctor approached them. His stethoscope hung loosely around his neck and his hair was dishevelled. From the immense bags under his eyes, it was obvious he'd worked a long shift.

'Inspector Ridpath?'

Ridpath stood up, realising how short the doctor was.

'My name's Dr Ahmed, I'm the senior registrar. I presume you are the investigating officer?'

'Not exactly,' Ridpath dissembled. 'But as Mrs Challinor is the senior coroner for East Manchester, the police obviously have an interest in the case. What can you tell me about her injuries?'

'We're just waiting for the X-ray reports, but it's obvious she was assaulted severely around the head and body. She appears to have a fractured skull, but we will confirm that shortly. I can't say any more at the moment...' The man's voice trailed off.

Ridpath glanced down at Sarah, listening to the conversation. 'Is she conscious, and can I talk to her?'

'She's not conscious, so that won't be possible, I'm afraid. Not at the moment.'

'This is her daughter.'

The doctor immediately went into patient relative mode, smiling and dropping the tone of his voice. 'We're just treating your mother, but she's unconscious and we will be admitting her as soon as a bed becomes available.'

'You said she had a fractured skull?'

He nodded. 'It's a bad fracture, she was struck with something heavy and solid.'

'Will she be OK?' Sarah's voice broke. 'Can I see her?'

'I'm afraid not. Your mother is in a very bad way.' He looked to the side for a moment, working out how to phrase the next sentence. 'Her injuries are severe with, I believe, a traumatic brain injury. I suggest you go home and return tomorrow morning. There's nothing you can do this evening.'

'I'd like to see her.'

'That won't be possible. She's under sedation while we ascertain the extent of her injuries.'

Sarah started crying.

'Please go home. Your mother is receiving the best care and attention. Now, if you'll excuse me, I have other patients I need to see.'

'One last thing, Doctor. Were her clothes bagged when she arrived?'

'Bagged?'

'In case the attacker left traces of DNA or evidence on them.'

'I don't think so.'

'Could you place them in a bag for me? And were her hands bagged?'

The doctor looked up and to the left. 'No, definitely not,' he answered finally.

'Could you also bag them for me? Knowing Mrs Challinor, she will have fought against her attacker. There may be DNA traces under her fingernails.'

'Inspector Ridpath, I am a doctor, not a policeman. Patients are my concern, not catching criminals.'

'Dr Ahmed, somebody has just assaulted a woman in broad daylight. You would like us to catch her attacker, wouldn't you?'

The doctor thought for a moment, before saying, 'I'll see what I can do.'

Chapter Twenty-five

Sarah was silent for most for the drive home. Ridpath didn't talk either, leaving her with her thoughts.

Eventually she said, 'Who would want to hurt Mum?'

Ridpath stayed silent. He had no answer to her question.

'I mean, Mum had no enemies, she was just a coroner. She always said the job was to find out the truth, not to decide guilt or innocence.'

'I'll ring up the investigating officer tomorrow and find out what I can.'

'Would you, Ridpath? It would help. I think it's not knowing what's going on that's the worst. The hospital tells you nothing and I haven't even talked to the police yet.'

'Nobody questioned you at the scene?'

'A sergeant asked me who I was but nothing else. I sat in the ambulance taking Mum to the hospital.' For a moment she was quiet. 'Her face was covered in blood. There was this little twig stuck in her hair, matted with blood. I reached over to take it out, Mum always loved her hair to be clean, but the medic wouldn't let me touch her, wouldn't let me touch my own mum.'

'He was just doing his job.'

'There was one time, just as we were nearing the hospital, her eyes opened. I could see the fear in her eyes, Ridpath. It was a look I'd never seen before, not on Mum, not on anybody.'

'You mum is the strongest, bravest woman I know, Sarah. If anybody can fight this, she can.'

They pulled up outside the house.

'Are you sure you're going to be OK here on your own?'

'I'm fine. I just need a shower, and the dog will keep me company.'

'How are you getting to the hospital tomorrow? Do you want me to take you there?'

'I can drive, and you probably have work. But if you can find out what's going on, I would be grateful. It's not knowing that makes it worse.' She opened the door. 'Thank you, Ridpath.'

'It's the least I could do.'

Despite it being close to the longest day of the year, the sun had long vanished beneath the horizon. Sarah walked slowly up the drive, Ridpath watching her all the way until she had switched on the lights and closed the front door. He waited a few minutes, checking everything was OK before deciding to leave.

He put the car in gear and drove down the road, seeing a lane off to his left, a single thread of crime scene tape and a large sign saying the road ahead was closed. He drove past before braking suddenly and reversing the car. It wouldn't hurt to look around for a few minutes.

Parking at the top of the lane, he locked the door. There were no police around, obviously none could be spared to guard a crime scene on a quiet country lane.

Above his head, a three-quarters moon shone brightly against a sea of stars. In the distance the dull yellow glow of the city suggested a hive of activity; people going home from the pub, shift workers keeping the factories going, burglars collecting their tools for a night on the prowl.

He ducked under the tape and walked slowly down the lane, hearing the sound of his shoes against the tarmac. Off to his left something howled at the moon. The pungent smell of freshly mown grass assaulted his nostrils and the shadows of the hedges and trees threw black shadows across the grey tarmac.

A shiver ran up his spine. Ridpath was a city boy, the countryside was unknown territory to him. Give him the neon-lit streets of urban Manchester any day of the week and twice on Sundays.

Up ahead, he spotted more police tape; an inner cordon, probably where Mrs Challinor had been attacked.

He looked over his shoulder. He had the strangest feeling somebody was watching him.

'Pull yourself together, Ridpath.'

Off to his right an animal screeched loudly. He saw a flutter of wings pounce on the ground, before rising up again against the night sky. Was it an owl, or something more sinister?

Ridpath walked on. The tape circled an area about ten yards across on one side of the lane. He looked all around him. The nearest house with its lights on was Mrs Challinor's home, at least one hundred yards away. The lane was fenced in on both sides by high hedges. A perfect place to attack somebody. How had the coroner escaped?

He stared at the verge of grass at the side of the lane. In the light of the moon, he could see clearly the grass and flowers had been trampled down, flattened from the tarmac to near the hedge. Was this where she was attacked? Had a struggle taken place here? He couldn't see Mrs Challinor giving in easily to any attacker.

Suddenly a movement to his left. A dark shape moving closer towards him.

Ridpath ducked but the blow struck him on the back of his head.

He stood there, swaying gently as if he was drunk, then his legs seemed to give way and he found himself falling in slow motion before his body reached the hard tarmac of the lane, landing heavily, sending a jolt through the back of his skull.

His last memory was of a pair of dark Nikes, the white swoosh close to his head.

Then all was black.

Chapter Twenty-six

Who the hell was he and what was he doing here so late at night?

I ran back to where I'd parked the motorbike and kicked it into gear, taking off without using the headlights.

What if there were more of them around? Had the police decided to mount a late-night search? But why was there only one of them?

All these questions seared through my head as I rode down the A56 back into town.

I'd gone back as the light had faded. A quick check showed me there were no coppers around and I'd started searching using my torch.

I'd been looking for fifteen minutes without success when I heard the sound of a car at the top of the road, the squeal of its gears as it reversed backwards.

I switched off the light on my phone and listened, my body haunting the shadows close to the fence, behind a tree stump.

After a minute or so, I heard the sound of shoes on the tarmac. A tall man appeared on the road. I held my breath, hoping he wouldn't see me.

He walked past, looking to where the police tape surrounded the scene of my work. He stood there for a moment, looking around him as if surveying the area. Then he turned his back on me to look down the lane.

I took my chance. I crept out onto the road and hit him across the head with a torch. He collapsed like a sack of rubbish thrown from a lorry.

I stood over him for a few seconds, deciding whether to hit him again.

But just as I was about to strike, I heard a loud screeching noise to my left.

It was then I took off, leaving the man lying in the road unconscious. Who was he? Another copper? Or just some curious local?

I guess I'll never know, but I need to be more careful.

I had broken my own rules, acted hastily without properly planning the operation. It won't happen again. From now on, I will go back to what had worked for me for so long.

Take my time.

Research properly.

Don't work fast.

Kill slowly.

Chapter Twenty-seven

Ridpath didn't know how long he'd been out. He sat up gingerly, feeling the back of his head. A bump the size of Old Trafford lying just beneath the skin.

He shook his head, trying to remove some of the fog still remaining. What had happened? Had he been attacked? Blurry images of a figure rushing in from his right. The blow cracking hard into his skull. His body falling limply to the tarmac.

He took out his phone and rang Operations. 'This is... this is...' What was his name? No matter how hard he tried, he couldn't remember his name.

'Hello, sir, this is the Operations Centre of Greater Manchester Police. How can I help?' A female voice answered on the other end of the line.

'I've just been attacked... I'm a serving police officer.'

'What is your name, rank and number, sir?'

Once again, Ridpath thought hard, but it just wouldn't come.

'Sir, what is your name, rank and number?'

And then the fog seemed to lift for a moment. 'My name is Thomas Ridpath, Detective Inspector Ridpath, number D2189.'

'Thank you, sir, And what is your location?'

From his sitting position, Ridpath looked around; all he could see were hedges. 'I don't know, I...'

'Not to worry, we've already tracked your phone. You're in Cheshire, just south of Little Bollington.'

Another flash of memory returned. 'Right, I took Mrs Challinor's daughter back to her home, I'm near Spodegreen Lane.'

'That's correct, sir. I've been on to Cheshire Police and they are dispatching a car from Knutsford, it should be with you in ten minutes. Are you bleeding? Do you need medical assistance?'

He rose shakily to his feet, stopping for a moment to rest on one knee, before finally finding his balance. Ridpath checked the back of his head. The skin didn't seem to be broken, just a large egg-shaped bump. 'No, I'm not bleeding, somebody hit me with something. Can you tell Cheshire Police I'm at the crime scene of an attack on a woman earlier today, Margaret Challinor, the coroner.'

'How do you spell the name?'

'C-H-A-L-L-I-N-O-R,' he said grumpily.

'Right, sir, are you sure you don't want medical assistance? You may be suffering from concussion.'

'No, I'm fine.' Suddenly, he felt an overwhelming desire to be sick. He ran across the road away from the crime scene and vomited the sandwich he had eaten at the hospital onto the grass.

'Inspector Ridpath, are you all right?'

'I'm fine.'

'I don't believe you are, sir. I'm sending a paramedic team to check you out.'

'It's not necessary.'

If a woman's voice could dig its heels in, this dispatcher was wearing six inch stilettos and they had buried themselves deep in the road. 'I believe it is, sir.'

Off in the distance, Ridpath could hear the sound of a police siren and see the flashing lights. 'OK, OK. Thank you for your help.'

A police car slid to a stop at the top of the lane. The sound of size ten police boots was running down the lane towards him.

'The cavalry are here, thank you for your time…'

'Laura, sir, Laura Kenyon.'

'Thank you, Laura.'

A slightly overweight and out-of-breath sergeant ran up to Ridpath. 'Who the bloody hell are you and what are you doing at our crime scene?'

Chapter Twenty-eight

It took another hour for the senior investigating officer, Detective Chief Inspector Tindall, to come in from Winsford.

In the meantime, Ridpath had been completely checked over by an emergency medical technician, advised to go to hospital for an X-ray, refused and then tested once more as a precaution.

Finally, he had been released with a warning that if he had any headaches, nausea, problems breathing or sudden pains anywhere in his body, he was to head straight to A&E. It was the last place he wanted to go, what with Mrs Challinor already there.

DCI Tindall greeted him with the same words as his sergeant. 'What the hell were you doing trampling all over my crime scene?'

'I didn't go anywhere near it. I returned the victim's daughter to her home and thought while I was here I'd take a look at where Mrs Challinor was attacked.'

'My sergeant tells me you're an inspector with Greater Manchester Police. What is Mrs Challinor to you?'

'My boss.'

The man's forehead creased in a heavy frown. 'I thought you were GMP?'

'I am. Margaret Challinor is the coroner. I'm seconded to her as a coroner's officer.' Did this man not know who his victim was?

'The victim was a coroner?'

Obviously he didn't. 'Nobody told you?'

'I was just given the job early this evening. I was still at the nick taking a statement from the man who found her when I received the call saying you'd been attacked.'

'So you haven't searched the crime scene?'

'Not yet – by the time I arrived, it was already late evening. I've arranged a search party and CSIs for tomorrow morning. With an assault like this, no point in starting in the dark,' he added defensively.

Ridpath shut his eyes. The first few hours were the most important in any investigation. It was on the tip of his tongue to point this truism out when he stopped himself. There was nothing to be gained by putting this man's back up.

'Well, I think the perp returned to the scene of the crime for some reason and whacked me.' Ridpath rubbed his head. 'Certainly feels that way.'

'You're lucky it wasn't a hammer like he used on the victim.'

'A hammer? So he meant business and came prepared?' Ridpath walked back to the inner cordon of tape. 'I think he was here for a reason; perhaps he dropped something. Why take the chance of coming back otherwise?'

'Rapists often return to the scene of their crimes, it turns them on.'

Ridpath eyed the stocky man standing in front of him. 'So you think it was an attempted rape?'

The man shrugged his shoulders. 'I don't know… yet.'

'You said a man found her?'

'A local farmer. He was cutting his field and stopped for second to move a nest when he heard the victim's screams and ran over.'

'What did he see?'

'Someone dressed in black on top of a woman. He shouted and whoever it was ran off. He thinks he heard the sound of a motorbike racing away.'

'You've checked CCTV and the traffic and ANPR cameras.'

Tindall looked around dramatically. 'Not a lot of CCTV in these hedges, no call for it. And we don't know what bike the perp was on, what they look like other than "dressed in black" nor the route they took after the assault.'

'Can I talk to this farmer?' As soon as he asked the question, Ridpath realised he had gone too far.

'Talk to him? This ain't your patch. Who do you think you are? Coming in here, telling me how to do my job. Piss off back to the city, you'll be more at home there.'

'Look, no offence was meant. It's just Mrs Challinor is my boss and my friend...'

'This is still my case and you have no jurisdiction, so piss off back to Manchester. That's no longer a request, but an order.' He turned to his sergeant. 'Take Inspector Ridpath back to his car and make sure he leaves the area.'

'But you haven't even taken a statement from me yet.'

In a voice dripping with sarcasm, he said, 'You're so right, silly me. Sergeant, take Inspector Ridpath back to his car, take a statement from him, and then make sure he leaves. Is that how I'm supposed to do it, Inspector Ridpath?'

Chapter Twenty-nine

It took Ridpath less than ten minutes to give and sign his statement.

There was nothing much to say. He hadn't seen his assailant, it was just a vague feeling of unease followed by a dark blur behind him and to his right.

When the sergeant returned to his boss. Ridpath was left with a dilemma. Should he go home and get some sleep, or should he go to the hospital and see Mrs Challinor?

Sleep won. He could get up early and go back to the hospital before going to the coroner's office.

At least Eve was taken care of. He was sure she was now enjoying herself in some campsite in the Lakes. At least he hoped she was enjoying herself. Should he ring Angela Wells to check?

No. That would be far too much the overprotective dad. Time for her to be on her own two feet. But at least it was a burden lifted from his shoulders; he didn't have to worry about his daughter.

He put the car in gear. The clock on the dashboard said 12.30. Another day gone.

As he drove home, the attack flashed through his mind. A black bulk behind him. Not thin, not fat. The blow across his head felt like it came from something soft, but sheathing a hard core.

A rubber truncheon?

A torch?

A cosh?

Definitely not the heavy metal of a hammer. If his assailant had used one like the Yorkshire Ripper, he wouldn't be driving his car home now. On the contrary, he'd be lying next to Mrs Challinor with a tangle of tubes attached to his body.

Flashes of the attack again. The attacker didn't feel tall, it was almost as if he was reaching up to Ridpath's height to hit him. The bump still growing beneath his skin was at the side of his head, not the top.

He wished he could have talked to the farmer, or at least seen the man's witness statement. DCI Tindall hadn't even given him a description.

Was it the same person who attacked Mrs Challinor? Then he remembered the phone call from the coroner earlier in the day. He was supposed to have a Zoom call with her. Well, it definitely wouldn't be happening now.

'I wonder what she wanted to tell me,' he said out loud.

The noise of the car engine was his only answer.

Saturday, June 19

Chapter Thirty

It was strange waking up and not having to make breakfast for Eve.

Lately, her love affair with her bed had deepened. It was becoming harder and harder to get her to perform the rituals of the morning; get up, wash her face and eat something before she went to school.

He realised he wasn't the only parent facing this problem. Talking with the others at the school, it was apparent this was a phase they all went through. Their first real romance happened with a set of springs, a headboard, a cuddly toy and three fluffy pillows.

Sitting alone in his kitchen drinking his coffee, he missed the daily battle. It gave a focus to his morning he lacked right now. Instead, it was going to be Angela Wells' problem. A problem no doubt doubled, with Maisie and Eve probably having spent most of last evening talking long into the night.

He'd already checked the bump on his head in the bathroom mirror. But other than the occasionally throb of dull pain, he felt OK. Actually better than normal. Perhaps he should get someone to hit him over the head at least once a week?

He took a few Panadol with his coffee and hoped for the best. The last place he wanted to go at the moment was A&E. Last night was enough to last him a lifetime.

He checked the clock on the oven. 7.35.

Time to go. If he hurried, he could check up on Mrs Challinor before going into Police HQ. With a bit of luck, she would be awake and able to tell him what had happened to her.

Last night, he'd checked on the hospital website. He needed a mask plus a recent lateral flow test to enter. Hospitals were one of the few places where pandemic rules were still in place. He'd had to follow exactly the same procedure when he went for his cancer check-up at Christie's.

Officially, most wards' visiting times started at ten a.m., and he was supposed to pre-arrange a time with the senior nurse, but he was sure judicious use of his warrant card would ensure an exception.

He found a test packet in the bathroom and swabbed inside his nostrils, hating the feeling of the cotton bud inside his nose. Putting the swab inside the small plastic tube, he swirled it around and around. He had done this so many times, it had almost become a routine.

He dropped the liquid into the small bowl and watched as it slowly rose through the paper. After fifteen minutes he had his result: just one solid line next to the C.

Once again, he heaved a sigh of relief. For some reason, both he and Eve had managed to avoid catching Covid. He put it down to luck and sensible precautions. But he also knew if he did, he would have to go straight back to Christie's for more tests. His bout with cancer meant he was classified as vulnerable even though, at the moment, he felt as fit as the proverbial butcher's dog.

It was almost as if he would be labelled a cancer survivor for the rest of his life. Despite having had no symptoms of myeloma for the last four years and being told he was in remission, the label still remained, hanging over him like an executioner's axe.

One day it might fall, or it might not. He never knew.

He took a picture of the test and popped it in a clear plastic bag in case the hospital wanted to see, packed his briefcase, grabbed a jacket and gave everything a last check before locking the front door.

Finding parking at the hospital was a pain even at eight a.m. He managed to grab an empty space in the outpatients department, just before an Audi, and ran into reception.

The person in charge was helpful once he had flashed his warrant card.

'Mrs Margaret Challinor?'

'That's correct.'

'She's on Ward A8. I'll just call the nurse in charge and check if you can go up.'

She made the call and Ridpath listened as she ummed and ahhed, nodding her head occasionally, before ending the call. 'The senior nurse says you can go to the ward, but the patient is still under sedation and you won't be able to question her.'

He followed the receptionist's directions to Ward A8 and, after walking on a green line for what seemed like hours along the same wide corridors, eventually arrived at the right place.

The sister was waiting for him. 'You're here early. We don't normally see the police until the patient is conscious.'

'Special case,' Ridpath mumbled, not revealing he wasn't the investigating officer. 'Mrs Challinor is the coroner for East Manchester.'

The relevance of her position seemed to be of no interest to the nurse, who began walking into a ward on the left-hand side of the corridor. 'She's still under sedation, so you won't be able to talk to her.'

She stopped outside a bed which had the curtains drawn and pulled one back to reveal Mrs Challinor. Two drips were attached to her arms and a heart monitor beeped quietly on her left. Other machines seemed to be monitoring her oxygen levels.

He stared at the coroner. For the first time since he knew her, she was totally helpless. Her grey curly hair had been cut back to the scalp and her head was swathed in bandages, her face a mass of livid bruises.

'She's booked in for a CAT scan at eleven a.m.; we'll know more then.'

He frowned. What did that mean?

'You'll know more about what?' he finally asked.

'The extent of her injuries. It seems she was hit about the head with a blunt object,' the nurse explained, before stopping and looking up at him. 'I thought you said you were the investigating officer? Surely you would know this woman had been attacked?'

Ridpath thought quickly. 'I'm just here to see if she can be interviewed yet. You know how it is, nobody tells me anything. Just a cog in the wheel doing as I'm told.'

The nurse smiled. 'Don't I know the feeling. Anyway, she won't be answering questions for a while.'

'How long?'

The nurse shrugged her shoulders. 'I don't know. With head trauma, one never knows.' The nurse stood next to Mrs Challinor and gently rearranged her drips so the tubes were no longer resting on her shoulders. 'The consultant will know more after the CAT scan this morning, I suggest you ring him later.'

Ridpath nodded and took the contact details for Mr Pereira, the consultant. He took a last few moments to look at the bruised face of Mrs Challinor and all the tubes attached to her. What had she wanted to tell him?

'Thank you, nurse…?'

'Ryan, Helen Ryan.'

'Thank you, I'll contact the consultant directly and let the relatives know her condition.'

'This is a short stay ward so she might be moved later. I don't know where we're going to find a bed though, the hospital is at capacity at the moment…'

Ridpath took one last look at Mrs Challinor and said goodbye, leaving the nurse to tidy another patient's bed. Once outside the confines of the hospital, he went to his car and rang Sarah Challinor.

'I've just been to see your mum and she's still under sedation.'

'Is that good or bad?'

'I don't know. The consultant is a Mr Pereira, you may want to call him later. They're doing more tests on your mother this morning.'

'That doesn't sound good.'

Ridpath tried his best to sound positive. 'I'm sure she will be fine. You know doctors, they always want to do more tests.'

'You didn't speak with her?'

'No, she's under sedation still.'

'I'll go at eleven a.m. and sit with her.'

'I'll follow up with the police and let you know. Have they contacted you yet?'

'Nothing.' A long pause. 'Why would anybody attack Mum?'

'I don't know, Cheshire Police need to find out. I'm sure they'll talk to you later today.' Ridpath made a mental note to call DCI Tindall. 'Anyway, I have to go to work now. I'll call later.'

'Thank you, Ridpath. You know how much Mum relies on you, don't you?'

Ridpath didn't know what to say for a moment, before he answered. 'I think the reverse is true; we all rely on Mrs Challinor. She's a strong woman; don't worry, she'll come through this.' For a moment, the image of Mrs Challinor's body lying inert in the hospital bed came to him. 'I'm sure she'll be fine,' he said again without conviction.

Sarah seemed to hear the hesitation in his voice. 'I hope so, Ridpath, I do hope so.'

Chapter Thirty-one

He had one more call to make. Taking three deep breaths, he instantly felt calmer, more controlled. 'Focus, Ridpath, focus, one thing at a time.'

He rang Jenny Oldfield on her mobile. The officer manager picked up the phone immediately, 'How is she?'

'Still under sedation, I'm afraid.'

'That's not good, is it? I heard last night about the attack, Sarah rang me. What are we going to do?'

'I think the best thing would be to keep the Coroner's Court running as smoothly as possible in Mrs Challinor's absence. Have you advised the chief coroner yet?'

'Not yet.'

'I suggest you call him immediately.'

'On it, Ridpath.'

'Does Helen know?'

'I told the her late last night.'

Helen Moore was Mrs Challinor's deputy. For some reason, Ridpath had little to do with her even though she had been working at the court for almost a year now.

'She should be in charge until the chief coroner decides differently. I have to go in to Police HQ now, but I'll come back to the Coroner's Court this afternoon. I know it's Saturday, but I think we should have an emergency meeting at two p.m. to handle this situation.'

'Even when Mrs Challinor isn't there?'

'*Because* Mrs Challinor isn't there. The court needs to run smoothly without her.'

'I'll get Helen to call the meeting. I think David Smail is in Manchester but I need to check. What should she say?'

Ridpath thought for a moment. Telling everyone Mrs Challinor had been attacked near her home wouldn't be right. 'Just say that unfortunately the coroner has been taken to hospital urgently.' At least it was the truth.

'OK, will do. We'll see you this afternoon at two?'

'Definitely. And Jenny, it's up to you to keep everything going, Mrs Challinor would want it.'

'I know, Ridpath.'

He put down the phone. Time to focus back on the case for Claire Trent. He hadn't finished reading all the materials yet. Somehow he would have to catch up. Too much to do and too little time.

Immediately he felt a sense of unease building in his stomach and pressing down on his chest. For a moment, the urgency of everything he had to do washed over him. He felt like he was being overwhelmed. Was it seeing Mrs Challinor lying in the hospital bed, tubes leading from her body to machines?

She had always been his rock, his source of stability when all around him was falling apart.

He closed his eyes and went to his safe space, as he had been taught by his therapist after Polly's death. High on the hill above Ladybower Reservoir, the wind swirling through his clothes and a skylark singing up above him.

'Focus, Ridpath, hold it all together,' he whispered to himself, putting the car in gear.

Chapter Thirty-two

Chrissy and Emily were waiting for him in one of the meeting rooms on the MIT floor. They had already placed a large hand-written sign on the door. To Ridpath, it looked more like a rehearsal room for a school play than an operations centre for a criminal investigation.

ROMEO AND JULIET.

DO NOT ENTER.

He walked in and saw the room had been transformed. White-boards had been set up with the photofit pictures of the two victims, the crime scene shots and a schematic of the third floor of the warehouse pinned to them.

In the corner, a stack of boxes reached to the ceiling, while assorted files were already lying open on the tables.

'Are those what I think they are?' Ridpath pointed to the boxes.

'The notes from Meredith. And guess what, there's no index or list of anything.'

'So he's decided to play silly buggers has he? Flood us with everything he has so we have no chance of getting to it all. Bastard.'

'I often wonder which side these people are on,' muttered Chrissy.

'Always their own. It's what makes them tick.'

Ridpath took his laptop out and placed it on the desk. 'Right then let's get down to work.'

'Aren't you going to tell us about Mrs Challinor?' asked Chrissy, adjusting the Manchester City scarf around her neck.

Ridpath raised his eyebrows. 'You've already heard about that?'

'Claire Trent asked me what happened this morning.'

Ridpath frowned. How had she found out so quickly? Did she have ears everywhere? 'I'll go tell the boss later. Let her know what's going on. Meanwhile, let's get going on this.'

They both stared at him.

'All right, all right. She was attacked last night as she was walking her dog. She's in hospital at the moment but still hasn't regained consciousness.'

'Not good…'

'I have to be back at the Coroner's Court in Stockfield this afternoon, so can we get on with this?'

'And what about you? Are you OK?'

He frowned again. 'What have you heard, Chrissy?'

'Nothing much. Claire Trent told me you were at the crime scene last night and you were also attacked.'

He decided to make light of it, rubbing the back of his skull. 'Somebody gave me a little tap on the head…'

'So now you have water on the brain?' Emily and Chrissy high-fived each other.

'Very funny ladies, but can we get back to work? Chrissy, you go first.'

'Right, I sent across the files on the server last night; the post-mortem report, the reports on PoliceWorks…'

'That pile of shit,' Emily shook her head.

'Yeah, the system is still a mess. The search function doesn't really work and I can see some copper has spent half his life inputting the data, but it's still pretty useless and there are lots of gaps.'

'Who was the copper?'

'A Rob Thomas.'

'I thought he retired years ago?'

'He did,' said Chrissy.

They both stared at her.

'I couldn't see any rank so I checked him out. He's an agency worker.'

'What?'

'He's one of the agency detectives hired by GMP.'

'Hang on, we're using temporary agency detectives to investigate major cases?'

'Not so temporary. He's been at Central for nearly a year now. We're short-staffed, not enough detectives. And I hate to tell you this, Ridpath, but it's why you've been brought back from the coroner's office.'

'Thanks for reminding me, Emily.' He ran his fingers through his receding hair. 'So let me get this right, PoliceWorks, the management tool supposed to consolidate and help us manage the workflows of each investigation, is a total mess…'

'An expletive deleted mess.'

'…And all the work on the case has been done by a temporary agency detective, probably working nine to five and costing us an arm and a leg.'

'That's about it.'

He pointed to the boxes of records. 'So the investigation is all in there?'

'Probably,' replied Chrissy. 'Some of it's on PoliceWorks but God only knows where.'

'We're back to paper records again.'

'Yep. Meredith did help by providing a separate timeline of the investigation.' She brought it up on the computer. 'At least we know what they did and when.'

'Thanks Chrissy.' He turned to Emily. 'How did you get on?'

'I went through the chief inspector's timeline. The investigation seems to have gone by the book. Interviewing possible witnesses, and checking the history of the building and its ownership.'

'Anything useful there?'

She checked her notes. 'Not a lot. It was built in 1885 by the Simpson's, a family of cotton exporters. They went out of business in the 1930s when it was bought by a cotton importer and used for storage. They closed in the early 1970s. For a while it was derelict, before being used by a wig manufacturer and exporter. Apparently they stored furs there too.'

'Perhaps that was when the additional room on the top floor was created, to store the valuable furs?' added Christy.

'They went out of business too, in the recession of the 1980s. From then, it was used mainly for storage and owned by a series of offshore companies based in the Cayman Islands.'

'So who owned the building in 2008?'

'Apparently it was Consolidated Building Services, a Cayman Island Company.'

'And who owned them?'

'Consolidated Building Factors.'

'Let me guess, another Cayman Island company?'

'Right first time, Ridpath.'

'I won't ask who owns them?'

'Good job, because Meredith never found out. He requested an investigation from a firm of forensic accountants.'

'And…'

'The decision hasn't been made yet to go ahead. Apparently the cost was too high.'

'When did Ronnie Hardcastle buy it?'

Emily checked the file again. '2016, from another Cayman Islands company, Burton's Active Management and Investment, which no longer exists. His company has held it ever since, finally receiving planning permission for a mixed-use commercial/retail/ housing development in early 2020. Then the pandemic hit…'

'And they were stuffed.'

'Weren't we all?'

Ridpath breathed out heavily. 'So we don't know who the true owners were, and in a week, we're not likely to find out? Is there anything we do know?'

Chrissy stuck her hand up. 'Meredith managed to track down a security guard who had been employed by Consolidated Building Services in 2008 to look after the property and prevent damage.'

'Well done, Chief Inspector Meredith.'

'The guard said they'd had some trouble with a few down-and-outs using it as a doss house but once they'd sealed it up, it went quiet.'

'He didn't notice a whole room had been bricked up on the top floor?'

'Nah, it was just one of the properties he had to visit on his rounds. His statement says he rarely went up to the third floor. But apparently the place was broken into some time in the summer of 2008; he didn't remember the exact date.'

'And?'

'He didn't find anything unusual. Thought it just some kids messing around.'

'Did he report it?'

'Nah, would've been a waste of time with nothing damaged or reported missing.'

'Anything on the date of the break-in?'

'He couldn't remember when, just sometime in the summer.'

'Right, we don't have much.'

'Probably less than that, Ridpath.'

'But we do have those.' He pointed to the boxes in the corner. 'I think we need to go through and sort them into a system. The answer must be buried in there somewhere.'

'What if it's not?' asked Emily.

'Then we have to start again from the beginning, but at least we'll know what Meredith missed.' He strode towards one of the boxes, picking it up and placing it on a desk. 'Let's get started.'

By lunchtime, they had finished sorting all the documents into a form of order: witness statements, local door-to-door inquiries, building history and ownership, scene of crime photos and forensic analysis, victim identification, missing persons reports, police notebook photocopies, intelligence databases, HOLMES printouts and, after the BBC *North West Tonight* programme, over four boxes of telephone transcripts from viewers.

The documents were stacked across six tables in the room and all carefully labelled by Chrissy.

'Shit,' said Emily. 'We're going to have to wade through all that?'

'Looks like it.'

Ridpath checked his watch. 'Let's get a sandwich from the canteen and start. Emily, you can take the witness statements, local door-to-door inquiries and missing persons reports. Chrissy, you tackle the building history, intelligence databases, newspaper reports, HOLMES printouts. I'll do the scene of crime and forensic reports plus the victim identification work.'

'What about the telephone transcripts and the newspaper reports?' asked Emily.

'We'll leave those to last. There may be something, but the problem with television crime watch programmes is they produce such a load of dross too.'

'All the nutters come out of the woodwork. I remember one time we were looking for a missing girl. One telephone respondent swore blind she'd watched her being abducted by aliens dressed as parking attendants. You couldn't make it up...'

'But she did.'

'The bad news is,' Ridpath interrupted as they laughed, 'I have to go to a meeting at the Coroner's Court at two this afternoon. We need to plan for Mrs Challinor's absence.'

Emily and Chrissy stopped laughing immediately. It was Emily who answered. 'Of course, Ridpath, do what you have to do.'

'I'll come in early tomorrow morning and start on these.'

'No worries, myself and Emily will go through it tonight. We'll message you if we find anything important.'

Ridpath took out his wallet. 'Right, ladies, the bacon butties are on me. And for you, Emily, I'll even cough to a vegan sausage roll.'

Chapter Thirty-three

As Ridpath was parking near the Coroner's Court, the call came in.

'Yes, boss.'

'You escaped before I had time to chat with you, Ridpath.' Claire Trent didn't sound pleased.

'Sorry, boss, I didn't know you wanted to see me.'

'What were you doing out in Cheshire in the middle of the night?'

'It was eleven o'clock, and I'd just taken Sarah Challinor, the coroner's daughter, home from the hospital.'

'That doesn't tell me what you were doing at a taped-off crime scene.'

Ridpath was quiet.

'Well…?'

'I just thought I'd check it out, boss.' Ridpath realised how weak he sounded. 'And I was hit on the head for my trouble.'

There was no sympathy from Claire Trent. 'Let me make it clear, Ridpath. Stay away. I'll say it again just in case the message, like the blow on the head, didn't penetrate your thick skull. This is Cheshire's case. STAY AWAY. Is that clear?'

Ridpath stayed silent.

'Is that clear?' Claire Trent repeated with more force.

'Yes, guvnor, quite clear.'

'It's a job for Cheshire Police, not us. Now get on with your real work and find out who murdered our bodies in the warehouse.'

'Yes, boss.'

The phone call ended abruptly. Ridpath stepped out of the car and walked slowly up the steps to the coroner's office.

The meeting had already started when he walked in. 'Sorry I'm late, a phone call.'

Instantly he felt embarrassed; he seemed to be making a lot of excuses lately.

Helen Moore was at the head of the table where Mrs Challinor normally sat. Next to here was the locum coroner from Derbyshire, David Smail.

Jenny Oldfield stood up and passed him the work-in-progress sheet prepared by Sophia yesterday. His assistant was in her normal place with an empty chair waiting for him.

She pushed a large Starbucks latte towards him as he sat down.

Helen Moore spoke as he sipped the first draught of warmed milk. There seemed to be no coffee taste at all.

'Ridpath, I was just updating everyone on the coroner's condition. Mrs Challinor is unfortunately still unconscious, according to her daughter, with the hospital apparently scheduling more tests.'

'Have the police followed up on her attacker?'

'I don't know, but she did mention a family liaison officer was with her.'

Despite Claire Trent's warning, Ridpath wrote a note to himself to ring DCI Tindall and inquire about the progress of the investigation. They certainly hadn't contacted him about his attack last night. He felt the back of his head. The bump was still there beneath the skin but at least it was smaller now.

'I have been on the phone to the chief coroner. He has urged us to continue as we are at the moment, and apparently they will be sending somebody to replace Mrs Challinor shortly.'

'When will that be?' asked Jenny.

'They didn't say. My feeling was they were looking for somebody, perhaps a retired coroner. Anyway, we need to make sure everything runs smoothly in Mrs Challinor's absence. It's what she would have wanted.'

'What about Mrs Challinor's cases? She was extremely busy,' asked Jenny.

'Again, I don't know. We'll go through her workload at this meeting and see what we can reassign and what we can postpone.'

Once again she scanned the people at the table, looking for agreement. Ridpath could sense her uncertainty. He was used to Mrs Challinor's decisive approach to these meetings. But without her leadership, they were all in new territory.

'Now, let's get started, shall we? Sophia, why don't you begin.'

His assistant opened the first page of her document. 'There were fifty-two deaths in our district last week. All the families have been contacted. Ridpath and I have highlighted the ones Mrs Challinor wanted to follow up.'

Ridpath drifted away as Sophia spoke. His mind was still on the Romeo and Juliet case. It suddenly occurred to him Meredith had approached it wrongly. What he should have done was...

'Ridpath, are you still with us?'

'Sorry, Helen, I was thinking about something else.'

A little cough of annoyance. 'I was asking if the death of Mr Watkins in Didsbury should be investigated more thoroughly. There are a few anomalies in the case that need to be clarified.'

Didsbury? Which case was it? And then it came to him. The man found at the bottom of the stairs. 'I agree, it does need to be followed up.' He made another note to himself.

'And how is your workload?'

'Yesterday, MIT assigned a new case to me. The Romeo and Juliet bodies found in the warehouse.'

Jenny turned a page. 'That's on Mrs Challinor's list too. She opened an inquest on it in January, postponing it pending police inquiries. It's still on the pending list.'

'It will probably stay there. The police have nothing so far.'

'There's still no identification of the bodies?'

Ridpath shook his head. 'Still Female A and Male B.'

'But why are you investigating?' asked Smail.

Ridpath explained the briefing from Claire Trent.

'So in a week you'll be free again?'

'I think so.'

Helen Moore coughed loudly. 'With Mrs Challinor... away, we need you here, Ridpath. We're up to our ears in work and I don't want to make mistakes with the chief coroner watching our every move.'

'There won't be any mistakes. Everything is under control,' said Sophia firmly.

Helen Moore stared at her, then turned to Ridpath. 'I'm not happy with this, not happy at all. I think it is a waste of your time to be investigating a six-month-old case when we are so busy. I've been unhappy about your... situation for a long time.'

'My situation?'

'Working for both MIT and the coroner's office. I have voiced by objections to Mrs Challinor repeatedly.'

'Mrs Challinor wanted me specifically to work this case. I...'

'But now Margaret isn't here and I'm in charge. I'll call Detective Superintendent Trent this afternoon.'

'I wouldn't bother. I can handle both jobs. There will be no errors.'

Ridpath stared across the table at her; finally she looked down.

'We'll leave it as it is for the moment, as it was Mrs Challinor's decision for you to be involved. But Jenny, if there are any problems, please let me know.'

Jenny looked across at Ridpath and rolled her eyes.

'Right, that's sorted. Shall we continue?'

The rest of the meeting passed quietly, everybody barely raising their heads from looking at their work sheets.

Finally, it came to an end. 'I know we all are going to miss Mrs Challinor, but we need to ensure that, in her absence, everything runs smoothly. The chief coroner's office is looking at us, looking at me. I don't want any mistakes. Clear?'

Helen Moore looked around the table for the last time, this time not looking for agreement but for obedience. Finally, she settled on Ridpath. 'And please try to be on time, Ridpath. I know you are busy, but aren't we all?'

She gathered up her files and left the room.

Ridpath was left clenching and unclenching his jaw. He hated being treated like a child.

Chapter Thirty-four

Ridpath spent the next couple of hours going through the work-load with Sophia, ensuring every 'i' had been dotted and all the 't's' crossed. He hated taking such a bureaucratic approach to work but felt there was no choice given the absence of Mrs Challinor.

They had finished about half of the cases when Sophia announced she had to go.

'Another date?'

'Yes, but this time it's with the mother. We're doing a mother/daughter bonding session down at the salon. Hair, nails, tummy lift, nose job – the usual drill.'

'Sorry to have to do this, but do you mind coming in and finishing these off with me tomorrow then? I know it's Sunday, but...'

'Not a problem. After a bonding session, I need a break anyway. There's only so much of my mum I can take.'

'See you tomorrow afternoon then.'

He quickly called Angela Wells only to be told Eve was halfway up a mountain and couldn't be reached, but apparently she was enjoying herself and the two girls, with only one dispute over breakfast that morning, were getting on well.

He heaved a sigh of relief. At least she was having fun, one less thing for him to worry about.

Having finished his work with Sophia, he decided to visit the coroner in hospital. With a bit of luck, she would be out of the coma by now.

He put a Bowie CD in the player and within seconds the power chords of 'Jean Genie' blasted through the fake plastic of the fascia, accompanied by Bowie's snarl and a thrust of the hips.

By the time he arrived at the hospital and parked at the hospital, he felt strangely elated. There was nothing better to drive away the cobwebs of bureaucracy than a bit of Bowie.

Up at the ward Mrs Challinor was still lying in bed, tubes and wires hanging off her. Next to her, Sarah Challinor was reading a book. Beside the coroner's daughter was a young woman in a police uniform, wearing bright purple gloves on her hands. She also had a green mask covering her face so all he could see were her eyes.

'Hi, Sarah, there's no change?'

The daughter shook her head. 'Still the same, Ridpath.'

The young police officer stood up. 'And you are?' she asked aggressively.

Ridpath produced his warrant card. 'Detective Inspector Thomas Ridpath.'

The woman stared at the card and reddened. 'Sorry, sir, I…'

'No worries, Constable…?'

'Ruston, sir. Alison Ruston.'

'You're the family liaison officer?'

'Yes, sir.'

'It's Ridpath, not sir.'

He looked back at the Mrs Challinor lying on the bed, her head swathed in a thick white bandage, the bruising on her face going from a dark purple to a vivid yellow.

He spoke directly to Sarah. 'Any news from the doctors?'

'They're still waiting for test results to come back. They're worried there might be brain damage.'

'When will we know for sure?'

'They'll tell me tomorrow when all the results are in.' A long pause. 'She may have bleeding on the brain.' After uttering those words, the tight control she had held over herself fell away and she dissolved into tears, her shoulders and body visibly shaking in front of Ridpath.

He put his arms around her. 'Don't worry, your mum is tough, she'll come through this.'

'But… but…'

He hugged her tighter. 'She's strong, resilient. She'll make it through. You also need to be strong for her.'

Sarah nodded, wiping her nose. 'Look at me,' she laughed, 'back to when I was a little girl crying over a grazed knee.'

When she had calmed down, Ridpath spoke to the constable. 'Can I have a word?'

They walked out into the corridor past a nurse's station and stopped outside the lifts. 'How's the investigation?'

The constable looked to either side. 'I don't know if I should say, sir.'

'It's Ridpath. Copper to copper, how's it going?'

Ruston thought for a moment, bringing up a gloved hand to scratch her face beneath the mask. 'DCI Tindall thinks it was an attempted rape that went wrong, sir.'

Ridpath heard the doubt in her voice. 'But you don't agree?'

'Maybe I'm talking out of turn, but I've been doing this job a long time. I'm the usual FLO, the one they go to on cases like this.'

Ridpath knew how that happened. Family liaison officers had one of the toughest jobs in the police, often having to tell people somebody had died or been severely injured, sitting with them afterwards listening to their worries and watching their grief. He had been hopeless at it, lacking the patience and empathy for the job. Even now as a coroner's officer he found it hard to handle grief; watching a family collapse in the face of tragedy was not something he could do every day.

'Go on…' he finally said to PC Ruston as she hesitated to tell him any more.

'Well, rapists don't normally attack their victims. They get off on the sense of power or control: a knife to the throat, a threat of physical harm, make the victim compliant and submissive.'

'They don't hit them with a hammer repeatedly about the head?'

'And the doctors tell me there was no sign of any sexual assault. Her clothes weren't removed. No semen traces on her jeans. There doesn't seem to have been a sexual element at all.'

'So why does Tindall think it's an attempted rape?'

She shrugged her shoulders.

'The forensic team have examined her clothes?'

She looked up at him. 'Was it you who asked the doctor to bag them up?'

Ridpath didn't answer.

'Anyway, we think we have some DNA off them.'

'And?'

'We're still waiting for the results. But it would be no use anyway, no chain of evidence. Too many people could have contaminated the evidence. The farmer, the medics. the doctors and nurses, even a hospital porter could have left trace elements on the clothes.'

'You'll have to test everybody. But he hasn't done that, has he?'

She shook her head.

'Let me guess again. It would cost too much.'

She smiled. 'You've been a copper too long.'

'As have you.' He thought for a moment. 'But he did test the DNA?'

She nodded again.

'And?'

She scratched the back of her gloved hand. 'Like I said, still waiting for the results.'

'Call me when you get them.'

'I don't...'

'Copper to copper. Mrs Challinor was a close personal friend as well as the coroner. I want to know what's happening in her case.'

The FLO finally nodded. 'I'll see what I can do.'

Ridpath was about to go back to say goodbye to Sarah, when something occurred to him. 'Why do you wear the gloves?'

'I spend a lot of my time in hospitals, which are full of disease. Just a safety precaution. Plus we have to wear the mask… rules.'

'You can't be too safe, can you?'

Chapter Thirty-five

As soon as he returned to the car, Ridpath made the call to DCI Tindall. He knew he shouldn't be doing it, Claire Trent had made it perfectly clear, but he had promised Sarah to follow up on the investigation. He wasn't interfering, merely asking for a progress update.

It was his justification and he was sticking with it.

The call was picked up after four rings.

'DCI Tindall, Cheshire Police.'

'Hi there, it's Inspector Ridpath.'

'Oh, hello Ridpath, are you ringing about your attack? Give me a second and I'll find the crime report number for you.'

Ridpath heard the clicks of an old-fashioned computer keyboard.

'Here it is. Have you a pen to write this down?'

'Actually, I was ringing to ask about how the investigation into the attack on Mrs Challinor was progressing.'

A long silence on the other end of the phone.

'Hello, I said I was ringing to...'

'I heard you the first time. It's progressing.'

Ridpath sighed. 'I'd just like to know what's going on. The coroner is both my employer and a good friend, I'd like to let her family know if there are any developments.'

'We have delegated a FLO to stay with the family and keep them informed of developments in the case; there is no need for you to become involved.'

Ridpath's eyes rolled upwards. He forced himself to stay calm. 'Copper to copper, I'd just like to know what's going on.'

'Copper to copper, it's none of your business. This is my case and I'm going to run it as I see fit. Understand?'

'Of course, I understand it's your case, but for the sake of professional courtesy it would be good to know if there are any developments.'

'You wouldn't know about professional courtesy, Ridpath, if it kicked you in the arse,' he snarled. 'A good mate of mine was sacked for no reason at all, so you go screw yourself. Am I clear?'

Turnbull. Why did the man continue to dog Ridpath like a bad smell? 'Listen, Chief Inspector Turnbull brought a false charge of assault against me. He got what was coming to him.'

'And you'll get what's coming to you. Which from me is absolutely nothing.'

The phone went dead in his hand. Ridpath slammed the steering wheel of his car, again and again in frustration. He hadn't even managed to ask Tindall why he thought it was an attempted rape.

'Shit, shit, shit.' Claire Trent's words came back to him clearly: 'This is Cheshire's case. STAY AWAY. Is that clear?'

He banged the steering wheel again.

Forget Tindall. Forget police politics. Forget them all.

Nothing was going to stop him finding out who attacked Mrs Challinor. He owed it to her. He owed it to her family. Above all, he owed it to the truth.

Chapter Thirty-six

He called Eve as soon as he arrived home. 'Are you enjoying yourself? How's the camping?'

'It's intense. Get it?'

He laughed dutifully.

'Sorry, one of Mr Wells' jokes. Maisie cringes even more than I do when you tell yours.'

'You cringe?'

'Inwardly all the time, Dad. Your jokes aren't that good.'

Brutal honesty: that's what teenagers gave you. 'You could sugar-coat it a little.'

'How's Mrs Challinor?'

'She's still in a coma. The doctors are doing tests.'

'How awful. I feel sorry for her daughter.'

There was a long pause. Was she thinking of when her mother died, and the feelings she had when it happened?

'Who would do such an awful thing to such a good person as Mrs Challinor?'

'I don't know, Eve, Cheshire Police are investigating it. Hopefully they'll find out who did it.'

'You're not involved in the investigation?'

He shook his head. 'It didn't happen in our area. Mrs Challinor lives in Cheshire.'

'But you know her better than anybody, Dad, I thought you would be involved.'

'I think I have enough on my plate, don't you? Have you eaten?' he asked, trying to change the subject.

'I've just had a peanut butter sandwich.'

'Peanut butter? When have you started liking peanut butter? Horrible stuff, sticks to the roof of your mouth.'

'What do you mean? It's the food of champions. Maisie's mum swears by it.'

'Swears at it more like. So what did you do today?'

'We walked the Great Langdale Round. We started at the Old Dungeon Ghyll and then bagged six Wainrights: Bowfell, Crinkle Crags, Pike of Stickle, Pike of Blisco, Loft Crag and Rossett Pike.'

'Sounds like you did a lot of walking?'

'A fair bit, and I'm a bit tired now. We even had a drink at the pub. But don't worry, I just had an orange juice. Mr Wells had two whole pints.'

'Lucky him.'

Ridpath stayed quiet as she described the countryside and mountains of the Lakes, the Herdwick sheep, Wordsworth's cottage and the Great Langdale valley. 'You know the flint quarried here in the past has been found as far away as Europe and Ireland.'

Ridpath stayed quiet. It was lovely to hear her talk about her day. So often these days they seemed to be passing ships in the night, rushing from place to place without connecting with each other.

He missed when she was a child and her whole world revolved around Polly and himself.

Polly.

How he missed his wife. Her voice, her kindness, the warmth of her body and soul as she lay beside him at night. Now, his bed was cold, but her shape was still there on the mattress. A ghostly impression and a constant reminder of what his life, and Eve's, was missing.

He felt his eyes beginning to moisten, so he quickly stood up and sniffed.

'Are you OK, Dad?'

'Fine, just a touch of hay fever,' he said, his voice beginning to break.

Her voice dropped a register. 'I miss her too, Dad.'

How did she know he was thinking of Polly?

'Remember the time we went to the Peak District with her and you got lost looking for a wartime bomber that had crashed in the mountains? Mum had to guide us out of the bog you lead us into.'

He smiled, remembering the day well.

'For a detective, you have the sense of direction of an amoeba.'

'Is that bad?' he finally managed.

'Worse than bad, non-existent.' A voice in the distance. 'I have to go now, Dad, we're going out to eat, some vegan restaurant or other. I hope there's no kale.' A long pause. 'I'll be back tomorrow. Miss you, Dad. And remember, Mum's always with us, even when she's not. If you want to talk just give me a call, OK?'

'Miss you too, Eve. See you tomorrow.'

After ten seconds, he heard the click as the phone was switched off.

He leant on the side of the sink, desperately trying to hold back the tears. What had she said? 'Mum's always with us, even when she's not.'

He heard the silence in the house, and he wondered who the adult really was in this relationship.

Chapter Thirty-seven

The steady beep of the machine next to the bed continued. Sarah no longer heard it. She had been sitting here for almost two days now, waiting for her mother to come round.

But still nothing. Just the steady beep, on and on and on.

She put down the magazine she had been reading on the table next to her chair. She called it reading, but actually she had been staring at the words as they swam in front of her eyes, none of it making much sense.

She pinched the soft skin at the top of her nose just above her mask, feeling the deep frown line between her fingers, pressing the ache behind her eyes. She glanced at the stack of plastic coffee cups on the table. How much more of the mud could she drink?

Not a lot.

The FLO had gone home hours ago, after finishing her shift. A good woman who did her job well, but Sarah was happy when she'd gone, leaving her alone with her mother.

She would have to go home soon too, if only to take a shower. Luckily Rufus was being taken care of by a neighbour. It was one less thing for her to worry about.

She stared across at her mother, lying there unmoving, a fresh bandage encircling her head. Her skin was as beautiful as ever, the peaches and cream complexion she was always so proud of. Shame she hadn't passed it on to her daughter. Her skin was more like her dad's: orange peel and freckles.

She remembered their last conversation.

'How do you keep it looking so good? Mine always looks like the inside of a peeled tangerine.'

'Soap and water.'

Her mother was putting the lead on the dog before taking him for a walk. He, as ever, was sweeping the kitchen floor with his tail in his excitement.

'That's all? No fancy creams or anything?'

'No point. Waste of money.'

Her mother took her blue fleece from its peg.

'Would you like anything to eat? I can make a salad and add a bit of leftover chicken.'

'Sounds good. I'll take Rufus for his walk. I have to do some thinking.'

'Work?'

'What else?'

'The salad will be ready when you get back.'

And that was it; she was dragged out of the door by the cocker spaniel eager to discover the sights and smells of the Cheshire countryside.

It was only later Sarah heard the police sirens and knew something bad had happened. And also knew, with an unerring sixth sense, it had happened to her mum.

Again, she looked at the bruised face lying on the pillow above the sheets. She wished they'd had a more profound conversation than 'Would you like anything it eat?' Wished she'd said something more meaningful, at least said she loved her before the door closed.

A shadow appeared next to her. It was the night nurse. What was her name? Catherine, that was it.

'You should go home. No point in you staying here. We can call you if she wakes up.'

She stared at her mum lying there and felt an immense wave of tiredness wash over her, drowning her with a desire for sleep, a desire to escape from the hospital and its smells and sadness.

'It's ten thirty now, go home, grab a shower and a good night's sleep, come back in the morning. We'll look after her while you are gone. She's in good hands.'

Sarah nodded. The nurse was right. She stood up, knocking over the stack of plastic cups.

'Don't mind them, I'll clean up after you go.'

She nodded again, picking up her bag and the magazines, walking past the other bed and its sleeping occupant towards the exit of the small ward. Taking one last glance at her mother, she stepped out, wishing she could tell her she loved her one more time.

Chapter Thirty-eight

Ridpath was about to go to bed when his phone rang.

He had already been through the scene of crime and forensic reports plus the victim identification work.

The forensic reports had revealed the victims' fingerprints were all over the room; on the walls, the mattress, the door, even the bucket in the corner. But there were no other prints at all and particularly none on the bricks and the plaster used to entomb the place.

Either the killer had been careful, or they had worn gloves all the time. Ridpath wrote a note.

Any tools found in the search?

The killer must have used a trowel and board for both the bricks and the mortar. He flicked through the scene of crime manager's document. They had searched all the dumpsters on the ground floor and cleared the remaining rubbish from the area in front of the room.

Nothing.

The killer must have taken all his tools. That suggested planning and a careful attitude to DNA. Bloody *CSI*, he thought, it had become a training manual for criminals and murderers.

He followed the steps Meredith had taken to identify the bodies. Obviously neither victim had a wallet or mobile phone with them. The killer must have removed both.

There were no tattoos on either victim nor had either of them had surgery or broken a bone. They had taken casts, pictures and X-rays of the teeth and circulated them to every dentist in Manchester, followed by Lancashire and then the rest of the north.

Not one dentist had come forward. A forensic dentist had been employed at great expense and he had come to the profound conclusion there was nothing special about these mouths. There was a distinctly sniffy tone in his report, as if the victims were beneath his expertise and dignity to examine.

Meredith had even traced the clothes they were wearing. Both the woman and the man's had been bought at a variety of chain stores according to the labels, none of which were still traceable to a particular outlet. Only Female A's shoes were more individual; a pair from a shop on Tib Street which had since closed down. Meredith had found the former owners but they had not kept any records.

As the pathologist had said, they were 'extraordinarily ordinary'.

Looking through the files again, the victim identification work in the case notes seemed a bit cursory to him, as if they were just going through the motions. He would have to check the missing persons files still in the boxes tomorrow morning before the meeting. Perhaps there would be more there.

He put down his notebook and pen and yawned. Just then his mobile rang. Without looking at the number, he answered. 'Ridpath.'

'Hi there, it's Alison Ruston, the FLO.'

He instantly leant forward.

'You asked me to call you if the DNA results came back from the lab. We found a large area of what looked like saliva close to Mrs Challinor's collar, probably from the assailant during the attack. There's no other reason for it to have been there.'

'And?'

'No hits on the National DNA database.'

'So whoever attacked Mrs Challinor has never been in trouble and never been arrested by the police.'

'Looks that way.'

'What about the coroner's nails? Anything there?'

'We checked for epithelials and the DNA was the same as on her clothes.'

'So no hits?'

'Nothing.'

'No link to anybody on the sexual offender's register?'

'None.'

'So why does Tindall still think it was attempted rape?'

'I dunno.'

From the tone of her voice, Ridpath could imagine the FLO shrugging her shoulders.

'So nothing from the DNA?' Ridpath persisted.

'No, it's a dead end. Tindall is working out what to do.'

'He hasn't got any leads, has he?'

'I don't think so.' There was a pause. 'There's one other thing. During the search of the area of the attack, they found a small bag with a hypodermic needle in it. The needle contained enough pure morphine to kill a horse. But Tindall isn't sure it's linked to the attack. No DNA or any fingerprints on it.'

'Where was it found?'

'In the hedge next to where Mrs Challinor was attacked.'

'And it's just a coincidence it was there?'

'I dunno, just giving you a heads-up.'

'Thanks, Alison.'

'No worries, Ridpath.' Another long pause. 'Why do you think the coroner was attacked?'

'I don't know, but I'm going to find out.' A long pause. 'And, unlike DCI Tindall, I don't believe it was an attempted rape.'

Chapter Thirty-nine

I've been busy today. The clothes I wore yesterday were washed and then taken to the tip. Shame, I rather liked the black hoodie. I'd also taken the bike to be detailed, just in case they could match the mud to the area near Mrs Challinor's home. I don't suppose they can, but I'd rather be safe than sorry.

Forensic services have improved immensely over the last few years. It was almost the same with medicine. Advances are made so quickly, it's so difficult to keep up. I could spend my whole life reading journals and still not cover half of it.

I poured myself a cold glass of sauvignon blanc. The air, the heat was oppressive. I had opened the doors leading to the patio from the kitchen but it didn't help much, simply attracting a swarm of insects and moths.

Ugly, brutish, dirty things.

In the twilight, the swifts whistled around the rear garden, sweeping up a late snack on the wing. How elegant they were compared with the ugliness of their food.

I needed another sip of wine.

Was there anything I'd missed?

I didn't think so.

In rushing the attack on Mrs Challinor, I had made too many mistakes. The bag was still hiding somewhere near the road but I couldn't go back now. The last time had been too close. The man, whoever he was, might be there again, lying in wait for me.

I would have to take my chances with the bag.

At least I knew there was no DNA on it. I would be safe.

The top of my wrist was painful where the bitch had scratched me with her nails. Three long, deep marks requiring antiseptic and a dressing. The last thing I needed now was to get an infection.

Would the police recover my epithelials from under her nails?

Probably not.

And even if they did, how would they match them to me? I'm not on any database and my DNA has never been taken.

Another weight lifted from my shoulders.

All I have to do now is wait and let the police investigation blow over. They always did in the past, when I killed the others. In Blackburn, Derby and Chester the police had run out of patience when they could find no evidence. I had even given evidence at the inquests, but nobody had made the connection.

They had all become cold cases.

Extremely cold cases.

Then I remembered Mrs Challinor. What had happened to her?

I'd checked the local news and papers and there was nothing. It was almost as if the police had requested no publicity.

If she had died, surely there would have been an announcement in the press? At least the local papers would have published an obituary, but there was nothing.

She must be in hospital somewhere.

Tomorrow, I would find out. It shouldn't be too difficult.

I took another sip of wine to discover I'd finished the glass. Time to open another bottle.

I needed to relax and plan the next moves.

Planning was key.

It had worked in the past and it would work again.

Sunday, June 20

Chapter Forty

Ridpath arrived at Police HQ early, at eight a.m.

It was another bright summer's day with nary a cloud in the sky. The weather report had said it was going to be a hot day, one of the hottest on record. Already Manchester was baking, a slight haze hanging over the roads as he drove in.

HQ was hot and stuffy when he arrived, the air-conditioning not yet on. Whoever had designed a glass building with windows which didn't open needed to be shot. Another cost-saving measure instituted by some accountant; anything to save a few pennies on the budget after a decade of cuts. No wonder they were now having to rely on rehiring the same coppers back as agency workers at three times the cost.

'Saving a penny to waste a pound,' he said out loud, remembering one of his mother's favourite sayings.

He couldn't worry about that now. It was time to focus. He pulled the missing person reports out of the boxes. Some poor bugger, a Detective Constable Briggs, had waded through every missing person report for 2008 and the preceding three years, over fifteen thousand of them, from the length and breadth of the country. He had started on reports of missing couples and then, when he had no success, moved on to the rest.

Lots of reports matched the age and description of the victims but still there was no positive ID. Instead a thick wad of possibles had been separated into different sexes, punched and placed in one bulging file containing over eight hundred reports.

The victims could have been inside. Or they might not. Nobody knew.

Chrissy and Emily drifted in at nine, each carrying a coffee and a bacon barm cake and each showing dark circles under their eyes from working late last night.

Ridpath instantly felt guilty again.

Emily placed her coffee and sandwich in front of him. 'For you, I bet you're starving.'

'What about you?'

'I've had mine already.'

Ridpath realised how hungry he felt. After wading through the results of six months of work, he suddenly was dying to eat. He took a large bite from the barm cake, instantly enjoying the salty crunch of crispy bacon contrasted with the oily loveliness of melting butter. Was there anything better than a bacon butty in the morning?

'Let's get started, shall we?' he mumbled, wiping away a slither of melted butter from the side of his mouth.

'I've been through most of the victim identification work. Meredith and his team have gone by the book, trying to ID our victims...'

'But no luck?' asked Emily.

'They've narrowed down the missing persons possibles to these males and females.' He pointed at the bulging box files on the desk in front of him.

'Those?' said Emily. 'There must be over a thousand names there.'

'Actually, there are 826. I counted them. We'll never be able to go through them one by one with just the three of us.'

'No shit, Sherlock,' said Chrissy chewing on her own bacon butty.

'How did you get on?'

Emily spoke first. 'Not a lot better for me. There was no CCTV in the building or in the surrounding area. And even if there had been, what company keeps its recorded images for more than fifteen years? Witness reports were hazy; nobody remembered seeing anything unusual. Our one security guard remembered having a few issues with kids but didn't go to the top floor too often. Too dark and scary, apparently.'

'It's always useful to employ a security guard frightened of the dark,' mumbled Chrissy.

'Door to door was worse than useless; many of the buildings had already been knocked down, were about to be knocked down or were empty and waiting to be knocked down.'

'Not a bad place to put a pair of bodies,' said Ridpath quietly. They both looked at him.

'Anywhere else they might have been found or at least noticed earlier, but in the old warehouse, the only people who went in were kids or tramps.'

'Talking about kids, they even found a couple who used to go inside to spray paint.'

'Where did they find them?'

'Inside.'

'What?'

'A nick. Or two nicks actually. Both had a long history of breaking and entering.'

'And?'

'They didn't remember anything useful. Said they only sprayed the place because it was in their territory.'

'So you have nothing, Emily?'

'Not a lot. One more thing. Meredith and his team tried to find out which trams had travelled from Altrincham to Manchester on August 18, only to be presented with a timetable and a predictable response that the transport authority only kept CCTV footage for thirty days. It had been destroyed "yonks" ago.'

Ridpath laughed to himself. He hadn't heard the word since he was a kid.

'So all in all, a lot of hard work in six months and they still came up with nothing. How about you, Chrissy?'

The civilian researcher put down her half-eaten butty and coughed once before taking a slurp of coffee. 'Not much better for me. I've been through the building history and everything tracks.'

'No chance of finding the real owners?'

'Not unless you have a couple of years and a lot of money. Offshore accounts are private for a reason. It's usually a way of avoiding tax, all perfectly legal of course...'

'If it's so legal, why hide it?'

Chrissy shrugged her shoulders. 'I'm on PAYE, no way I can avoid tax, so I haven't a clue. Anyway, it could be legal tax avoidance or it could be money laundering; ill-gotten gains from drug dealing, corrupt payments, bent money from any number of different sources or just creative accountancy. Unless we appoint a firm of forensic accountants we're unlikely to get anywhere. And they will certainly take more than a week to dig up the real owners in 2008.'

'Anything from intelligence or HOLMES?'

'No intelligence reports. No whispers about cons with an MO of bricking people up in buildings. HOLMES has even less. Meredith entered the MO and even the presence of the water bottle into the database and came up with a big fat zilch. I did the same and came up with less.'

'So we've got nothing?'

'We haven't been through the newspaper reports of the responses to the TV programmes yet,' said Emily hopefully.

'Did Meredith find anything?'

She shook her head. 'He would have followed it up if he did.'

'Like I said. We've got nothing.'

Ridpath stared at the whiteboard. On it the pictures of the two victims from the post-mortem stared back at him.

A thought that had occurred to him yesterday flashed through his brain again. 'We have to look at this differently from Meredith,' he said finally.

'How do you mean?'

'We have less than a week now. If we just replicate Meredith's work over the last six months, we'll get nowhere.'

'I know, but what can we do differently? It looks to me like Meredith covered most of the bases.'

'Ending up down a lot of dead ends.' Ridpath glanced at the victims again. 'I think we need to start in a different place.'

Emily sat forward. 'What do you mean?'

Ridpath tossed a marker to his detective sergeant. 'Let's write down a few questions we need to answer. The first is obvious.'

Emily walked over to the whiteboard and wrote.

Who are the victims?

'Exactly. If we don't know who they are, we can't ever work out who killed them.'

Chrissy sat forward. 'It leads us to ask why they were there.'

Ridpath tilted his head. 'Why 2008? What's important about the date to our victims? Write it down, Emily.' Ridpath scratched his head. Somehow, thinking always made his scalp itchy.

She stepped back from the whiteboard, admiring her handiwork.

Who are the victims?

Why were they there?

Why 2008?

Ridpath looked at the questions. 'Anything we've missed?'

'Probably the most important ones.' Emily strode back the road and wrote.

Who killed them?

Why?

'It's a start,' said Emily.

Ridpath stood up and walked to the window. Outside, the sun was blazing down from an almost cloudless sky. Even the hills to the north looked parched and yellow, covered in a shimmering haze.

He turned back quickly. 'It's a strange way to kill someone, isn't it? Bricking them up in a room. Why do it? Why not knife them? Or shoot them? Why brick them up to die from lack of water or slowly starve to death?'

'A sadist?' said Chrissy. 'Somebody who wants to inflict a slow and painful death.'

'But surely a sadist would have found some way of watching them die? We found no method of watching, the room was completely sealed.'

Emily lifted her chin. 'So he just bricked them in and walked away, knowing they would die but not wanting to watch. What sort of sick sod does that?'

'Perhaps our killer is mentally disturbed. Or perhaps...'

'What is it, Ridpath?'

'Perhaps he didn't want to see them die.' He paused for a moment, knowing he was winging it but feeling he was on to something. 'Perhaps... he wanted them dead but didn't want it to be up close and personal. Didn't want to see the blood after a knife attack or the impact of a bullet on a human skull. It's a curiously dispassionate way of killing someone, don't you think?'

Emily sighed. 'This is all well and good, Ridpath, but how does it help us? We have less than a week to find out who he is.'

'I know, Emily, I don't need another reminder.' Then a thought struck him. 'Perhaps Meredith used HOLMES incorrectly. He looked for a similar MO – deaths in locked rooms or bricked-up rooms...'

'That's what he searched for,' Chrissy acknowledged.

'Perhaps we should be looking for a similar signature, not the same MO?'

'What do you mean?'

He searched for the words. 'Perhaps instead of looking at what our killer did, we should look at what emotional satisfaction he gained from the death?'

Chrissy and Emily remained quiet.

'He killed them without seeing the effects of his actions,' Emily finally whispered.

'He wasn't there to see the pain, the struggle as they died. He's not into the process of death. He's not like the Yorkshire Ripper, who wanted to stare into the eyes of his victims as he killed them, to see their pain.'

'Or Shipman, who would relish the control, injecting his victims, sitting back in an armchair beside their bed, watching life ebb from their old bodies,' added Chrissy.

'Death is functional for him or her. He wanted these two people dead but he didn't want to see it. I wonder...' A long pause. 'Chrissy, could we search HOLMES for murders when the killer is not there?'

'You mean when the killer is not physically present? Long-arm murders? So not anything normal like a stabbing, shooting or a strangulation.' She paused for a moment. 'I can't believe I used the word normal. What have I become?'

Ridpath snapped his fingers. 'Exactly that, cases where the killer isn't there. A long-arm murder. Can HOLMES collate those?'

'I dunno, but I can try.'

'Great.'

'But if the killer had a reason to murder our two victims, it's still going to be difficult to identify him... or her... without knowing who *they* are.' Emily pointed to the two pictures on the board.

Ridpath held out his hand and begin to count off his fingers. 'We have no forensic evidence. No fingerprints on any database. No dental ID. No physical uniqueness like a tattoo. And nobody has come forward to identify our victims from the photofit. We have nothing to identify them.'

'But we do have the one thing which identifies them,' Emily interjected, 'their DNA. Nothing is more conclusive.'

'But we've compared it with the database and there are no hits,' said Ridpath.

'Even though in number terms the National DNA Database is large, in actuality its scope is limited,' said Chrissy.

'Why?' Ridpath asked the question, hoping he wasn't going to get a long, convoluted answer.

'NDNAD was only created in 1995, and until 2001 only DNA from recordable crimes was uploaded to the database. After a couple of legal challenges, the government amended the law to ensure profiles belonging to individuals who had not been convicted of any crime, but taken when they were arrested, were now lawful. The UK forensic DNA database quickly became the largest in the world.'

'You've been on a course, haven't you?'

Chrissy nodded. 'Last year, slept through most of it. There is nothing more boring than a government scientist talking about their favourite hobby horse. The NHS should prescribe their talks as a cure for insomnia. Anyway, even with the new law, DNA was only added to the database from less than five per cent of the crime scenes which were forensically examined, and with less than seventeen per cent of crimes having any forensics at all…'

'A lot still fell though the net,' added Ridpath.

'After 2012, the law changed again so only the DNA of those convicted of recordable crimes could be retained.'

'So you're saying, the chances of getting a match are pretty low?'

'If our victims hadn't been convicted of a crime, been at a crime scene or been arrested at any point in their lives…'

'Like most people…'

'…they would not be on the database. And it gets worse.'

'How could it get worse?'

'The Home Office is involved, how could it NOT get worse? In most cases, NDNAD only looks for direct matches: Does this sample of DNA match somebody on our database? I can think of only one case when an indirect match produced a conviction.'

'What was that?'

'The Melanie Road murder in Bath in 1984. For some reason, the investigators at the time swabbed seventy-one blood spots found at the scene and, even more strangely, they kept them and uploaded the DNA to the database in 1996.'

'Some copper did his job and wouldn't give up.'

'Exactly. But it wasn't until 2014 that the DNA proved useful. That year a woman was arrested in a domestic dispute and her DNA was taken. In 2015, they ran familial DNA for Melanie's murder and got a hit for a Christopher Hampton, the father of the woman arrested in 2014. He was swabbed and his DNA matched that found at the crime scene.'

'Why don't we do a familial DNA test using the NDNAD?' asked Ridpath.

Chrissy clicked her tongue. 'We could do, but we'd have to get approval from a government quango called the Forensic Inform-ation Database Strategy Board, known catchily as FINDS...'

'Why am I not surprised there is another government acronym?'

Chrissy ignored him, carrying on talking. 'Since 2012 only a hundred and twenty searches have been approved by the board and it takes about two months to obtain approval.'

'Time we don't have.'

Chrissy thought for a moment. 'Perhaps we could use genetic genealogy.'

'What's that?' said Ridpath.

She shook her head. 'Sometimes you can be such an old fogey, Ridpath. It's one of the latest tools in solving cases, particu-larly cold cases. How do you think the Americans found the Golden State Killer in California in 2018? A man who prob-ably committed thirteen murders, at least fifty rapes and multiple home burglaries throughout California in the 1970s and 1980s and whose last known crime was in 1986.'

'I remember. Wasn't he a copper?'

'His name was Joseph DeAngelo. They had his DNA from a crime scene in 1980 and plugged it into a genealogy database.

Based on the pool of people on the genealogy website, investigators built a family tree of the killer's relatives which eventually led them to DeAngelo.'

'But we have a problem, Chrissy, just a teeny one.' Ridpath pinched his two fingers together. 'We don't have any DNA from our killer.'

'We don't need any.'

'What? I don't understand.'

'We have the DNA of our victims. We need to find out who they are first.'

Suddenly it was as if a lightbulb exploded in Ridpath's head. His eyes lit up. 'It's worth a shot, we have nothing else. And, if we can find out who they are,' he pointed to the pictures on the whiteboard, 'we're halfway to solving this.'

'There are just a couple of problems.'

'I knew it couldn't be easy.'

'First, I haven't a clue where to start. We need somebody who understands genetic genealogy and who can do the research for us.'

The room went quiet again before Emily spoke. 'I know somebody.'

The both stared at her.

'Her name is Jayne Sinclair. I trained with her. She used to be a copper, a good one too.'

'Jayne Sinclair? Why do I know the name?'

'She was the partner of Dave Gilmour.'

'The copper killed in Moss Side?'

'Yeah, shot through the door on a routine house call. She was standing next to him.'

'How awful,' whispered Chrissy, tightening the City scarf around her neck.

'She tried to come back to work but couldn't hack it any more. PTSD I think.'

At the mention of the letters PTSD, Ridpath immediately went back to his own struggles, remembering long hours with the therapist after Polly had died. He focused quickly back on Emily. 'How can she help us?'

'I'm not sure she can. But I had lunch with her a year ago. She now has a new career as a genealogical investigator.'

'What's one of those?'

'She told me it was looking into people's pasts to find lost relatives or ancestors.'

'Do you think she could help us?'

'It's worth a try.'

'Call her and set up a meeting. At the moment, we've got nothing and time is wasting away.'

At that moment a knock came on the door. A young officer who Ridpath didn't know popped his head round the door and looked straight at Ridpath.

'Sorry to disturb, but the boss sent me. Can you go to see her?'

'She's here? On Sunday?'

'Yep.'

'Sure, won't be a minute, let me just finish here.'

'I think she means right away. Her exact words were, "Get me bloody Ridpath and get him now."'

Chapter Forty-one

Even though it was Sunday, quite a few of the desks in MIT were occupied with detectives staring earnestly at computer screens.

Ridpath knocked gently on Claire Trent's door and waited for permission to enter.

'Come in, Ridpath.'

He entered, surprised to also see Steve Carruthers sitting on the other side of Claire Trent's table, facing him.

'How did you know it was me, boss?'

'Who else would it be?' She obviously wasn't in the mood for small talk.

Ridpath entered the room as if treading on eggshells, which, in a proverbial way, he was. The opening question was gentle.

'How's the investigation going?'

She hadn't asked him to sit down, leaving him standing like an errant schoolboy in the headmaster's office.

'It's going, boss. We've been through all of DCI Meredith's work on the case.'

'You've read it all in twenty-four hours?' It was the Scots burr of Carruthers.

'Yes, sir. We still have the responses to the TV programme to do but as we know, most of those are dross so we're not expecting any big breakthroughs.'

'And?'

'And what, boss?'

Claire Trent let out a long, exasperated sigh. 'And what have you found?'

Ridpath clicked his tongue. 'Not a lot, to be honest. DCI Meredith has done the investigation by the book. A lot of work went into the background of the building, interviewing witnesses, ploughing through missing person lists and door-to-door inquiries...'

'But he's turned up nothing, hasn't any leads and is nowhere near even having any suspects.'

'That seems to be the gist of what we discovered, boss.'

Claire Trent threw her pen down on the desk. 'I could have told you that from reading the executive summary.'

'But we had to do the work, boss. DCI Meredith may have missed something.'

'But he didn't.'

'I don't think so.'

'So what are you planning to do next?'

'We've identified some possible avenues of inquiry and are pursuing them.'

'Less of the copperspeak, Ridpath, you're not on *Crimewatch* now. I'll ask you again, what are you planning next?'

Ridpath scratched his head. Letting the boss know where he was going before he had any evidence for his line of inquiry was a sure way to get shut down before he even started.

'We've decided to approach the inquiry from a different angle to DCI Meredith.'

'Which is?'

It was time to dig his heels in. 'I'd rather not say at the moment, boss. It might be nothing, we're just following a hunch.'

'A hunch? I have to report to the chief constable tomorrow with a plan for the Inspectorate visit. Why do you think I'm in here today with Steve? And I'm supposed to tell him not to worry, not to be concerned, because Ridpath is following a hunch?' Her voice rose, becoming more shrill by the end of the sentence.

Ridpath had the good sense to remain silent. His knight in shining armour, when he arrived, came from an unexpected source and with a strong Scottish burr.

'Boss, we gave Ridpath the job because we wanted him to follow his hunches, his intuitions. We already knew Meredith had got nowhere. Unless we allow him to go with his ideas, we may as well pull him off the case right now. We can use the manpower on the Urmston stabbing.'

Claire Trent stared into mid-air, her eyes fixed. Finally she said, 'You have the rest of the day to follow this "hunch", but I want more details about where you are going with this tomorrow morning at…' She flicked open her diary. 'Shit, I have yet another meeting tomorrow first thing. Operational readiness in case of strike disruptions.'

'You want me to do it without you?' asked Carruthers.

'No, we both need to be at this one. Let's meet at eleven a.m., Ridpath. Don't be late, understood? I have the chief at noon.'

'Understood, boss.'

He turned to go, eager to get out of the office.

'I haven't finished with you yet, Ridpath.'

He turned back to face the music. It wasn't Bowie.

'What did I tell you yesterday?' She continued before he had time to answer. 'I made it clear in no uncertain terms you were to stay away from Mrs Challinor's case. It was a job for Cheshire Police, not us. But now I find out you rang the investigating officer, DCI Tindall, asking for an update and berating him for a lack of progress.'

'Boss, I was ringing on behalf of the family. Mrs Challinor's daughter had been kept in the dark, I just wanted to know what I could tell her.'

Claire Trent opened a folder in front of her. 'That's not what I have been told. There is an unofficial complaint about your involvement in the case from their assistant chief constable.' She held up a piece of paper. 'So far it's been kept beneath the radar and handled between mates, but if it ever becomes an official complaint, well…'

She left the rest of the sentence unsaid.

'Boss, can I lay my cards on the table?'

Claire Trent sat back, interlocked her fingers, and said, 'Lay away, Ridpath.'

'Boss, I think they've bolloxed the investigation.'

'Is that the technical term, Ridpath?'

'They didn't start going over the crime scene till the following morning. When I visited the crime scene in the evening—'

'Which you should not have done.'

Ridpath continued, '—when I visited the crime scene and received a blow on the head for my troubles...' He stopped for a second, hoping for some words of sympathy. None came. 'I think the perp had returned. Maybe he dropped something, or was missing something...'

Claire Trent was about to speak, so Ridpath carried on.

'...anyway, talking with his FLO, it's apparent Tindall thinks it's an attempted rape. But she wasn't so sure. The attack had more of the hallmarks of the Yorkshire Ripper than a rape. When you hit somebody over the head with a hammer, you're trying to kill them, not incapacitate them prior to a rape.'

'Have you finished?'

Ridpath nodded slowly.

The voice when it came was surprisingly gentle, with just a hint of admonishment. 'I'll say this once and just once. This. Is. Not. Your. Case. Understand? It has been assigned to the investigative control of Cheshire Police. Their head of crime happens to be a friend of mine and she is all over this like poison ivy. She was also a friend of Mrs Challinor. We are all in the Women in Law society. And before you think it, Ridpath, we do know it's called the Muffia by the less enlightened male members of the law and justice circles...'

Ridpath was about to defend himself, but stopped when Claire Trent raised her finger.

'Do not get involved. If you do and we get a formal complaint, I can no longer defend you, is that clear?'

Ridpath mumbled a reply.

'Is that clear?' she repeated.

'Yes, boss.'

This time Ridpath didn't have his fingers crossed behind his back.

Chapter Forty-two

His ears still burning from the latest reprimand, Ridpath saw Emily in her usual place leaning against the wall smoking a cigarette.

He was beginning to think these meetings weren't as haphazard as he imagined. Was this Emily's way of finding out exactly what was going on in Ridpath's head?

She gestured for him to join her. He sauntered over, checking Carruthers hadn't also nipped out for a crafty fag.

'What did Claire Trent want?'

'To give me a bollocking.'

She smiled. 'You probably deserved it.'

'Thanks for the support.'

'What had you done wrong this time?'

'Annoyed some copper in Cheshire apparently.'

'Haven't you annoyed coppers in every force within one hundred miles? Last time I heard, Merseyside were going to arrest you on sight if you ever went near their manor.'

'Nah, I patched it up with Merseyside. It was West Yorks who wanted to arrest me.'

'Doesn't surprise me. Coppers from Yorkshire were always a little Neanderthal.'

'I wouldn't say it too loudly,' he said, looking over his shoulder.

'Doesn't it tell you something when every force can't stand you?'

'It tells me I'm doing my job.'

The door to the left swooshed open and Carruthers stepped out into the open air, immediately flicking open a pack of Marlboros and shuffling one into his mouth.

He spotted Ridpath and Emily and walked over to join them.

'I didn't know you were one of the outcasts, Ridpath.' He checked around him. Because it was Sunday, not many coppers were smoking around the ashtray but it was still full of stubs. 'Not so many walking dead today.'

'Too hot, sir.'

'It's Steve or guvnor, DS Parkinson. I see you out here quite often.'

'Its Emily, sir, and I'm afraid I've a habit. Also it's a break from staring at a computer screen.'

He lit his cigarette. 'Tried to stop three times. Patches, hypnosis, willpower, even bloody acupuncture. Nothing works. I started behind the school cludgie in Govan when I was fourteen.'

Emily looked around her. 'You've come a long way, sir.'

'Aye, I have. The smells are slightly better though.' He focused on Ridpath. 'I wouldn't take the bollocking to heart. The boss has a lot on her plate at the moment, what with the inspection.'

'I won't, guvnor.'

'But don't take it with a pinch of salt either. Ringing the SIO and telling him how to run his case was stupid, to say the least. In any police force, there are ways of doing things without getting caught or getting up people's noses.'

Was Carruthers telling him how to get around Claire Trent's restrictions?

'I always found the FLO on any case a great source of inform-ation.'

He crushed the dimp of the cigarette beneath an expensive Oxford brogue. 'Anyway, I'll leave you to it. I'm away to my desk. Staffing for the next three years needed by yesterday. Keep your nose clean, Ridpath.'

He sauntered back through the automatic doors into the dark, stuffy lobby of Police HQ.

'What was all that about?' asked Emily.

'I think our new boss is trying to get us on side.'

'It's better than having somebody like Turnbull constantly in your face.'

'I don't know, Emily, the jury's still out.'

'God, you're a trusting man, Ridpath.'

Ridpath inhaled as Emily lit another cigarette and expelled a long stream of blue smoke.

'Anyway, can you follow up on your friend, Jayne Whatshername, the boss wants a briefing at eleven a.m. tomorrow.'

'Already done. She can meet you tomorrow morning any time.'

'It better be early. Let's say nine. Let her choose where as long as it isn't Ibiza.'

'OK, I'll message you later. Meanwhile, I'll go through the responses to the television appeal. Meredith may have missed something.'

'Ta, Emily, you're a star.'

'Don't try turning on the charm, Ridpath, it doesn't work with me, remember?'

'You're a hard-hearted copper then, DS Parkinson. Eve's still away in the Lakes so I'm off to spend the rest of the day at the Coroner's Court and then I'll go to see Mrs Challinor.'

'Send her my best wishes.'

'I will, if she's awake.'

He turned to go, before stopping as he heard her voice.

'Ridpath.'

He looked back at her, leaning against the wall, a half-smoked cigarette in her hand.

'Take it easy. You're going to burn yourself out at this rate.'

'Look who's talking.'

'I mean it, Ridpath. You can't solve all the world's problems.'

He smiled. 'No, I can't. Just a few. The ones we know about.'

Chapter Forty-three

He drove back to the Coroner's Court without getting anything to eat for lunch. Once again, he just didn't feel hungry. This morning, he noticed his trousers were even looser around his waist than before.

He knew it wasn't such a good sign. Eve, his thirty-three-year-old teenager, constantly nagged him to eat healthy food. He remembered her words as he drove.

'A Greggs sausage roll is not good for you, Dad.'

'It tastes great though, and at just over a quid, who's complaining?'

'Your stomach and cholesterol count is. You have to eat healthily. Make a start with breakfast.'

'What's wrong with black coffee to get me going in the morning? Your mother swore by it.'

As soon as he mentioned Polly he knew he had gone too far.

Eve paused before speaking again. 'Listen, Dad, you need to look after yourself better. I don't want to be an orphan.'

There it was. The guilt trip, in all its beautiful simplicity. A kick to the gut with size five Doc Martens.

He parked in Stockford and walked to the local cafe to buy a salad. It always felt like he was eating grass, munching away like a cow, but he knew the green stuff was good for him.

He was greeted immediately by Sophia with, 'So Eve's been nagging you again.'

He looked longingly at his assistant's crispy fried chicken. 'Says I have to eat better.'

'She's right.'

'Looks who's talking.' He pointed to the fried chicken leg on its short journey to Sophia's mouth; it halted just before entering.

'Oh, I forgot to tell you. There's news about the replacement for Mrs Challinor from the chief coroner's office. He's arriving tomorrow.'

'Who is it?'

'I dunno. Some retired geezer according to Jenny. Helen Moore isn't chuffed at all. She thought she had at least two weeks to show how well things could run in Mrs Challinor's absence.'

The mention of the coroner's name reminded him he hadn't heard anything about her condition. 'Any news from the hospital?'

'Nothing so far. Jenny went this morning and Mrs Challinor was still unconscious. They're moving her to another ward tomorrow though.'

'Oh? Why?'

Sophia shrugged her shoulders.

'When you've finished your bits of deep fried battery hen, we'll go through the work. Let's at least be up to date for when Fred or whatever he's called gets here tomorrow.'

'His name is Clarence Montague...' Jenny was at the door, '...and he used to be senior coroner for Berkshire for thirty years before he retired. Apparently he was educated at Winchester and Oxford, before taking his articles at Graey's Inn.'

'I've never met a Clarence before,' said Sophia.

'Well, you will tomorrow. What time are you free for a meeting, Ridpath?'

'I'm out in the morning, how about after lunch. Two p.m.?'

'I'll set it up. Apparently, Mr Montague is a stickler for time-keeping according to the clerk at the chief coroner.'

'I'll be there.'

Sophia wiped her mouth, removing a smear of chicken fat coating her top lip. 'Anything we should do for the meeting?'

'I was about to tell you, Sophia. He's requested a full update on every extant case.'

'"Extant case"?'

'Those were his words. It means our work-in-progress, in case you didn't know.'

Sophia rolled her eyes.

'And it has to be in this form. He emailed an example to me.' She handed across a copy of an Excel spreadsheet. 'Apparently, he doesn't look at them unless they are like this.'

Sophia rolled her eyes again. 'We'll get on it this afternoon. How was Mrs Challinor this morning?'

For the first time Jenny's face softened. 'Exactly the same. Just lying there, her head bandaged. I'm so worried about her.'

Ridpath checked the new format. He couldn't see any difference from the old one. 'I'll go to the hospital later, see if there is any change.'

'Let me know if there is, Ridpath.'

'I will, but in the meantime, let's get on with our work for Mr Clarence Montague. We'll be on time, even if he isn't.'

Chapter Forty-four

For the rest of the afternoon, Ridpath went through the remaining cases with the possibility of an inquest.

The family of the man who had fallen downstairs in the care home in Didsbury, Mr Watkins, had been notified and the casework completed. Ridpath had checked the pathologist's report, and nothing seemed to indicate any possibility of foul play. It had just been one of those tragic accidents that happen, particularly to the old and fragile. Before the inquest, Ridpath would have to go to the care home and check out the location of the fall. Was there anything which could have been done to prevent it?

He made a note for himself. All that remained was for Jenny to find time on the calendar and a coroner to oversee the case. Helen Moore probably.

Another case of a death in a fire in Fallowfield was more troubling. A man who lived alone, a Mr Sambini, had died in a fire starting in the living room. The fire had been noticed by a neighbour and the timely arrival of the pumps had prevented it spreading. Only after it was put out was Mr Sambini's body discovered sitting in an armchair in front of the television.

As ever, Sophia had everything else under the control. The paperwork was completed and each family had been individually informed of the status of their loved one's case.

There were only a couple of phone calls Ridpath had to make. For each one, Sophia's notes had been precise and accurate.

The call to the fire consultant went smoothly. He promised the report would be on Ridpath's desk by first thing tomorrow morning. He also rang a colleague who had been the SIO on the death in the care home. The police investigation would be sent over in an hour. They had found nothing suspicious about the death so there would probably be no need for an inquest, but that was for the coroner to decide.

By four p.m., they were done.

'Where are you off to tonight? Another date?'

'I do have a date as a matter of fact.'

'With the Irishman?'

'With an Irishman. I don't know if he is *the* Irishman yet.'

Ridpath began to whistle the tune to the 'Wedding March'.

'Don't you start. I'm still working out how to tell my mum.'

'She'll accept your choice, surely.'

'You don't know my mum.'

Ridpath glanced at the clock. 'Is that the time? I want to go to see the coroner before I see Eve.'

'Running to catch up again?'

'Tell me about it.'

He packed everything in his briefcase, including the notes for the fire in Fallowfield and the Romeo and Juliet case. 'Don't work too late.'

'No worries, I won't. I just need to put all this into chummy's template and I'm done.'

On his way out, Ridpath glanced back at his assistant, hunched over her laptop, staring at the screen intently. He didn't know what he would do without her. His life, with all its complexity and juggling of balls, would have been impossible.

'Thanks, Sophia.'

'You're welcome,' she said without raising her head.

'I mean, thanks for everything, I don't think I could function without you.'

She looked up. 'Are you going all soppy on me, Ridpath? It's not what I need in the middle of formatting this bugger.'

'I know I don't say it enough, but thank you. Is there anything I can get you?'

'No,' she said, glancing back at her computer, 'you don't say it enough. But now's not the time. Unless you want Mr Clarence

Montague of Winchester, Oxford and Gray's Inn to have a blank sheet of paper in front of him tomorrow.'

'Thanks once again.' He smiled and closed the door.

She was right, he didn't say it enough.

Chapter Forty-five

The hospital was as busy as ever when he arrived; nurses hurrying purposefully along wide corridors, porters pushing gurneys, some empty and some with patients lying wearily on them, harassed doctors rushing hither and thither. And always the constant refrain of messages on a tannoy, calling numbers, consultants and names.

It was a microcosm of a city; a vast operation where everything, hopefully, ran smoothly.

He completed all the Covid formalities and walked to Mrs Challinor's ward. The nurse he had met on the first morning, Helen Ryan, was sat at her station.

'Is she still unconscious?'

The nurse nodded. 'No change, I'm afraid.'

'Is her daughter there?'

'And one of your colleagues.'

He nodded once and strode to the ward. The bed next to the coroner was now empty; what had happened to its occupant?

The coroner was lying in exactly the same position as when he left her yesterday. Both her daughter and the FLO stood up when he arrived.

There was no need for him to ask but he did anyway. He couldn't think of anything else to say. 'No change?'

Sarah Challinor shook her head. 'I'm beginning to get worried, Ridpath. I talked to Mr Pereira at lunchtime and I could tell he wasn't happy. He said the tests had shown the fractured skull and the subsequent trauma might be more severe than they thought. She may have internal bleeding in her brain.'

'All we can do is wait. The doctors know what they are doing.' He turned to the FLO. 'Any news of the investigation?'

She stared back at him. 'I'm not at liberty to say.'

Had she received a bollocking too?

'You must know something?' he persisted.

'They are investigating the attack, that's all I know.'

'Haven't they told you anything?'

She shook her head. 'Not since I called you last night. I've heard nothing.'

Ridpath sighed, glancing at Sarah Challinor. They could treat him badly, but this was no way to treat the relative of a victim.

He was just about to have a go at the FLO when Mrs Challinor mumbled something. They all turned to look at her. Her arm had moved from its position on her chest to near her head, as if she was trying to remove her bandage.

The machine beside her bed began to beep more quickly. She mumbled something again.

'You'd better get the nurse,' Ridpath ordered the FLO.

As she ran off, Mrs Challinor spoke again clearer this time.

'What is it?' Ridpath bent nearer to her mouth to listen to the words.

'Don't… deaths…'

The machine beeped faster and Mrs Challinor's body went rigid, before thrashing about against the confines of the bedclothes.

'Have to stop them… stop…' she shouted, struggling against the tightness of the sheets.

Her IV drips were ripped from her arms and she was flailing about, banging her head against the pillow.

The nurse arrived, pressing a button beside the bed. 'Mr Pereira to Ward A8, immediately please.'

She bent over Mrs Challinor, forcing her shoulders back onto the bed, trying to keep her body still. The doctor hurried to the bed with another nurse, shoving the FLO aside.

'Please move away from the bed and leave the ward,' he ordered. 'NOW.'

They stepped away and he closed the curtains, shutting off the coroner from view. From the outside, they could hear commands from the doctor and the sound of the machine almost screeching in pain.

Another nurse and a doctor arrived and began to usher them away.

'What's happening with my mum? What's going on?'

'You're not helping . You have to leave us to do our work.' Then his voice changed, becoming softer. 'Please let us do our work.'

Ridpath put his arm around Sarah and led her away.

As he did, the last words the coroner said flashed into his mind. 'Stop.'

What did it mean? Stop who? Stop what?

Chapter Forty-six

Ridpath stayed with Sarah Challinor until the doctor came out to talk to them an hour later.

'We've moved your mother into the ICU. She's had a relapse.'

'Will she be all right?'

Mr Pereira swallowed and then answered. 'There has been an intra-cranial haematoma, bleeding within the brain. After she was attacked, our test showed both contrecoup and counter contre-coup injuries along with a fractured skull.'

'I'm sorry, I don't understand.'

'When she was hit, the brain suffered internal contusions at the point of impact and on the opposite side of the brain, too. We had hoped these injuries were not life threatening, but...'

'But what?'

'The bleeding on her brain has become so severe we need to operate to relieve the internal pressure.'

'When?'

'Now. She's being prepped for surgery as we speak. We will need you to sign these release forms before we proceed.'

He produced a lengthy form attached to a clipboard.

'You want me to sign this now?'

'Yes.'

'Can't I see my mum?'

'I'm afraid that won't be possible. She's being prepared for surgery.'

He handed her a ballpoint pen. She took it and began to sign before stopping and staring at the doctor.

'Be honest with me — what is the likelihood of this surgery being successful? Fifty-fifty, or better?'

'I don't do percentages, not when a human life is at stake. On the plus side, your mother is healthy, fit and strong. On the negative side, she has suffered a dangerous brain trauma. Each brain injury is different, as is each person's reaction to it, We will know more after the operation.'

Sarah took a deep breath and signed the form.

'Thank you,' said Mr Pereira, 'I know it wasn't an easy decision. Now, I need to prepare myself and my team. I'll come out after the operation and let you know how it went.'

Ridpath eyes followed him as he walked down the ward. Would the coroner survive? She seemed so pale, so weak, her voice a mere imitation of the woman she had been just three days ago.

Sarah Challinor sat beside him, staring into mid-air. 'I can't lose Mum, not now, I haven't...' Her voice trailed off.

Ridpath put his arm round her shoulders while the FLO looked on.

The coroner had to survive. He couldn't imagine a world without her.

Once again, his mind flashed to Polly. Lying in her casket before burial. He hadn't imagined living without her either, but he had.

Life carried on. Death wasn't the end.

It just wasn't the same any more. Nothing was the same.

Chapter Forty-seven

Mrs Challinor was still in surgery when Ridpath had to go and meet Eve. Luckily the coroner's sister, Susan, arrived just as he was about to leave.

'How is she?' The woman was the spitting image of the coroner, even down to the wildly spinning grey corkscrew curls of her hair.

Sarah Challinor stood up, throwing her arms round the new arrival's neck. 'Oh, Aunt Sue, I don't know, Mum, she…'

'She's a strong woman, Sarah, she'll pull through. Your mum won't give up without a fight.'

Ridpath had left them both to console each other. Even the FLO had pulled away, sitting to one side.

Before he left, he took her aside. 'If the coroner dies, this becomes a murder case. I suggest you make DCI Tindall get his finger out of his arse and start working.'

She had simply nodded once without replying.

Ridpath had thrown himself into his car, still angry at the situation, slamming his hand on the hard edge of the steering wheel. He knew it was useless to get angry but frustration had begun to get to him.

Usually he knew what to do, but today, he was powerless. He couldn't even investigate the case, having been warned off it repeatedly. He had to calm down before he saw Eve. There was no point infecting her with his frustration.

He took three deep breaths before starting the engine, going once again to his safe place in the Peak District. Luckily, by the time he reached the Wells' he was back to some sort of equilibrium… just.

Eve was pleased to see him, running up and throwing her arms around his neck.

'Rescue me,' she whispered, 'I can't face any more kale.'

She then turned and thanked Mrs Wells for a lovely trip, giving Maisie a big hug while Ridpath carried the backpack and sleeping bag out to the car.

'Thank you so much, Angela and Rick. It was so kind of you to include Eve in your trip.'

'Not a worry, Tom,' said Angela Wells, 'she's such a lovely, polite girl, you've done an amazing job of raising her.'

'Thank you, but it's nothing to do with me.'

Eve thanked the Wells one more time and sat in the car. They pulled away, waving goodbye.

'Sorry, Dad, Angela and Rick are lovely people but I can't eat, or even look at, kale any more.'

'You still hungry?'

'Starving.'

'What can I cook for you? Lasagne?'

'Cook? Is that what we're calling taking frozen lasagne out of the freezer and zapping it to within an inch of its life in a microwave?'

Ridpath nodded. 'Yep.'

'Sounds great. Can we zap some frozen tomato sauce too? And add a lot more cheese so it goes brown and crunchy at the edges.'

'Of course, wouldn't be the same without the crunchy bits.'

'I love your cooking, Dad.'

And for a second, Ridpath forgot about the two desiccated bodies and Mrs Challinor's pale, pained face, just basking for a few seconds in the uncomplicated love of his daughter.

There were still things to look forward to in life.

Chapter Forty-eight

As soon as they returned home, Ridpath pulled the lasagne out of the freezer and stuck it in the microwave as Eve changed her clothes.

The frozen tomato sauce was removed from it's freezer bag and placed into a bowl in the microwave next to the warming lasagne. Ridpath turned on the grill in the normal oven ramping it up to high.

'When's it going to be ready, Dad, I'm starving,' she said from the doorway, now wearing her pyjamas.

'Coming in exactly... three minutes, thirty-four seconds.'

She looked at her watch. 'I'm timing you, Dad.'

He stopped the microwave with one minute to go. 'Now for the finishing touches to the recipe.' He took out the now warmed lasagne, grated over some more cheddar and a sprinkling of parmesan, and placed the dish under the grill.

Two minutes later the kitchen oozed with the aroma of grilled cheese. 'Extra crunchy bits for Eve and a big helping for Dad. I'm starving, too.'

While they ate the lasagne, drizzled with spoonfuls of the hot tomato sauce, Eve chatted about school; the competing factions and cliques, the petty jealousies, who was in and who was out, her thoughts about the teachers and their idiosyncrasies.

He just sat there and listened to her voice, not caring what she said, just enjoying the moment.

A daughter and Dad moment.

Finally she pushed her plate away. 'I'm stuffed.'

'There's still more crunchy bits.'

'I can't, Dad, I'm as fat as a walrus and we have PE tomorrow.'
She stood up and kissed him on the head. 'You want me to wash the dishes?'

'I can't risk losing any more plates, we only have four left.'

'That wasn't my fault. They were wet.'

'They usually are when they are being washed. No, you go to bed, you must have some reading to do for school.'

'Yeah, a lot.'

'I'll come and turn the light off later.'

Another kiss on the top of the head. 'Night, Dad.'

'Night, Eve.'

And she was gone, leaving Ridpath alone in the kitchen.

He placed the plates and cutlery into the sink and filled it with hot water. He had an important call to make.

'Sarah, how is Mrs Challinor?'

'She's out of surgery now and Mr Pereira said it went as well as can be expected. They've moved her to ICU. We're here now.'

'You and the FLO?'

'No, myself and my aunt. The FLO left as soon as we heard the news the operation had been successful.'

'You should go home.'

'I can't, Ridpath, not tonight, we need to be here, just in case...' Her voice drifted away. 'Are you coming here tomorrow morning?'

'I have a meeting, but I'll be there in the afternoon. Anything you need?'

'Nothing, just for Mum to get better.'

'I'm sure she will, Sarah, she's a strong woman.'

They carried on talking for a while before ending the call. It was just a question of waiting now. Something Ridpath wasn't good at. He shut his eyes, suddenly feeling exhausted, as if all the energy in his body had been drained, like air from a balloon.

He thought about pouring himself a small glass of Glenmorangie but decided against it. There was too much to do, too much to think about, whisky wouldn't help.

He checked his notes one more time.

The questions they had written on the whiteboards shouted out at him.

Who are the victims?

Why were they there?

Why 2008?

They hadn't even begun to answer any of them.

'What have we missed?' he said out loud. 'What have we done wrong?'

Then he scanned down to the last two questions.

Who killed them?

Why?

In his head, he went over the case once more. A couple found dead in a bricked-up room. No leads. No ID. No suspects. Nothing.

Meredith had spent six months investigating and got nowhere. They had spent three days and discovered even less.

He sighed out loud.

Still no suspects. Still no answers.

He closed his eyes again and felt a headache coming on. Not what he needed right now.

Monday, June 21

Chapter Forty-nine

Ridpath knew who Jayne Sinclair was the second he stepped into the cafe on Barlow Moor Road in Didsbury. Like most police, he had a built in copdar, recognising another member or even ex-member of the force across a crowded room even if he had never met them before. It was the way they held themselves: a stiffness, a formality in both dress and posture, even in the most casual of settings.

The fact she was sitting in the classic cop position – facing the door, with a view of the cafe – was a dead giveaway.

'Jayne Sinclair, I presume?'

She held out her hand. 'Tom Ridpath, I've heard a lot about you.'

'Most of it good, I hope.'

'Most of it.'

He was expecting her to continue speaking but she didn't. He saw she had a half drunk latte in front of her. 'Can I get you anything else?'

She shook her head, 'I've drunk enough coffee to float the *Titanic* this morning.'

He looked at her quizzically.

'A client in Australia. I've been awake since five a.m.'

He wasn't the only person who worked hard then.

'But the coffee's good, and I recommend the lemon drizzle cake if you can eat in the morning.'

He had tried to eat this morning – a bowl of cornflakes with a yoghurt on the side. Having slept fitfully, he'd also risen early, intending to go over his notes before meeting Jayne. He'd taken a couple of mouthfuls of the cereal before stopping, leaving the yoghurt to continue to ferment in the morning warmth. It was probably the nearest he had been to culture in a long time. Years of just having black coffee for breakfast had spoilt his stomach for anything else.

For some reason, Eve had been particularly uncommunicative.

'What do you want for breakfast?'

'Nothing.'

He gave her some cornflakes and milk, which she devoured.

'Do you have choir after school?'

'No.'

'I thought it was today.'

'Cancelled.'

It was like talking to one of the living dead in a school uniform, but without the chattiness.

'I'll try and pick you up from school but if I'm not there you know what to do.'

Silence.

He lost it a little. 'Did you hear me? A response now and again might be useful.'

'Yeah, I heard you.'

Four words. Better than nothing.

'I'll try to pick you up.'

'Yeah.'

She'd been fine last night after her return from the Lakes. Now she was giving him the cold shoulder. He'd have to chat with her later, find out what was going on in the minestrone of hormones that was the teenage mind.

He walked over to the counter, past the other diners – mostly mums who'd just finished the school run – ordered a black coffee, and turned back to look at Jayne Sinclair.

She was both as he'd expected and yet not. Her short blonde hair was cut fashionably, her clothes casual and comfortable. Yet there was a quiet intensity about her Ridpath appreciated, and the row of silver rings piercing her left ear suggested more. A free, rather unconventional spirit.

He paid for his Americano and sat down opposite her. 'Who was the client?'

'An old man, in his seventies. One of those poor kids who were packed off to Australia in the late 1950s when the UK was exporting its orphans to the colonies. The problem was he wasn't an orphan. His father was still alive, and he had a brother and sister who remained in England.'

'That's terrible.'

'For forty years, he was told he was alone, everybody in his family had died. Imagine the shock when he found out his brother and sister were still alive? I'm just finding other members of the family for him before he visits in September. Lost cousins he didn't even know existed.' She stopped speaking for a second, and looked at him directly. 'But you didn't come to meet me in the wilds of Didsbury to hear me rabbiting on. How can I help you?'

He liked this woman, she was direct and business-like.

'Did DS Parkinson fill you in?'

'Emily gave me a broad sketch. You're looking into the Romeo and Juliet case?'

He nodded. 'After six months of work, the investigating team have nothing. Somebody killed those two young people by bricking them up in a room, but we don't know who did it, why they did it or even who the victims were.'

'That's why they brought you in?'

'And the rest of the team. We have a week to make a breakthrough.'

'How can I help?'

'The previous team spent a long time looking for the killer. We've decided to concentrate our time looking for the victims.'

'If you find out who they are, you could possibly find out why they died.'

She was a quick read.

'Exactly. The problem is we have too little to go on. Two dead bodies, a tram ticket for August 2008, the clothes they were wearing and that's it. No wallet, no phone, no ID.'

'Any identifying marks?'

'Nothing. Exceptionally unexceptional.'

'But if you have a body, you do have their DNA.'

Emily *had* briefed her.

'...and you're wondering if genetic genealogy can help you discover who the victims are.'

Ridpath sipped his Americano. It was good; bitter without being acerbic. 'Can it?'

'Possibly. I presume NDNAD has given you nothing?'

'The database didn't give us any hits.'

'Not surprising, it only searches for direct matches, genetic genealogy is far more than comprehensive.'

'Go on...'

'Put simply, genetic genealogy is the use of DNA tests, in combination with traditional genealogical methods, to infer genetic relationships between individuals.'

'How can it help me?'

'As of 2019, about thirty million people had been tested by the main genealogy organisations. It's enabled groups of people to trace their ancestry even though they are not able to use conventional techniques. Police officers in the States have used genetic genealogy to track down perpetrators of violent crimes such as murder or sexual assault. The arrests of the Golden State Killer, the Chameleon, and the Cobb County Rapist are examples of its use. So far, over eighty cold cases in the United States have been solved by using genetic genealogy.'

'Yeah, Chrissy told me about them.'

'There have been cases in the UK too. The Shoe Rapist, the Bristol Murderer and the White Van Man were all caught using familial DNA searches.'

'Familial DNA?'

'A search of the NDNAD to look for a list of potential candidates who may be close biological relatives to the perpetrator whose DNA was found at the crime scene. I don't know the latest figures but at least two hundred searches of familial DNA have been authorised leading to over sixty arrests so far for crimes such as murder or rape.'

'The problem for us is that the killer left no DNA at the crime scene.'

'But Emily told me you were looking to identify the victims, not the killer. You have their DNA, don't you?'

Ridpath smiled. 'How would genetic genealogy work in the Romeo and Juliet case?'

'We would try to find out the relatives of your victims by comparing their DNA with other people on the various DNA databases using centimorgans.'

'What's a centimorgan when it's at home?'

'It's a unit of genetic measurement, describing how much DNA and the length of specific segments of DNA you share with other people. Put simply, the more centimorgans you share with someone, the more closely you are related.'

'How do we know how many centimorgans we share with other people?'

'Your DNA test will give you a number. For example, your parents will have roughly 3,500 cMs each which they share with you, a grandparent will only have about 1,750, while a second cousin would have only 250.'

'So the number changes with each different relationship?'

'Correct. We can use this information to start building a family tree. And once we have their family chart...'

'...we can work out who our Romeo and Juliet are.' Ridpath finished her sentence.

Jayne took a long swallow of her coffee, carefully placing the cup down on the table. 'But there are a couple of caveats you must know...'

'Go on,' said Ridpath warily.

'It all depends if your victim's relatives have completed DNA testing and, more importantly, uploaded the results to a site like GEDmatch.'

'If they haven't?'

'We're stuffed. Plus there's one other issue. Since 2019, GEDmatch has required people to opt in to have their results used by the police.'

'But people have opted in, haven't they?'

'Quite a lot, luckily. The good news is if the results are there, I should be able to construct a family tree for each of your victims.'

'So what are we waiting for? Let's get started.'

'There is another major problem.'

'What?'

'GDPR.'

'I hate these bloody acronyms. What's privacy law got to do with it?'

'Under the General Data Protection Regulations, people's data is protected.'

'Even if it's a bunch of DNA numbers?'

'Even if it's DNA.'

'How do we get around this? I have to investigate the death of two young people and we don't even know who they are. We need to think of the parents. How are they feeling, not knowing where their son or daughter is?'

'I understand. There is a possible way. The BFEG—'

Ridpath rolled his eyes skyward. 'Another bloody acronym?'

'The Biometrics and Forensics Ethics Group has only recommended genetic searches be approved, it's still not mandatory...'

'So we could go ahead?'

'Somebody senior at GMP would have to give the go-ahead. Familial searches are generally allowed when murder or extreme violence has been used to commit a crime. This case is slightly different in that we are looking for the identity of the victims, not the killer, so we may have more leeway.'

'I'll do it. Go ahead.'

'Somebody senior, Ridpath. Not a probationary inspector attached to the coroner's office.'

'Ouch. Emily was right when she said you don't take prisoners.'

'No point beating about the bush. This is a murder case.'

'If I can get the permissions – *when* I can get the permissions, how long will it take you to complete the work?'

'If I'm lucky, twenty-four hours. If the families are small and the search on GEDmatch gives me a fairly close relative, a cousin or an uncle.'

'And if you're not lucky?'

She held her arms open. 'How long is a piece of string?'

'Let's hope you're lucky then.'

'Let's hope you get the permissions. There's one other problem, Ridpath.'

'I thought you said this was going to be easy.'

'We have to convert the crime scene DNA results into a usable kit on GEDmatch.'

'OK, let's do it.'

'I know a lab which can make the conversion but we needed to start it yesterday if you want me to begin the genetic genealogy investigation as soon as possible.'

'I'll get somebody to courier over the DNA results from the crime scene.'

'Great. I'll contact the lab and warn them. The owner is a friend so we'll be able to rush it through.'

'Good, let's get started.'

'You need the permissions before I can begin.'

Ridpath was silent. He would have to talk to Claire Trent... again. It was a conversation he wasn't looking forward to.

'One final thing, Jayne, how much will your work cost?' he asked tentatively.

'I'm not too busy at the moment, and I do owe GMP a lot, so, as long as it doesn't take me weeks, there will be no charge at my end.'

'Free?' Said Ridpath raising his eyebrows.

'That's right. Like I said, I feel I owe GMP for my training, time to pay them back. But this is a one-time offer, Ridpath.'

'Got it. Claire Trent will be pleased and the bean counters delirious.'

They chatted about mutual colleagues in the police, life and everything for a few minutes, before Jayne looked at her watch and said she had to leave.

'I'll wait to hear from you, Ridpath.'

'Thank you, Jayne, I'll call you in a couple of hours to confirm we're going ahead.'

She left quickly, rushing off to meet another client.

As he was in the area, Ridpath decided to visit the nursing home where Mr Watkins had fallen down the stairs. He trusted the SIO who had reviewed the accident, she was a good and thorough copper, but there was nothing like seeing a scene for yourself.

Chapter Fifty

After checking the nursing home, and finding nothing out of order, he rushed back to Police HQ, pulling Claire Trent and Steve Carruthers out of their operational readiness meeting which was running late.

'Make it quick, Ridpath.'

She obviously wasn't a happy bunny.

'As I explained yesterday, boss, DCI Meredith has done a lot of great legwork on the building and the investigation—'

'Cut the crap, Ridpath, you've no need to butter up Meredith, he isn't here. And besides, he had six months on this and got nowhere.'

He ploughed on. 'But we've decided to approach the case from a different angle.'

His boss glanced at her watch.

'We believe the key to understanding this case is the two victims. Who are they? Why were they in the room? Why were they killed? But we won't answer the last two questions without answering the first. Who are they?'

'Go on…' said Carruthers.

'DCI Meredith has used all the tools at his disposal; missing person reports, analysis of clothes, CCTV, even checked their DNA against the national database…'

'And got nowhere. What are you suggesting we do?'

Now was the time to take the plunge. 'I want to use genetic genealogy.'

She glanced across at Carruthers. 'What the hell is that?'

Ridpath explained in great detail the process for tracing a missing person through discovering their ancestors combined with traditional genealogical research.

'You mean like the discovery of the Golden State Killer?'

Ridpath nodded.

'So you want me to approve this… search?'

Ridpath let out a breath, 'Exactly, boss.'

'No, absolutely not. I can't sanction it.'

'Why not?'

Claire Trent threw her pen down on the desk in front of her. 'For starters, it might have ethical, legal and safeguarding considerations, breaking the European Convention on Human Rights and the Human Rights Act of 1998, as well as infringing the Data Protection Act of 2018. Not to mention the fact all familial searches have to be approved by a committee.'

Trust Claire Trent to know the procedures to protect privacy.

'It's only a recommendation for genetic searches to be approved, boss, not mandatory. And we won't be searching on the police database, but in GEDmatch. Luckily, the people who have uploaded their DNA to GEDmatch have already opted in if the data is used by the police.'

'But the legality of using informed consent as the sole appropriate legal basis to obtain highly sensitive data is a doubtful area,' interrupted Carruthers.

They both stared at him.

'I'm doing a part-time degree in law at the Open University. The ethics of privacy is one of the core modules.' He paused, placing his forefinger across his lips. 'The key question here is whether such research meets the tests of necessity and proportionality. I think there is a good case for necessity. We have spent the last six months trying to find out who these people are and have failed miserably. As for proportionality, the measure must be reasonable, considering the competing interests of different groups. Here, I would argue, it is reasonable to uncover the identity of a murderer, particularly when all other attempts have failed.'

'There may be another couple of problems, boss,' added Ridpath.

Claire Trent raised her eyebrows.

'First, to manage expectations, it is quite possible when we upload the DNA to GEDmatch, we won't get any hits. The relatives of our victims may never have looked into their family history.'

'Understood, it's the same as searching for fingerprints on IDENT1, you never know what you will find.'

'And the second is a request from our genealogist, Jayne Sinclair.'

'The name rings a bell. Wasn't she a copper?'

'She left GMP in 2016, and has since set herself up as a professional genealogist.'

'There is life after the police.'

'Anyway, she needs written permission from us before she embarks on the research.' He shrugged his shoulders. 'The privacy issues mentioned by you are a bit of a sticking point for her.'

Claire Trent went silent, staring out of her window at the sun shining down on the streets of Manchester. Ridpath could hear the ticking of a clock on the wall, loud in the silence.

Finally. 'What do you think, Steve?'

The new DCI blew across the tips of his fingers again. 'As I see it, it is our only way forward. Everything else has failed. Unless we do this, there is no chance we are going to crack this case in the next four years, never mind four days. But...'

'But?'

'I would cover our arses. We should make sure we maintain the security of data and of the genealogical research. Treat it like we would any other piece of evidence; ensure it meets chain of custody and security requirements. So I would suggest Ms Sinclair conducts her research here at HQ and before we appoint her, we check her qualifications and make sure she signs a confidentiality agreement.'

'Cover our arses properly.'

'As ever, boss.'

'Can you draw up a non-disclosure agreement for Ms Sinclair to sign? And you will take full responsibility for this course of action?'

Again, silence descended on the room, before Carruthers nodded his head. 'I will take responsibility, we have no other options.'

'I'll have a quiet word in the ear of the assistant chief, get his take on it.' She turned back to Ridpath. 'In principle, Ridpath, you have our agreement to proceed. How much is this going to cost us?'

'It's free, boss. Ms Sinclair is offering her services for free.'

'That's a first. And how long will it take?'

'She thinks she can have preliminary findings for us in twenty-four hours.'

'What are you waiting for? Get on with it, both of you.'

They both stood. 'Thanks boss, you won't regret this.'

'I hope not, Ridpath, and I hope you don't either.' With those words, she snatched her budget files and marched out.

Inside the room, only Carruthers and Ridpath remained.

'I've stuck my neck out for you today. Make sure you deliver. But just so you know, I think it's the right thing to do, otherwise I wouldn't have agreed. We have nowhere else to go.'

For the first time in a long time, Ridpath was actually thankful for the support of one of his bosses. 'Thank you, Steve.'

'Let me get on with writing the agreement. You should get Ms Sinclair in to start her research as soon as you can.'

'Should we wait for the boss to talk to the assistant chief?'

'Sometimes your naivety surprises me, Ridpath, she's never going to talk to him. Her reluctance to agree was to ensure I took responsibility. If it's a success, then she'll claim it. And if it's a failure, it's my signature on the memo. In her position, I would have done exactly the same, it's the only way to proceed. Good luck with your work.'

Carruthers rose quickly and walked out of the office, leaving Ridpath all alone.

Ridpath let him leave, before clenching his fist and punching the air. 'Get in.'

Chapter Fifty-one

Ridpath walked into the small room they had designated as their operations area. On the door, Chrissy had changed the hand-written notice to say 'Operation Romeo and Juliet'. At least it now had a slightly more professional ring to it and sounded less like some amateur night at the local dramatic society.

'Right, we're on. Can you ring Jayne and get her to come in as soon as possible? She needs to sign a non-disclosure agreement and work here, not at home.'

'I'm sure she'll be OK,' said Emily dialling the number.

'How did you get on with your new HOLMES search, Chrissy?'

'It was interesting...'

In the background he could hear Emily speaking. She looked across and gave him the thumbs up. 'She'll be here at three p.m.'

'Great. Sorry Chrissy, carry on.'

'Like I was saying, it was interesting. I went all the way back to the year 2000, putting in the parameters you suggested. Deaths where the killer was not present when the murder was committed. After a throwing a conniption—'

'Is that the technical term?'

Chrissy ignored him. '—the computer isolated with three possibilities in the north of England. I only asked HOLMES to check in a sixty-mile radius around Manchester. There may have been more deaths elsewhere.'

'Can we expand the search to cover the UK?'

'Sure, the programme might spontaneously combust but it's worth a shot.' She wrote a note to herself. 'One more thing,

HOLMES has only flagged deaths delineated as murders. If the death was ascribed to suicide or any other reason, it wouldn't show up.'

'Can we check suicides?'

Chrissy began tapping on her laptop. 'The latest figures for 2019 show there were 5,691 suicides in England and Wales. If we were to look at all of them since 2000, we'd have to go through over 100,000 cases, Ridpath – we'd need an army, not the three of us.'

Ridpath held his hands up in mock surrender. 'OK, bad idea, I get it. What did HOLMES find?'

Chrissy's voice suddenly became as excited as that of a kid with a new toy. 'This is where it gets interesting. In 2015, a couple in Blackburn, the Singhs, were found dead in the kitchen along with their six-month-old child. At first, the cause of death was unknown, but then the toxicology examination showed high levels of diazepam in their blood with injection marks on their arms.'

'Suicide?'

'The post-mortem suggested they had been murdered. Testing the milk for their breakfast and in the baby's bottle showed it had been poisoned with cyanide.'

'But nobody was arrested or charged with murder?'

'And no suspects either.'

'Now why does that sound familiar.'

'The second was a single woman, Joan Blackledge in Derbyshire in 2017. Her body was found on a hillside. She'd been out walking alone in the countryside.'

'Why was that seen as a murder?'

'She was a diabetic and had died from ketoacidosis. When they examined her meds, they found her insulin had been replaced by water.'

'What a horrible way to die.'

'And again, HOLMES flagged it because whoever murdered her wasn't present at her death.'

'No suspects or arrests?'

Chrissy nodded.

Ridpath stared at the whiteboards. This case was becoming more and more complicated.

'Sorry, Chrissy, you said there were three cases?'

'The final result from HOLMES was more recent, 2018. A twenty-year-old man, Tony Snellgrove in Chester, found in a car in his garage, a pipe leading from the exhaust to the car.'

'Sounds like a suicide.'

'But then they found his hands had been tied to the steering wheel and toxicology showed he had been pumped full of morphine. A couple of needle marks on his arms but no works anywhere near the body. An inquest ruled it as unlawful killing.'

'No suspects again?'

'A witness reported seeing a figure in black near the garage but nobody was arrested or charged.'

'But there is a big gap in years between our deaths and these on HOLMES,' said Emily. 'Seven years for the Blackburn murder.'

'Right, so why?'

'And these are just links thrown up by HOLMES. We have no evidence any of these deaths are connected.'

'None, so far,' said Ridpath, 'but nobody has been looking for connections.'

'You're not thinking what I think you're thinking, Ridpath?'

'We could have had a serial killer operating for the last fifteen years in the north, and nobody knew.' Ridpath clenched his jaw and lent forward. 'Now let's find the evidence to prove it.'

'How are we going to do that?'

'We look for what ties these deaths together, the killer's signature. You have your marker, Emily, let's get started.'

Chapter Fifty-two

I had a quiet couple of days.

This was quite deliberate. It was useful to establish an equilibrium, to fall back into the usual routine, to become as boring as before.

Pottering around the house, meeting friends, doing the shopping. All those banal activities with which we fill our days.

My mind, though, was still ticking over, searching for an answer to the problem.

I had rushed the attack on Mrs Challinor, moving far too early. I should have acted as I usually did. Taken my time, planned the operation, made sure I was as far away as possible when the actual death occurred.

Instead, hubris had kicked me in the arse and it wasn't pleasant. I was just as fallible as all the others I had dealt with over the years.

But not any more.

The problem of Mrs Challinor still remained, though. It had been relatively easy to discover which hospital she had been taken to. A few calls to all the local A&Es pretending to be a concerned relative ringing from London always worked.

She was in the ICU in an induced coma.

Brilliant. I had time to make my plans. But I still had to move quickly. If she woke, she would be able to tell them who I was, and it would all be finished.

Everything I had worked for all those years, the seeding of the world, over and done with.

I couldn't allow the work to be tarnished, not after so many years.

She was in my domain now, and in a coma. All I had to do was make sure she never woke again.

It was time to start planning.

Chapter Fifty-three

By the time reception had rung to say a Jayne Sinclair had arrived, they had virtually finished.

On a new board on the left-hand side of the room, Emily had written the toplines of the three new cases.

2015 – BLACKBURN – COUPLE AND CHILD – THE SINGHS, 22, 23, 6 MONTHS OLD – CYANIDE POISONING.

2017 – DERBYSHIRE – JOAN BLACKLEDGE, 32 – INSULIN SWITCHED.

2018 – CHESTER – TONY SNELLGROVE, 28 – MORPHINE + CARBON MONOXIDE POISONING.

Next to it were two other whiteboards.

OBSERVATIONS

No links between any of those who died.

Different parts of the country.

No evidence our killer witnessed murders.

No forensic evidence.

No clues.

No suspects.

SIGNATURE

Use of drugs.

Killer not present.

No forensics.

No obvious motive for murders.

All MOs different.

'It looks weak to me, Ridpath,' said Emily. 'A signature is still not admissible in a court of law last time I looked. We need to find evidence, so far this is just a theory, a hunch. If you take this to Claire Trent, you're going to be chopped into so many pieces, even a taxidermist couldn't put you back together again.'

Ridpath frowned. 'I know, but I feel it in my water they are linked. This is all about the victims…'

Emily's phone buzzed. 'Jayne's here.'

While Emily went down to escort Jayne into the building, Ridpath stared at the boards. He knew the answer was here somewhere. Why couldn't he see it? This was someone who killed from afar, who didn't look into the eyes of the victims. But why?

His thoughts were interrupted by the return of Emily with Jayne Sinclair.

'Great to see you, and welcome aboard the good ship Romeo and Juliet.'

'Is that what you're calling this?'

'It seems to have stuck. Officially it's case number 2022/478569B.'

'Far catchier. Where can I set up?'

Ridpath pointed to table in the corner. 'There's a password for the internet if you need one.'

She looked around. 'Where's the rest of the team?'

'The rest?' Ridpath shrugged his shoulders, pointing to himself, Emily and Chrissy. 'You're looking it.'

'Three of you? The cuts have bitten hard. Back in the day, there would have been at least fifteen detectives attached to a case like this.'

'We're lean but we're mean,' said Emily.

'Mean as in you're doing this for free,' added Ridpath.

'As I said, I don't need the money and I'm not busy.' She noticed the boards on the wall; the pictures of the couple in the blocked-up room, the crime scene, plus the new boards with the details of the other crimes and their observations.

'You're linking this to other crimes?'

She *was* a quick read.

Ridpath shrugged his shoulders. 'To be honest, we don't know yet. HOLMES has flagged these possible links.'

She walked over to the boards.

'So you're looking for a signature rather than an MO. Smart.'

They all stared at her.

'I may have left the police, but the work never leaves you. I still keep myself up to date on the latest developments.'

'Like the Golden State Killer?'

'That, and others. Can I get started?'

'Take me through what you're going to do.'

She produced a notebook. 'Each of our victims' DNA has now been uploaded and a kit number produced. Only two DNA sites allow the police to use their DNA profiles to identify families: GEDmatch and FamilyTreeDNA. The two largest ones, Ancestry and 23andMe, won't allow us to search without a warrant.'

'Do you want me to get one?'

'You may have to eventually, but first let's try the other two and see if we get any hits. We'll start with GEDmatch.'

'Why not the other one, FamilyTreeDNA?'

'I need to get permission first. I sent the email and it should come back later with a bit of luck.'

She opened the GEDmatch site and logged in, selected a tab and began uploading Female A and Male B's DNA kits to the site. All the time, Ridpath was standing over her, watching her every move like a hawk.

'What happens now?'

'We wait.'

'What?'

'It takes a couple of hours for the site to process the data, and then we can analyse it using one of their tools, One-to-Many.'

'What?'

'It's a tool which compares our victims' DNA to all the others on the site.'

'Can't we do anything else?'

'Not until it uploads.' She tapped her fingers on the table and turned to him. 'Ridpath, if you stand over me asking questions continually, it's just going to slow down the process. Let me do my job, OK?'

He was just about to argue that he needed to know exactly what was going on in order to understand the process, when his phone rang.

'Ridpath.'

'It's Sophia. You'd better get over here.'

'Why?'

'Clarence Montague has arrived, and he wants a staff meeting now.'

Ridpath looked around the room, finally focusing on the portraits of the two victims on the board. 'Can't you tell him to wait until tomorrow? I'm in the middle of something.'

'He doesn't want to wait, Ridpath. The meeting is going to start with or without you in thirty minutes. He was insistent you be here.'

Ridpath closed his eyes. The last thing he needed right now was a London bureaucrat throwing his toys out of the pram. Didn't the man realise there was a murder to solve?

He sighed audibly.

'Are you coming?'

He looked at Jayne, who was writing in her notebook while Emily and Chrissy were deep in their laptops.

'I'll be there as soon as I can.'

Chapter Fifty-four

Once again the meeting had already started by the time Ridpath arrived.

Helen Moore was back in her usual place beside David Smail. Jenny was at the top of the table to the left of an old man dressed formally in a black jacket, starched white shirt and diagonally striped tie.

'Ah, the infamous Mr Ridpath has finally arrived.' A flashing smile appeared on the curiously unlined face, dominated by the brightest green eyes Ridpath had ever seen. 'Do take a seat.'

He pointed to Ridpath's usual place next to Sophia. The voice was patrician, beautifully modulated and phrased. A voice one didn't often hear on the mean streets of Manchester.

'Let us carry on, shall we? As you are late I will repeat what I have already told the rest of the office. My name is Clarence Montague and I have been appointed by the chief coroner, due to Mrs Challinor's unfortunate indisposition, to take charge of the East Manchester Coroner's Court. You will have all received a notice of my appointment from the chief coroner.'

'I didn't,' said Ridpath.

'Why is that, Miss Oldfield?'

For once Jenny wasn't dressed in one of her vintage orange or purple skirts. Even her make-up owed more to Giorgio Armani than to Sephora.

'Officially, Ridpath isn't on the staff list for East Manchester. He is actually employed by Greater Manchester Police and is on their payroll.'

'So he doesn't form any part of our precept from local government?'

It was one of the strange oddities of the English judicial system that coroners were funded by local councils rather than central government. Consequently, they had been affected more than most by the recent cutbacks to council funding.

'Ridpath isn't part of our settlement from the local authority.'

Montague frowned and his voice rose an octave. 'How strange? A coroner's officer not officially employed by the coroner's office.'

'It was an agreement reached by Mrs Challinor and Detective Superintendent Claire Trent. It's worked well so far,' Jenny added as an afterthought.

It was as if Ridpath was a minor servant at a gentleman's club being talked about by a pair of senior members.

'Hmmm, let me look into it. In the meantime, let us continue with our meeting.'

Jenny handed out the WIP sheets.

'I presume this has been formulated in the manner to which I am accustomed. This format has been introduced by the chief coroner to allow him to standardise the reports from the individual coroner's offices.'

Ridpath glanced at it. Other than a few indents being in different places and the action section being removed, he couldn't see any difference from their previous form.

'I introduced it in Berkshire in 2016 and I was very pleased when it was adopted for the rest of the country. I'm surprised it wasn't used before in East Manchester.'

'Mrs Challinor liked the way we used to do it. She could tell at a glance what action was needed.'

'Didn't the chief coroner's office complain?'

Jenny laughed. 'We don't send these work-in-progress sheets to their office.'

Montague's face clouded over for a second, before relaxing once again. 'We will be sending them in from now on. When I was seconded to the chief coroner in 2018, I found them useful as a means of isolating potential problems before they became actual issues. Anyway, we will be sending them in starting today. Please continue, Miss Oldfield.'

Ridpath zoned out as Jenny went through each of the cases, highlighting their status and which required further investigation. The ongoing inquests were explained fully with details of the coroner appointed to head each one. It was apparent how busy Mrs Challinor had been. The recent inquest on the death of Mr Davies was looked at last.

'It is a shame the jury had already returned a verdict before Mrs Challinor's indisposition. I have read her summation of the evidence and it does strike me as overly critical of both the health authority and the social services department.' He sniffed.

'Mrs Challinor was about to send a Regulation 28 notice to the local health trust,' said Ridpath.

Mr Montague sniffed again. 'I hardly think it is necessary.'

'But what about the family? Mr Davies' wife suffered immensely at the last inquest. She felt they had let her husband down. The support services failed in their duty of care to her husband.'

'Thank you for your input, Mr Ridpath, but this is a legal matter, not an investigative one. I have made a decision.' He looked around the table. 'There is one thing I have noticed. We are investigating far too many cases which compromise time, money and resources, and end with us submitting Regulation 28 notices critical of government and health departments.'

'Mrs Challinor felt it was our job to serve families, ensuring all possible failures in the system were highlighted and remedied.' Ridpath found himself speaking in the same way as the man opposite. 'She saw the coroner's role as to represent the dead in the court of the living.'

Clarence Montague cleared his throat this time. 'An estimable sentiment I am sure, but not terribly useful in a twenty-first century coronial service.'

Ridpath was about to speak again when Montague continued.

'Now if there is nothing else, I suggest we carry on with our duties. I know how much you all appreciated Mrs Challinor's work and passion, but this office has been on the watch list of the chief coroner for some time now. In my time here, we will return it to more efficient and effective working practices to ensure we deliver value for money for the customer and follow the rules and regulations laid down by the chief coroner's office to the letter. Thank you all for your attendance at such short notice.'

He capped his fountain pen, collected his files and went into Mrs Challinor's office, closing the door behind him.

'Well, that's us put in our place,' said Sophia.

'It's about time,' said Helen Moore. 'This place has been run as private fiefdom for far too long. I for one am going to enjoy the new coroner's no-nonsense approach.' She picked up her files and flounced out, followed puppy-like by David Smail.

The worms were turning and it wasn't pretty to see, thought Ridpath.

'Jenny, have you heard anything from the hospital?' he asked.

She shook her head. 'She's still unconscious and in ICU.'

'Could you spare me a few minutes?'

'What's it about, Ridpath?'

He glanced across at Sophia. 'If we could talk in private.'

'I know when I'm not wanted. I'll be in our office if you need me.' She was the last to leave.

'What's so important even Sophia can't know, Ridpath?'

Chapter Fifty-five

'Was Mrs Challinor acting in any way…' Ridpath stumbled over the words, '…strangely, before the attack?'

Jenny shook her head vigorously. 'Almost the opposite. She was focused on her work. The Davies case had taken a lot of her time. She was convinced the Health Authority had been so decimated by the pandemic and staff absences it was no longer fit for purpose. She was determined to sort it out.'

Ridpath touched his mouth with the tip of his index finger. 'When I met her, she seemed to be keen I take over the Romeo and Juliet case for GMP, despite us being extremely busy. Do you know why?'

'She never said anything to me. But she rarely talked about staffing matters unless it involved the scheduling of inquests or court appearances.' She smiled. 'If you're worried, Ridpath, we never discussed you. You would be the last thing we talked about.'

He stood. 'Just my imagination then. I thought she had something on her mind. Sorry to bother you.'

'No worries.'

He turned to leave, but just as he reached the door, she said, 'Now you mention it, there was one other strange thing.'

'What?'

'Well… the night before the attack, she had an appointment in her diary. There was no name, just a time. Seven thirty. I thought it was strange because she was normally so difficult about agreeing to outside meetings. She saw most of them as a waste of time, taking her away from her work.'

'No name or place?'

Jenny shook her head. 'Nothing. There was just a handwritten note of the time in her diary.'

'You didn't ask her about it?'

'Perhaps I should have done. But I learnt long ago, the coroner had her own way of doing things. She would let me know if she needed anything from me.' She looked up for a moment. 'And, if I'm honest, I had a jitterbug night that evening and I didn't want to miss it.'

Before he realised it, Ridpath had asked, 'Jitterbug?'

'You know, swing dancing. I never miss those nights, they are so much fun.' The smile vanished from her face. 'I would be careful about Mr Montague if I were you.'

'What do you mean?'

'He wasn't just sent here to keep everything running smoothly.'

'I'll remember that, but I have too much on my plate to deal with some bureaucrat who takes more delight in reformatting documents than actually doing his job of protecting people.'

Jenny shrugged her shoulders. 'Those types of people are always the most dangerous, Ridpath.'

'Yeah, sometimes it's easier to face a thug with a machete than some bureaucrat trying to knife you in the back.'

Chapter Fifty-six

The rest of the afternoon passed without incident. Ridpath rang Emily twice only to be told in no uncertain terms that Jayne was 'working on it'.

At five p.m., he decided to go to see Mrs Challinor in hospital. On his way out he bumped into Clarence Montague coming from the coroner's office.

'Off so early, Mr Ridpath?'

He ignored the passive-aggressive tone and just carried on walking out of the door. It probably wasn't the smartest thing to do but Ridpath had had enough of the black-suited bat.

Only the healing powers of Saint Bowie and Bishop Ronson would work, the strident power chords of 'The Width of a Circle' on *The Man Who Sold the World* brightening his mood as he drove to hospital.

Inside the ICU, Sarah Challinor was sitting in the corridor with Alison Ruston, the FLO. Both had been kitted out in clinical aprons and hairnets. Sarah's aunt was no longer there, presumably taking a break.

Mrs Challinor was secreted in one of the isolation cubicles in the unit. Through the glass, Ridpath could see the tubes leading from her throat to the intubation machine beside her bed.

'Mum's been put in an induced coma. It's for her own good, the doctor said.'

Ridpath glanced back at Mrs Challinor. Her head was swathed in a new bandage and her face looked gaunt and pale.

'They've eased the bleeding on her brain though. It's all a question of time now.'

A nurse dressed in PPE entered the room and checked Mrs Challinor's vital signs, adjusting the saline drip feeding a colourless solution into a catheter on her hand.

'Your mum is a formidable woman. I'm sure the doctors are doing the best they can,' Ridpath tried to soothe her.

'It's the waiting I can't stand. But I don't want to go home in case anything happens.'

Sarah was looking in almost as bad a shape as her mother. Her hair was straggly and unwashed, the lines deep on her forehead, the bags dark beneath her eyes.

'You should go home too. It won't help your mum if you get ill. Alison can drive you back to your house.'

Ridpath glanced once again at Mrs Challinor lying motionless on the bed, the sound of the machines she was attached to a constant orchestra of discordant noises.

'Come back tomorrow, get some sleep now.'

The FLO stepped forward. 'I can drive you back if you want and pick you up again tomorrow morning. You might want to use the restroom before we go.'

Sarah thought for a moment and then nodded her head, slowly walking down the antiseptic corridor, looking back continually at the isolation room as if, in her absence, her mother would suddenly take a turn for the worse.

When she had finally turned the corner, Ridpath faced the FLO. 'Anything from the investigation?'

'I haven't heard anything new.'

'No arrests or suspects?'

'Not that I know.'

'Will you promise to let me know if you hear anything? Copper to copper.'

'It worked out well last time, didn't it? I had a bollocking from my boss.'

Ridpath held his hands up in mock surrender. 'My fault, totally. I shouldn't have called Tindall and spoken to him. But we are dealing with a family here, and they have a right to know how the investigation is progressing.'

'You don't though. You're not family.'

Ridpath sighed. This was going nowhere. 'Look, help me will you? I still need to know what's going on and frankly, I don't have a lot of trust Tindall is going to find out who did this.'

He pointedly stared at the coroner through the glass wall.

'She is the victim here, not Tindall and his mates.'

Alison Ruston also looked at the coroner and sighed. 'OK, if I hear anything, I'll call you. But you know as well as I do, if the detectives haven't made a breakthrough in the first forty-eight hours, it's unlikely anything will happen.'

'How long are you going to be assigned here?'

Alison Ruston shrugged her broad shoulders. 'I dunno. Because it's the coroner, probably longer than normal, but I could be pulled off tomorrow, particularly if another case comes up.'

Sarah Challinor appeared at the top of the corridor. They both walked towards her.

'Let me know whatever you can,' Ridpath whispered.

Chapter Fifty-seven

Ridpath was sitting in front of the television, the sound down and the screen flickering. He'd gone to pick up Eve from Mrs Wells' and already cooked an evening meal for her. It had been eaten in relative silence.

It was one of *those* days.

She finally went upstairs to finish her homework and he was left on his own. He thought about going through the calls in response to the TV announcement but couldn't face them at the moment. He even called Emily one more time only to receive a sharp rebuke about constantly interrupting their work.

He had a strange, disquieting feeling he had missed something. It was like he had gone out and left something behind in the house, but couldn't work out what it was.

The words of Charlie Whitworth, his ex-boss and mentor, came back to him. 'Evidence, lad, you have to find evidence. Everything else is speculation until you find evidence.'

God, he missed Charlie. He would have been the voice of reason now, telling them to work harder, to dig deeper.

'It's all there, lad, you just have to sweat the work.'

His phone rang. He looked at the screen, not recognising the number.

'Ridpath speaking.'

'Hiya, it's Jenny, sorry for calling so late.'

She sounded out of breath, as if she had been running for the bus.

'I've been thinking about what you asked me.'

A long pause.

'And?'

'It may be nothing, but about two months ago, Mrs Challinor asked me to request ten files from other coroners' offices.'

'Files?'

'Proceedings and transcripts of inquests going all the way back to 2015.'

'Was this unusual?'

'Occasionally she would ask for one or two, particularly if she was checking a point of law or wanted to read the reasoning of a coroner in a case.'

'But never ten all at the same time?'

'Never.'

'You don't happen to know the inquests she wanted you to look at?'

'There's an email she sent me on my laptop at work, I can send it to you tomorrow when I get in.'

'That would be great, Jenny.'

'It may be nothing, but you did ask me if she'd done anything out of the ordinary recently. And there's one other thing, Ridpath. I had the impression she was only interested in a few of the files.'

'I don't understand.'

'It was as if she didn't want me to know the ones she wanted to see, so ordered more.'

'Why would she do that?'

'I don't know. It was just a feeling.'

'Thanks, Jenny. Send me the details tomorrow. Now you can get back to your dancing.'

'We're doing the cha-cha-cha, it don't half take it out of me.' A voice in the background. 'I have to go, Mr Lawrence is calling us back. You are coming in to the Coroner's Court tomorrow? Montague will be checking up on you.'

'I'll try to make it in the afternoon, but this inquiry is taking a lot of my time.'

'See you tomorrow then.'

'Don't forget to send me—' Ridpath never finished as the phone went dead in his hand.

He put it down on the table beside him and stared at the silent television.

Why had Mrs Challinor requested so many inquest transcripts?

Ridpath rubbed his head. He could feel another headache coming on.

It was the end of the longest day and, outside in his garden, the birds were just singing their last chorus as the sun went down.

But he still had work to do.

What was Mrs Challinor investigating? Had she discovered something that everybody else had missed? And was her investigation linked to the attack?

Too many questions, and not enough answers.

What had she found?

Tuesday, June 22

Chapter Fifty-eight

Ridpath parked his car outside Police HQ at exactly nine a.m. He'd thought about going in early, but after last night's rebuke from Emily, thought it better to leave the team alone to get on with it. He could do nothing to accelerate the process, so he just had to be patient. A virtue that didn't come naturally to him.

He was also being patient with Eve. Her mood hadn't improved this morning. If anything she was even more uncommunicative. Grunts had replaced words as her preferred mode of communication.

Not good. Not good at all.

It was obviously time to sit down and chat with his daughter, but finding time was going to be the problem. It had to be tonight at the latest.

Once again, Ridpath found himself running desperately trying to catch up with life.

As he walked into the meeting room on the MIT floor, Jayne Sinclair was explaining something to Emily and Chrissy. Behind her, what looked like a small family tree was written on a board.

'Ah, Ridpath, you've arrived just at the right time,' she said to him.

Looking around the room, it was obvious they had been there all night. Pizza boxes, used plastic coffee cups and sheets of discarded paper were strewn across the tables.

Instantly, a wave of guilt flooded his body. As team leader, he should have been with them, not snoring loudly in his pit at home.

'You worked all night?'

'Had to be done, but we finally cracked it,' answered Jayne.

'I didn't,' said Chrissy. 'I left at eleven. Need my beauty sleep, otherwise I'm a basket case.'

Ridpath sat down, staring at the wall behind Jayne. It made absolutely no sense to him. 'Tell me what you have.'

'I think we have a living relative of Male B, plus a possible name.'

'You did all the work in a night?'

'It's not difficult, and luckily Emily was here to help.'

'I made coffee,' said Emily.

'Let me take you through what we have.' Jayne Sinclair pointed to a board behind her. 'Firstly, our two victims, Female A and Male B, were not the star-crossed lovers Romeo and Juliet, as portrayed by the papers. At least I hope they weren't.'

'Why?'

'Because I think they were half-siblings.'

'What? Why? How do you know?' Ridpath spluttered.

'GEDmatch has a lovely little tool called One-to-One. It means I can compare one set of DNA with another set. If you remember, the amount of shared DNA is usually expressed in something called centimorgans. I loaded the DNA data of our victims into GEDmatch and did the comparison. Siblings share around fifty per cent of their DNA, with an average centimorgan number of 2,629, while half-siblings only share around twenty-five per cent, with an average of 1,783 centimorgans.'

'So what was the result of your comparison?'

'The numbers of centimorgans our victims shared was high, around 1,804. There's a number of possible relationships between them but, given their ages, it's a fair bet they were half-siblings, or aunt and uncle. Are you with me so far?'

Ridpath nodded. It was complicated but he was beginning to understand it. For him, it was just a different type of forensic evidence. He didn't have to understand the science behind it all, just comprehend the implications for the investigation.

'If we were to proceed further, we had to start to compile family trees. And for that we use a mixture of GEDmatch and traditional documentary genealogy.'

'What does that mean?'

'We started with Female A's DNA and loaded it into another GEDmatch tool called One-to-Many. This compares a person's DNA with everybody else who has registered on the website. Unfortunately, we found no matches.'

'Why?'

'Her relatives may not have been interested in family history or they simply hadn't uploaded their DNA data to the site. However, when we uploaded Male B's GEDmatch data and compared it, we had one good hit. A man with a centimorgan shared relationship number of 1,405. This number gave us possible relationships of uncle, great uncle or grandparent to Male B.' She wrote uncle, great uncle or grandparent on the whiteboard. 'It also gave us a name, an email address and a date of birth.'

'Who was it?'

'Frederick Orwell, born in 1949.'

'How does it help us discover the name of our male victim?'

'First, I wanted to find out Frederick Orwell's mother's name.'

'Why?'

'It's a way of checking we are looking at the right person. If we know the father's surname and the mother's too, I can use other tools to find out more.' She sighed, obviously having explained this a thousand times before. 'It's a bit like a line of dominos. Knowing one bit of information allows to find out more and so on, until all the dominos have fallen and we have a complete family tree. The first domino is Frederick's mother's name.'

'So how did you find it out?'

'We went on a website called FreeBMD which gives the details of all the births, deaths and marriages in England and Wales from 1837. Luckily his name is not common and we had the date of birth. I'll show you.'

Jayne turned around her laptop to face Ridpath. On it was long list of names all beginning with O.

'This is the register for April to June 1949. Here's Frederick's name, and his mother's surname, Harcourt. The other numbers are the pages for the register where the birth certificate is found. We then did another search using both the Orwell and Harcourt names and two more births came up: Ellen Orwell, born between October and December, 1951, and Stephen Orwell, born between July and September, 1956.'

'You know they had other children, so what?'

'It helps to build a family tree, and from this we can work out how this man, Frederick, is related to our Male B.'

'OK…' Ridpath said slowly.

'I wanted to know the full name of Frederick's parents, so I went on one of the other family history search engines and searched in the Marriages section for the names Orwell and Harcourt. The search came back with a church marriage certificate for a Samuel Orwell to a Mathilda Harcourt in 1948. It also gave me Frederik's grandfather's name, Harold Orwell, and his maternal grandfather, Ronald Harcourt.' She pointed to the family tree on the whiteboard. 'I checked out the family of Ronald Harcourt; Mathilda was an only child. Whereas Harold Orwell had two sons; Ellis, born in 1922, and Samuel in 1924.'

'So you now have to trace the lines of those two sons to get all the possible matches, right?'

'Correct. And this was where we had a bit of luck. Ellis was killed in Normandy during the D–Day landings. He was a paratrooper with the 7th Parachute Battalion and he died without getting married or having any children.'

'Lucky for us, unlucky for him.'

'Ellen, Samuel's daughter, died in 1960 at the young age of nine. So there were no great uncles or aunts.' She crossed out the next word, leaving only one left.

'Frederick Orwell must be the uncle of Male B.'

'Correct. I checked on Frederick. He emigrated to Australia in 1975 with his wife, Rachel. They had two children in that city, Michael, born in 1977, and Toni, born in 1979.'

'Both too old to be our vic.'

'And too young to have produced children to match the age of our victims.' Jayne tapped one name on her family history chart. 'So that leaves only one brother as the father of Male B. Stephen Orwell. Over to you, Chrissy.'

'I checked him on the electoral register. Guess what? He lives in Manchester. Altrincham, to be precise. He's a medical doctor, but now semi-retired. He married Alexandra Weston in 1985.'

'So Male B could be their son?'

Jayne stepped forward. 'He could be, but we can only find one child registered to Stephen Orwell and his wife: Michael Orwell, born in 1987.'

'So is that our victim? Slightly older than the pathologist thought, though.'

Chrissy raised her hand. 'Unfortunately, the electoral register shows a Michael Orwell living at an address in Altrincham with his parents from 2012 until today. He is still alive.'

Ridpath scratched his head. 'So we're stuffed again.'

'No,' Jayne spoke firmly. 'The science doesn't lie. Our Male B must be a child of Stephen Orwell.'

'I get it, but you said he only had one child.'

Jayne put her finger up. 'I said he only had one child with his wife. We just rang the registry office and there was a Ralph Orwell born in Manchester in 1990. The mother's name was Moira Travis and the father was…'

'…Stephen Orwell.'

'Right first time, Ridpath. But there are no records for the birth of a daughter, at least not in Manchester.'

He stood, suddenly energised. 'We know his address, right? What are we waiting for? We'll go interview him.'

'You're not going to call first?' asked Jayne.

'No, let's surprise him. Emily you're with me. Chrissy, find out all you can about this Stephen Orwell, dig deep.'

'On it.'

'What do you want me to do?' asked Jayne.

'Go home, if you've been working all night.'

'I'm not tired yet. I'd like to continue looking for Female A's relatives if I can.'

'Fine by me, but don't push yourself too hard.'

Jayne stared at him. 'One more thing. You do realise this man could have killed two young people, Ridpath – his son and an unknown young woman. You're going to just walk up to the house and knock on the door without tactical support?'

Ridpath remembered Jayne's history. A partner shot through a door on a cold call.

'I can't see any other way, Jayne. We need to interview this man as soon as we can. If nothing else to eliminate him from our inquiries. At the moment, he's our only lead.'

Jayne Sinclair stared back at him and slowly nodded her head. 'Just be careful.'

Chapter Fifty-nine

The address they had was on one of the most expensive roads in Greater Manchester. The house wasn't as large as some on the street, but still comfortably elegant. An elegance that shouted quietly about the wealth of its occupants.

Altrincham had once been a small town on the old Roman road out of Manchester. It had always had a stuffy, rather self-satisfied air about it. Now, it had reinvented itself as an 'in' place to live, with bistros, an old market redesigned as a foodie heaven, and a Sainsbury's actually selling fresh sushi.

Ridpath was used to taking Eve here for her school, but was less used to visiting it as part of an investigation. It was a place where crime happened behind closed curtains rather than out on the streets.

Aware of Jayne Sinclair's worries, he knocked on the door and stepped to one side. This wasn't Moss Side but you couldn't be too careful.

The door was answered almost immediately by a woman dressed in a large coat who was obviously on her way out. She was tall and refined, with a casual elegance that suited the house.

'Can I help you?'

Definitely not a Manchester accent.

Both Ridpath and Emily Parkinson pulled out their warrant cards. 'Inspector Thomas Ridpath, are you Mrs Alexandra Orwell?'

The woman frowned. 'I am. What is this concerning?'

Again, the pronunciation and the words were clear and refined.

'Is your husband, Stephen Orwell, at home?'

She glanced back into the house. 'He's in the drawing room. What is this about?'

A house like this would have a drawing room.

'We'd like to have a chat with him, if we may. Can we come inside?'

'I don't know. I'm just going out, I...'

'It won't take more than a few minutes. It's to help with one of our inquiries.'

She thought for a moment and her eyes glanced once more back into the house, before she opened the door and stepped back.

'Come in, but wipe your shoes on the doormat first.'

Ridpath did as he was told and walked across the threshold, followed by Emily.

The hallway was spacious and stylish, with the far wall painted in a rich midnight blue. There was an antique dresser to the left, a long mirror to the right, and black and white tiles stretching into the distance.

'This way.'

Mrs Orwell walked down the hallway to a room on the right. She opened the door, announcing, 'Stephen, the police are here for some reason.'

An older man looked up from doing his crossword in *The Times*. 'The police,' he said loudly. 'What are they doing here?'

'I'm about to ask them the same question.'

Ridpath moved into the room, feeling himself sinking into a carpet up to his ankles.

He took out his warrant card again. 'I'm Inspector Thomas Ridpath and this is Detective Sergeant Parkinson. We'd just like to ask you a few questions, Dr Orwell, if that would be possible.'

'What's it about?'

'Your name has been flagged in connection with one of our investigations.'

'My name? Are you sure you have the right person, Inspector?'

'We think so, that's why we're here. To ask you a few questions.'

'I'm not sure it's convenient right now, Inspector.'

'We could do the interview here or down at the station, whichever is more convenient?'

'Altrincham Police Station?'

'No, we would be going to Police HQ on Oldham Road.'

Mrs Orwell spoke for the first time. 'They said it was just going to take a few minutes, dear, so I let them in.'

Was there fear in the explanation? She was certainly a lot younger than her husband and seemed almost subservient to him.

Stephen Orwell rolled his eyes extravagantly, putting down the newspaper on the small side table beside the armchair. 'I suppose we'd better get this over with. But before I answer any questions, I would like to know how my name came up in one of your inquiries.'

'Do you need me to stay? It's just I'm late for my Women's Institute meeting.'

'No, dear, I can handle this. Unless you'd like my wife to stay, Inspector?'

'No, sir, won't be necessary.'

'Make sure you get the smoked salmon and pâté for tonight's party.'

'Of course, dear. Goodbye, Inspector Ridpath and Sergeant…'

'Parkinson.'

'Well, I'm off. There's tea, coffee and biscuits in the annex if you need them.'

'I'm sure Inspector Ridpath and his colleague won't be staying long enough for tea or coffee, dear.'

She frowned and then waved her hand absent-mindedly. 'We're learning how to fix a broken pipe today. I am looking forward to it.'

With those last words she was off, shutting the drawing room door behind her.

Stephen Orwell waited until he heard the front door close before saying, 'My wife loves DIY. Personally I can't stand it. She likes fixing things, while I much prefer doing my crosswords. Sit down, won't you, and tell me why you are here?'

Ridpath took a seat on the couch opposite, as did Emily Parkinson. She took out her notebook and began writing.

Ridpath chose his words carefully. He wanted this man to cooperate. 'As you may have already guessed, we are based at Police HQ.'

'I'd worked that out, Inspector. Please credit me with a modicum of intelligence.'

This man was used to speaking down to people, lecturing them as if he was the fount of all wisdom and they were mere mortals, playthings for the gods.

Ridpath decided he could use this sense of superiority. He immediately assumed a more humble tone of voice.

'Sorry, sir, I'll explain…'

'That would be helpful… and more efficient.'

'We are currently investigating the discovery of two bodies found in a warehouse in the Northern Quarter.'

'Surely you would need to talk to a pathologist rather than somebody of my specialisation.'

'We have already performed a post-mortem, sir. Today, we are talking with you because your name has come up in relationship to one of the victims.'

Stephen Orwell frowned. 'Really? I don't think I know any criminals, Inspector…'

The man had forgotten his surname on purpose.

'Inspector Ridpath, sir, Thomas Ridpath.'

'As I was saying, I don't know any criminals. Not part of my social circle.'

'I didn't say they were criminals, sir, I said their bodies had been found. In fact, one of the victims, a male, shares your DNA.'

'My DNA? What are you saying, Inspector? My DNA was found on this man's body?'

'No, sir. We tested the man's DNA and it came back as having a close relationship to you.'

'But I've never tested my DNA, and I have no interest in doing so.'

'But your brother tested his and uploaded his results onto the website.'

'Just a minute. Are you saying, you found a link to me through my brother's DNA? Isn't that illegal, Inspector? Surely privacy laws would apply?'

'Your brother opted in on the website to allow his DNA to be used for law-enforcement purposes.'

'He did, but I didn't.'

'Nonetheless, sir, we are dealing with a murder inquiry here, and if you could help us, we would be grateful. We are sure you would agree that law-abiding citizens such as yourself have nothing to hide and would be willing to help solve a murder.'

Ridpath knew he was laying it on a bit thick but after the man's reaction to the news about the DNA website, he had to appeal to his vanity. 'Frankly, sir, we have been unable to identify the male victim. You are our last chance.'

A smug smile crept like a thief across Stephen Orwell's face. 'You need my help, Inspector?'

'Yes, sir... please.'

'Since you have asked politely, how may I help you?'

'The DNA obtained from the male victim shows a close relationship to you.'

'A close relationship? What does that mean?'

'It shows you are possibly his father, sir.'

The man snorted. 'His father? Preposterous. Do you see any children running round this house, Inspector? Do you hear the patter of tiny feet? See any pictures on the walls or on the piano over there?'

'No, sir.'

'That's because my wife and I have only one son, and he is now thirty-five.'

Right on cue, Ridpath heard the heavy tread of someone coming down the stairs.

'Ah, speak of the devil. Michael, can you come into the drawing room?'

'What is it? I'm on my way out,' answered a querulous voice from the hallway.

'Just come in, will you. I want you to meet some people.'

The door slowly opened and a man dressed in motorcycle leathers with a mask covering his face and an unfastened helmet on his head entered the room. He was short and stocky, the leathers giving him a squat, ungainly manner.

'What do you want?' he said roughly.

'How many times have I told you not to wear those ghastly clothes in the house.'

'I'm going out, I need to wear them.'

Stephen Orwell harrumphed loudly. 'See, Inspector, this is my son, Michael. He is not lying in some mortuary in Manchester, even though, occasionally, his mother and I wish it were the case.'

'Inspector?' asked Michael Orwell.

Ridpath fished out his warrant card again. 'Greater Manchester Police. Detective Inspector Ridpath and Detective Sergeant Parkinson from Police HQ.'

'What have I done now? I'm going to pay the bloody speeding fine soon, I told them last week.'

'We're not here for you, just to ask your father some questions.'

A smile crossed his face. 'Been up to no good, Father? I warned you about your ways, didn't I?'

Stephen Orwell sighed and pointedly looked away.

His son jerked his thumb towards the hallway. 'So I can go? I need to drop into the clinic.'

'Just go, Michael,' his father said irritably.

The son didn't wait any longer. He left the room, leaving the door open. Stephen Orwell slowly rose from his chair to close it. 'You wouldn't believe my son is a doctor, would you? A failed marriage and two kids, but still came running home into the welcoming arms of his mother. Even worse, he rides a motorbike like a teenager. Do you have children, Inspector?'

'A daughter, sir.'

'A daughter. I wanted a daughter, but Michael's birth was a difficult one. Afterwards, my wife had a total hysterectomy, her uterus and cervix were removed. An extremely traumatic time for her – one from which she has never fully recovered. One of the reasons she throws herself into her charity and community work at the Women's Institute.'

The front door slammed and was followed by the roar of a motorbike engine as it revved before pulling away from the house.

Ridpath was silent for a moment, before leaning forward and clasping his hands together. He had to trust Jayne Sinclair was right with her research.

'As I said, sir, the DNA shows a close relationship to you and the science does not lie. Our male victim shares your DNA. Is there any way that could have happened?' he asked in a low voice, staring at the man sitting in front of him the whole time.

The man looked away.

Ridpath asked again. 'Is there any way this male victim could be related to you?'

'How old was he?' Stephen Orwell asked quietly.

'We think about eighteen years old. He probably died in the summer of 2008.'

The man's shoulders slumped and he let out a gasp of air. It was as if he visibly shrank in front of Ridpath, all his pomposity and smugness escaping like air from a punctured balloon.

He looked at Ridpath, then glanced at the door, as if checking his wife was no longer there.

'I had an affair,' he finally said in a whisper.

'When was it?'

'In 1989. With one of my patients. It just happened, I have no idea why.'

Emily stopped writing in her notebook and asked, 'Was a child born from this affair?'

The man nodded.

'A male child?'

'I think so.'

'You think so?' She raised her voice. Ridpath signalled with his eyes she should back off.

'I'd already finished the affair when she told me she was pregnant. My wife found out, you see. Saw my credit card bills from the hotel and worked it all out. I had to end it.'

'When was this child born?'

'I'm not sure. It would have been the summer of 1990, I think.'

'You didn't keep in touch with the mother?'

'I moved to a clinic in America to work and continue my research in September of that year.'

'So you never saw this child?'

The man shook his head. 'We had to move, I had to save my marriage.' Stephen Orwell's voice trailed off weakly.

'And you could have been struck off, barred from working as a doctor by the General Medical Council. I believe they frown on doctors having affairs with their patients.'

The man's eyes flamed with anger at Emily's words. 'Don't you dare judge me. I made a mistake, and I'll have to live with it for the rest of my life. I never even saw the child and his mother never asked me for anything. No money, nothing.'

'What was her name? The woman with whom you had the affair.'

'Moira Travis.'

'Any other details? Her age? Address?'

'I don't know. I never spoke to her again after the affair was ended. I remember she was about twenty-four and lived in Chorlton when we were...' His voice trailed off.

'And she never contacted you?'

Stephen Orwell stared into mid-air. 'Once. She contacted me once afterwards. She sent me a picture of the child and said she had called him Ralph. Ralph Orwell.'

'Your name is on the birth register as the father.'

Orwell looked up. 'Is it? I didn't know. How dare she use my name—'

'Do you still have the picture?' asked Emily Parkinson aggressively.

The man shook his head. 'I burnt it immediately. I couldn't have my wife finding the bloody thing, discovering the evidence of my... indiscretion.'

The DS sat forward. 'Indiscretion? It was a child...'

Ridpath waved his arm at her, forcing her to sit back on the couch.

'It's something I regretted all my life, burning the picture. You say this body, this man you found, was her son, Ralph?'

'We're not sure, but if you would agree to having a simple DNA test we could confirm the relationship.'

'I wouldn't have to do it here?'

Ridpath didn't understand the question.

'I could do the test at Police HQ? I wouldn't want my wife to find out. Painful memories for her...'

Ridpath sighed. 'Of course, you could do it at the station if you want. A couple of more questions. Did you have other affairs?' he asked bluntly.

The man seemed affronted. 'Of course not, how dare you suggest such an idea. One mistake was more than enough for me.'

'You see, we found a female body with the male. She was younger, perhaps seventeen years old and, according to her DNA, was probably his half-sister.'

'I know nothing about her. As I said, I moved to the US in 1990 for my work, staying there until 1997.'

'You never came back to Manchester?'

'Just once, in 1994, for a conference. I didn't meet with Moira.'

'And where did you work in the USA?'

'At the Halson Clinic in Boston. You can check with the hospital. I'm sure they will confirm my work with them.'

'Oh, we will be contacting them, don't worry, sir.'

Ridpath glanced across at Emily to see if she had any other questions. She shook her head.

'I think we have spent enough of your time, Dr Orwell. If you can give DS Parkinson your contact details, we'll arrange for you to come in for the DNA test.'

He stood and picked up a card from the mantlepiece. 'Here they are. Please use my mobile number to contact me.'

Ridpath checked the card. Orwell had a long list of letters after his name, obviously medical degrees and diplomas. At the top were the words THE ORWELL CLINIC.

'Thank you for your time. We'll be in touch.' Ridpath moved towards the door before stopping. 'Just one more question, sir. Where were you in 2008?'

'Back in America, Los Angeles this time, at the Boulevard Hospital. We moved there in 2005, returning in 2012.'

'You stayed there the whole time?'

'Yes, I had no desire to return to England.'

'Thank you for your time.'

Ridpath turned to leave.

'Er… Inspector. Can we keep this quiet, just between us two? I wouldn't want my wife to find out. She would be awfully distressed if she knew.' The man smiled hopefully.

Ridpath was in no mood to ease his fears. 'I'm sorry, I can't promise, Dr Orwell. We may have to question her to confirm your story – your recollection of the events. Terribly sorry, it has to be done.'

It did have to be done, and Ridpath wasn't sorry.

Chapter Sixty

As soon as he was out of the house, Ridpath was on the phone.

'Chrissy, I need you to find a Moira Travis, asap. In 1989 she was roughly twenty-four years old and living in Chorlton.'

'Is her son, Ralph Orwell, Male B?'

'Could be. We need the answer as quickly as you can.'

'Will do, Ridpath. I've put you on speaker, Jayne wants a word.'

Another voice came through. 'I'm afraid still nothing on Female A. She's proving elusive.'

'Stephen Orwell denies being her father, said he was in America.'

'That may explain it, Ridpath. I'm been searching on the UK directories and registers, but if Female A was American it's a completely different ball game.'

'He denies being the father though.'

'Let me work on it.'

'Aren't you tired, Jayne? Why don't you go home?'

'No point, Ridpath, too much adrenaline running through my veins to sleep. I'll carry on for a bit longer.'

'Great, Emily and I are coming back now. See you in thirty minutes or so.'

'Ridpath, Jenny Oldfield rang from the coroner. She said she sent through the email she promised yesterday. She wants you to call her.'

'OK, will do. We're getting close everybody, I can feel it in my water.'

He switched off his phone and turned to Emily. 'As soon as we return, I want you to get on to those American hospitals. I want the exact dates he was working and any possible absences from work.'

'You think he could be our man, Ridpath?'

'I'm not sure. He fits the bill, but his surprise when we talked about Ralph Orwell's body being discovered seemed genuine. What do you think?'

'I think he's a slimeball. Got his girlfriend pregnant, and then did a runner, leaving her holding the baby, literally. The fact he would have been disbarred if the General Medical Council had found out makes it worse.'

'But does it make him a killer? It was eighteen years after the birth, why kill the young man?'

'Blackmail. Perhaps Male B—'

'Ralph Orwell.'

'Perhaps Ralph Orwell was blackmailing him? Holding the threat of revealing his existence and the affair to the BMC, demanding money.'

'I don't know...' His phone rang.

'Ridpath.'

'Hi, it's Jenny. I sent you the email this morning. Did you get it?'

'Sorry, Jenny, I've been stuffed until now. I'll look at it soon.'

'One more thing. Mr Montague is on the warpath, asking where you are. He wants to see you about the Didsbury case.'

This was exactly what Ridpath didn't need.

'Can you tell him I'll be in this afternoon?'

'He's not going to be a happy bunny.'

'His happiness is the least of my concerns, Jenny.'

Ridpath rang off and opened the door to his car. He was about to start the engine when he stopped. 'Won't be a second. Let me just check something.'

He opened Jenny's email. There was the usual polite introduction and an attachment at the bottom. He clicked on the attachment and a document opened with a list of case numbers and details for the inquests Mrs Challinor had requested.

Ridpath's mouth opened wide. 'That can't be right.'
And another piece of the puzzle slotted into place.

Chapter Sixty-one

'The police are finally on to me. How? It must have been the warehouse deaths. Six months after the discovery of the bodies, they had finally found a clue to my identity.

Or was it the coroner? Had she found something and that was why she wanted to meet?

What were their names? Ridpath and Parkinson, that was it. I was surprised when I saw them both. One badly dressed in some threadbare outfit bought at Burton's years ago. The other with sensible shoes and short hair, every inch the butch copper.

If they had any hard evidence, they would have arrested me. Instead, they were just there asking questions, searching for answers.

Luckily the police, especially these two, were plodders, too slow to wipe their own noses. Like snails chasing a cheetah. After all, it had taken them six months to get here.

I needed to act, though.

One person had seen me and knew who I really was.

Mrs Challinor.

In a coma now, but who knew when she would awake.

I had to make sure that would never happen. There would be no more errors, no more mistakes. I wasn't going to rush, and she wouldn't escape this time.

She would never come out of her coma.

Chapter Sixty-two

When Ridpath and Emily Parkinson arrived back in the situation room at Police HQ, there was a palpable sense of excitement in the air.

'Tell me what you have, Chrissy.'

'Moira Travis, now fifty-six years old, living in a flat in Withington.'

'She's not moved far from Chorlton,' said Emily.

'Divorced from a Peter Travis in 1990. One son, Ralph Orwell, born on June 22 of that year. Worked as a secretary and part-time barmaid. Now living on Universal Credit. Doesn't seem to have previous, Ridpath, no criminal history except one DUI back in 1996.'

'Do you have an address?'

'It's on the board.'

Ridpath checked it out. Flat 3, Stalybridge Road, Withington. 'Let's go,' he said to Emily.

'Hang on, there's more.'

Ridpath knew he was rushing, not thinking things through. He forced himself to take a few breaths and sat down at the table.

'Sorry, Chrissy, take me through everything you have.'

'The son, Ralph, left school at sixteen, no qualifications. He seems to have spent a couple of years doing nothing and then vanishes in 2008. I've checked the usual places: DVLA, the electoral register, passport applications. Nothing. The mother made a police report when he vanished but, as he was over eighteen, it was assigned a low priority. No real follow-up, it was one of those that fell through the cracks. They are searching for the original report for me in the archives but there's the usual problems.'

'Right, great work, Chrissy. Can you contact the school…'

'Parrs Wood.'

'See if any teachers remember him. Even better, check if they have any school pictures, I'd love to see a photo.'

'Will do.'

'Anything, Jayne?'

The genealogist looked tired, her usual energy now sadly depleted. 'Nothing on my end, Female A is being elusive. I'm still waiting for the go-ahead from FamilyTreeDNA. Once I have it, I should be able to get some movement.'

'Thank you, Jayne. As for Emily and I, we met Stephen Orwell—'

'Not a nice man, a bit of a prick actually…' interrupted Emily Parkinson.

'He admitted to having an affair with Moira Travis in 1989 and knowing she gave birth to a baby boy in 1990.'

'So there's the DNA link,' said Jayne. 'He was the father.'

'It seems so. Apparently, he never met or even wanted to see his son.'

'The bastard did a runner to America, leaving Moira Travis alone with the baby.'

Both Jayne and Chrissy mouthed, 'Bastard.'

'He still denies having any other affairs though, so how can he have been the father of Female A?'

'Men often deny affairs, Ridpath, until they have actually been caught in the act.' Jayne wrote a note to herself. 'Let me continue to search for her. Once we discover who she was, we can find out if there is a link to Stephen Orwell.'

'Thanks Jayne. There's one more piece of information that just came in from Jenny Oldfield at the Coroner's Court. Recently, Mrs Challinor asked her to dig out some transcripts from old inquests. And guess what?'

They all shook their heads.

'Three of the transcripts she asked for were inquests into the deaths of the Singhs in Blackburn, Joan Blackledge in Derbyshire and Tony Snellgrove in Chester.'

Chrissy's mouth opened wide. 'What?'

'It seems like the coroner was also looking into our deaths before she was attacked. I wonder if she noticed something when she opened the inquest into our victims in the warehouse.'

'Noticed a connection, you mean?'

'After Harold Shipman slipped through the net, she was always wary of something similar happening. I'll ask Jenny for the transcripts and send them to you.'

'OK, we're getting somewhere, Ridpath.'

He nodded. 'I know, but we are running out of time. One more thing – it strikes me as a bit of a coincidence that Mrs Challinor was attacked just as she was looking into these deaths.'

Emily tapped the table. 'Are you suggesting the attack was somehow linked?'

'I don't know, but I'm not a great believer in coincidences. Right now, though, we need to focus on this case. Chrissy, can you also check with these hospitals in America? Stephen Orwell said he was working at them from 1990 to 1997 and again from 2005 to 2012.'

Chrissy glanced at the clock. 'Their HR will be closed right now, but Boston will open in a couple of hours, I'll give them a call.'

'I thought you wanted me to follow up with the hospitals?' said Emily.

'You need to come with me to see Moira Travis.' He stood. 'Let's go.'

'Now?'

'No time like the present.'

'Are we going to eat?' A pause from Emily as her eyes lit up. 'Greggs again?'

'There's one on the way.'

She pocketed her notebook, 'Why don't we just pay my salary direct to them? I can have a standing order for veggie sausage rolls.'

'Not a bad idea, Emily. Come on.'

'Shouldn't you tell Claire Trent about the breakthrough?' said Jayne.

Ridpath thought for a moment. 'Later, after the interview with Moira Travis. I want something more concrete to tell her and Steve Carruthers.'

'Are you going to inform Moira Travis that Male B could be her son, Ralph? We still don't have a confirmed ID,' asked Chrissy.

'Thanks for reminding me. Here's Orwell's card. Can you call him and arrange a time for a DNA test here at Police HQ? Do it as soon as possible, Chrissy.'

'Will do. But you still haven't answered my question, Ridpath?'

'I'll handle it... somehow.'

Chapter Sixty-three

A shiver went down Ridpath's back as he approached Moira Travis' home. It was situated in the same area as a place he had spent far too much of his time: Christie's hospital.

It was here his myeloma had been diagnosed and treated. A place where he still had to return every three months for a check-up. On the road past the hospital he could practically smell the unique blend of antiseptic, bleach, furniture polish and fear that shrouded the place.

He tried to keep his eyes on the road, staring straight ahead, not looking at the white buildings with their aluminium chimneys, willing himself to get past them.

It was not that his treatment at the hospital was bad – on the contrary, it was probably one of the best places in the world to be looked after if you have cancer. It was just that he associated these bland white buildings with intimate pain; being told he had cancer, suffering the ignominy of losing his hair, isolation as the chemotherapy took hold, endless painful bruises on the back of his hands where catheters had leached chemicals and drugs into his body.

Next to him, Emily Parkinson was re-reading her notes quietly, unaware of what he was going through.

The satnav saved him from any more memories.

'Turn right at the next junction in two hundred metres.'

He waited for a car to pass, then swung right into a small street lined with large old Victorian houses converted into flats.

'You have reached your destination.'

It was the fifth house along the street. In older, more splendid days, these would have been the houses of rich cotton merchants, served by acres of liveried servants. These days, they were rather down-at-heel shoddy flats for students, indigents and those who could not afford to live anywhere better, rented out by landlords renowned for their greed and slowness at making repairs.

They stepped out of the car and walked up to the door with its blizzard of buttons on the right-hand side.

'It's flat three,' said Emily.

Ridpath pressed the bell. After ten seconds a light came on and a small, squeaky voice came over the intercom.

'Who is it?'

'Is that Moira Travis?'

'Speaking.'

'I'm Inspector Thomas Ridpath from Greater Manchester Police. Could we have a word, Mrs Travis?'

'What's it about?'

'We'd rather come in and talk to you directly. It's about your son, Ralph.'

Instantly, there was a loud click and the door opened slightly. Ridpath pushed through into a dark, dingy hallway with the stark smell of cooked cabbage. At the top of the stairs, a woman wearing a pink housecoat was waiting for them.

'You've heard from Ralph?' she shouted down from above.

'If we could come up, Mrs Travis, we can explain more.'

A minute later they were sat in a large, comfortably furnished one-bedroom apartment. A large bay window filled the sitting room with light, picking out the largely pink furniture. On the left a sideboard was laden with pictures of a young woman in colourful dresses with frilly petticoats, bouffant brown hair in a large beehive and a number attached to her wrist.

'I used to dance a lot at the Palace and Finnigans. I loved to dance.' The woman sitting opposite them now was small and frail, her once splendid dark hair reduced to a few wispy strands of grey.

'Would you like anything to drink, tea perhaps? I may even have some biscuits, if I haven't eaten them all.'

Ridpath noticed her hands were shaking, just a slight tremor but still noticeable.

'Thank you, no, Mrs Travis, I think we're full.'

They had stopped briefly at Greggs where Emily had her usual order. Ridpath just bought himself a large coffee, he couldn't face food before an interview. He knew he should eat, but somehow couldn't manage it.

'Are you sure?' asked Moira Travis again. 'It's no trouble.'

He glanced across at Emily. 'Thank you, we're sure.' He took a deep breath. 'We're here today to talk about your son, Ralph.'

'You've found him? I knew he would turn up one day. Where is he?'

Ridpath didn't answer.

'You do have a son called Ralph Orwell?'

'Of course, he was a beautiful boy.'

'And he was born on June 22, 1990?'

She frowned. 'That's correct. How do you know his birth date?'

Ridpath lowered his voice. 'We have some bad news, I'm afraid. We think we may have found his body.'

The woman made an audible shriek and her hand flew to her mouth.

Ridpath was tempted to try to comfort the woman, but realised he needed to press ahead, no matter how painful for her. And for him.

'We are still waiting for confirmation it is him. But we thought we would come to see you and let you know as soon as we could.'

'So it might not be my Ralph?'

'As I said, we are waiting for confirmation, but we are fairly sure from DNA tests it is your son.'

'Can I see the body? I'd like to see my son again.'

'I'm sure it can be arranged, but first I'd like to ask you a few questions, if I may?'

She nodded slightly, her eyes veiled in tears, here hand still covering her mouth.

'To confirm, Ralph was born on June 22, 1990?'

She nodded again.

'Where was he born?'

'At Park Hospital. It wasn't an easy birth, I was in labour for over eighteen hours.'

'And who was the father?'

The woman hesitated for a moment before saying, 'My husband, Peter Travis.'

Ridpath took a second. 'That isn't true, is it Mrs Travis? The father was a man called Stephen Orwell, wasn't it?'

The woman glanced away, staring at the bay window, looking at nothing. Then Ridpath saw a barely noticeable movement of her head.

'I'm sorry, Mrs Travis, but I'm going to have to get you to confirm it verbally. The father of your son was Stephen Orwell?'

Her eyes turned back to him and they were no longer full of tears, but of anger. 'I was his patient and he took advantage of me. I know that now. He groomed me and wined and dined me, made me feel special. My marriage wasn't great but with him I felt like a million dollars.'

'And after you told him you were pregnant?'

'He dropped me like a stone. Didn't want to see me any more. The bitch gave me some money to take care of it, but I wanted my baby, wanted him more than anything.'

'The bitch? You mean his wife, Alexandra Orwell?'

'Who else? He told me about her. "As frigid as an iceberg," he said. Didn't actually like sex, thought it was dirty. He wouldn't even see me, but she did. Offered to buy my baby off me, but I wouldn't give him to the likes of her. He was my child.'

Ridpath glanced across at Emily. 'So you had a meeting with Mrs Orwell?'

'We met twice.'

'Was her husband there?'

She snorted. 'That coward? He got me pregnant but couldn't bear to see me again.'

'And the wife offered to adopt your child with Stephen Orwell?' asked Emily.

'Adopt? She offered to buy my baby. Five thousand quid was her price. I told her where to go. Nobody was buying my child.'

'Did you send Dr Orwell a picture of your child?'

She looked away once more and nodded, her bottom lip coming up to cover the top one. 'But there was no answer. I even went to his house in Altrincham. I knew where it was because he had taken me back there one time when his wife was away. But the house was empty, they had already gone to America, a neighbour said.'

Ridpath frowned. 'Yet you named your child after him? You called him Ralph Orwell.'

She looked back, staring right through him. 'That was the stupid part. After everything, I still loved him, still wanted him to leave her and come to me. What a fool I was?'

Ridpath decided to move on. 'So you brought up your son alone.'

'I'd told Peter the boy wasn't his and he left. I couldn't work, so I had to sell the house in Chorlton. Peter wanted his share of course. The money didn't last long. So I got a job working as a dancer on the cruise ships.'

'And what happened to your baby?'

'He went to stay with my mother, she looked after him as best she could while I was away. And then...'

'What happened?'

'I met Roger. For some reason, he and Ralph didn't get on. There were constant fights. Ralph wouldn't go to school and he was always getting into trouble with the police; on the streets, nicking from shops, a bit of weed.'

'So what did you do?'

'Sent him back to his granny, but she couldn't handle him either. He ran away when he was sixteen, then came back and ran away again. I never saw him afterwards...' Her eyes filled with tears and she began to sob quietly. 'I wanted to do the best for him, but I couldn't.'

'You never heard from him after he ran away?'

She shook her head. 'Not a word. I thought he hated me so much. All these years, I hoped he had built a new life for himself, somewhere good, somewhere happy.' She stopped sobbing for a moment and glanced again at Ridpath. 'When did he pass away?'

'We're not certain. We think it was in the summer of 2008. When was the last time you saw him?'

'I think it was about the end of April 2008. He just left my mum's one day without saying a word.'

'Did you report it to the police?'

She nodded her head. 'But they didn't do too much. We thought he'd be back when he ran out of money. He always came back… except this time, he didn't.' She paused for a moment and stared sightlessly into mid-air as if remembering a time long lost. 'Ralph could look after himself. He was very grown up, an adult in a kid's body.'

Ridpath felt his phone buzz on his pocket but he ignored it. 'Did Ralph have any close female friends? A girlfriend perhaps?'

'I don't think so. Roger always thought he was the other way inclined. It was one of the reasons they fought. Roger was an ex-soldier, loved his sport and his football. Ralph was smaller, quieter, preferred to stay in and read a book. Liked his books, did Ralph.'

'Where is Roger? Could we speak to him?'

Moira Travis snorted again. 'He's long gone. Found another barmaid to screw, didn't he?'

Ridpath closed his notepad. 'I think that is all we need at the moment, Mrs Travis.'

'When can I see my son?'

'I'll check with the mort— the place where he is and let you know. Here is my card if you want to contact me, the mobile number is on the bottom.'

She took the card and stared at it for a long time.

'There's one thing you haven't told me, Inspector.'

'What's that? I'm happy to help you in any way.'

She looked at him, her blue eyes sparkling through the smudged mascara. 'How did my son die?'

Chapter Sixty-four

'That was... interesting,' said Emily as they walked to Ridpath's car.

'If by interesting you mean harrowing, it was.'

Ridpath pulled out his phone. There were three messages from Sophia.

> I know you're busy but His Lordship, Clarence Montague, would like to see you asap. It's about the fall in the nursing home in Didsbury. He seems to have a bee in his bonnet about it. But I can't work out what the problem is.

> He definitely wants to see you, Ridpath. I've told him you are busy and will be in later but he's not a happy camper. When are you coming in?

> He wants to see you NOW. He's just been demanding I give him your mobile number. He could find it in the directory if he bothered to look. When are you coming in?

Quickly, Ridpath texted back.

> There in fifteen, Sophia. Can you pull the case file and I'll take him through it when I get there?

An answer appeared almost immediately.

> He's ranting at Jenny now. I'll let him know you are coming. Sorry Ridpath, I know you are busy.

> Not your fault, Sophia. Keep your chin up.

Ridpath finished the text and pressed send. He didn't need somebody throwing their toys out of the pram at the moment.

'I have to go to the Coroner's Court, Emily. Are you OK getting back to HQ on your own?'

'No problem, I'll call an Uber. What do you want me to do?'

'Follow up on those American hospitals with Chrissy. I want to know the exact dates the Orwell's were in America. And see what you can find out about Alexandra Orwell. She sounds like a piece of work, Women's Institute and all.'

'Will do, Ridpath.'

As Emily walked away to call her Uber, he opened the car door and then stopped. Something had occurred to him.

Was it just a coincidence the tram ticket found in Ralph Orwell's pocket was from Altrincham, where the Orwell's lived?

Ridpath didn't believe in coincidences.

Chapter Sixty-five

As soon as he arrived at the coroner's office, Ridpath gathered the case file for the Didsbury death from Sophia.

'I'm sorry I sent you the texts, Ridpath, he just kept on and on at me. Where were you? When would you be coming back? What were you doing?'

'No worries, Sophia, let me handle him. I've met his sort before.'

'He's like my mum. Thinks his needs are the most important thing in the world and nothing else matters. Another narcissist.'

'He's not like your mum.'

'You haven't met her, Ridpath. If I said "Giant Haystacks" would it give you a better idea of her?'

Ridpath laughed and walked to the office, knocking on the closed door.

'Just a second.' The rustling of papers was followed by a peremptory command. 'Come.'

He opened the door and walked in.

The office had changed. Gone were Mrs Challinor's pictures of her family and the stacks of case files on top of the wooden cabinets. All were replaced by pictures of gun dogs, and an anaemic photo of a woman wearing tortoiseshell glasses next to a picture of a younger male version of Montague wearing a shirt and tie and a bad haircut.

'You wanted to see me?'

'I did, Mr Ridpath. It's good to see you've finally made it to the office. I've been checking our files and there is the death of a Mr Watkins in a nursing home in Didsbury.'

'That's right, he fell down the stairs. I rang the SIO on the case and she told me they had found nothing suspicious in the death. Here's a copy of the police report.'

He took out the document and passed it across the desk.

It was ignored by Clarence Montague.

'It's not the police file that interests me.' He turned a page. 'In our documents, you were supposed to go to the nursing home to check the location of the fall. Helen Moore tells me this was agreed in a meeting.'

So that was what this was about. 'The meeting was on Saturday. I went there yesterday morning.'

'I can see no indication of a visit or notes in the file,' he sniffed.

'I haven't had time to update the files yet.'

Montague smiled like a cat who'd just bitten the head off a canary. 'Before we can close this case, and notify the family, we need you to complete the applicable forms in duplicate. There is a note asking you check the location of the death but no indication that you have done so.'

'But I—'

Montague held his hand up to stop Ridpath from speaking. 'I'm sure you would agree, it is basic investigative practice. To keep up-to-date case notes.'

Ridpath closed his eyes and breathed out. 'It is, I should have entered my visit into the file by now.'

Another smile.

'There is one more matter I would like to discuss with you.' A long pause and a scratch of the nose. 'As you know, there is a basic standard of dress for a coroner's officer. I have noticed you have fallen short of the standards we require. What may be allowed in Greater Manchester Police is certainly not suitable for the coronial services.'

Ridpath's mouth opened, flapped a few times but no words came out. He looked down at his suit. The elbows were rather threadbare and the lapel slightly frayed. His tie had an unknown stain on it, but the detective in him guessed it was brown sauce from a bacon butty.

'Please attend to it. That will be all, Mr Ridpath.'

Clarence Montague returned to writing his memos. Ridpath got up from the chair and pushed it back under the desk, leaving the office quietly.

Chapter Sixty-six

Ridpath was in a foul mood after updating the Watkins case file with the notes from his visit to the nursing home.

He shouldn't have allowed Montague to treat him so badly. The man was a bully and needed to be stopped before he did any more damage. The next time would be different.

'What a toerag,' he whispered under his breath.

'What did you say?'

'Nothing, Jenny. I was miles away.'

'You looked it. Had a good day?'

He frowned.

'You had a scowl as wide as a cow's arse.'

'Some days you win, some days you lose. This is one of the latter days.' He needed to forget Clarence Montague and focus back on the investigation. They were getting close now. 'But you could make it better by doing me a little favour.'

The office manager's eyes narrowed. 'Which is?'

'I saw the list you sent and I wondered if you had the actual transcripts and notes from the inquests?'

Jenny scratched her head. 'That's exactly what Mrs Challinor wanted. I have them somewhere, unless she took them home.'

'Can you look through your files and email them to me? Tonight if possible?'

As Ridpath spoke, the clock above Jenny's head chimed five p.m. The door to Montague's office opened and the man stepped out, complete with briefcase and rolled umbrella.

He ignored Ridpath.

'I am going back to the hotel, Miss Oldfield. Don't forget our scheduled meeting at nine a.m. tomorrow morning. Will you be ready?'

'Of course, Mr Montague.'

With a curt nod towards Ridpath, he strolled out of the door and down the front steps.

'Looks like I'm going to be working late anyway. Shame, it's the amateur night at the Palais tonight. I always enjoy a bit of paso doble.' She took a deep breath. 'I'll look for your transcripts first, Ridpath, he can wait.'

'Thank you, Jenny. Have you heard from the hospital?'

'Nothing since this morning.'

'I'll call Sarah and find out.'

'Please let me know.' She checked the door where Montague had exited, leant forward and whispered, 'I don't know how long I can stand him. You know he had me redo a complete case report because he doesn't like to see the Oxford comma.'

'I would have thought there were more important things to focus on.'

'So would I. But apparently not. Can I ask you something, Ridpath?'

'Ask away.'

'What's going on? I mean, you suddenly seem so interested in the files Mrs Challinor requested, she has a secret meeting with somebody and then the following evening she is attacked and put in hospital. Something is up.'

Ridpath held his arms out wide, palms facing forward. 'I don't know, Jenny, but I'll tell you one thing, I'm determined to find out. The inquest files may hold the key.'

'Right, I'll get on it straight away. Even if Mrs Challinor took the original files home, the copies should still be in the system, somewhere. I found them once, I can do it again.'

Chapter Sixty-seven

Security is always lax at hospitals.

People come and go all the time. Some for outpatient visits. Others to visit relatives. Still more to see consultants for check-ups or to receive the results of tests.

There was a constant stream of people which meant I could blend in with the crowd and work out my plan.

And the fear of Covid meant I had an ideal opportunity. Everybody was masked, covering half their face, revealing only the eyes. What better way to blend in?

When the traffic was particularly heavy and there was a queue in front of reception, I walked forward, paper in hand as if I were looking for a particular ward.

I followed the red line on the floor to the ICU.

As usual, everybody ignored me. Nurses rushed past, patients being pushed by porters on gurneys or in wheelchairs, doctors hurrying, white coats fluttering in the breeze, late for appointments.

It was a scene which could have been witnessed at any hospital in any country all over the world.

It was only as I approached my destination that the pace slowed down a little. Here there were fewer visitors and more doctors and nurses, some dressed head-to-toe in PPE.

I stopped in front of a door labelled 'ICU'. It suddenly opened and a patient lying on a gurney came out, pushed by a porter. I held the door open for him and he nodded his thanks.

Still gripping my protective paper, I wandered into the ICU unit. There was a long corridor with a bank of windowed wards on the right. Entry to these wards was restricted to the unit's doctors and nurses.

I wandered down the corridor. On benches and chairs, relatives sat, waiting for news about their loved ones. At the third window, I saw the spitting image of the coroner.

Was she already awake and walking around?

It couldn't be. The hospital had told me she was in an induced coma yesterday. She couldn't have recovered so quickly.

Next to her was another woman, younger than the coroner. As I approached, I saw I had been mistaken. The hair was the same, but this woman was older than Margaret Challinor, with features which weren't as fine. A sister perhaps?

As I walked past, I glanced through the window and saw somebody lying in bed, tubes attached to their throat and body, a bandage wrapped around their head.

This was the coroner, I was certain.

'Excuse me, can I help you?'

A nurse in PPE was standing in front of me. The coroner's sister and the other young woman raised their heads.

I showed the nurse the paper I was holding.

'I'm looking for Ward A11, but I seem to be lost. Do you know where it is?' I answered.

Above her mask, I saw her eyes laughing. 'You're miles away, I'm afraid, this is ICU. You need to retrace your steps and look for the green line to take you there. Do you want me to ring the ward?'

'No, that's OK, I'm sure I can find my way. Thanks for your help.'

I retreated out of the ICU past the two women, both staring at me.

Stare as much as you want. I now know where Mrs Challinor is, and I know how to kill her.

It's just a question of time.

Chapter Sixty-eight

Before going home to see Eve, Ridpath rang Sarah Challinor.

'How is your mum?'

'No change, she's still in a coma. She could remain unconscious for five hours, five days or even five months.'

'I'm so sorry to hear it, Sarah. You should go home.'

'Not yet, I will later. There is good news, the doctor says the bleeding on her brain has stopped, the operation was successful, it's just a question of time. Waiting and hoping for the best.'

'Mrs Challinor won't be made better if you fall ill too. You need to go home and get a good night's rest. I'll try to come early tomorrow morning before I go into work.'

'Would you? My children are coming back from their father tomorrow morning. I'd love to spend some time with them.'

'I'll come in before work, but unfortunately I have to be at Police HQ by nine.'

'That's great, Ridpath. I can get there by noon, once I settle the children back home.' She laughed. 'I call them children, but they are really teenagers. They grow up so quickly.'

Ridpath immediately flashed to Eve. He had to make more time for her, somehow. 'Tell me about it,' he replied. 'One moment they are happy little toddlers and the next they're angst-filled teenagers, with only seconds in between.'

She laughed.

'So I'll come tomorrow morning. Could I speak to Alison for a second?'

'The FLO? She's not here. I was told she wasn't coming back. I no longer needed her services apparently and she was wanted elsewhere.'

It wasn't a good sign. It meant Tindall had started to pull resources off the case. He had either already made up his mind or was no longer investigating it as a priority. Ridpath wondered if he could risk a phone call to the DCI. He'd already claimed one favour from Claire Trent today, he couldn't push his luck too far.

'Let me call the officer in charge of the case at Cheshire Police and see what's happening,' he said anyway. Police egos could take a running jump.

'Would you, Ridpath? That would be great, nobody is telling me anything.'

'No worries, I'll do it as soon as I can.'

Chapter Sixty-nine

Ridpath had barely opened the door when Eve came rushing out of the kitchen and smothered him in a big hug.

'I'm sorry I've been such a grinch the last few days.'

He hugged her back, surprised at the strength in his daughter's arms. 'No worries, I just thought you were on your period or something.'

She stopped hugging and looked him straight in the eye. 'Just because I'm in a bad mood, it doesn't mean my period has come. That particular time of the month is a couple of weeks away.'

'No, of course not,' Ridpath spluttered.

She stepped back. Her school shirt was stained on the front with something.

'Listen, Dad, for an otherwise supposedly smart detective, you can be incredibly dumb about women and their moods.'

Ridpath smiled. 'Guilty as charged. Sorry, I won't presume in the future.'

'You'd better not. Actually, Maisie and I have been going through a bad time. We fell out again after we returned from the Lakes. Apparently her mum had been comparing me to Maisie and then I mistakenly on purpose threw the ball at her during netball practice and she didn't like it. You should see the bruise on her arm.'

'Doesn't sound like good behaviour, Eve.'

'She deserved it. Anyway, I apologised profusely this morning and we're good friends again.'

'Till the next time. How often have you two rowed this year?' Ridpath began counting off his fingers. 'There was the economy, and the eco day, and the trip to Dunham Park, and—'

'I get the message, Dad. Anyway, we're friends again now.' She walked back to the kitchen. 'Is there anything to eat, I'm starving?'

'You're always starving.' He looked at his daughter; she was as thin as a stick of liquorish with a head on top. 'I don't know where you put it all.'

'So what's for tea?'

'How about pizza. I could cook a Margarita for both of us.'

'You mean take it out of the freezer, switch on the oven, set the temperature to two hundred degrees and let it cook for twenty minutes. Same as the lasagne sort of cooking?'

'Exactly. I would probably take it out of the box before I put it in the oven though. But that's just my own personal preference.'

'Sounds great, Dad. Can we have some baked beans with it?'

'Baked beans?'

'Yeah, I fancy them. You take them out of the cupboard...'

'I get it, but baked beans and pizza?'

'A Manchester speciality. Gordon Ramsay rates it and Anthony Bourdain raved over the complex flavours. Did you know there's a baked bean museum in South Wales? The Welsh love them, go great with laverbread and bara brith. And guess where the biggest baked bean factory is in the world?'

'Wigan.'

'How did you know?'

'I arrested a rapist who worked there once. Had the guided tour.'

'*The Magical Places Where I Have Arrested People*, a travelogue by Detective Inspector Thomas Ridpath. You should write the book, Dad.'

He put the pizza in the oven – taking it out of the cardboard box first, of course. 'What do you want to drink?'

'Water, I've given up on all the sugary stuff.'

'Good, I always said it was bad for you.'

Ridpath took a bottle of Heineken out of the fridge. He needed a beer, something cold and wet to take away the dryness of the heat parching his throat. He had done a lot of interviewing today.

'You need to change your uniform. I should wash the shirt for you.'

She looked at the stain. 'It's blood from Rachel Green's nose.'

He waited for an explanation that didn't come. Finally he said, 'Well get changed. Do you have a clean uniform for tomorrow?'

'Cleanish. I've only worn the shirt twice.'

Ridpath closed his eyes. When he was buried deep in a case, the basics of everyday life, like laundering school uniforms and his own clothes, escaped him. He would have to catch up on the weekend.

'It's OK to wear?'

'Yeah, everybody else is in the same boat. Parents these days…'

She went out shaking her head.

Ridpath was left alone. He had to get on top of the other stuff soon, he couldn't let the cases dominate his life. Eve and her welfare mattered too.

But he knew it was an empty promise and the phone ringing seconds later merely confirmed it for him.

'Ridpath.'

'Hi there, it's Jenny. I found the transcripts for two of the cases and sent them to you. Sophia is helping me search for the others. We'll send them as soon as we have them.'

'Thanks, Jenny, but don't work too late. I'll read the two you've sent me this evening.'

'No worries, we have to be here for the scheduling pro forma. Montague called me, he wants the format changed again. Apparently there is a new diktat from the chief coroner's office and Montague wants to be the first to use it. Anyway, we'll keep looking.'

'Thanks, Jen—' but the phone was already dead in Ridpath's hand.

He opened his laptop and the message with its attachments was there. He downloaded both of them ready to read after dinner.

Eve walked back into the kitchen, now dressed in the long T-shirt she slept in.

'Pizza ready yet?'

'Just waiting for the cheese to brown and the base to crisp.'

'There's nothing worse than soggy pizza.'

'I'll put the baked beans on.'

'Yay, Carbs-R-Us.'

Ridpath ate as Eve talked non-stop. The words gushed out of her like a waterfall of impressions, experiences and events, all seen through the eyes of a thirteen-year-old girl. He realised for her the world was full of light and colour and the joy of experiencing something new. For him, the world was darker, as if he had seen it all before and it was covered in a grey shroud.

He knew he had to try to be brighter, more bubbly for her. To see the world, in all its possibilities, through her eyes. But the transcripts of two inquests were waiting for him on his laptop. Two events when people had died and a coroner had spent time judging how it had happened.

'Hello, earth to Planet Dad. Come in Planet Dad.'

'Sorry, lost in my thoughts for a second. What were you saying?'

'I was telling you about the chemistry teacher, Mr Reynolds, who is forever picking his nose and staring at the stuff he just mined. It's like he's going to find some rare jewels buried in there.' A slight pause. 'You were thinking about work again, weren't you?'

He was tempted to deny it but instead he just nodded his head.

'You have to relax more, take time off, Dad. There's always going to be work, it never stops.'

She walked to the sink and placed her now clean plate on the drainer.

'There's still some beans left if you want more.'

'No thanks, I'm full,' she said with her back to him before turning round. 'You do need to relax more, Dad, I worry about you.'

'I just have to get through this case, Eve, and then—'

'There'll always be another case, Dad, and another, and another. And then I'll go away to university and get married and have kids and you'll still be working your cases.' The words gushed out of her and she took a deep breath. 'When are you going to make time for me?'

Chapter Seventy

After Eve had gone upstairs to finish her homework, Ridpath was left alone.

Her question had cut him to the core. Did he have time to properly care for his daughter, or would his work always get in the way?

And what about himself? Montague's words came back to haunt him: 'I have noticed you have fallen short of the standards we require.'

Another desk warrior. 'The man wouldn't know an investigation if it bit him on the arse,' he said out loud. But he should have already updated the file after the visit to the nursing home, or asked Sophia to do it. He couldn't find enough hours in the day to do everything that needed to be done.

And now there was Eve. She was growing so quickly and he had so little time left with her. Soon she would be doing her GCSEs and saying sayonara to home and he would be left alone, rattling around the house, waiting for her phone calls and her rare returns from university.

One thing he did know. He was a good copper and an even better detective. It was a job he loved and one he cared about. It was unfashionable these days to talk about protecting the public, but it was how he saw his role; to look after those who couldn't look after themselves.

'Enough,' he said out loud to the empty living room. He wasn't going to solve this today, but what he could work on was the case. The others were probably still at the office. The least he could do was pull his weight.

He opened his laptop and found the email from Jenny.

I've found two of the inquest transcripts. I know the coroner definitely read both of these because she wrote a note on both of them to follow up with C, L and D. Whoever they are? I'll look for the other ones and try to get them to you asap. I've scanned the originals and attached them.

Regards,

Jenny

He forwarded it to Emily and Chrissy for them to read and then opened the attachment for the first inquest. Reading the coroner's summary to the jury, it was obvious Tony Snellgrove had been murdered by person or persons unknown. He had been injected with a solution of almost pure medical-grade morphine, his wrists tied to a steering wheel and a pipe leading from his exhaust into the cockpit of the car. The coroner, a Mr Willoughby, had discussed the possibility that Snellgrove had bound his own hands to prevent himself escaping. But he had concluded it was impossible given the police and pathologist's evidence. The man had definitely been murdered by persons unknown and he instructed the jury to come to that conclusion.

It was when Ridpath read the witness testimony that he started to put it all together. The senior investigating officer had traced Snellgrove's movements on the day he was killed. Apparently, he had taken a train to Manchester early in the day, returning the same evening. The officer had not found out where he had gone, nor could he trace his movements.

Ridpath wrote a note for himself.

Where did Snellgrove go in Manchester?

Did they check CCTV?

Were GMP or Cheshire Police involved?

Investigation notes????

Contact Tindall?

His wife had reported that he seemed unsettled and unhappy when he arrived home. She had gone to bed, while he had gone out for a late night walk.

Meeting someone?

She woke at three in the morning and, finding the bed empty, had gone downstairs. In the kitchen, she could hear a car engine and wandered into the garage to find her husband. The estimated time of death was one a.m.

But other than the absence of a killer there was little to tie the death of Snellgrove to the bodies found in the warehouse. Why had Mrs Challinor requested the transcript of this particular inquest? What had she seen that he was missing?

He put his pad down and rubbed his eyes. Constantly staring at the computer screen made him tired. It had been a long day. He thought about going to bed and getting up early the following morning to finish the other inquest report, but remembered he had promised to visit Mrs Challinor. A promise he couldn't and wouldn't go back on.

He clicked the second inquest file; the death of the young couple and their six-month old baby in Blackburn. Once again, he began with the coroner's summary. The bodies had been found one morning by a next-door neighbour, all sitting around the kitchen table, the baby in his high chair. Toxicology reported a massive level of cyanide in the milk in the baby's bottle and in the jug on the table. Enough to kill everyone three times over. Traces of diazepam were found in the couple's bodies too, along with injection marks on their arms, but no hypodermics were found in the house.

Lancashire Police had investigated, finding the couple had no links to organised crime, no debts, no history of mental illness in anybody in the family. On the contrary, they seemed to be a happily married young couple, enjoying the birth of their young son and relishing the role of being parents. Was it suicide, an accident or murder? The coroner's jury finally opted for unlawful killing by a person or persons unknown based on the evidence and the forensic discoveries.

Ridpath wrote a note.

> **Three inquests, all with the same verdict and one still not concluded.**
>
> **No links between any of those who died.**
>
> **Different socio-economic status.**

He checked the two summations on the two inquests again plus the notes from the Romeo and Juliet case. There were only a couple of links he could see and he wrote them down.

> **Three different drugs but all medical grade.**
>
> **No suspects.**

Was the first one the link?

Was that what Mrs Challinor had seen?

But it was too flimsy, drugs could be obtained from anywhere and there were countless cases of pharmaceutical quality drugs being used in suicides and murders. What made these cases different?

He yawned and stretched his arms above his head. It was time for bed; the transcript of the Blackburn case would have to wait till tomorrow. Perhaps he could read it quickly before he went to see Mrs Challinor.

Then his phone rang.

'Ridpath,' he said lazily.

'Have you seen it yet?' It was Emily, and she sounded excited.

'Seen what?'

'The transcript of the Blackburn case.'

'I'm just about to read it.' Ridpath crossed his fingers as he told his little white lie.

'Guess who was the doctor treating Mrs Singh?'

Ridpath was too tired to play guessing games. 'I give in, who?'

'Stephen Orwell.'

'What?'

'He was her gynaecologist before and after the birth. She was a patient at his clinic.'

Ridpath forced his mind to focus. Was this the link between the deaths?

'Which page, Emily?'

'It's page thirty-seven of the transcript.'

Ridpath quickly scrolled to the page.

'The inquest heard testimony she visited him a couple of days before her death. She was apparently worried about something and Valium was prescribed, even though she was still breast-feeding. We have a link, Ridpath.'

'Great work, Emily. How's the rest working out?'

'Not so good. The American hospitals are refusing to release any details of Orwell's work or time with them, citing doctor-patient confidentiality.'

'Christ, we don't want any medical records, just the dates he was working.'

'Still, it's a problem.'

'No worries, I'll sort it out tomorrow. How are Chrissy and Jayne?'

'Chrissy is looking for the police reports on the cases in Black-burn and Chester, they should be here tomorrow. Jayne is still deep in the American archives looking for Female A, but with no success so far.'

'Right. Now listen to me, you've done great work so far but we're all tired. Speaking for myself, I'm exhausted.'

'But we have a deadline...'

'Hitting a deadline is pointless if we have nothing to show. I would rather we all turned up at nine a.m. tomorrow morning, fresh as the proverbial sunflower.'

'It's a daisy...'

'What is?'

'The idiom, fresh as a daisy.'

'Whatever. I am now ordering you to go home and I am ordering myself to go to bed.'

'But Ridpath—'

'Is that clear? All of you GO. HOME. NOW.'

'OK, we're out of here.'

'We regroup at nine a.m. tomorrow. I have a feeling a good night's sleep will help us find new threads we've missed.'

'Chrissy and Jayne are packing up.'

'As are you, Emily.'

'Me too, see you tomorrow.'

Ridpath put the phone down. He had ordered them to go home and sleep but he knew the night was still young for him, and he now had to read the transcripts for the Blackburn inquest tonight.

And then he suddenly understood Mrs Challinor's note about following up with C, L and D. It was so obvious.

Cheshire.

Lancashire.

Derbyshire.

He should have worked it out much earlier. Was he too tired, missing the obvious?

Wednesday, June 23

Chapter Seventy-one

The next morning, Eve was back to her normal zombie-like self. Dishevelled hair, school uniform thrown on, garbled noises coming from her mouth as she ate breakfast.

'I hate school' was the one coherent sentence she managed to squeeze out between mouthfuls of Coco Pops, followed by, 'Why am I awake so early?'

'I have to visit Mrs Challinor in hospital. She's still in a coma.' She perked up at the mention of the coroner's name.

'Are you OK going to school early?'

'No probs. I can sit in the homework club.'

'I thought you finished it last night.'

'I did, but there's the extra challenges in maths. I usually ignore them but Mr Abernathy will be chuffed if I do a few.'

'Is Mr Abernathy the one with the toupee?'

'No, that's Mr Wright. Abernathy has a limp.'

'Do all your teachers have something wrong with them?'

She looked up from her Coco Pops, a single pop hanging disconsolately from the side of her mouth.

'Yeah.'

He reached over and brushed the Coco Pop away. 'Hurry and brush your teeth, we're leaving in five.'

'Minutes?'

'No, seconds. Get a move on.'

Ten minutes later they were out of the door and he was about to start the car when Eve remembered she had forgotten her school iPad. A dash into the house, hunting for it high and low, before finally finding it charging in the kitchen.

Meanwhile, Ridpath was tapping his fingers on the steering wheel, counting slowly to ten and imagining he was in his safe place high on the hills in the Peak District.

Finally, she jumped in the car. 'What are you waiting for? Let's go. You can drop me at the tram station. I'll take one to school.'

'You're sure?'

'No probs. Look, by the time you've driven all the way to school then to the hospital, you'll be far too late. Have you done your Covid test?'

'Yeah, while you were getting ready. Still negative.'

She pointed with her head.

'What?'

'Drive, Tonto. You need to put it in gear if we're going to move.'

'Yes, Kemo Sabe. Your wish is my command.'

'I'll remember those words.'

He dropped her off at the tram station and she leapt out of the car without looking back. For some reason, his heart fell seeing her walking away. He wished she would look back just once. But teenagers never looked back, it wasn't in their nature. The whole point of being a teenager was to look forward.

He shrugged his shoulders, put Bowie on the stereo to keep himself happy and drove to the hospital.

After completing all the Covid formalities, he found himself stood behind the glass wearing a green PPE apron and gloves, staring at Mrs Challinor lying in her bed.

She hadn't moved since the last time he was there, stuck in exactly the same place with tubes leading from her mouth to a machine keeping her alive. Her face looked paler than before, as if all the energy and life had been leeched out of it and passed to the machine beside her bed.

'She's doing very well.'

Ridpath turned and Mr Pereira was standing next to him, dressed in scrubs with a hairnet over his head and protective covers on his feet.

'It doesn't look like it.'

'I think the worst is over. Now it's just a matter of time as the brain heals itself. An induced coma allows it to do exactly that.'

Ridpath glanced back at the coroner. 'She looks so… vulnerable.'

'Not the person you knew?'

Ridpath shook his head.

'She was lucky. The blows were not as strong as we feared, but it's still going be a long road to recovery.'

'How long?'

'Nobody knows. A brain injury can affect different functions. Speech, motor abilities, memory. We won't know until she comes round.' The doctor moved his gaze from Mrs Challinor. 'It's Inspector Ridpath, isn't it?'

'That's right, I work for the coroner.'

They didn't shake hands.

'I met your colleague, Chief Inspector Tindall. He seemed quite convinced Mrs Challinor was the victim of an attempted rape. We examined her and found no evidence of any sexual molestation. Of course the rapist may have been disturbed before he…' His voice trailed off. 'Not a pleasant man, your colleague. A bit of a bull in a china shop.'

'He's not my colleague.'

The doctor raised an eyebrow.

'Two different forces, GMP and Cheshire Police.' Just then, Ridpath remembered something. 'Thank you for giving him the clothes she was wearing.'

'I think my colleague passed the bag to him, but I'll pass on your thanks.'

Ridpath made a mental note to ask Tindall about the clothes and the DNA result. The FLO had already told him but it wouldn't hurt to get the official line from the horse's mouth. He wasn't supposed to have any contact, but sod that. This was about the coroner and her family, fragile police egos could take a back seat.

'Anyway, I need to continue my rounds. You will be here later?'

'Probably not, but her daughter and sister will come in.'

'Good, it's important to have someone here. Even in a coma, patients can be aware of their surroundings. That's why we constantly speak to our patients even though we cannot be certain they can hear us.'

'It's like suspended animation, isn't it?'

'I prefer to think of a coma as a pause button to allow the brain to heal itself. One day, she can start to move forward again.'

'Hopefully that will be soon.'

'When the day comes, we may have to move her to our specialist neuropathy unit at Salford Royal, where she can begin to rebuild her life.'

The consultant glanced at the clock. 'I must be off – goodbye, Inspector Ridpath,' and he hurried away as silently as he'd arrived. Just then, Ridpath remembered a question he had forgotten to ask.

'Mr Pereira, have you ever heard of a Dr Orwell?'

The consultant stopped. 'Orwell? Do you mean Stephen Orwell?'

Ridpath nodded.

'I went to a few of his lectures as an undergrad, a brilliant man in his field. Did some amazing research in America when he was there, Boston, I believe. He wouldn't have received funding in the UK.'

'His field? What exactly did he specialise in?'

'Assisted reproductive technology. He practically wrote the textbook on the subject. But I believe he's semi-retired now. Do you know him? Pass along my regards if you do, a brilliant man.' Another glance at the clock. 'I must be going. Bye once again, Inspector.'

Ridpath was left alone with only the rhythmic sound of Mrs Challinor's ventilator for company.

He stared at her right hand lying limply by her side, soft and white, the long nails with spots of varnish rubbed away.

Had she found a connection to Stephen Orwell they had missed?

Chapter Seventy-two

When Ridpath arrived late to the meeting in Police HQ, the rest of the team were already there. All of them working hard, staring at their laptops or writing notes.

Instantly, a wave of guilt flowed through his body. He stared at the investigation board. At the centre, a large photo of Stephen Orwell had been placed.

This man was now their main suspect.

'Morning, Ridpath,' said Chrissy looking over the top of her laptop. 'The boss wants a meeting with you at ten thirty.'

'She was in here this morning?'

'About ten minutes ago. I said you were on your way in.'

'Thanks, Chrissy. Right, everyone, let's go through an update on the case.' Everybody except Jayne looked up. She continued to tap away on her computer. 'I'll go first. I went through the inquest transcripts last night for two of the three cases which appeared on both Mrs Challinor's list and in the search on HOLMES conducted by Chrissy.'

He walked to the whiteboards and underlined two of the cases in red.

2015 – BLACKBURN – COUPLE AND CHILD – THE SINGHS, 22, 23, 6 MONTHS OLD – CYANIDE POISONING.

2017 – DERBYSHIRE – JOAN BLACKLEDGE, 32 – INSULIN SWITCHED.

'I'm still waiting for the transcript from the third inquest. Jenny should get it to us today. Have you requested the case notes from the Lancashire, Cheshire and Derbyshire police, Chrissy?'

'They are coming today with a bit of luck, Ridpath.'

'With a bit of luck?'

'Same archival problems, as we have.'

Ridpath scratched his head. 'We need to read them as soon as they arrive, I'm sure the information we need is buried in there. Hassle them as much as you have to, Chrissy. We need them yesterday.'

'Will do, Ridpath.'

'There is one link to Stephen Orwell. He was the doctor who treated Mrs Singh during her pregnancy. In fact, he saw her two days before her death.'

He stepped away from the board and stared at it.

'So Orwell is connected to two of the four cases. His illegitimate son, Ralph Orwell, died in Manchester, and the Singh's in Blackburn. That reminds me, Emily, when is he coming in for DNA testing?'

'Ten thirty.'

'Good. When will we get the results back from the lab?'

'They've promised to rush the comparison. End of day today.'

'Even better.' He walked to the boards again. 'We need to solve these questions.' He wrote in the scrawl that passed for his handwriting:

Can we link Stephen Orwell to the other cases?

Was he in the country at the time?

Are there any witness reports placing him at or near the scenes of these deaths?

Emily stuck up her hand. 'You've forgotten the most important question, Ridpath.'

'No, I haven't.' He went back to the board and wrote in large, capital letters.

WHY???

'That's the biggie, isn't it?'

'And what worries me is, after five days, we're no closer to finding an answer.'

Chapter Seventy-three

Sarah Challinor stood in front of the window looking into her mother's ICU ward. A nurse was adjusting the endotracheal tube which snaked from the ventilator into her mother's mouth and down into the lungs.

On her left arm, a blood pressure cuff and an oxygen saturation monitor fed information to two constantly blinking screens next to the bed. The nurse checked her heart rate and rhythm, blood pressure, body temperature, breathing rate, oxygen saturation and intra-cranial pressure.

Next to her mum's neck a catheter in the vein provided liquids and drugs from a syringe pump while down at the bottom of the bed another catheter drained her pee.

All this had been explained to her by Mr Pereira this morning as he finished his rounds. She had pressed the intercom on the wall below the glass and asked him directly, 'How long is Mum going to be like this?'

He had shrugged his shoulders. 'To be honest, we don't know.'

She could hear his voice clearly through the tiny speaker.

'Comas can last six hours or six days, but they rarely last longer than a month. You must remember your mother has had a severe brain trauma. On the Glasgow Coma Scale, I have assigned her a rating of six which is an indication of how badly she was injured. As you can see now, she is not verbally responsive, has no ability to follow commands and her eyes are closed. It will take a while for her to recover. We just have to be patient. It's something all neurologists have in common. We are incredibly patient.'

'It's been five days now.'

'The good news is the intra-cranial bleeding has stopped and your mother is remarkably fit and healthy for a woman her age. Like I said, it's just a matter of time.'

'And when she does wake up, how will she be? Will she be the same?'

'Again, we don't know. In such injuries there can be severe after-effects, particularly in terms of language, memory and behaviour. We will conduct a full assessment when she regains consciousness, creating a personal rehab plan for your mother.' He glanced at his watch. 'I'm sorry, but I have to continue my rounds. I'll be back this afternoon to check on her again.'

Sarah was joined at the window by her Aunt Sue.

'I'm going for coffee, do you want one?'

Sarah shook her head.

'Why don't you go home and spend some time with the kids. Come back tomorrow. I'll stay here and watch Margaret for the rest of the day. I'll call you if there is any change.'

Sarah glanced back at her mother. The monitors were still blinking, the ventilator still humming and her mother was still lying there motionless.

She nodded.

There was nothing more she could do here. It was just a matter of time.

Chapter Seventy-four

They all stared at Ridpath's question on the whiteboard.

WHY???

They realised they didn't have a clue why all these people had been killed.

'Let's park the question for the moment. Chrissy, what did you find? Do we have confirmed dates for his time in the US?'

The civilian researcher cleared her throat and took off her City scarf, laying it beside her laptop. 'The hospitals in Boston and LA are still refusing to release the details of Orwell's working years unless we provide them with a signed warrant from a judge. Even then, in my opinion, they will continue to play silly buggers.'

'Did you explain this was a murder investigation and we are trying to confirm an alibi?'

'Done all that. They are citing confidentiality and not budging.'

'Do we know anybody with the Boston Police Department or LAPD?'

Everybody shook their heads.

'I've checked at the International Crime Coordination Centre. Apparently, we have to go through our international liaison officer.'

'Who's that?'

Emily checked her notes. 'A Detective Inspector Jonathan Blake.'

'Great, get on it.'

'He's on holiday and won't be back until the middle of August.'

'Typical. There must be somebody covering for him?'

'There is, but it's just the first hurdle.'

Ridpath sighed.

'We have to send an international letter of request to ask for mutual legal assistance.'

Ridpath sighed again. 'Go on.'

'These letters are drafted and issued by a court or designated prosecutor. For us, it's the Crown Prosecution Service. The letters must outline the case, specify the information requested and, I quote,' she made a brackets sign with her fingers, '"any legislation that should be adhered to in order to ensure the evidence is gathered in a way admissible in the requesting state's criminal proceedings." End quote.'

'That could take months.'

'Possibly years, if the hospitals still refuse to release the information and we have to initiate court proceedings in America.'

'We don't have the time.'

'I realised, Ridpath, so I thought of a simpler way.'

'Go on...'

'I checked the Whitepages in the USA, paying 9.99 for a full report which gave me an address for Stephen Orwell in LA for 2011.'

'Great, you're sure this was the right Stephen Orwell?'

'Yeah, it lists the people living with him as Alexandra and Michael Orwell. But to be sure I went onto another website called True People Search. This not only gave me the LA address but has a feature to check past addresses. Up popped an address in Boston, occupied from 1990 to 1997.'

'So we know he was definitely living in the US for the dates he claims. 1990 to 1997 and 2005 to 2012.'

'I could keep searching on ZabaSearch and Infobel. If they owned the house in Boston or LA, their records would be available on the local tax assessor website.'

Emily started typing on her laptop. She stopped and smiled. 'Or we could just Google him. In 0.1374 seconds, it's found over a thousand hits.' She turned her laptop around so everybody could see. 'Here he is in 1994 receiving an award in New York for his medical work on the role of inhibin B, follicle stimulating hormone and luteinizing hormone prediction in patients with non-obstructive azoospermia, whatever that is. It seems his specialty is reproductive endocrinology. Apparently that's IVF, test tube babies, that sort of stuff.'

'Great work, now we're moving.'

Jayne Sinclair raised her head from her laptop for a second. 'There is a slight problem, Ridpath. Two slight problems, actually. None of this is evidentiary, it won't stand up in a court of law. And secondly, it does show he wasn't in the UK for the period when our victims in the warehouse died in 2008.'

'He may have been on holiday,' said Chrissy. 'I can check with the passenger name record.'

'What?'

'Since the 1971 Immigration Act, airlines have had to send their passenger records for every flight to the Home Office. In serious cases, I can access them but I don't know if they still keep the early records.'

'And America? Do they keep the same records?'

'Yeah, the system tightened up after 9/11. They are heading towards a total information awareness system combining passenger names, translation of texts, facial analysis, computer data and algorithm pattern programmes to try to spot terrorists in the system.'

'Sounds scary,' said Emily.

'Bingo,' shouted Jayne. 'Got you!'

Everybody stared at her.

She looked up, a broad smile on her face. 'I think I've found Female A through her grandma. The age and profile fit. Even better, her mother is still alive.'

'Who is she?'

'Her name was Skylar Robinson, born in Mystic, Connecticut in 1991.'

'Connecticut? Isn't that close to Boston?'

'Only a hundred or so miles away. The mother was an Audrey Robinson, no father listed.'

'Are you sure, Jayne?' asked Ridpath.

'Pretty sure. I'll need to go over the family trees to check one more time, but she is the only female in that part of the family, all the rest were males.'

'Good work, Jayne.'

'If you have an address or even a town, I could try to find a telephone number for Audrey Robinson.'

As Jayne relayed the information, Chrissy typed away on her laptop.

'Here she is. Still living in the same small town on her own, it would seem, from the Whitepages.'

'Can we set up a call, Ridpath? If we could tie her to Stephen Orwell, we may be getting close.'

Ridpath glanced at the clock. 'Let me clear it with the boss. I don't want to start treading on international toes…'

'You've trodden on enough in Manchester.'

Ridpath ignored Emily as the others laughed.

'…and besides, they are six hours behind us so it would be four twenty-five in the morning over there.'

'While I'm with Claire Trent, can you handle Stephen Orwell, Emily? Not a word to him about what we're doing. Just take him to another room to do his DNA test.'

'I've asked a police nurse to help me. She'll handle the chain of evidence.'

'Great. Chrissy, follow up on the case notes from Derbyshire and Cheshire. We need to see if Orwell was involved in any way, shape or form with the other cases.'

'On it.'

'Jayne, thank you for all your help…'

'I'm not leaving now, Ridpath, I'll check my work and help Chrissy when she needs it.'

Ridpath knew there was no point arguing. He glanced again at the clock. Ten twenty-eight. It was time to face Claire Trent.

Had they done enough to convince her Stephen Orwell was a person of interest, and perhaps even a suspect? Would they be able to pull him in for questioning?

He stared at the boards.

Was it enough?

He just didn't know.

Chapter Seventy-five

At exactly ten thirty, Claire Trent and Steve Carruthers came into the room, took one look at the boards and sat down.

'This had better be good, Ridpath, I have a meeting with the chief constable this afternoon and I want to give him some good news. It's been a ton of shit so far.' She looked around the room, spotting Jayne Sinclair and Chrissy. 'Where's DS Parkinson?'

'She's busy,' said Ridpath without revealing why.

'And you must be the genealogist?' She reached over to shake Jayne's hand. 'You worked for GMP before?'

'I was a DS in Moss Side but then retired.'

Claire Trent sighed. 'It's one of those days when I'd like to retire too. But perhaps Ridpath can make it slightly better. What are you waiting for? Get on with it.'

He took three deep breaths. 'This is our prime suspect so far.' He pointed to the large picture at the centre of the boards on the wall. 'Stephen Orwell. A medical doctor who had an affair in 1989 with Moira Travis, the mother of the male victim in this case, Ralph Orwell.' He tapped the crime scene picture of the body in the warehouse. 'Stephen Orwell is Male B's father.'

'Have we confirmed it?' asked Carruthers.

'We will know for certain by the end of today. Emily is just arranging a DNA test for him.'

'He has come in voluntarily?'

'He has, boss.'

'That shows a stunning self-confidence, or a belief he's not involved. Take us through the rest of this.'

'We interviewed Moira Travis and she admitted Orwell was the father of her son. Apparently, the young man went missing in 2008 aged just eighteen.'

'Did she submit a missing person's report?'

'Yes, boss, but as he was eighteen, there was little police follow-up at the time.' He looked at Chrissy, who passed a printout to Claire Trent.

'We have the original missing person report. His mother always thought her son had just run away and would come back.'

'Even fourteen years later?'

'She still held out hope. We will test her DNA to see if she is actually the mother.'

'Again, make sure it's voluntarily given.'

'Will do, Steve.' Ridpath tapped the photofit picture of the young woman. 'We also discovered Female A's identity through Jayne's genetic genealogy work. She is an American, Skylar Robinson, born in 1991 in Connecticut. Orwell was living in the States at the time. Again, we will do a comparison test with his DNA to confirm whether he was her father this afternoon.'

'So you have the identities of both our victims in the Romeo and Juliet case and a possible suspect. What are the other boards for?'

'Chrissy used HOLMES and searched for similar MOs, where the victim died but the killer wasn't present at the death, with an added filter of the use of drugs. This revealed five other suspicious deaths in the period from 2008 to 2019.'

'You saying the Romeo and Juliet deaths weren't a one-off? The same person may have killed other people?'

'We think so, boss.'

Clare Trent glanced across at Carruthers.

'It appears Mrs Challinor was also looking into these cases. She requested the inquest notes on these deaths.'

'Margaret Challinor? Why do you think she was looking at these cases?'

'I think she came to the same conclusion we did, boss.'

'And what was that?'

'A serial killer was operating unknown to everybody.'

Another glance at Carruthers. 'Another possible Shipman?'

Ridpath nodded.

'And you didn't know anything about these investigations by the coroner?'

'Nothing, boss. She mentioned to me she was looking into something but I didn't realise how big it was.'

'Right, carry on.'

'We've looked at the inquest transcripts for four of these deaths so far; the couple in Blackburn, a Mr and Mrs Singh and their six-month-old child, and a man in Chester, a Mr Tony Snellgrove.'

'Both places out of our jurisdiction.'

'Correct, boss.'

'Have you checked the investigation files from the relevant forces?' asked Carruthers.

'We've sent for them and they should come in today,' said Chrissy.

'Have you found any links between these cases and Orwell?'

'Just one so far. From the evidence at the Blackburn inquest, he was Mrs Singh's gynaecologist. We haven't found a link to the Chester or Derbyshire cases yet.'

'So you've found a link to Stephen Orwell, however perfunctory, in our case and Blackburn but not the others?'

Ridpath didn't like the tone of the question. 'We haven't finished searching yet, we'll know more later today.'

'Are there any forensic links between Orwell and the Romeo and Juliet victims?'

'Other than he was the father of one of them, nothing so far, boss. But if you remember, the CSIs found no forensic evidence at the scene other than the DNA and fingerprints of the two victims.'

'Was there any forensic evidence linking Orwell to the scene of the other deaths in Blackburn and Chester?'

'Not that we have found yet. We'll know more—'

'—later today. We've heard that before, Ridpath.' Claire Trent stared at the boards. 'So you have a suspect, but no evidence linking him to the crime scenes.'

'There's more, boss. Stephen Orwell claims he was out of the country, in the USA, when the Romeo and Juliet murders were committed in 2008. He claims he was working in America from 1990 to 1997 and 2005 to 2012.'

'Have you checked the alibi?'

'The hospitals have refused to give us his employment records, but using other means, we confirmed he was in the States during this time period.'

Clare Trent thought for a long time.

'It's good work, people, but it's not good enough, all too circumstantial. There is no evidence linking Stephen Orwell with any of these deaths, and particularly not with the Romeo and Juliet case. What do you think, Steve?'

'Ridpath and his team have come a long way in a short time, Claire. I would give them the rest of today to push on. For me, if his DNA links him to one of the victims, Male B, then we have a case for pulling him in and questioning him. Perhaps, under pressure, he might cough to something.'

She stood. 'It's not strong enough, Steve, a decent solicitor would blow holes in this in three seconds, still leaving time to brush their hair. Pulling him in without more concrete evidence would be a mistake. We've come a long way, but not far enough. I'm going to brief the chief constable this afternoon we haven't cracked the case yet.'

She went to leave.

'Boss, can we carry on working for the rest of the day? We might come up with something new. Find the link to Stephen Orwell...'

'You think so, Ridpath? You're going to pull something out of the bag? I've had the temporary coroner, what's his name...'

'Clarence Montague.'

'That's it. Sounds a patronising bastard. Anyway, he's been on the phone today, complaining you are not doing your job as coroner's officer.'

'That's untrue, boss, despite all the work here, my department at the coroner is running as smoothly as ever.'

'Well, he's threatening to replace you with a new officer. Silly southern chough doesn't realise I pay for everything. We're so short-staffed here I would be quite happy to pull you back to MIT. Let him find the dosh to fund another officer from the local council. They have more problems with funding than we have. Anyway, the last thing I need is some southern nonce up my bum, moaning like a banshee.'

'I'll sort it out, boss. I may need your help.'

'You'd better, Ridpath. And call me if you need anything. I've got better things to do with my time than dealing with some sweaty southerner.'

With those last words, she strode out.

Steve Carruthers was left behind. 'It's good work, but the boss is right. As it is at the moment, nothing will be conclusive in a court of law. You've got a few links, but no hard evidence.'

'You agree questioning Orwell is the right way to go?'

'Of course – if he is the father of Male B, we have reason to question him. But he will probably have a brief with him and unless there is concrete evidence linking him to the scene of the crime, I doubt you will break him.'

Ridpath nodded.

'Find the evidence.'

And with that, he too strode out, leaving the team staring at the closed door.

Chapter Seventy-six

After Carruthers left, everybody was silent for a long time. Eventually, Jayne spoke. 'Now I remember why I left GMP.'

As she finished speaking, Emily bustled back into the room. 'How did it go? I just saw Carruthers in Claire Trent's office. They seemed to be having a bit of a barney.'

'We were good, but not good enough.'

'Jeez, what did they expect? We've only been working on this for five days and we've made far more progress than Meredith and his army of minions and agency workers did in six months.'

'Still not good enough, apparently.' Chrissy rested her head on her folded arms on the table.

'Look, it's not the end, it just means we have to do more work, more digging. Chrissy, get on to Lancashire, Cheshire and Derbyshire, get those investigation notes for us, asap. I don't care what you use, bribes, threats, charm or insults, but get them today.'

'I'm on it,' said Chrissy, picking up her mobile phone.

'Emily, I want you to go through the inquest transcripts again. See if we missed something, anything, linking Orwell to any of the cases. And talking about Orwell, how was he?'

'Fine, we swabbed his mouth and he was as cooperative as a puppy having his stomach scratched. Even made us do an extra swab in case the lab screwed up his first test. "Labs make mistakes, you know." Either he's innocent or he's the cockiest sod I've ever met.'

'Push the lab to come back with the results this evening. We need confirm that he was Ralph Orwell's father. Plus, make sure they test his DNA against that of Female A...'

'Skylar Robinson.'

'Check if he is her father, too.'

'I'll be on their case, Ridpath.'

'Finally, Jayne, I know this isn't part of your role, but could you read Meredith's case notes? We may have missed something important.'

'What are you going to do, Ridpath?'

'I'm going to take a drive. Go to see somebody I've avoided, but now it needs to be done. If the coroner was investigating the same connections as we are, then the attack on her becomes a little bit too coincidental for my liking.'

Just then, Carruthers knocked on the door and stepped into the room.

'Do you want the good news or the bad news?'

'Good news first, always,' said Chrissy.

'I've persuaded Claire to allow you to bring in Orwell for questioning. If, and it's a big if, he tests positive as the father of Male B.'

Ridpath punched the air.

'Don't be too excited. If he's as smart as you think he is, he's going to have solicitors coming out of his wee arse, and without evidence, you are unlikely to get him to admit anything.' He scratched the end of his long nose. 'This is what we are going to do. Spend the rest of the day finding any links between Orwell and the victims. We need to put him at the crime scenes. If he is the father of Male B, you can pull him in for questioning tomorrow. Nothing too heavy, mind, we don't want him squealing to his MP or the papers. But you need more evidence. It's all too thin at the moment. Well done so far, we just need more.'

'You said there was bad news,' Chrissy spoke again.

'This is the last throw of the dice. If nothing comes from today's work or tomorrow's interview, Clare is pulling the plug. At the moment, it's not strong enough to bring in the chief constable and the Inspector of Police is due on Monday. We can't keep throwing resources at an investigation which has been going for six months with no suspects and no evidence.'

'Even if is there is the possibility a serial killer has been operating for the last fourteen years and we knew nothing about them?'

'We won't close the case, it will still be investigated. We simply won't throw so many resources at it.'

'Two detectives, a civilian researcher and a freelance genealogist is a lot of resources?' asked Jayne Sinclair.

'You mustn't forget there has been six months of painstaking detective work and over a million quid thrown at this case. There has to be a time when we say enough is enough.'

'Tell that to the two victims; Ralph Orwell and Skylar Robinson.'

Carruthers stared at Jayne Sinclair. 'It's the nature of modern policing. You have one more day to get some traction, and more importantly, evidence, against Stephen Orwell. That's it. Remember, it's tenacity which gives us success. Look for the detail, it's always the detail which catches them out.'

He walked towards the door, stopped and turned round. 'Great work, by the way. I don't think I've said this before, but when we started, I couldn't imagine coming this far so quickly. Good luck.'

The door closed quietly behind the DCI.

'We'd better get working,' said Ridpath quietly.

Chapter Seventy-seven

Even as he drove down the A523, Ridpath knew this was a long shot. Even worse, if it got back to Claire Trent, he might be under attack from both her and Clarence Montague.

But it had to be done. He had called DI Tindall before he left HQ.

'Look, I think we started off on the wrong foot. I'm concerned about the coroner and her family and I'd like to meet. I also think there's a link to a case I'm working on.'

After much umming and ahhing, Tindall had agreed to meet him at Macclesfield Police Station. The hot, sticky red brick of Manchester soon gave way to the more leafy lanes of Cheshire, cooler beneath the canopy of trees lining the route.

The station was located in the old part of Macclesfield town close to rows of elegant Georgian townhouses and the public library. But of course the station itself was one of those ugly, half-metal, half-brick structures created by architects whose brief was to make something as cheap, shoddy and as much of an eyesore as possible.

Ridpath parked behind the station and was soon shown to Tindall's small, temporary office on the second floor overlooking the car park.

'How's the head?'

Ridpath touched the back of his skull, realising he hadn't even thought about the attack, or felt its effects, for the last couple of days.

'Fine, I think I have a thick skull.'

'So I've heard.' He pointed to a small chair in front of his desk. 'How can I help you?'

Ridpath sensed a certain wariness from Tindall, like a poker player holding a royal flush who doesn't want to reveal his hand.

'It's more how I can help you.'

'Really? I heard you were at the hospital this morning.'

How did he know?

As if reading his thoughts, Tindall went on to answer his question. 'The FLO, Alison, went to the hospital at ten a.m. and had a chat with the doctors. She also met Mrs Challinor's daughter, Sarah, and the aunt, Susan.'

'I thought you'd pulled her off the case?'

'We have, full-time, but she still needs to liaise with the family while we are investigating.'

'Short-staffed?'

'Tell me about it.'

Ridpath decided to plunge in. 'So you haven't come to any conclusions about the attack yet?'

Tindall stared at him for a long time, before finally answering. 'We thought for a long time it was an attempted rape. But we went through all the local men on the pervs register and nobody came up. We even contacted your sexual attack team in Manchester and still nothing. The more I worked on it, the less it seemed like a sexual assault and the more it felt like attempted murder.'

'The hammer and the absence of any tearing of the clothes or attempted sexual contact?'

'Exactly, it bore none of the usual features.'

'You had the hammer examined?'

'Bog standard. B&Q sells them by the barrow load. By the way, thanks for asking the hospital to bag her hands and her clothes. Useless for evidentiary purposes, too many people had touched them and there was no chain of evidence, but helpful nonetheless.'

'How?'

'We pulled some epithelials from under her nails. She probably scratched her assailant during the attack.'

'But?'

'No hits on NDNAD. Either her assailant has no history of violence, has never been arrested or never been caught.'

Why was Tindall being so open? Only a couple of days ago he had told Ridpath to piss off in not so many words.

'So you've got nothing?'

Tindall nodded his head. 'There seems to be no reason for the attack, there are no suspects and the only witness, the farmer, has given a description of a tall person, wearing a black mask and hoodie.'

Ridpath finally understood the change in attitude. 'That's it?'

'We've got nothing. And because the attack was on one of Her Majesty's coroners, I am under pressure to get it sorted... sharpish.'

He held his hands out wide.

'One more thing. I checked with my mates at GMP – apparently Paul Turnbull did try to fit you up. I don't know what went wrong with him, he was a good copper when we worked together.'

'I don't know either. I think my personality rubbed him up the wrong way.'

'You don't say? I can't imagine how that would happen, can you?'

They both smiled at the tone.

'Anyway, back to our case. Why would someone assault a woman on her own in broad daylight of it wasn't a sexual attack? I don't get it. Was it something she had done in the past? One of her inquests? I checked and there were no threats made against her. On the contrary, she seems to have been admired by everyone as a hard-working, conscientious member of the local community.'

Ridpath brought his bottom lip to cover the top one. He had to trust this man, otherwise he had nothing.

'I think I can help. Mrs Challinor was looking into something. She never told me what it was but I think it had to do with unexplained deaths in the north in the last fourteen years.'

Tindall frowned, the crease between his eyes becoming even deeper.

'She asked for inquest reports from around the region. The same cases were highlighted when we did a search on HOLMES.'

'What are you working on?'

'The Romeo and Juliet case. Have you heard about it?'

Tindall whistled. 'Who hasn't? Do you have somebody in the frame?'

'We think a man, a doctor called Stephen Orwell, may be involved. But to be honest, we have no evidence linking him to the crime scenes.'

'Have you asked him where he was last Friday night?'

'Not yet. With a bit of luck, we'll interview him tomorrow.'

'Let me know how it goes. If we could tie this doctor to our assault on the coroner...'

'I don't want to hold out too much hope. Like I said, we have no evidence at the moment, but by tomorrow, we hope to tie him to at least one of the crime scenes.'

'Good luck.'

'There's one way you can help me.'

Tindall sat forward, suddenly interested. 'How?'

'Was there anything in your investigation pointing to a doctor, and particularly our doctor, being involved?'

Tindall thought hard, shook his head, then smiled.

'What is it?'

'During the search of the area, we found a small bag underneath a hedge, about twenty feet away from the attack.'

'And?'

'We couldn't link it to the assault, thought perhaps it had been thrown from a passing car.'

'But...'

'The bag contained a hypodermic loaded with morphine, enough to kill somebody.'

'Really?'

'It's still not evidence; there were no prints or DNA on the hypodermic or the bag.'

'Doesn't it strike you as strange her attacker should have a hammer *and* a needle?' asked Ridpath quietly, as if talking to himself.

'It seems like overkill.'

'Exactly, our attacker was making sure they did the job properly.'

'There was one other thing, or should I say, two other things in the bag.'

'What?' Ridpath waited for the answer.

'Two small feathers, dove's feathers apparently, according to the lab.'

'What did you just say?'

'Two dove's feathers. We found them in the bag with the hypodermic.'

Feathers? Where had he read about feathers before?

Then it hit him like a brick between the eyes. He knew then he had found his connection between the attack on Mrs Challinor and the Romeo and Juliet case.

Chapter Seventy-eight

On the drive back into Manchester, Ridpath began to fit the pieces of the jigsaw together in his head.

The feathers.

The inquest transcripts.

The strange deaths.

It all led back to Stephen Orwell.

Now if only the DNA swab he had given this morning confirmed the man was the father of Ralph Orwell, aka Male B, they would at least be able to bring him in for questioning as a person of interest tomorrow.

He was tempted to ring Emily to see if the results were back yet, but he held off. There was no point in hassling her and besides, he was certain she would call him if something had come in.

Should he go into the coroner's office? Clarence Montague would be expecting him to show his face sometime today and it was on his way back. He decided to ring Sophia instead, pressing the speaker phone.

'Hiya, how's it going?'

'Missing you.'

'Really?'

'Montague is proving to be a real pain. He's just sent us every update issued by the chief coroner in the last five years and requested we read and follow them to the letter.'

'Even the ones issued during the pandemic?'

'Especially the ones issued during the pandemic. He's also withdrawn all the Regulation 28 notices sent out by Mrs Challinor.'

'Withdrawn them, why?'

'Apparently, "At this time, it is incumbent on us to support the various offices and officers of the state and its departments, not require them to spend time and money answering our notices."'

'What? Mrs Challinor only sends out Regulation 28s when she feels there is a danger to the general public.'

'It is no longer our concern. We are, and I quote again, "to follow the precepts of the chief coroner's office to the letter".'

Ridpath stopped at a red light. He could either turn now and go into the coroner's office, or return to Police HQ.

'Do you need me to come in, Sophia?'

'His Lord and Highness has been requesting your presence. He now wants to discuss the Fallowfield case, the death in the fire.'

'Can't he just read the report we wrote?'

'Apparently not...'

There was a rustling on the phone and a new voice came on. 'Mr Ridpath? This is Clarence Montague. I need you to come to the coroner's office immediately. That is not a request, but an order. Come back now.'

Ridpath pursed his lips and counted to three. 'Certainly, Coroner, I'll be there in twenty minutes.'

'I look forward to seeing you, Mr Ridpath.'

As the lights turned to green, he signalled right, incurring the beeped ire of the motorist behind him.

These problems with the coroner had to end, and end today. Time to sort it out.

Chapter Seventy-nine

Clarence Montague was waiting for him in Mrs Challinor's office.

'Ah, Mr Ridpath, just a moment as I finish this memo.'

The man carried on scribbling on the paper, scratching away in crabbed handwriting.

Ridpath stood there like an errant schoolboy standing in front of a stern headmaster. As Montague carried on writing, he pulled out a chair and sat down, occasioning a surprised glance from the coroner.

Finishing the memo with a flourish of a signature, Montague finally looked up properly. 'I've called you here to discuss the death of a Mr Sambini in a fire in Fallowfield. Have we shown conclusively the fire was caused by a lit cigarette igniting a sofa as the man slept?'

Ridpath opened the case file. 'If you look on page seven, you will see the preliminary report by the senior fire officer at the scene. An independent fire investigator also looked into the death of Mr Sambini. His report is on page twelve. It indicates conclusively the source was a lit cigarette falling from the man's fingers, igniting the fabric and stuffing of the sofa. From the empty bottles of wine near the body, the fire investigator concluded he was probably intoxicated at the time of his death. They found more empties in the waste bin in the kitchen. There was no indication of the use of accelerants or of any electrical fault. I questioned both Mr Sambini's relatives and his neighbours and they confirmed he was an alcoholic who smoked at least forty cigarettes a day. In addition, we found cigarette burns on the upstairs mattress which indicates this had happened before.' Ridpath paused. 'It's all in the case file.'

'Good, I just wanted you to explain it to me. It is the role and duty of a coroner's officer, is it not? To investigate and then explain the investigation to the coroner?'

'Or you could just read the report. Mrs Challinor preferred everything to be documented and written down.'

'I don't have to remind you Mrs Challinor is no longer here, Ridpath. I expect you to explain the cases to me when I need an explanation.'

'Look, Mr Montague, you know I am working a case for MIT. Mrs Challinor agreed my services would be shared between the coroner's office and the police.'

'As I have already told you, Mrs Challinor is no longer here. There is a new sheriff in town, Ridpath, and I would like to work a different way. I want you to be available when and where I need you. Is that clear?'

'So you want me to stop working at MIT?'

'You need to do your job properly as a coroner's officer, not spend your time on a meaningless investigation for the police.'

'It's a murder investigation.'

'Whatever it is, you need to do *your* job, not somebody else's. Is that clear?' He opened a file in front of him and began reading, indicating the meeting was over.

Ridpath took out his phone and pressed the speed dial button.

'Detective Superintendent Trent, I have you on speaker phone. This is Ridpath, and I am sitting with the temporary senior coroner, Clarence Montague.'

The man looked up, surprised.

Claire Trent's voice sounded loud and clear from the mobile. 'Welcome to Manchester, Mr Montague. I'm sure we will enjoy working together.'

The coroner didn't speak. His face was flushed bright red.

'Mr Montague would like to remove me from the Romeo and Juliet case, ma'am.'

'I'm afraid it's not possible, Mr Montague. Ridpath is making progress on the case and I need him. I believe this coincides with the work of the coroner's office. Mrs Challinor opened a file on the case on January 4, 2022, postponing the inquest pending our investigation. Ridpath has made important strides in the last few days and we believe we may be close to a breakthrough.'

Montague coughed. 'Thank you for your update, Mrs Trent...'

'Please call me Claire.'

'Thank you, Claire. This is the first I've heard about the case. Mr Ridpath has been remiss in keeping me informed...'

'One of his many failings. He does tend to go off on his own.'

'...but I am sorry to say the coroner's office is far too busy at the moment to have one of its most important staff away for most of the day.' There was a long silence at the other end of the phone which Montague tried to fill by saying, 'I'm sure you understand my position.'

'No I don't, actually. GMP and the coroner's office have a long-standing agreement regarding Ridpath's position. Now is not the time to renege on the agreement.'

'There is no question of reneging, but I have been sent here by the chief coroner to ensure the smooth running of this office in the absence of Mrs Challinor. And frankly, I have been appalled by some of the practices I have seen.'

'You must do your job and I must do mine. The only thing I am concerned with at the moment is the investigation into two bodies found in the centre of Manchester. An investigation agreed with Mrs Challinor prior to your arrival. Now if you would like me to call the chief coroner and explain this to him, I would be more than happy. But the last time I met him in London, he was extremely complimentary about the arrangement. In fact, he called it an outstanding example of cooperation between the differing branches of the legal world. The fact I pay all of Ridpath's salary was probably one of the factors in his enthusiasm.'

This was the first Ridpath had heard of these compliments. They were obviously above his pay grade.

Claire Trent finished off with a Manchester kiss, otherwise known as a kick to the goolies. 'But, as I said, I am more than happy to call and tell him you have decided to cancel the arrangement.' The sound of shuffling papers. 'I have his number somewhere...'

'That won't be necessary, Claire. I'm sure Mr Ridpath is needed on your investigation. How much longer will it last?'

Montague was trying to save face, but Claire Trent wasn't even going to allow him that.

'I'm not sure, but it won't be too long. I'll let you know when he has finished. Have we sorted our little problem out? Unfortunately, I need to rush off to a meeting with the chief constable. Thank you for your time, Mr Montague.'

The phone went dead.

The coroner stared at the phone and then looked at him. 'That is all, Mr Ridpath.'

'There is one other thing, Mr Montague.' Ridpath slid his card onto the table in front of the temporary coroner. 'I do not like you harassing my assistant or any of the other staff here. If you want to get hold of me, here is my number. Call me anytime. I'm always available.'

Ridpath stood and walked out, leaving Montague staring dead-eyed at the white card he was holding in his hand.

Chapter Eighty

Ridpath drove all the way back to Police HQ with a smile plastered on his face. Briefing his problem with Montague to Claire Trent before the meeting had helped immensely. She was more than willing to take him on, firstly because the investigation was finally making progress, and secondly because he was a southerner.

He took the lift up to the MIT floor, still smiling. However, the smile was wiped off his face as soon as he entered their operations room.

It looked like a bomb had hit it.

The boards and pictures stuck on the wall were still as neat as ever but the rest of the room was a jumble of files, pizza boxes, coffee cups, more files, Sellotape, and more boxes.

Jayne, Chrissy and Emily Parkinson all looked up at the same time as he came into the room. All three looked tired, with bags under their eyes and wrinkles on their foreheads.

'Any luck wherever you went?' asked Emily.

'Yep. I went to see DCI Tindall, the SIO in charge of investigating the attack on the coroner.'

'You two are friends now?'

'Not bosom buddies, but not enemies either. I took him through what we discovered regarding the inquests. And guess what?'

'We're too tired for guessing games, Ridpath.'

'A bag with a hypodermic full of morphine and two dove's feathers was found near the scene of the attack.'

'What?' All three chorused at the same time.

'Medical equipment again, and feathers. Chrissy, remember the list of stuff found in the room with Romeo and Juliet compiled by the CSIs?'

Chrissy tapped away on her laptop before showing him the list from the forensic report. The others stood and walked over to where she was sitting.

'See...' he pointed at the list, 'the seventh line down.'

Two mattresses, both new, bought from IKEA.

A red bucket from B&Q.

One empty Evian bottle, traces of barbiturate found inside.

One bottle cap, the outside grooves containing traces of plaster dust.

A used candle in its holder, only a small nub of wax remaining.

A book of used matches.

Two dove feathers.

A tram ticket found on Male B dated August 18, 2008.

'Two dove's feathers. Same as were found in the bag close to Mrs Challinor's body.'

'It's a bit thin, Ridpath,' said Emily. 'The feathers probably drifted into the room when the two workmen broke in. The floor in the warehouse was covered in the stuff.'

'But what if they didn't? What if they were placed there?'

'Hang on,' said Chrissy. She turned her laptop around and typed again. 'I knew I'd seen it before. The case notes from Chester came in. Remember the man who died from carbon monoxide poisoning? Well, the CSIs also found two feathers on the seat next to him. The local police couldn't explain it and wondered if the man had picked them up by chance earlier in the day.'

'They weren't mentioned in the coroner's inquest.'

'Probably not thought to be relevant.'

Ridpath walked back to the boards. 'So we have our signature. The perp leaves dove's feathers at the scene of his crimes. Or at least at three of them.'

'Why?' asked Emily.

Ridpath shrugged his shoulders. 'I don't know. Childhood trauma? An association with death? They turn him on? Why does any serial killer do anything? But what I do know is we need to look at the other two cases HOLMES pinpointed in Blackburn and Derbyshire. Were feathers found at those scenes too?'

'I didn't see anything in the inquest transcripts,' said Emily.

'We have the case notes for both places but I haven't been through them yet,' said Chrissy.

'Give me Derbyshire, you handle Blackburn, Emily.'

'I'll finish going through Chester, see if there is anything else,' added Chrissy.

Jayne Sinclair raised her hand. 'I hate to rain on your parade, but you haven't linked Orwell to any of the crimes yet. The feathers may give you a link to a perp, but not to Orwell.'

'That's not rain, it's a thunderstorm. We need to find the links, people. Final question, Emily...'

'The answer is not yet, Ridpath. I can't ring the lab again, I think they'll put me against a wall and shoot me.'

'OK, let them get on with the job. They have another set of DNA to compare.'

'What?'

'Cheshire Police pulled epithelials from Mrs Challinor's attacker, they think she scratched the man during the assault. Can you get the lab to work on them?'

'Asap?' asked Emily.

'Quicker. We need them yesterday. If we can connect Orwell to the attack on the coroner...'

'We have him, hung, drawn and quartered.'

'Not quite. There's no chain of evidence, but it's a start, and a bloody good one too.'

Just then, Emily's mobile phone rang. 'It's the lab.'

Chapter Eighty-one

Emily slowly, tentatively held the phone to her ear.

'Uh-huh,' she said, 'Uh-huh.' She frowned. 'Can you send the results over to us asap? And Julie, we have another rush job for you, is that OK? I'll make it up to you with a bottle of something fizzy.'

She listened for a while before finally saying, 'Thanks again, you're a star,' and switching off her phone.

Everybody in the room was staring at her.

'Well?' asked Ridpath, stepping forward.

A broad smile broke across her face like the sun coming out after a Manchester shower. 'Stephen Orwell is definitely the father of Ralph, aka Male B. One hundred per cent sure.'

Ridpath punched the air like he'd just scored a hat-trick in the dying seconds of a cup final for United. Chrissy did the same but for City. The normally taciturn Jayne even shouted 'Get in!'

When they had all recovered, it was left to Ridpath to start organising their next moves.

'Emily, make sure the DNA for the attack on the coroner gets across to the lab and finish the case notes from Blackburn. We need to see if dove's feathers were found at the scene of the Singh deaths.'

'On it, Ridpath.'

'Chrissy, carry on going through the Chester case. Was there a link to Stephen Orwell or his clinic anywhere? Also, send me the case notes from Derbyshire, I'll go through them now and later this evening.'

'Right, will do.' She tapped a few more keys. 'The case notes are in your inbox.'

'And Jayne, please go home, I'm conscious you've been working harder than any of us.'

'No chance, Ridpath, not till I finish Meredith's notes. But it looks so far as if you covered everything.'

Ridpath clapped his hands. 'We have a big day ahead of us tomorrow and I want everybody to be fresh. Looking at you all, I've seen more life in the morgue. You all look like death warmed up.'

'You do know how to charm women, Ridpath.'

'One of my unique strengths. But seriously, killing ourselves isn't going to solve this case, not when we are on the cusp of something big.'

He gathered his file and notes, and walked towards the door.

'Where are you going?' asked Emily.

'To tell Claire Trent and Steve Carruthers the good news, and get them to agree to us bringing in Stephen Orwell for an interview at ten a.m. tomorrow. I think it would be best if we did it quietly rather than have every reporter this side of London hanging outside our front door, pen ready to write a lurid headline.'

'There's one thing I don't understand, Ridpath.'

'What's that, Jayne?'

'Why did he come in voluntarily to give his DNA? He could have refused, and then we would have had to get a court order. And with the best brief money can buy, that could have been postponed indefinitely.'

Ridpath made a moue with his mouth. 'Cockiness. Or perhaps he knew we'd discover he was the father eventually and better get it over and done with.'

'It doesn't make sense. You should have seen him as we were swabbing his cheek. Telling us how to make sure we did it properly to get the right amount of cells on the sample,' said Emily.

'Isn't it because the only thing we have against him is the paternity of his son, Ralph Orwell? Everything else is only conjecture. We can't put him at the scene of any crime nor can we directly link him to any death.'

After Jayne Sinclair spoke a shroud of silence descended on the room.

'I need to see Claire Trent,' said Ridpath, closing the door quietly behind him.

Chapter Eighty-two

I've decided to kill her tomorrow.

She might remain in a post-coma state for weeks, or she might wake at any time. There may be memory loss from post-traumatic amnesia but that could wear off after a couple of months.

Whatever state she is in, I can't take the chance any more, particularly after the police visit.

I don't know how close they are but the mere fact they are looking means I have a problem. And the biggest issue is Mrs Challinor. I won't enjoy killing her, but it has to be done. I won't fail again.

I've checked the hospital plan from the internet and worked out a better route to the ICU. It should be easy to gain access and, once inside, it will only take a matter of seconds to kill the coroner and get out again before anybody knows.

There is the problem of the staff, but it should be easy to solve. It's all about blending in, and I know how hospitals work and how they think.

It's time to become a chameleon, albeit one armed with a hypodermic needle full of morphine.

The good news is a patient dying in ICU is not uncommon. There probably won't even be a post-mortem or an inquest.

And I can be free again.

The inspector and his sidekick will probably carry on investigating, but without Margaret Challinor they have nothing. Just a few coincidences and some circumstantial evidence. Nothing able to stand up in a court of law.

Tomorrow it is then. This time I won't fail.

Chapter Eighty-three

Ridpath parked outside the Wells' house. At seven thirty, he was slightly early to pick up Eve, so he decided to take a few moments to himself.

The bosses had decided Ridpath and Emily Parkinson were to go to the house tomorrow morning and invite Stephen Orwell to come in for a voluntary interview. If he refused, officers from Trafford police division would be on standby to support an arrest. Orwell would then be taken to Stretford Police Station rather than Police HQ for the interview. It was felt using neutral ground was better and less confrontational.

For Ridpath, the reasons seemed political and less to do with the investigation, but there was no point arguing. He was going to be able to question Orwell directly and that was the most important thing.

Officially, he would be cautioned but not charged and was free to leave at any time. It was Ridpath's job to keep him there and talking, preferably without a solicitor. He would have to plan and prepare for the interview tonight.

First though, time to pick up his daughter.

He opened the gate to the Wells' and knocked on the door. It was immediately answered.

'Come in, Ridpath, Eve is just finishing her tea.'

The girls were both sat at the kitchen table fighting with what looked like thin green rubber tyres. Neither of them seemed to be winning.

'How has she been? As good as gold, I hope.'

'She's been a dream. She and Maisie even finished their maths homework before tea. A world's first for my daughter. They've been watching *Gilmore Girls* together as a treat.'

'I want to live in Stars Hollow,' said Maisie.

'Me too,' agreed Eve.

'Where?'

'It's the town in the programme, somewhere in Connecticut I think.'

The mention of the state reminded Ridpath they should contact Audrey Robinson as soon as possible. They would need a sample of her DNA to confirm the relationship to her daughter.

'And I want to go to Yale just like Rory.'

Eve nudged her friend, rolling her eyes. 'It's only TV, Maisie, it's not real.'

'Harvard is real.'

Ridpath realised then how little TV he had watched recently. It was as if the world outside the investigation no longer existed. He never saw the news. Never read any papers. Didn't even know which striker United were attempting to buy this weekend.

He had to get a life.

After the investigation was finished, of course.

'Come on, Eve, we'd best be going.'

Eve stared at the kale sitting stolidly on her plate. 'I'm full, Mrs Wells.'

'No worries, dear, I'll wrap it up and you can eat it later.'

She bustled about in the cupboard looking for her tinfoil while Eve went to get her school jacket.

'See you tomorrow, Maisie, I bet I'm going to be at school early tomorrow.'

Ridpath nodded. 'Yeah, I think you are.'

'Can I go to school early too?' asked Maisie.

'I can collect her tomorrow morning and take them both before I go to work.'

'It's too much trouble, Ridpath, and Maisie has such a problem waking in the morning.'

'But I'll wake early tomorrow. Eve and I can get work done while we're waiting for classes to begin.'

'I'm afraid I have to leave at seven thirty on the dot.'

Angela shrugged her shoulders. 'OK, I suppose so. But I want you bright and bushy-tailed tomorrow morning, Maisie Wells, and not a sign of Little Miss Grumpy.'

Ridpath laughed. 'The same name could be used for Eve.'

Angela handed Ridpath the foil package of baked kale. 'Just a minute or so in the microwave and it's ready, and it keeps ever so long in the fridge.'

They were now stood at the door. A quick hug for the girls and an even quicker 'thank you' from Ridpath and they were out of the door heading for the car.

Eve leant into him and whispered, 'You ever put that stuff near the microwave and I'm no longer your daughter. I'll run away to Stars Hollow and you'll never see me again.'

Chapter Eighty-four

After Eve had gone to bed, Ridpath was left alone with a small glass of Glenmorangie for company.

He had already been through the Derbyshire case notes. There it was staring them in the face. In Joan Blackledge's bag, the CSIs had found two dove's feathers. The police had assumed the woman had found them during her walk.

Emily rang him at ten.

'I hope you're not still in the office?'

'On my way out.'

'With Jayne and Chrissy?'

'We're just leaving, Ridpath. If you let me speak, I can pack my bags and get out of here.'

He stayed silent.

'You were right. The police in Blackburn found two feathers on the kitchen table next to the baby's milk. They couldn't explain them so put them to one side. It looks like we have a confirmed signature for all four cases.'

'Well done. We're getting there, Em.'

'There's more. The police in Chester tracked down where Tony Snellgrove visited in Manchester.'

'The Orwell Clinic?'

'Right first time. Apparently he and his wife had been trying for another baby. She was much older than him and undergoing IVF at the clinic.'

'Great, another link. It's all coming into place now, Em. I'm just going through the Derbyshire case report, no links to Orwell anywhere. It doesn't mean there weren't any, just the police never found them. Three out of four is pretty good.'

'But we still haven't put him at any of the crime scenes, Ridpath.'

'He's too clever. Remember, there was no DNA found at any of the scenes. And wouldn't a doctor have access to all the right PPE to make sure he never left a trace of himself anywhere?'

'Still, it's going to make it harder to get him to cough to the murders.'

'I know, Em, but you've done enough now. Go home and I'll see you tomorrow. I want us to be sharp and focused.'

He ended the call.

So they now had found different deaths, all with a consistent signature:

The killer wasn't at the scene when they died.

The victims were drugged.

Efforts were made to make the victims as comfortable as possible.

Two dove's feathers were found at each scene.

It was enough to convince him the same killer, or killers, had been involved in all four murders. They had the consistent signature of a serial killer.

The only exception was the attack on Mrs Challinor. Drugs had been found near the scene of the crime as well as two dove's feathers, but this was a brutal assault, not like any of the other cases.

Had the killer been flustered? Did they not plan this murder as well as the others, rushing into an attack? Was the unknown meeting in the diary the catalyst?

He didn't know.

He scratched his head, before taking a small sip of Glenmorangie, enjoying the burn of the spirit as it slid down his throat and spread its sweet fire across his chest.

Jayne's words came back to him. 'Isn't it because the only thing we have against him is the paternity of his son, Ralph Orwell?

Everything else is only conjecture. We can't put him at the scene of any crime nor can we directly link him to any death.'

She was right.

It was up to him tomorrow to force a confession out of Stephen Orwell.

A shiver went down his spine.

Was he up to the job?

Thursday, June 24

Chapter Eighty-five

Ridpath and Emily Parkinson sat in a car just around the corner from Stephen Orwell's home.

They had met at eight fifteen that morning in the Starbucks on Lloyd Street. Far enough away from the Orwell's not to be seen yet close enough to get there in five minutes even in the heaviest rush hour traffic.

Ridpath hadn't bothered to drive all the way into Police HQ after dropping Eve and Maisie off. It was better to stay out in Altrincham close to where he was needed.

'Hiya, all set?' asked Emily when she arrived.

'As ready as I'll ever be.'

She sat down next to him, staring at him all the time. 'If you don't mind me saying, you look nervous, Ridpath.'

'Second coffee of the morning,' he joked. But he was nervous; if he couldn't get Orwell to admit his guilt, they had nothing.

'You want anything to eat?'

'Nah, I'm good.'

Trafford Division had sent a plain clothes detective to sit outside the house from six a.m. that morning on surveillance. The only movement he had reported was the son leaving on his motorbike at eight thirty-six a.m. They could even hear the roar of the engine through the comms.

'Do you want me to follow him?'

'Stay where you are,' ordered Ridpath, 'he's probably off to the clinic.'

The man returned at nine fifteen, so he hadn't been to work. Ridpath made a note in his book to follow up where he had been.

After going through the plan one more time and finishing their drinks, they drove round and parked in the street near the Orwells.

Ridpath glanced at the clock on the dashboard and checked with his watch.

9.45.

Emily wrote the time down in her notebook.

He contacted the plain clothes detective with eyes on the house. 'Any movement?'

'Nothing that I can see at the front.'

'They are still inside?'

'Nobody except the son has left since I arrived at six.'

'Great. When you see us pull round the corner, you drive away and we'll take your spot.'

'Roger that.'

Ridpath found himself tapping on the steering wheel, impatient to get going. The clock on the dashboard flickered electronically, the numbers taking hours to change rather than minutes.

9.46.

9.47.

9.48.

9.49.

At exactly 9.50, a patrol car pulled beside them. The passenger wound his window down, saying, 'Detective Inspector Ridpath?'

'That's me.'

'Sergeant Poulson and Constable Harrison. We're to support your detention of a suspect. Expecting any trouble?'

Ridpath shook his head. 'We're inviting him in for an interview but I may need to arrest him if he refuses to come. I'll give you a signal if I need you to act.'

'OK, we'll follow your lead.'

'Park the patrol car here and walk round to join me. I want to give him the opportunity to come in quietly.'

The clock ticked over slowly again.

9.54.

9.55.

9.56.

Ridpath started the engine and pulled away from the kerb. They were slightly early but he couldn't wait any longer.

He drove slowly around the corner. Ahead of him, a grey Mondeo pulled out of a parking space opposite the driveway to the house.

He flashed his lights and pulled into the vacant spot. They waited for the two uniformed officers to round the corner to approach their car.

'Ready, Em.'

'Let's go get him,' she said, opening the door.

Chapter Eighty-six

They strode up the path followed by the two uniformed police officers, knocking loudly at the door.

No answer.

Ridpath knocked again.

The door opened slowly and they were faced with Stephen Orwell.

'It's you again, Inspector...?'

'Detective Inspector Ridpath and Detective Sergeant Parkinson. We'd like you to accompany us to the station, if you could.'

Orwell was joined by his wife.

'What?'

'We'd like you to accompany us to the station.'

'I heard what you said, Inspector, I just couldn't believe you said it.'

'Nonetheless, I did. Please come with us, sir.' Ridpath gently touched the man's elbow but his hand was shaken off.

'Why?'

'We'd like to ask you some more questions, down at the station this time.'

'And if I say I don't want to go?'

'This is a voluntary invitation, Dr Orwell. I'm sure as a citizen you would like to help the police with their inquiries, particularly into a murder.'

Orwell planted his feet in the hall and refused to move. 'It's not convenient at the moment. I don't want to go.'

'Listen, sir, I have made a polite request for your help. If you refuse to come with us, I will instruct the sergeant to bring round his patrol car with all the lights flashing. We will also call for backup from at least three other units who will arrive with sirens blaring, attracting the attention of the neighbours. You will then be cautioned and taken in handcuffs down the path and placed in the back of a police car with a burly police officer sitting beside you.' A long pause. 'Or you could simply come with me to Stretford Police Station and answer a few questions on a voluntary basis. Which is it to be? The choice is yours.'

Throughout Ridpath's speech, Stephen Orwell had stood there with his chest puffed out, his wife by his side.

'What are you going to do, Dr Orwell?'

The man sighed, took a look outside the door at the unmarked police car and said, 'Let me get my jacket.'

'Stephen, what's happening?'

'I don't know, dear, but it seems I will be accompanying these two...' he paused for a second and looked back at the two detectives, '...people to Stretford Police Station. Call my solicitor and have him join me there as soon as possible.'

'Do you want me to come with you?'

'That won't be possible, Mrs Orwell.'

'You can't stop me from coming to the station to be with my husband, Inspector.'

Ridpath stayed silent.

They were joined at the door by Michael Orwell. 'What's all the racket? What's happening?'

Constable Harrison moved round to cover him in case of trouble.

'I'll call the solicitor and then go to the station,' announced Mrs Orwell.

'Are they arresting Father? What's he done? Do you want me to come, Mother?' asked Michael Orwell.

'No, you go to the clinic. Somebody has to be there today.'

'Are you sure?'

She put her hand on his face, stroking it tenderly. 'Let me handle this, Michael. You need to be at the clinic.'

Stephen Orwell took his jacket from a peg on the dresser and walked back to join the two detectives.

Ridpath signalled to Sergeant Poulson. The uniformed officer stepped forward.

'Stephen Orwell, you do not have to say anything. But it may harm your defence if you do not mention when questioned something which you later rely on in court. Anything you do say may be given in evidence.'

Sergeant Poulson took the man's arm and gently pushed him down the path.

'Am I being arrested, Inspector Ridpath?' Orwell asked over his shoulder.

'No, sir, as I said this is a voluntary interview. The caution is merely to remind you of your rights.'

Orwell stopped for a second and turned back. 'You are going to regret this, Inspector Ridpath. I am well known and respected in this community. After today, I am going to make it my life's work to make sure you never serve as a police officer again.'

'Is that a threat, sir?'

'No, a promise, Inspector.'

'Put him in the car, Sergeant Poulson. Not mine though. Constable Harrison, bring the patrol car round and make sure your lights are flashing and the siren's blaring.' Ridpath could see a few curtains already twitching on the quiet road. 'I'm sure the neighbours won't want to miss the action.'

Chapter Eighty-seven

'Was that wise, Ridpath?' Emily Parkinson asked after they had placed Stephen Orwell in one of the interview rooms in Stretford nick, after booking him in at the front desk.

'I don't know, but I found it funny. This man need to be knocked off his pedestal, Emily. The angrier he is, the more likely he will give us something.'

'Are we going to interview him now?'

'No, we'll let him stew for an hour or so. I've always found sitting alone in an interview room with nothing to do helps concentrate the mind. It's amazing what the imagination does even to the most hardened criminal. Besides, he has already asked for a solicitor to be present so we have to wait.'

Right on cue, a small dapper man arrived with Orwell's wife.

'Inspector Ridpath, my name is Leach, Harold Leach, Dr Orwell's solicitor. I hope you haven't tried to interview my client yet?'

'No, he's requested a solicitor be present even though this is only a voluntary interview.'

'I'd like to see my client before the interview begins.'

'Of course.' Ridpath stepped aside, allowing the solicitor to enter the corridor where the interview rooms were located. Mrs Orwell tried to follow him.

He barred her way. 'I'm sorry, ma'am, it won't be possible.'

'But I want to see my husband.'

'That's not possible, I'm afraid. Not when he is waiting to be interviewed.'

She tried to push past him but Ridpath stood his ground.

'Let me past, Inspector.'

'As I said, Mrs Orwell, it is not possible at the moment. You can see your husband when I have decided he is free to go.' He signalled to Harrison. 'Take Mrs Orwell down to the canteen and buy her a cup of coffee on GMP.'

'I don't want your coffee,' she shouted.

'Alexandra, let me handle this.' The solicitor stepped close to her and whispered in her ear.

She nodded once. 'You won't hear the last of this, Inspector, I know people.'

'So I've been told, Mrs Orwell. I know people too, but probably not the same ones. Sergeant Poulson, can you show Mr Leach to interview room four? In ten minutes we will begin the interview.'

Chapter Eighty-eight

Ridpath entered the interview room followed by Emily Parkinson. Orwell and his solicitor were sat on the same side of the table facing the door. Both looked up as he entered.

He placed the files down on the table in front of him. The room was hot and stuffy, Ridpath had ordered the air-conditioning to be switched off an hour ago. Anything and everything to make Stephen Orwell a little more uncomfortable.

He pulled out a chair and sat down, pressing the recording button on the tape.

'The time is 12.06 p.m. on June 24, 2002. This voluntary interview is being recorded and filmed. Present are Detective Inspector Ridpath and Detective Sergeant Parkinson of Greater Manchester Police. The interviewee is Dr Stephen Orwell, accompanied by his solicitor, Mr Harold Leach.'

He paused for a moment to let the information sink in.

'The purpose of this interview is to ask questions concerning the deaths of two young people found in a warehouse in Manchester in January. Their identities have been confirmed as Ralph Orwell, aged eighteen, and Skylar Robinson, aged seventeen. It has been ascertained that these two people were killed by a person or persons unknown around August, 2008. This is therefore a murder inquiry.

'In view of the seriousness of this investigation, Detective Parkinson will now repeat the caution given earlier to Dr Orwell on the steps of his home.'

Emily Parkinson coughed once. 'Stephen Orwell, you do not have to say anything. But it may harm your defence if you do not mention when questioned something which you later rely on in court. Anything you do say may be given in evidence.'

The solicitor interrupted. 'The important part here, Stephen, is you do not need to say anything at all. In fact, I would advise you not to answer any of the detectives' questions.'

'As I've already said, Harry, I have nothing to hide.'

'This seems to be the right moment. Inspector Ridpath, we have a statement to read before you begin your questions.'

With a nod of the head, Ridpath asked him to proceed.

'On behalf of my client, I would like to read this statement.' It was Harold Leach's turn to cough. 'I have come voluntarily into the police station today as I have nothing to hide. I will answer any questions posed by the police as long as I believe I have answers. I would like to place on the record my unhappiness with the conduct of Inspector Ridpath and Detective Sergeant Parkinson and will be making a formal complaint in due course.'

'Thank you, Dr Orwell, your complaint has been noted and will be give the attention it deserves from Greater Manchester Police. Now if we can begin, I would like to ask Dr Orwell a few questions.'

'Ask away, Inspector.' Orwell smiled across the table and sat back, crossing his legs.

'Did you have an affair with Mrs Moira Travis beginning in 1989?'

Stephen Orwell smiled and said one word. 'No.'

Ridpath nodded his head. It was going to be like that, was it? He opened the case file and thumbed to a page of case notes.

'When you were questioned on June 22, 2022 at your home, I asked you the same question and you admitted to having an affair with her.'

'The affair didn't begin in 1989, that was the year it ended. The relationship began in 1987.'

It *was* going to be like that.

'Mrs Travis was a patient of yours?'

'You don't have to answer, Stephen,' his solicitor interrupted.

'It's OK, Harry, I want to answer. I'm retired now and I don't think the General Medical Council are going to bother with something which happened over thirty-five years ago.' He scratched his nose. 'Mrs Travis was a patient. She came to my office seeking help to have a baby. IVF, in vitro fertilisation, for the uninitiated, was in its relative infancy during this period, having only started in 1978. I am proud to say I was one of the leading practitioners in the UK.'

'But Mrs Travis became pregnant in a far more traditional way, didn't she, Mr Orwell? You impregnated her.'

The smile vanished from the man's face.

'A son was born to Mrs Travis on June 22, 1990. She called him, Ralph, Ralph Orwell. She named you as the father.'

Emily Parkinson passed across the birth certificate Mrs Travis had given them.

Stephen Orwell picked it up and stared at it, reading his own name. 'I was the father according to this. But she was still married at the time. The husband could have fathered this... baby.'

'No, he couldn't. You gave us your DNA yesterday and we compared it with Ralph Orwell's DNA. Document 5B shows you are definitely the father.'

Orwell shrugged his shoulders.

'Ralph Orwell was eighteen when he was murdered by being bricked up in a small room in a warehouse with no food or water. He died from dehydration.'

'I had nothing to do with his death. I was in America at the time, working in California.'

Ridpath ignored his words. 'Another person died of dehydration with Ralph Orwell, his half-sister, Skylar Robinson.' A long pause by Ridpath to let the import of the relationship he had just described sink in. 'We also compared Ms Robinson's DNA with yours. It turns out you were her father too.'

'Impossible, you're lying.'

'Here is document 6; the results from the lab.' It was snatched from his hands by Orwell. 'As you can see quite clearly, you are the father of Skylar Robinson.'

Orwell's eyes scanned the paper frantically. 'It can't be... Impossible.'

'The science doesn't lie, Dr Orwell, as you know.'

'You must have mixed the samples, they were contaminated.'

'We checked the results with the second sample you were kind enough to give us. Document 7 confirms the fact you were her father.'

That paper was snatched from Ridpath's hands too. He waited while the man looked through it, twice. 'It's wrong, I had no affairs in America with any women, it's impossible.'

'What happened, Dr Orwell? Did these two young people somehow find out the truth; you had fathered both of them with two different women? Did they come to you asking for money? Threatening to blackmail you? Is that why you killed them?'

'I... I... I...'

The solicitor placed his hand on Orwell's arm. 'Don't answer, Stephen. Inspector, I would like a few moments to confer with my client if you please.'

Ridpath thought for a moment. Would the solicitor stop Orwell answering the questions? Or would Orwell give in and admit the truth? The man was definitely rattled, the science had shocked him. But they still couldn't put him at the scene of any of the crimes. He had to take the chance.

'I'll give you ten minutes, Mr Leach, but when I come back I would like some honesty from your client. As he knows, the science does not lie.'

He leant into the mike and announced, 'At the request of Dr Orwell's solicitor, we will now pause the interview. The time is twelve forty-five. We will resume at one p.m.'

Chapter Eighty-nine

Ridpath joined Emily Parkinson outside Stretford station on Talbot Road. For the first time in ages, he desperately craved a cigarette.

As she lit and inhaled, he was about to bludge one off her, but the words lodged in his throat. He couldn't do it. Not now. He had made a promise to Eve and this time he was going to keep it.

'It's going well,' said Emily, exhaling a long stream of blue smoke, the best Gallaher could provide. 'I thought he was going to crack for a second, until the solicitor intervened.'

'It was the science that got to him. He couldn't deny the science.'

'Why did you allow the break?'

'I had to. We still only have circumstantial evidence against him, we can't place him at any of the crime scenes…'

'…yet. But we're working on it. I just had a text from Chrissy. She rang Audrey Robinson in America. She said her daughter went to study in the UK in 2008 at a summer school in Brighton but never returned. She made a missing person report to Sussex police, even visiting the area three times over following years to search for her daughter, but with no success. She always thought she had vanished into some religious cult and that's why there was no contact. She also confirmed she knew Orwell and was a patient of his but denied having a sexual relationship with him.'

'Again, the science says something different. I wonder why she lied?'

'Chrissy said she didn't handle the news about the death of her daughter well, didn't believe she was dead. Apparently, she's flying over on the next available flight, wants to see her body.'

'There's no chance the lab could have screwed up?'

'Not according to them.'

Emily had been puffing away nervously throughout their conversation. She lit another cigarette with the end of the first.

'Any news on the flight data from the Americans? Did Orwell fly back to the UK in 2008?'

'Nothing so far.'

'What about the comparison of the DNA from Mrs Challinor's attacker with Orwell?'

'I messaged the lab, no reply.'

'Call them, we need to know.'

Ridpath's phone buzzed while Emily made the call.

It was Steve Carruthers asking how it was going. He typed a quick message.

> On a break now. All going well so far but Orwell still hasn't admitted anything. Going back in now.

Emily finished her call. 'They are still waiting for the results. They will let us know just as soon as they have them.'

'Message Chrissy to get on to the Americans, we need the flight data. Was he in the UK in August 2008?'

'What are you going to do in the next session?'

'Time to pile pressure on him by introducing the other deaths. He doesn't know we are aware of them yet. With a bit of luck, he'll crack. Are you ready?'

She took a long toke at the end of the cigarette and stubbed it out with the heel of her shoe. 'As ready as I'll ever be.'

They walked back through the foyer of the station. Ridpath spotted Mrs Orwell sitting on her own in the corner; her eyes were red and a deep frown spoilt her otherwise perfect make-up. She looked down as he strode past her.

You should be worried, he thought, damn worried.

Chapter Ninety

'Dr Orwell, do you know a family in Blackburn, the Singhs?'

Ridpath had already been through the formalities of restarting the interview. It was time to dive into the other deaths.

'No comment.'

So that's what he and his solicitor had decided in the break.

'Mr and Mrs Singh and their six-month-old baby were murdered in 2015. Their bodies were found in the kitchen of their terraced home. Both had been injected with a barbiturate and had drunk cyanide. They were your clients, were they not?'

'Yes, they were, but—'

The solicitor's hand came down on the back of Stephen Orwell's arm.

'No, Harry, I'm going to answer his questions. I have nothing to hide and I would be bored stiff saying "no comment" for the next two hours. This lot have nothing on me.'

Ridpath smiled. 'Mrs Singh came to see you two days before her death, didn't she?'

'She did. She was suffering from post-natal depression. I prescribed Valium for her even though she was breastfeeding. It is better to treat the mother's illness than worry about complications from her passing the drug onto her baby.'

'Did she tell you why she was depressed?'

'Something to do with her husband being unhappy, I think. I am always busy. My clinic has two consulting rooms so I can treat two patients at any one time. Sometimes, you have to give the bad news to a patient that they are infertile or the IVF has failed. My wife then takes care of them while I move on to a new patient in another room.'

'Very caring.' Emily spoke for the first time.

'I presume that was sarcasm. It may seem uncaring to you, but it means I can treat twice as many people in the same time, solving twice as many fertility problems.'

'And making twice as much money.'

'I think that remark is uncalled for, Inspector Ridpath. I have to remind you this is a voluntary interview. Against my advice, my client has decided to answer your questions. I would advise your junior colleague to keep her sarcasm to herself, otherwise we will walk out of here.'

Ridpath glanced across at Emily and signalled with his eyes. He opened another file.

'In 2017, a diabetic, Joan Blackledge, died on a hillside in Derbyshire. She was your client too, wasn't she?'

'She was a patient.'

'She also visited you shortly before she died, didn't she?' Ridpath crossed his fingers beneath the table. He didn't know whether she had or not, but going by the rest of the cases, it was a strong possibility.

'She did. A couple of days before, I think. She'd already had one child with her husband using our services and we did a scan to confirm she was pregnant again.'

What? Why wasn't these fact in the police report? Ridpath slowly turned the pages of the file over to give himself time to think.

'So she was pregnant, yet still went out walking, alone in the hills?'

'It was my advice to her. She enjoyed doing it and exercise is good for diabetics.'

'But her insulin had been tampered with, hadn't it? She died halfway up a hill with nobody to care for or look after her?'

'A sad case.' A long pause, and then his face showed surprise. 'Are you suggesting I tampered with her insulin, Inspector?'

'Did you?'

'No,' he said firmly. 'Let me remind you I took the Hippocratic Oath many years ago to protect human life, not take it.'

'The oath didn't stop Crippen from killing—' said Emily.

'If your colleague insults my client one more time, this interview is over,' interjected the solicitor.

'My colleague is only making an observation, I'm sure no insult was meant.' He quickly continued before Emily could speak again. 'A third death is linked to you. In 2018, a Mr Tony Snellgrove from Chester was found dead in his garage, a tube leading from the exhaust to his car. A case of suicide you might say, except he had been bound to the steering wheel and injected with a large dose of morphine. Mr Snellgrove visited you in Manchester on the day of his death, didn't he?'

'Yes, he did.'

'What did he want?'

It was Orwell's turn to smile. 'I don't think I can tell you. Doctor–patient confidentiality is something I take extremely seriously.'

'You told us about the other cases.'

'This one was of a more personal nature.'

'But Mr Snellgrove is dead.'

'I still won't reveal what he said to me.'

Harold Leach stood. 'I think it is time for us to leave. This is a voluntary interview, but it has now started to compromise my client's relationship with his patients and former patients. So far you have produced no evidence linking my client with any of these deaths, just a litany of coincidence and circumstance.'

'I'm not finished with your client yet.'

'But my client is finished with you. Come on, Stephen, it's time to go.'

'I'm free to leave?'

'You are, unless the inspector would like to file formal charges and make an arrest.'

He stared directly down at Ridpath.

Emily's phone buzzed on the table.

'So, Inspector, are you going to file charges?'

Ridpath thought desperately. How could he keep Orwell in the room?

'I thought not. Let's go, Stephen.' The solicitor took his client's arm.

'Where were you last Friday?' Ridpath finally blurted out.

'Friday the eighteenth?'

'Correct.'

Orwell thought for a moment. 'In London, at a dinner for the Royal Society. I left on the Friday morning with Michael. We both returned on Saturday afternoon.'

'You have witnesses to confirm this?'

'Around two hundred and fifty. I even gave a short speech welcoming the guest of honour.'

Ridpath was stunned. If he was in London, he couldn't have attacked Mrs Challinor.

'If that was your final question, it is time for us to leave.'

As Leach and Orwell strode through the door, Emily showed him her phone. There was a message from Chrissy.

> The lab results confirm there is NO MATCH, repeat NO MATCH between the DNA found on Mrs Challinor's clothes and Stephen Orwell.

Chapter Ninety-one

Ridpath sat alone in his sitting room. The television was off. No music was playing. The lights were dimmed. The air was hot and stuffy even though the windows were open.

Next to him, on the side table, the bottle of whisky was open and he was on his third glass of Glenmorangie.

After Stephen Orwell and his solicitor had left Stretford station, the day didn't get any better.

Chrissy rang to confirm the DNA found on Mrs Challinor's clothes did not match that of Stephen Orwell. Even worse, it wasn't even male at all.

'It must have been contaminated, or perhaps the emergency medical technician or a nurse left her DNA.'

The news didn't improve with another call five minutes later.

'Hi there, Chrissy again. The results have come back from the Department of Homeland Security. Stephen Orwell made no flights to the UK in 2008 or 2009. There is a recorded fight for him in February 2010 but he only stayed two days before returning to California.'

They had of course checked Orwell's alibi for the night of Mrs Challinor's attack and his presence was confirmed at a dinner at Mansion House. There was even footage on YouTube of him introducing the guest speaker that night.

The final kick to the teeth (if another one was needed) came from Jayne Sinclair.

'I've finally been allowed on the FamilyTreeDNA site and I'm afraid it's bad news. After I entered the data from Orwell's kit, I saw close matches to over fifty other kits from across the United States, all people born between 1990 to 1997.'

'So what does it mean, Jayne?'

'I think Stephen Orwell must have been a sperm donor. It's the only explanation. It also explains why Audrey Robinson denied having an affair with him. She probably conceived Skylar through an anonymous donation from a sperm bank. There is no way Stephen Orwell would know who used his sperm once it was donated. I'm sorry, Ridpath, it looks like there's no direct link from him to Skylar Robinson.'

'Is sperm used in more than one country?'

'It is. I've checked and the international trade has a value of nearly $100 million with most of it coming from the United States.'

'So it could have been used in the UK?'

'Perhaps; we'll never know. But it does render any genetic genealogy work invalid unless we can show direct contact between Stephen Orwell and a woman. The only person so far to have such a contact is Moira Travis.' A long pause. 'I'm sorry, Ridpath.'

'Don't worry, it's not your fault. You should go home and get some sleep.'

'What are you going to do?'

'I think I have to go and see Claire Trent and Steve Carruthers. It's not going to be a happy meeting.'

He had immediately returned to Police HQ and taken both of his bosses through the interview and the subsequent events.

They were quiet when he finished.

'That's it then, we're stuffed,' said the DCI in his Scots brogue.

'I'll have to tell the chief. He was hoping for some good news before the meeting with the Inspectorate.'

'At least we now know who our victims are. That's one great result from Ridpath's investigation.'

'But it's not enough.' Claire Trent counted off on the fingers of her hand. 'No suspects. No clues. No evidence. No DNA.' She exhaled loudly. 'Right, we've wasted enough time on this, it's time to shut it down.'

'Just give me one more week, boss,' Ridpath had pleaded. 'I'm sure if we go through it all one more time, we will find something we missed.'

'Give you another week on it? No point, Ridpath, it wouldn't be an effective use of resources. Remember, the whole building is just going to be another hole in the ground in Manchester city centre soon. It's time to bury this investigation too.'

'Please, boss.'

'No, it's over, Ridpath. You need to go back to being a coroner's officer. The last thing I need at the moment is Clarence bloody Montague ringing me every half hour complaining you're not doing your job. I need it like I need another hole in my head.'

'I'm sorry, Ridpath,' Carruthers had added, 'it was good work.'

'Good, but not good enough,' were Claire Trent's final words.

Now here he was sitting in the dark, a nearly empty whisky glass in his hand. Eve had sensed his mood and had left him alone after eating dinner, retreating to her room to chat with Maisie on Messenger.

He had screwed it up royally.

Stephen Orwell's words came back to haunt him. 'You are going to regret this, Inspector Ridpath. I am well known and respected in this community. After today, I am going to make it my life's work to make sure you never serve as a police officer again.'

At least he had that to look forward to.

He drained the dregs of the whisky remaining in his glass and poured himself another treble.

It was going to be a long, hot night.

Chapter Ninety-two

That was close.

Seeing Ridpath and his colleague with two uniformed police on my doorstep had sent my heart racing.

But I survived. Luckily, they hadn't worked it out yet. Would they ever?

Ridpath surprised me, he was far more tenacious than I thought. And they had done their work putting together the links from the various coroners' offices.

Had Margaret Challinor left notes for them? Is that how they had managed to link the inquests?

She was the problem now.

Only she could identify me.

I had to move quickly to get rid of her before she came out of her coma.

It would have to be done tomorrow, before the police could interview her or even realise she was in danger.

The plans were in place. The method simple. There would be no enjoyment in it. Killing somebody was never easy, but this had to be done.

Sweet dreams, Margaret Challinor.

Friday, June 25

Chapter Ninety-three

Ridpath woke with a headache which wasn't helped by a bright, intense sun shining through the open curtains. His mouth felt dry and wasted, and he could still taste the sweet bitter residue of the whisky.

He shouldn't drink. Firstly because he wasn't good at it and secondly because it always made him feel like death warmed up the following morning.

He stumbled down to the kitchen to find Eve already sat at the table, dressed in her school uniform and eating her Coco Pops.

'You're awake early,' he said.

'Actually, you're awake late.'

He looked around for the clock. 'What time is it?' He saw the small green numbers on the stove. 8.00.

'Sorry, love, I overslept. Let me get dressed and I'll drive you to school.'

'Are you sure you're fit to drive?'

He remembered he had gone to bed at 2.30, when the last of the bottle had finally been finished.

'I'll be fine after a quick shower.'

'You're not working early today?'

The events of yesterday flooded back into his brain in a series of increasingly calamitous images. 'Not today,' he answered weakly. He would go into Police HQ after taking her to school. Chrissy, Emily and Jayne Sinclair deserved an explanation for the decision to end the investigation, or at least, the active part of the investigation.

'Give me ten minutes. Are you ready?'

She opened her arms, indicating her school uniform. 'Duh… but I'm going to need some fresh clothes.' She smelt her shirt. 'These are beginning to walk out of the closet on their own.'

It was something he had to do. Life, as ever, had gotten away from him in the last week or so. 'Sorry, I'll sort it out at the weekend.'

Ten minutes later they were in the car driving down the A56. Eve had put her earphones in, singing along to some song on her phone. Ridpath was focusing on the road, trying to make sure he made no more mistakes.

He dropped her off at school.

'You coming to meet me tonight?'

He nodded. 'Wouldn't miss it for the world.'

'Great.' Then, for the first time in a long time, she leant over and kissed him on the cheek. 'It's good to have you back, Dad.'

And with that, she was out of the car and walking into the school without looking back.

'It's good to be back,' Ridpath whispered, watching her go. She was taller now, becoming more grown up with every passing day. He had to spend more time with her before he lost her to the terrible disease known as becoming an adult.

He put Bowie in the CD player and put the car in gear to drive to Police HQ before going on to face the day working with Clarence Montague.

It wasn't something he was looking forward to.

Chapter Ninety-four

I drove to the hospital and parked outside, sitting in my car.

There was no rush. I wanted to wait until ten a.m. when the whole place would be busy. Visitors coming to see relatives. Outpatients arriving for the first appointments of the day. Doctors, nurses and porters already halfway through their shifts, thinking about when they could take a break to grab a quick coffee and a cigarette.

That would be the time to walk in unnoticed.

It was the same in hospitals the world over, and this one was no different.

I would bide my time. There was no rush.

Chapter Ninety-five

As Ridpath entered MIT, only two desks had detectives sitting behind them. Either every detective was out on the streets working, or he was early.

Eight fifty.

Neither Chrissy nor Emily were in yet. He didn't blame them, perhaps they had been told separately by Steve Carruthers the investigation was over. At least it would save him the job.

He wandered in to the room they had commandeered, taking down the sign from the door. Operation Romeo and Juliet was now finished. He tore the paper into little bits and threw it in the bin.

Inside, somebody had already tidied up. There were no more used coffee cups, no pizza boxes and the stacks of used paper had all been thrown in a bin. The computers Jayne, Emily and Chrissy had worked on lay closed and cold.

All that remained were the whiteboards with their questions and notes and pictures. He looked again at the photofit images of Ralph Orwell and Skylar Robinson. Young people whose lives had been cruelly and painfully ended.

He mouthed the word, 'Sorry.'

Next to them, in the centre of the wall, Stephen Orwell's picture stared out at him. Chrissy had taken it from some physician's yearbook she had found.

He looked into the eyes of the man he had interviewed. Where had they going wrong? He was certain this man was involved. There were just too many coincidences, too many connections.

Charlie Whitworth's advice came back to him. 'It's all about the evidence, son, the evidence sets you free. Everything else is just confetti blowing in the wind.'

The door opened and both Chrissy and Emily stood in the entrance, carrying coffee and sandwiches.

'Sorry Ridpath,' said Chrissy, 'didn't know you were here.'

'Thought I'd tidy up before going to the coroner's office.' A long pause. 'I'm sorry about yesterday. I thought we had him, but I screwed up. We should have waited before interviewing him. We rushed it. Sorry.'

'Don't blame yourself,' said Emily coming into the room. 'I thought we had him too.' She placed the coffee and sandwich on the table in front of him. 'We did our best in the time we had.'

'But it wasn't good enough was it?'

He began taking down the notes from the whiteboards.

'We were so close,' said Emily. 'It was when we talked about the science I thought we had him.'

'Yeah, me too. Did we check whether he was a sperm donor or not?'

'I sent emails to the main companies who run sperm banks in Boston, but I don't expect an answer. Confidentiality and all that. But the hospital there did finally confirm himself and his wife were employed in the Halson Clinic from 1990 to 1997.'

Ridpath frowned. 'Orwell *and* his wife?'

Chrissy logged onto her laptop, retrieving the email. 'Yeah, from September 1990. He was a doctor specialising in IVF and she was a counsellor.'

'What?'

'According to this, she ran his clinics and gave his patients psychological counselling as they needed it. Particularly if they lost a child, miscarried or were unable to conceive even with IVF.'

'She met all the patients?'

Chrissy shrugged her shoulders. 'I guess so.'

And then a series of images flooded into Ridpath's head. For a moment, he struggled to make them make sense as they flickered past, scraps of information tumbling around his brain like clothes in a drier.

Orwell's words in the interview. 'My wife then takes care of them while I move on to a new patient in another room.'

The DNA on Mrs Challinor's clothes was from a woman, not a man.

The figure in black that attacked him, slight not muscular. Was it a woman?

Her own words. 'We're learning how to fix a broken pipe today. I am looking forward to it.'

His words. 'She likes fixing things, while I much prefer doing my crosswords.'

How could he have been so stupid?

Chapter Ninety-six

It was time.

The number of people standing round the ashtray having a cigarette break had increased to a crowd, all with masks rolled down to their necks and wearing a variety of hospital outfits. Visitors, porters, nurses, even a few doctors in scrubs.

I opened the car door, adjusted my face mask, pulled the cap down over my eyes and went round to the boot to get the bag.

A quick check. Everything was packed and ready, the hypodermic needle and the bottle of morphine secreted in another small pocket inside.

I glanced once more at the smokers. Some of them were beginning to drift back into the hospital, break time over.

I followed them through the door carrying the bag, looking for the long red line leading to the ICU. I followed it carefully, ignoring everybody else in the hospital and looking straight ahead.

On the ICU floor, there should be a washroom next to the lifts.

There it was.

Into an empty cubicle and breathe. All was going to plan. I checked my watch. The shift change should happen in twenty minutes, plenty of time to prepare.

I opened the bag, taking out the same PPE used by the ICU staff; a long white gown, plastic surgical boots, purple protective gloves, a light green apron over the top of the gown, a hairnet, FFP3 face mask and clear plastic eye protector.

Slowly, carefully, I put it all on, adjusting the hairnet and the mask so only my eyes were visible through the Perspex protector.

Now to sit and wait. I was used to waiting. Normally, I sat just outside Stephen's consulting room as he gave the good or the bad news to a patient. Comforting them if they had been told they were unable to conceive.

Or calming them down if he had just told them they were finally pregnant.

Stephen wasn't interested in either outcome. It was the science which excited him. The ability to create life when none had existed before. To manipulate the minutest of materials, spermatozoa and zygotes, to create a human being.

It was the closest anybody came to being God. It took him six days to create man, Stephen could do it in six minutes.

I could no longer have children after Michael was born. I always thought it ironic my husband created so many babies for other women but couldn't do it for me.

Perhaps God does have a sense of humour after all.

The awful woman wouldn't let me have the baby she had created with Stephen, but after her refusal, I conceived a better idea.

Why not simply make more children?

After all, I had the raw materials: wombs desperate for children. All the equipment needed for IVF. Stephen's amazing ability to create life.

And, even better, his own sperm, which he used for experimentation.

Moving to America helped. We were new there, nobody was aware of us, and the American hospital left us alone to do exactly what we wanted as long as the patients continued to flock through the doors and pay their fees.

Stephen was extraordinarily successful and good at what he did. A brilliant man and a brilliant mind. Why shouldn't those women be happy to bear his offspring?

Substituting his sperm was easy if they wanted a donor, and even if there was a husband ready and willing, it was possible to use his instead of theirs. All life was created in a lab anyway. Nobody would ever know I had used Stephen's sperm, not the husband's.

Of course, back in 1990, I wasn't aware how important DNA was going to become. Nobody was. As far as I knew it was just something being discussed in obscure journals by scientists obsessed with recreating the human genome.

It was Ralph Orwell who worked it all out. What a clever young man he was. Taking after his father no doubt. Somehow, he had met his half-sister, Skylar, online. She had been the result of one of my first interventions on Stephen's behalf. A woman who wanted a child but didn't want the hassle that went with having a husband. She had chosen some Greek hunk as the donor but I used Stephen's sperm instead.

Nobody was any the wiser until Ralph Orwell worked it out and began to send messages to the clinic, threatening to reveal the truth unless he was paid. Stephen hadn't contributed anything to his upbringing, perhaps he felt he was owed the money.

But I couldn't allow Stephen's work to be interrupted or questioned. He was far too brilliant a man to have a lifetime of service to science destroyed by some snot-nosed brat.

Enticing them to the warehouse was easy with a promise of money. I knew the area well as we had used it for storage for many years in my family's fur business. The most difficult thing was bricking them up in the room. It took far longer than I thought and hearing them scrambling at the door was heartbreaking.

For the others, I always made sure I was far enough away when they died. I didn't want to hear them fighting for life.

The Singhs, Joan Blackledge and Tony Snellgrove all had to die, but I didn't enjoy killing them. They had all worked out through DNA testing that the husbands weren't the father of their children.

Their deaths were simply necessary to protect Stephen and his work. I couldn't take the risk of exposure.

I checked my watch. Five more minutes and then I would move.

Perhaps I should have stopped when we returned to the UK, but the power of creation obsessed me. Shouldn't other women also enjoy the intelligence Stephen offered? They tended to choose donors for their physical prowess when what was most important was the mind. The body was just a vehicle, a container for intelligence. Why didn't more people realise?

The attack on the coroner had been a mistake. I shouldn't have moved so quickly. Even worse was imagining I could kill somebody up close and personal.

They police had almost worked it out, but missed the most obvious answer.

It wasn't Stephen, but me.

I checked my watch again. Time had slowed now, just four minutes to go.

I took out the bag with the hypodermic and placed into the pocket of my apron. I hung a fake ID around my neck. It wouldn't stand up to close scrutiny, but from afar I would look like all the other staff.

I was ready.

It was time to kill Mrs Challinor.

Chapter Ninety-seven

'Chrissy, when the Americans told you Stephen Orwell had not flown to the UK in 2008 and 2009, did they check if any other members of the family came back?'

'I don't think so, but they gave me a spreadsheet for those years of all people with the surname Orwell.'

'Did they? Can you open it?'

'Just a minute.' She tapped a few keys on her laptop.

Ridpath ran over and looked over her shoulder, scanning the list. 'There it is. Alexandra Orwell, aged forty-three, flying from Los Angeles to Manchester on August 16, 2008. Flying out again on August 30. The exact dates when our bodies were incarcerated according to the tram ticket found in Ralph Orwell's pocket.'

They were joined by Emily. 'What are you saying?'

'I wonder if were looking at the wrong person. Who testified for the clinic in the inquests in Cheshire, Lancashire and Derbyshire?'

Chrissy opened the attachments. 'In Derbyshire, it was a Mrs Orwell, Alexandra Orwell, she is down as practice manager and counsellor.'

'And in Cheshire and Lancashire?'

Chrissy's finger flew across the keyboard. 'The same. Stephen Orwell didn't testify, it was his wife.'

'Emily, where was Mrs Orwell on the night the coroner was attacked?'

'I don't know, Ridpath, Stephen Orwell said only himself and his son, Michael, went to London. They are both captured in pictures from the evening.'

Chrissy looked at him. 'But if Mrs Orwell was the one who attacked the coroner, wouldn't she have been seen? Wouldn't the coroner have seen her face?'

Ridpath stopped what he was doing and froze.

'My God, I've been so stupid.'

He suddenly burst into action. 'Chrissy, get a team to go to the Orwells' house in Altrincham. I want them to arrest Alexandra Orwell immediately if she is there. Emily, get on to Claire Trent and Steve Carruthers. Pull them out of whatever budget meeting they are in and tell them what we have discovered. It was Alexandra Orwell who murdered our Romeo and Juliet as well as killing at least five other people.'

He ran towards the door.

'Where are you going, Ridpath?'

'The hospital. I think the coroner and her family are in danger.'

Chapter Ninety-eight

Sarah Challinor turned the page of her magazine and yawned. Next to her, a flask of coffee lay empty. She had finally had enough of the hospital's dishwater and brought her own to keep her awake.

She had been there all night watching over her mother, but there had been no change. Her aunt would come in for the day shift at eleven o'clock. That way, there would be somebody here in case her mum regained consciousness.

This was the seventh day since the attack. Other than the few strange and unintelligible words spoken when she had her relapse, her mother had said nothing.

How Sarah missed her voice.

Just chatting about her day over breakfast. Or working out what to do with the kids at the weekend. Or simply talking over the latest challenges she was facing.

Anything would be better than silence.

Her mother's voice had been a constant in Sarah's life, particularly after her painful divorce, when Margaret had been the rock on which she had rebuilt her life.

She stood, stretched and walked over to the window looking into the ICU ward. Her mother was still lying there, unmoving, wires attached to her body and her fingers.

Around her head, the bandage had been changed by the nurse an hour ago. All her mother's beautiful hair had been lost. The spiralling grey corkscrew curls that were constantly unmanageable, but which Sarah loved, gone now, shaved off.

They were the essence of her mother. A free spirit, uncontrollable, a force of nature.

Would she be the same when she woke?
Sarah didn't know.
She just wanted her mum back.

Chapter Ninety-nine

Ridpath ran out of Police HQ and jumped into his car, immediately placing the blue light onto the roof.

He accelerated out of the car park.

Which way would be quickest?

Through the city centre, or use the M60?

Decide.

Decide.

He turned left onto Oldham Road, the opposite direction from where he wanted to go. But now he was driving against the flow of traffic into town. He would get on to the M60 and with his blues and twos blaring should be able to race round to the hospital.

Maybe he was panicking or over-reacting. Mrs Challinor would still be in a coma in her hospital bed in the ICU when he arrived, unmoving and silent.

But for some reason, he felt she was in danger. After yesterday, Alexandra Orwell wouldn't take any more chances. Mrs Challinor was the only person who may have seen her.

All their other evidence was circumstantial. The coroner was the only one who knew for sure.

As he turned onto the M60 ring road, the phone rang.

'Ridpath.'

'The uniforms went round to the Orwells' house, she wasn't there. Stephen Orwell was livid, screaming blue murder about harassment, but he finally said his wife wasn't at home. Apparently she had left the house early in the morning to visit a friend in hospital.'

'Chrissy, is Emily there?'

'Listening, Ridpath.'

'Get a tactical team to the hospital immediately. Code Red. Now. Have you told Trent and Carruthers?'

'We're here, Ridpath.' The Scottish brogue of his DCI came over the phone.

'I think Alexandra Orwell is trying to kill the coroner.'

'Tactical team, on its way. Their ETA is fifteen minutes,' answered Emily.

'Get them there quicker.'

'We're on our way, Ridpath, keep the phone lines open.'

Ridpath pressed the accelerator and the car surged ahead.

He had to get there in time.

Chapter One Hundred

A quick check in the bathroom mirror before I left.

The hairnet needed to cover my eyebrows more, so I pulled it down. Now all anybody could see was a pair of bright blue eyes staring out from behind a Perspex visor.

I adjusted the apron and gown. It needed to be more ruffled, as if I had been working hard on my shift. But it shouldn't look too dirty. The orders were always to change PPE after finishing a procedure.

I pulled the purple plastic gloves tighter around my hands, smoothing down in between each finger. I loved the smell of PPE, that fresh clinical smell reminding me of labs and science and working next to Stephen.

The hypodermic nestled in its bag in my apron. I initially thought about simply switching off the coroner's life support system and ventilator, but alarms would have sounded and staff would come rushing from all over the ICU.

Instead I had found an easier way to kill her. A way that would be invisible, with no need for a post-mortem or an inquest. Even better, I would not have to watch but be far away when she died. I'd thought I would enjoy attacking her, seeing the life flee from her eyes.

But I didn't, it wasn't in my nature.

After I injected the morphine into her neck, I could just walk out and go home to Stephen. Nobody would be any the wiser and the coroner would die a slow and relatively painless death.

I picked up the Styrofoam cold box with its stickers for fragile and dangerous medicines plastered on each side. This would give me a reason for being out of the ICU.

Time to go.

Time to kill.

This time there would be no mistakes.

Chapter One Hundred and One

Ridpath accelerated to a stop outside the main entrance, the car's rear end swerving wildly and the tyres screeching.

He opened the car door and ran into reception.

'Oi, you can't leave that here,' he heard one of the porters shouting.

A security guard grabbed his arm, trying to stop him.

'You can't come into the hospital without a mask.'

'Police, let go of me.'

'I don't care who you are, you can't come in here without a mask. Rules—'

Ridpath tried to shake him off, pulling out his warrant card. 'Let go of me, I'm Inspector Ridpath, GMP.'

The security guard held on tighter. 'I don't care if you're PC Plod, nobody comes in here without a mask.'

Ridpath shoved him backwards and the man finally let go, falling heavily against a carousel full of Covid pamphlets.

He ran down the corridor, hearing the man on his radio behind him.

'Security alert. We have an intruder heading towards ICU. All security to ICU now.'

Ridpath could hear his shoes against the tiles of the hospital corridor. Ahead, people seemed to recognise the wildness in his eyes and moved quickly out of his way.

Take the lift or up the stairs?

The lift was on the second floor and moving slowly. Ridpath dodged round an old man in a wheelchair being pushed by a hospital porter.

'Hey you—'

But Ridpath was already racing up the stairs.

Chapter One Hundred and Two

I waited outside the ICU carrying the Styrofoam cold box, pressing the call button until somebody answered. A person in a mask and a face shield looked through the clear window cut into the door.

'Sorry, forgot my swipe card,' I shouted.

The door was opened by the male nurse. 'Haven't seen you here before?'

'Agency nurse working in the pharmacy. Need to get these shots into the fridge quickly before the temp rises. The lift was slow.'

'It's on your right.'

He stepped aside and I walked in.

The ICU was calm and quiet. On my right, a doctor was looking at a readout from one of the monitors. Two nurses were moving a bed back onto the ward while another nurse wrote on a patient's chart.

Nobody paid any attention to me. I blended in perfectly.

'It's over there.'

The male nurse pointed at the fridge. I'd forgotten about him.

I moved towards the fridge, putting the box down next to it, and glanced over my shoulder.

The male nurse had moved on now, I couldn't see him.

I left the box on the counter and walked towards the ICU wards. Mrs Challinor's room was the third on the right.

Hold your head up. Do not look to the left or right. You are just another nurse going about your duties.

I opened the door. The bed next to the coroner was empty.

Perfect.

Mrs Challinor was still lying exactly where she had been two days ago, wires and tubes coming out of her into a ventilator. Would she ever come out of her coma? Maybe not, but I couldn't take the chance.

I looked over to my left. Her daughter was standing at the glass looking at her mother.

Shame; I would have preferred nobody to be there, but it couldn't be helped. I would simply block her view of what I was doing with my body. She would be none the wiser; just another nurse taking care of her mother.

I had to act now.

It was time to take care of her.

I said my usual benediction, 'I give life and I take it away,' as I pulled the hypodermic out of my pocket and held it in front of me.

Chapter One Hundred and Three

The nurse had just entered the room. What was she going to do this time? Make Mum more comfortable? Change the bandages again?

This wasn't the usual nurse. Mum's was short and stocky, this one was quite tall and walked elegantly, almost like a ballerina rather than the normal nurse's bustling gait.

She was standing over Mum now, looking down at her.

What was she doing? Was she speaking to Mum?

She heard a shout to her left and Ridpath was at the end of the corridor. What was he doing here?

He ran towards her, immediately looking through the glass.

'Your mother, how is she?'

He was out of breath, panting heavily.

'Still the same. She hasn't come out the coma yet. Why have you been running?'

'We've found out who attacked your mum,' he said, doubling over, trying to catch his breath. 'It was Alexandra Orwell.'

'Who?'

'Our suspect's wife, I took too long to work it out, I should have seen it earlier...'

As Ridpath spoke, Sarah Challinor stared through the glass into her mother's room. The nurse turned around. She had the brightest blue eyes Sarah had ever seen. But there was something cold about them, something cruel.

Then she looked down at the nurse's hand.

There was a hypodermic needle. Why was she holding a hypodermic needle?

A thin stream of liquid erupted from it.

The nurse held the hypodermic near her mum's neck. What *was* she doing?

Then she looked back towards the glass.

Sarah Challinor screamed.

Chapter One Hundred and Four

Ridpath looked up. What was the nurse doing with the hypodermic?

As she turned and looked back towards him, he recognised those blue eyes. He had seen them before.

Alexandra Orwell.

Sarah Challinor screamed.

Ridpath looked around. The entrance to ICU was back near the lifts.

Too far.

The hypodermic was hovering close to Mrs Challinor's neck. He banged on the glass. For a second she stopped, and then moved forward again, the hypodermic about to enter the coroner's neck.

He remembered the intercom on the wall. He pressed the button. 'Alexandra, stop.'

The nurse halted and looked back towards the glass.

'You can't get away with it. More police will be here any minute. There's no escape.'

She straightened up and spoke. 'How did you work out it was me, Inspector?'

'It could only have been you. I should have seen it earlier. But why did you kill them?'

The eyes blinked slowly. 'I didn't want to, I received no pleasure from killing at first, but they were going to expose everything we had achieved over the years. All my husband's children...' her voice trailed off. 'I couldn't allow it.'

'You murdered the Singhs, Joan Blackledge and Tony Snellgrove as well as the couple in the warehouse?'

She nodded slowly. 'As I said, I didn't enjoy it, not with any of them…'

'You killed Ralph Orwell and Skylar Robinson?'

'They were so young and innocent, but so greedy. They had to die.'

'And the others?'

'They got in the way, threatening to expose everything. They had worked out the children were fathered by Stephen. It was my gift to them, but they didn't appreciate how privileged they were.'

'It's over, Alexandra, you don't have to kill, not any more.'

She turned her head to look down on Mrs Challinor before looking back. Ridpath saw the madness in those blue eyes.

'But I do, Inspector. I have to finish the job and it's too late to stop now.' She moved the hypodermic closer to the coroner's neck.

Ridpath scrambled for something to say, anything, he had to keep her talking. 'Just answer one question. Why the feathers? Why did you leave them behind?'

She laughed, pulling off her mask so he could see her face. 'When I gave birth to Michael, there were two small feathers on the bed next to me. I remember staring at those feathers all through the pain of his birth. Something died in me that day, the day he was born. I felt the other deaths should be remembered properly.'

A doctor dressed in PPE ran down the corridor followed by two security guards. 'She's locked the room from the inside. We're trying to get in.'

Ridpath could hear the banging on the door as the ICU staff tried to break it down.

Alexandra Orwell heard it too.

'Looks like you are right, Inspector, there is no escape. Shame, I thought I planned it so well.'

'Alexandra, you don't have to do this. Move away from the bed.'

'But I do, Inspector. One last thing. Stephen knew nothing. He is entirely innocent…' she paused, '…perhaps too innocent.'

The banging became louder, more intense.

Ridpath had to keep her talking. The hypodermic moved closer to the coroner's neck.

'I... I...' Ridpath mumbled. 'One more question...'

'Too late, Inspector.'

The hypodermic stabbed into Mrs Challinor's neck and the plunger was slowly depressed.

'MUM!' screamed Sarah.

Ridpath picked up the chair and smashed it against the plate glass separating him from the ward. It shattered with an almighty crash.

He kicked the remaining shards out of the way and scrambled over the divider, followed by the doctor.

Was the coroner still alive?

Two Weeks Later.

Chapter One Hundred and Five

Ridpath stood in the corridor overlooking Mrs Challinor's room.

The glass he had smashed had been repaired, the intercom was now working.

Inside Mr Pereira was making one final note in Mrs Challinor's chart, handing it off to a nurse to be hung at the end of the bed.

Mrs Challinor was still lying there, tubes leading from her throat to the incubator. The screens above her head still beeped with an almost musical rhythm, the orchestra of life.

It had been a close run thing. He remembered grabbing hold of Alexandra Orwell and flinging the hypodermic to the ground.

The doctor had rushed over to Mrs Challinor. The monitors above her head were beeping loudly, each one flashing a bright orange warning.

Outside the room, Sarah Challinor was still screaming, her face a mask of terror.

'What did you inject into her neck?' The doctor shouted.

The door to the room crashed down and two security guards rushed in followed by the rest of the ICU staff.

'What did you inject into her neck?' The doctor repeated his question, even louder this time.

Alexandra Orwell stayed silent.

Ridpath increased his hold on her.

Another nurse came in. 'I found this empty morphine bottle in the bathroom along with a bag full of clothes.'

The warning sounds became louder, screaming their unhappiness.

'Did you give her morphine?'

'She's used it before to kill,' answered Ridpath.

'Five milligrams of naloxone quickly. MOVE!' the doctor shouted and a nurse rushed out.

The monitors continued to beep their alarms, louder still.

Then they stopped and the room went silent.

The doctor reached his hand towards her neck to take her pulse.

Ridpath stared at the coroner lying motionless in bed. A dark shadow seemed to pass across her face.

The machines stopped.

The nurse ran in and handed a filled hypodermic to the doctor. He checked it before injecting the whole syringe into the crook of the coroner's arm.

Everybody was staring at him as he worked, not saying anything, not even daring to breathe.

Ridpath noticed, for the first time, the Police Tactical Group were standing there, Heckler & Koch rifles levelled at the people in the room.

He pushed Alexandra Orwell towards them. 'Arrest and caution her.'

'What's the charge?' A gruff voice came from behind a black mask.

Ridpath looked down at the still motionless body of the coroner. 'Murder.'

Just then, the monitors began to beep again, starting slowly and gradually increasing in tempo.

The doctor took her pulse once more before ordering everybody to leave the room immediately.

The last words Ridpath heard were from Sarah. 'Is Mum alive? Is she OK? What's happening? Is Mum OK?'

He had been coming to the hospital every day since, seeing the coroner lying in her bed, still deep in the induced coma.

Today, Sarah Challinor was sat behind him reading a book, passing time, waiting for her mother to return to the land of the living.

When the doctor and nurse left, Ridpath pressed the intercom. 'Morning, Coroner,' he began.

They had been instructed to talk to Mrs Challinor when they could, to encourage her mind to return to consciousness. At first Ridpath felt uncomfortable as there had never been any replies from the inert body lying on the bed behind the glass. But, gradually, he had become used to the situation, chatting with her as casually as if she were wide awake and listening to every word.

'We finally submitted the papers to CPS today. It's up to them now whether they proceed with the case or if Alexandra Orwell is quietly sentenced to a mental hospital for the rest of her life.'

The machines whirred on in reply.

'The husband has been shouting in the newspapers of course, proclaiming her innocence and denouncing us for abusing his data protection rights. He seems to have forgotten seven people died at his wife's hand. She was open in her interviews at first, answering all our questions, telling us exactly what she did and when. But then she clammed up, becoming almost comatose in her answers, repeating the words "no comment" again and again. But don't worry, we've found evidence on her mobile phone putting her at the scene of your attack, plus there is the second attempt on your life. She won't get away, not this time.'

He was joined at the window by Sarah Challinor. 'Are you sure, Ridpath? I've seen his statements in the press accusing the police and threatening to sue them for damages.'

'He can do his worst, Sarah, I don't care. We pulled a killer off the streets, a woman who had murdered seven people including a young baby simply to protect her husband, as well as attacking your mother. Jayne Sinclair has continued her work on her own and found another eleven children in the United States who were fathered by Stephen Orwell. It wouldn't surprise me if the man, and the hospitals who employed him, spend the next couple of years in court being sued for medical malpractice. What goes around, comes around.'

Ridpath smiled and turned back, pressing the intercom once again. 'Jenny and Sophia send their love, they are missing you immensely and hope you get well soon. I'm afraid your replacement, Mr Montague, is making their life hell. He's also withdrawn all of your Regulation 28 notices. Apparently now is not the right time to create additional work for the local health authorities. I've tried to argue with him but he won't listen. It seems my work is not appreciated by Mr Montague.'

Sarah Challinor laid her hand on Ridpath's arm. 'I appreciate what you've done. Without you, Mum wouldn't be alive today.'

Ridpath reddened but had no response.

Instead, he turned back to look at the coroner. When would she come out of her coma? And if she did, would she be the same person? Would her memory or behaviour be affected?

The doctors didn't have an answer and neither did he.

Ridpath offered up a silent prayer for her recovery. He wasn't usually a praying man but right now, he was going to do anything, ask anything, to see the coroner happy and healthy again.

'Do you want a coffee, Ridpath? I'm sure Mum won't mind if we take a break for half an hour,' said Sarah.

Ridpath nodded, realising that, for the first time in ages, he was actually hungry.

'I wouldn't mind getting something to eat too.'

'My treat,' Sarah replied. 'It's the least I can do.'

As they walked down the corridor towards the lifts, Ridpath took one last look back at Mrs Challinor, lying motionless on her bed in the sterile isolation room, her face hidden in the shadows of the machines that were keeping her alive.

Would she ever recover?

 **CANELO**CRIME

Do you love crime fiction and are always on the lookout for brilliant authors?

Canelo Crime is home to some of the most exciting novels around. Thousands of readers are already enjoying our compulsive stories. Are you ready to find your new favourite writer?

Find out more and sign up to our newsletter at canelocrime.com